C000019520

BARRINGTON
(COMPLETE)

LECTOR HOUSE PUBLIC DOMAIN WORKS

This book is a result of an effort made by Lector House towards making a contribution to the preservation and repair of original classic literature. The original text is in the public domain in the United States of America, and possibly other countries depending upon their specific copyright laws.

In an attempt to preserve, improve and recreate the original content, certain conventional norms with regard to typographical mistakes, hyphenations, punctuations and/or other related subject matters, have been corrected upon our consideration. However, few such imperfections might not have been rectified as they were inherited and preserved from the original content to maintain the authenticity and construct, relevant to the work. The work might contain a few prior copyright references as well as page references which have been retained, wherever considered relevant to the part of the construct. We believe that this work holds historical, cultural and/or intellectual importance in the literary works community, therefore despite the oddities, we accounted the work for print as a part of our continuing effort towards preservation of literary work and our contribution towards the development of the society as a whole, driven by our beliefs.

We are grateful to our readers for putting their faith in us and accepting our imperfections with regard to preservation of the historical content. We shall strive hard to meet up to the expectations to improve further to provide an enriching reading experience.

Though, we conduct extensive research in ascertaining the status of copyright before redeveloping a version of the content, in rare cases, a classic work might be incorrectly marked as not-in-copyright. In such cases, if you are the copyright holder, then kindly contact us or write to us, and we shall get back to you with an immediate course of action.

HAPPY READING!

BARRINGTON
(COMPLETE)

CHARLES JAMES LEVER

ISBN: 978-93-90294-42-8

Published: 1907

© 2020
LECTOR HOUSE LLP

LECTOR HOUSE LLP
E-MAIL: lectorpublishing@gmail.com

BARRINGTON
(COMPLETE)

BY

CHARLES JAMES LEVER

WITH ILLUSTRATIONS
BY PHIZ.

COMPLETE EDITION OF TWO VOLUMES

1907.

CONTENTS

VOLUME II.

CONTENTS

LIST OF ILLUSTRATIONS

Page

VOLUME I.

THE FISHERMAN'S HOME

BARRINGTON.

CHAPTER I.

THE FISHERMAN'S HOME

If there should be, at this day we live in, any one bold enough to confess that he fished the river Nore, in Ireland, some forty years ago, he might assist me by calling to mind a small inn, about two miles from the confluence of that river with the Barrow, a spot in great favor with those who followed the "gentle craft."

It was a very unpretending hostel, something wherein cottage and farmhouse were blended, and only recognizable as a place of entertainment by a tin trout suspended over the doorway, with the modest inscription underneath, — "Fisherman's Home." Very seldom is it, indeed, that hotel pledges are as honestly fulfilled as they were in this simple announcement. The house was, in all that quiet comfort and unostentatious excellence can make, a veritable Home! Standing in a fine old orchard of pear and damson trees, it was only approachable by a path which led from the highroad, about two miles off, or by the river, which wound round the little grassy promontory beneath the cottage. On the opposite side of the stream arose cliffs of considerable height, their terraced sides covered with larch and ash, around whose stems the holly, the laurel, and arbutus grew in a wild and rich profusion. A high mountain, rugged with rock and precipice, shut in the picture, and gave to the river all the semblance of a narrow lake.

The Home, as may be imagined, was only resorted to by fishermen, and of these not many; for the chosen few who knew the spot, with the churlishness of true anglers, were strenuously careful to keep the secret to themselves. But another and stronger cause contributed to this seclusion. The landlord was a reduced gentleman, who, only anxious to add a little to his narrow fortune, would not have accepted a greater prosperity at the cost of more publicity, and who probably only consented to his occupation on finding how scrupulously his guests respected his position.

Indeed, it was only on leave-taking, and then far from painfully, you were reminded of being in an inn. There was no noise, no bustle; books, magazines, flowers, lay about; cupboards lay open, with all their cordials free to take. You might dine under the spreading sycamore beside the well, and have your dessert for the plucking. No obsequious waiter shook his napkin as you passed, no ringleted barmaid crossed your musing steps, no jingling of bells, or discordant cries, or high-voiced remonstrances disturbed you. The hum of the summer bee, or the flapping plash of a trout, were about the only sounds in the stillness, and all was as peaceful and as calm and as dreamy as the most world-weary could have wished it.

Of those who frequented the spot, some merely knew that the host had seen better days. Others, however, were aware that Peter Barrington had once been a man of large fortune, and represented his county in the Irish Parliament. Though not eminent as a politician, he was one of the great convivial celebrities of a time that boasted of Curran, and Avanmore, and Parsons, and a score of others, any one of whom, in our day, would have made a society famous. Barrington, too, was the almoner of the monks of the screw, and "Peter's pence" was immortalized in a song by Ned Lysaght, of which I once possessed, but have lost a copy.

One might imagine there could be no difficulty in showing how in that wild period of riotous living and costly rivalry an Irish gentleman ran through all his property and left himself penniless. It was, indeed, a time of utter recklessness, many seeming possessed of that devil-may-care spirit that drives a drowning crew to break open the spirit-room and go down in an orgie. But Barrington's fortune was so large, and his successes on the turf so considerable, that it appeared incredible, when his estates came to the hammer, and all his personal property was sold off; so complete his ruin, that, as he said himself, the "only shelter he had was an umbrella, and even that he borrowed from Dan Driscoll, the sheriff's officer."

Of course there were theories in plenty to account for the disaster, and, as usual, so many knew, many a long day ago, how hard pressed he had been for money, and what ruinous interest he was obliged to pay, till at last rumors filtered all down to one channel, and the world agreed that it was all his son's doing, and that the scamp George had ruined his father. This son, his only child, had gone out to India in a cavalry regiment, and was celebrated all over the East for a costly splendor that rivalled the great Government officials. From every retired or invalided officer who came back from Bengal were heard stories of mad Barring-ton's extravagance: his palace on the Hooghly, his racing stud, his elephants, his army of retainers,—all narratives which, no matter in what spirit retailed, seemed to delight old Peter, who, at every fresh story of his son's spendthrift magnificence, would be sure to toast his health with a racy enthusiasm whose sincerity was not to be doubted.

Little wonder need there be if in feeding such extravagance a vast estate melted away, and acre followed acre, till all that remained of a property that ranked next to the Ormonds' was the little cottage over whose door the tin-trout dangled, and the few roods of land around it: sorry remnant of a princely fortune!

But Barrington himself had a passion, which, inordinately indulged, has brought many to their ruin. He was intensely fond of law. It was to him all that gambling is to other men. All that gamesters feel of hope and fear, all the intense excitement they derive from the vacillating fortunes of play, Barrington enjoyed in a lawsuit. Every step of the proceeding had for him an intense interest. The driest legal documents, musty declarations, demurrers, pleadings, replies, affidavits, and counter-affidavits were his choicest reading; and never did a young lady hurry to her room with the last new novel with a stronger anticipation of delight than did Barrington when carrying away to his little snuggery a roll of parchments or rough drafts, whose very iterations and jargon would have driven most men half crazy. This same snuggery of his was a curiosity, too, the walls being all decorated with portraits of legal celebrities, not selected with reference to their merit or distinction, but solely from their connection with some suit in which he had been engaged; and thus under the likeness of Chief Baron O'Grady might be read, "Barring-ton versus Brazier, 1802; a juror withdrawn:" Justice Moore's portrait was inscribed, "Argument in Chambers, 1808," and so on; even to the portraits of leading counsel, all were marked and dated only as they figured in the great campaign,—the more than thirty years' war he carried on against Fortune.

Let not my reader suppose for one moment that this litigious taste grew out of a spirit of jarring discontent or distrust. Nothing of the kind. Barrington was merely a gambler; and with whatever dissatisfaction the declaration may be met, I am prepared to show that gambling, however faulty in itself, is not the vice of cold, selfish, and sordid men, but of warm, rash, sometimes over-generous temperaments. Be it well remembered that the professional play-man is, of all others, the one who has least of a gamester in his heart; his superiority lying in the simple fact that his passions are never engaged, his interest never stirred. Oh! beware of yourself in company with the polished antagonist, who only smiles when he loses, whom nothing adverse ever disturbs, but is calmly serene under the most pitiless pelting of luck. To come back: Barrington's passion for law was an intense thirst for a certain species of excitement; a verdict was to him the odd trick. Let him, however, but win the game, there never was a man so indifferent about the stakes.

For many a year back he had ceased to follow the great events of the world. For the stupendous changes in Europe he cared next to nothing. He scarcely knew who reigned over this empire or that kingdom. Indifferent to art, science, letters, and even society, his interest was intense about all that went on in the law courts, and it was an interest so catholic that it took in everything and everybody, from the great judge upon the bench to the small taxing-officer who nibbled at the bill of costs.

Fortunately for him, his sister, a maiden lady of some eighteen or twenty years his junior, had imbibed nothing of this passion, and, by her prudent opposition to it, stemmed at least the force of that current which was bearing him to ruin. Miss Dinah Barrington had been the great belle of the Irish court,—I am ashamed to say how long ago,—and though at the period my tale opens there was not much to revive the impression, her high nose, and full blue eyes, and a mass of wonderfully unchanged brown hair, proclaimed her to be—what she was very proud to call herself—a thorough Barrington, a strong type of a frank nature, with a bold, resolute will, and a very womanly heart beneath it.

When their reverses of fortune first befell them, Miss Barrington wished to emigrate. She thought that in Canada, or some other far-away land, their altered condition might be borne less painfully, and that they could more easily bend themselves to humble offices where none but strangers were to look on them; but Barrington clung to his country with the tenacity of an old captain to a wreck. He declared he could not bring himself to the thought of leaving his bones in a strange land, but he never confessed what he felt to be the strongest tie of all, two unfinished lawsuits, the old record of Barrington v. Brazier, and a Privy Council case of Barrington and Lot Rammadahn Mohr against the India Company. To have left his country with these still undecided seemed to him—like the act of a commander taking flight on the morning of a general action—an amount of cowardice he could not contemplate. Not that he confided this opinion to his sister, though he did so in the very fullest manner to his old follower and servant, Darby Cassan. Darby was the last remnant of a once princely retinue, and in his master's choice of him to accompany his fallen fortunes, there was something strangely indicative of the man. Had Darby been an old butler or a body-servant, had he been a favorite groom, or, in some other capacity, one whose daily duties had made his a familiar face, and whose functions could still be available in an humble state, there would have seemed good reason for the selection; but Darby was none of these: he had never served in hall or pantry; he had never brushed the cobweb from a bottle, or led a nag to the door. Of all human professions his were about the last that could address themselves to the cares of a little household; for Darby was reared, bred, and passed fifty-odd years of his life as an earth-stopper!

A very ingenious German writer has attempted to show that the sympathies of the humble classes with pursuits far above their own has always its origin in something of their daily life and habits, just as the sacristan of a cathedral comes to be occasionally a tolerable art critic from his continual reference to Rubens and Vandyck. It is possible that Darby may have illustrated the theory, and that his avocations as earth-stopper may have suggested what he assuredly possessed, a perfect passion for law. If a suit was a great game to Barrington, to Darby it was a hunt! and though his personal experiences never soared beyond Quarter Sessions, he gloried in all he saw there of violence and altercation, of vituperative language and impassioned abuse. Had he been a rich man, free to enjoy his leisure, he would have passed all his days listening to these hot discussions. They were to him a sort of intellectual bull-fight, which never could be too bloody or too cruel. Have I said enough, therefore, to show the secret link which bound the master to the man? I hope so; and that my reader is proud of a confidence with which Miss Barrington herself was never intrusted. She believed that Darby had been taken into favor from some marvellous ability he was supposed to possess, applicable to their new venture as innkeepers. Phrenology would perhaps have pronounced Darby a heaven-born host, for his organ of acquisitiveness was grandly developed. Amidst that great household, where the thriftless habits of the master had descended to the servants, and rendered all reckless and wasteful alike, Darby had thriven and grown almost rich. Was it that the Irish climate used its influence over him; for in his practice to "put by something for a rainy day," his savings had many promptings? As the reputation of having money soon attached to him, he was often applied to in the hunting-field, or at the kennel, for small loans, by the young bloods who frequented the Hall, and, being always repaid three or four fold, he grew to have a very high conception of what banking must be when done on a large scale. Besides all this, he quickly learned that no character attracts more sympathy, especially amongst the class of young squires and sporting-men, than a certain quaint simplicity, so flattering in its contrast to their own consummate acuteness. Now, he was simple to their hearts' content. He usually spoke of himself as "Poor Darby, God help him!" and, in casting up those wonderful accounts, which he kept by notches on a tally-stick, nothing was more amusing than to witness his bewilderment and confusion, the inconceivable blunders he would make, even to his own disadvantage, all sure to end at last in the heart-spoken confession that it was "clean beyand him," and "he 'd leave it all to your honor; pay just what ye plaze, and long life to ye!"

Is it that women have some shrewd perception of character denied to men? Certainly Darby never imposed on Miss Barrington. She read him like a book, and he felt it. The consequence was a very cordial dislike, which strengthened with every year of their acquaintance.

Though Miss Barrington ever believed that the notion of keeping an inn originated with her brother, it was Darby first conceived the project, and, indeed, by his own skill and crafty intelligence was it carried on; and while the words "Peter Barrington" figured in very small letters, it is true, over the door to comply with a legal necessity, to most of the visitors he was a mere myth. Now, if Peter Barrington was very happy to be represented by deputy,—or, better still, not represented at all,—Miss Dinah regarded the matter in a very different light. Her theory was that, in accepting the humble station to which reverse of fortune brought them, the world ought to see all the heroism and courage of the sacrifice. She insisted on being a foreground figure, just to show them, as she said, "that I take nothing upon me. I am the hostess of a little wayside inn,—no more!" How little did she know of her own heart, and how far was she from even suspecting that it was the *ci-devant* belle making one last throw for the admiration and homage which once were offered her freely.

Such were the three chief personages who dwelt under that secluded roof, half overgrown with honeysuckle and dog-roses,—specimens of that wider world without, where jealousies, and distrusts, and petty rivalries are warring: for as in one tiny globule of water are represented the elements which make oceans and seas, so is it in the moral world; and "the family" is only humanity, as the artists say, "reduced."

For years back Miss Barrington had been plotting to depose Darby. With an ingenuity quite feminine, she managed to connect him with every chagrin that crossed and every annoyance that befell them. If the pig ploughed up the new peas in the garden, it was Darby had left the gate open; it was *his* hand overwound the clock; and a very significant hint showed that when the thunder soured the beer, Mr. Darby knew more of the matter than he was likely to tell. Against such charges as these, iterated and reiterated to satiety, Barrington would reply by a smile, or a good-natured excuse, or a mere gesture to suggest patience, till his sister, fairly worn out, resolved on another line of action. "As she could not banish the rats," to use her own words, "she would scuttle the ship."

To explain her project, I must go back in my story, and state that her nephew, George Barrington, had sent over to England, some fifteen years before, a little girl, whom he, called his daughter. She was consigned to the care of his banker in London, with directions that he should communicate with Mr. Peter Barrington, announce the child's safe arrival, and consult with him as to her future destination. Now, when the event took place, Barrington was in the very crisis of his disasters. Overwhelmed with debts, pursued by creditors, regularly hunted down, he was driven day by day to sign away most valuable securities for mere passing considerations, and obliged to accept any conditions for daily support He answered the banker's letter, briefly stating his great embarrassment, and begging him to give the child his protection for a few weeks or so, till some arrangement of his affairs might enable him to offer her a home.

This time, however, glided over, and the hoped-for amendment never came, — far from it. Writs were out against him, and he was driven to seek a refuge in the Isle of Man, at that time the special sanctuary of insolvent sinners. Mr. Leonard Gower wrote again, and proposed that, if no objection would be made to the plan, the child should be sent to a certain convent near Namur, in the Netherlands, where his own daughter was then placed for her education. Aunt Dinah would have rejected, —ay, or would have resented such a proposal as an insult, had the world but gone on better with them. That her grand-niece should be brought up a Catholic was an outrage on the whole Barring-ton blood. But calamity had brought her low, —very low, indeed. The child, too, was a heathen, —a Hindoo or a Buddhist, perhaps, —for the mother was a native woman, reputed, indeed, to be a princess. But who could know this? Who could vouch that George was ever married at all, or if such a ceremony were possible? All these were "attenuating circumstances," and as such she accepted them; and the measure of her submission was filled up when she received a portrait of the little girl, painted by a native artist. It represented a dark-skinned, heavy-browed child, with wide, full eyes, thick lips, and an expression at once florid and sullen, —not any of the traits one likes to associate with infancy, —and it was with a half shudder Aunt Dinah closed the miniature, and declared that "the sight of the little savage actually frightened her."

Not so poor Barrington. He professed to see a great resemblance to his son. It was George all over. To be sure, his eyes were deep blue, and his hair a rich brown; but there was something in the nose, or perhaps it was in the mouth, —no, it was the chin, —ay, it was the chin was George's. It was the Barrington chin, and no mistake about it.

At all events, no opposition was made to the banker's project, and the little girl was sent off to the convent of the Holy Cross, on the banks of the Meuse. She was inscribed on the roll as the Princess Doondiah, and bore the name till her father's death, when Mr. Gower suggested that she should be called by her family name. The letter with the proposal, by some accident, was not acknowledged, and the writer, taking silence to mean consent, desired the superior to address her, henceforth, as Miss Barrington; the first startling intimation of the change being a strangely, quaintly written note, addressed to her grand-aunt, and signed "Josephine Barrington." It was a cold, formal letter, —so very formal, indeed, as to read like the copy of a document, —asking for leave to enter upon a novitiate of two years' duration, at the expiration of which she would be nineteen years of age, and in a position to decide upon taking the veil for life. The permission, very urgently pressed for by Mr. Gower in another letter, was accorded, and now we have arrived at that period in which but three months only remained of the two years whose closure was to decide her fate forever.

Barrington had long yearned to see her. It was with deep and bitter self-reproach he thought over the cold neglect they had shown her. She was all that remained of poor George, his boy,—for so he called him, and so he thought of him,—long after the bronzed cheek and the prematurely whitened hair had tempered his manhood. To be sure, all the world said, and he knew himself, how it was chiefly through the "boy's" extravagance he came to ruin. But it was over now. The event that sobers down reproach to sorrow had come. He was dead! All that arose to memory of him were the traits that suggested hopes of his childhood, or gave triumph in his riper years; and oh, is it not better thus? for what hearts would be left us if we were to carry in them the petty rancors and jealousies which once filled them, but which, one day, we buried in the cold clay of the churchyard.

Aunt Dinah, moved by reasons long canvassed over in her own mind, at last began to think of recalling her grand-niece. It was so very bold a project that, at first, she could scarcely entertain it. The Popery was very dreadful! Her imagination conjured up the cottage converted into a little Baal, with false gods and graven images, and holy-water fonts at every turn; but the doubtful legitimacy was worse again. She had a theory that it was by lapses of this kind the "blue blood" of old families grew deteriorated, and that the downfall of many an ancient house was traceable to these corruptions. Far better, she deemed it, that the Barringtons should die out forever than their line be continued by this base and ignoble grafting.

There is a *contre* for every *pour* in this world. It may be a weak and an insufficient one, it is true; but it is a certainty that all our projects must come to a debtor or creditor reckoning, and the very best we can do is to strike an honest balance!

How Miss Dinah essayed to do this we shall learn in the next chapter and what follows it.

CHAPTER II.

A WET MORNING AT HOME

If there was anything that possessed more than common terror for Barrington, it was a wet day at the cottage! It was on these dreary visitations that his sister took the opportunity of going into "committee of supply,"—an occasion not merely for the discussion of fiscal matters, but for asking the most vexatious questions and demanding the most unpleasant explanations.

We can all, more or less, appreciate the happiness of that right honorable gentleman on the Treasury bench who has to reply to the crude and unmeaning inquiries of some aspiring Oppositionist, and who wishes to know if her Majesty's Government have demanded an indemnity from the King of Dahomey for the consul's family eaten by him at the last court ceremonial? What compensation is to be given to Captain Balrothery for his week's imprisonment at Leghorn, in consequence of his having thrown the customs officer and a landing waiter into the sea? Or what mark of her Majesty's favor will the noble lord recommend should be conferred upon Ensign Digges for the admirable imitation he gave of the dancing dervishes at Benares, and the just ridicule he thus threw upon these degrading and heathenish rites?

It was to a torture of this order, far more reasonable and pertinent, however, that Barrington usually saw himself reduced whenever the weather was so decidedly unfavorable that egress was impossible. Poor fellow, what shallow pretexts would he stammer out for absenting himself from home, what despicable subterfuges to put off an audience! He had forgotten to put down the frame on that melon-bed.

There was that awning over the boat not taken in. He 'd step out to the stable and give Billy, the pony, a touch of the white oils on that swelled hock. He 'd see if they had got the young lambs under cover. In fact, from his perturbed and agitated manner, you would have imagined that rain was one of the rarest incidents of an Irish climate, and only the very promptest measures could mitigate the calamity.

"May I ask where you are off to in such haste, Peter?" asked Miss Dinah one morning, just as Barrington had completed all his arrangements for a retreat; far readier to brave the elements than the more pitiless pelting that awaited him within doors.

"I just remembered," said he, mildly, "that I had left two night-lines out at the point, and with this fresh in the river it would be as well if I 'd step down and see—"

"And see if the river was where it was yesterday," broke she in, sneeringly.

"No, Dinah. But you see that there 's this to be remarked about night-lines—"

"That they never catch any fish!" said she, sternly. "It's no weather for you to go tramping about in the wet grass. You made fuss enough about your lumbago last week, and I suppose you don't want it back again. Besides,"—and here her tongue grew authoritative,—"I have got up the books." And with these words she threw on the table a number of little greasy-looking volumes, over which poor Barrington's sad glances wandered, pretty much as might a victim's over the thumb-screws and the flesh-nippers of the Holy Inquisition.

"I've a slight touch of a headache this morning, Dinah."

"It won't be cured by going out in the rain. Sit down there," said she, peremptorily, "and see with your own eyes how much longer your means will enable you to continue these habits of waste and extravagance."

"These what?" said he, perfectly astounded.

"These habits of waste and extravagance, Peter Barring-ton. I repeat my words."

Had a venerable divine, being asked on the conclusion of an edifying discourse, for how much longer it might be his intention to persist in such ribaldries, his astonishment could scarce have been greater than Barrington's.

"Why, sister Dinah, are we not keeping an inn? Is not this the 'Fisherman's Home'?"

"I should think it is, Peter," said she, with scorn. "I suspect he finds it so. A very excellent name for it it is!"

"Must I own that I don't understand you, Dinah?"

"Of course you don't. You never did all your life. You never knew you were wet till you were half drowned, and that's what the world calls having such an amiable disposition! Ain't your friends nice friends? They are always telling you how generous you are,—how free-handed,—how benevolent. What a heart he has! Ay, but thank Providence there's very little of that charming docility about *me*, is there?"

"None, Dinah,—none," said he, not in the least suspecting to what he was bearing testimony.

She became crimson in a minute, and in a tone of some emotion said, "And if there had been, where should you and where should I be to-day? On the parish, Peter Barrington,—on the parish; for it 's neither *your* head nor *your* hands would have saved us from it."

"You're right, Dinah; you're right there. You never spoke a truer word." And his voice trembled as he said it.

"I did n't mean *that*, Peter," said she, eagerly; "but you are too confiding, too trustful. Perhaps it takes a woman to detect all the little wiles and snares that entangle us in our daily life?"

"Perhaps it does," said he, with a deep sigh.

"At all events, you needn't sigh over it, Peter Barring-ton. It's not one of those blemishes in human nature that have to be deplored so feelingly. I hope women are as good as men."

"Fifty thousand times better, in every quality of kindliness and generosity."

"Humph!" said she, tossing her head impatiently. "We 're not here for a question in ethics; it is to the very lowly task of examining the house accounts I would invite your attention. Matters cannot go on as they do now, if we mean to keep a roof over us."

"But I have always supposed we were doing pretty well, Dinah. You know we never promised ourselves to gain a fortune by this venture; the very utmost we ever hoped for was to help us along,—to aid us to make both ends meet at the end of the year And as Darby tells me—"

"Oh, Darby tells you! What a reliable authority to quote from! Oh, don't groan so heavily! I forgot myself. I would n't for the world impeach such fidelity or honesty as his."

"Be reasonable, sister Dinah,—do be reasonable; and if there is anything to lay to his charge—"

"You 'll hear the case, I suppose," cried she, in a voice high-pitched in passion. "You 'll sit up there, like one of your favorite judges, and call on Dinah Barrington against Cassan; and perhaps when the cause is concluded we shall reverse our places, and *I* become the defendant! But if this is your intention, brother Barrington, give me a little time. I beg I may have a little time."

Now, this was a very favorite request of Miss Barring-ton's, and she usually made it in the tone of a martyr; but truth obliges us to own that never was a demand less justifiable. Not a three-decker of the Channel fleet was readier for a broadside than herself. She was always at quarters and with a port-fire burning.

Barrington did not answer this appeal; he never moved,—he scarcely appeared to breathe, so guarded was he lest his most unintentional gesture should be the subject of comment.

"When you have recovered from your stupefaction," said she, calmly, "will you look over that line of figures, and then give a glance at this total? After that I will ask you what fortune could stand it."

"This looks formidable, indeed," said he, poring over the page through his spectacles.

"It is worse, Peter. It *is* formidable."

"After all, Dinah, this is expenditure. Now for the incomings!"

"I suspect you 'll have to ask your prime minister for *them*. Perhaps he may vouchsafe to tell you how many twenty-pound notes have gone to America, who it was that consigned a cargo of new potatoes to Liverpool, and what amount he invested in yarn at the last fair of Graigue? and when you have learned these facts, you will know all you are ever likely to know of your *profits!*" I have no means of conveying the intense scorn with which she uttered the last word of this speech.

"And he told me—not a week back—that we were going on famously!"

"Why wouldn't he? I'd like to hear what else he could say. Famously, indeed, for *him* with a strong balance in the savings-bank, and a gold watch—yes, Peter, a gold watch—in his pocket. This is no delusion, nor illusion, or whatever you call it, of mine, but a fact,—a downright fact."

"He has been toiling hard many a year for it, Dinah, don't forget that."

"I believe you want to drive me mad, Peter. You know these are things that I can't bear, and that's the reason you say them. Toil, indeed! *I* never saw him do anything except sit on a gate at the Lock Meadows, with a pipe in his mouth; and if you asked him what he was there for, it was a 'track' he was watching, a 'dog-fox that went by every afternoon to the turnip field.' Very great toil that was!"

"There wasn't an earth-stopper like him in the three next counties; and if I was to have a pack of foxhounds tomorrow—"

"You'd just be as great a foot as ever you were, and the more sorry I am to hear it; but you're not going to be tempted, Peter Barrington. It's not foxes we have to think of, but where we're to find shelter for ourselves."

"Do you know of anything we could turn to, more profitable, Dinah?" asked he, mildly.

"There's nothing could be much less so, I know *that!* You are not very observant, Peter, but even to you it must have become apparent that great changes have come over the world in a few years. The persons who formerly indulged their leisure were all men of rank and fortune. Who are the people who come over here now to amuse themselves? Staleybridge and Manchester creatures, with factory morals and bagman manners; treating our house like a commercial inn, and actually disputing the bill and asking for items. Yes, Peter, I overheard a fellow telling Darby last week that the "'ouse was dearer than the Halbion!'"

"Travellers will do these things, Dinah."

"And if they do, they shall be shown the door for it, as sure as my name is Dinah Barrington."

"Let us give up the inn altogether, then," said he, with a sudden impatience.

"The very thing I was going to propose, Peter," said she, solemnly.

"What!—how?" cried he, for the acceptance of what only escaped him in a moment of anger overwhelmed and stunned him. "How are we to live, Dinah?"

"Better without than with it,—there's my answer to that. Let us look the matter fairly in the face, Peter," said she, with a calm and measured utterance. "This dealing with the world 'on honor' must ever be a losing game. To screen ourselves from the vulgar necessities of our condition, we must submit to any terms. So long as our intercourse with life gave us none but gentlemen to deal with, we escaped well and safely. That race would seem to have thinned off of late, however; or, what comes to the same, there is such a deluge of spurious coin one never knows what is real gold."

"You may be right, Dinah; you may be right."

"I know I am right; the experience has been the growth of years too. All our efforts to escape the odious contact of these people have multiplied our expenses. Where one man used to suffice, we keep three. You yourself, who felt it no indignity to go out a-fishing formerly with a chance traveller, have to own with what reserve and caution you would accept such companionship now."

"Nay, nay, Dinah, not exactly so far as that—"

"And why not? Was it not less than a fortnight ago three Birmingham men crossed the threshold, calling out for old Peter,—was old Peter to the good yet?"

"They were a little elevated with wine, sister, remember that; and, besides, they never knew, never had heard of me in my once condition."

"And are we so changed that they cannot recognize the class we pertain to?"

"Not *you*, Dinah, certainly not you; but I frankly own I can put up with rudeness and incivility better than a certain showy courtesy some vulgar people practise towards me. In the one case I feel I am not known, and my secret is safe. In the other, I have to stand out as the ruined gentleman, and I am not always sure that I play the part as gracefully as I ought."

"Let us leave emotions, Peter, and descend to the lowland of arithmetic, by giving up two boatmen, John and Terry—"

"Poor Terry!" sighed he, with a faint, low accent

"Oh! if it be 'poor Terry!' I 've done," said she, closing the book, and throwing it down with a slap that made him start.

"Nay, dear Dinah; but if we could manage to let him have something,—say five shillings a week,—he 'd not need it long; and the port wine that was doing his rheumatism such good is nearly finished; he'll miss it sorely."

"Were you giving him Henderson's wine,—the '11 vintage?" cried she, pale with indignation.

"Just a bottle or two, Dinah; only as medicine."

"As a fiddlestick, sir! I declare I have no patience with you; there 's no excuse for such folly, not to say the ignorance of giving these creatures what they never were used to. Did not Dr. Dill tell you that tonics, to be effective, must always have some relation to the daily habits of the patient?"

"Very true, Dinah; but the discourse was pronounced when I saw him putting a bottle of old Madeira in his gig that I had left for Anne M'Cafferty, adding, he 'd send her something far more strengthening."

"Right or wrong, I don't care; but this I know, Terry Dogherty is n't going to finish off Henderson's port. It is rather too much to stand, that we are to be treating beggars to luxuries, when we can't say to-morrow where we shall find salt for our potatoes." This was a somewhat favorite illustration of Miss Barrington,—either implying that the commodity was an essential to human life, or the use of it an emblem of extreme destitution.

"I conclude we may dispense with Tom Divett's services," resumed she. "We can assuredly get on without a professional rat-catcher."

"If we should, Dinah, we'll feel the loss; the rats make sad havoc of the spawn, and destroy quantities of the young fish, besides."

"His two ugly terriers eat just as many chickens, and never leave us an egg in the place. And now for Mr. Darby—"

"You surely don't think of parting with Darby, sister Dinah?"

"He shall lead the way," replied she, in a firm and peremptory voice; "the very first of the batch! And it will, doubtless, be a great comfort to you to know that you need not distress yourself about any provision for his declining years. It is a care that he has attended to on his own part. He 'll go back to a very well-feathered nest, I promise you."

Barrington sighed heavily, for he had a secret sorrow on that score. He knew, though his sister did not, that he had from year to year been borrowing every pound of Darby's savings to pay the cost of law charges, always hoping and looking for the time when a verdict in his favor would enable him to restore the money twice told. With a very dreary sigh, then, did he here allude "to the well-feathered nest" of one he had left bare and destitute. He cleared his throat, and made an effort to avow the whole matter; but his courage failed him, and he sat mournfully shaking his head, partly in sorrow, partly in shame. His sister noticed none of these signs; she was rapidly enumerating all the reductions that could be made,—all the dependencies cut off; there were the boats, which constantly required repairs; the nets, eternally being renewed,—all to be discarded; the island, a very pretty little object in the middle of the river, need no longer be rented. "Indeed," said she, "I don't know why we took it, except it was to give those memorable picnics you used to have there."

"How pleasant they were, Dinah; how delightful!" said he, totally overlooking the spirit of her remark.

"Oh! they were charming, and your own popularity was boundless; but I 'd have you to bear in mind, brother Peter, that popularity is no more a poor man's luxury than champagne. It is a very costly indulgence, and can rarely be had on 'credit.'"

Miss Barrington had pared down retrenchment to the very quick. She had shown that they could live not only without boatmen, rat-catchers, gardener, and manservant, but that, as they were to give up their daily newspaper, they could dispense with a full ration of candle-light; and yet, with all these reductions, she declared that there was still another encumbrance to be pruned away, and she proudly asked her brother if he could guess what it was?

Now Barrington felt that he could not live without a certain allowance of food, nor would it be convenient, or even decent, to dispense with raiment; so he began, as a last resource, to conjecture that his sister was darkly hinting at something which might be a substitute for a home, and save house-rent; and he half testily exclaimed, "I suppose we 're to have a roof over us, Dinah!"

"Yes," said she, dryly, "I never proposed we should go and live in the woods. What I meant had a reference, to Josephine—"

Barrington's cheek flushed deeply in an instant, and, with a voice trembling with emotion, he said,—

"If you mean, Dinah, that I'm to cut off that miserable pittance—that forty pounds a year—I give to poor George's girl—" He stopped, for he saw that in his sister's face which might have appalled a bolder heart than his own; for while her eyes flashed fire, her thin lips trembled with passion; and so, in a very faltering humility, he added: "But you never meant *that* sister Dinah. You would be the very last in the world to do it."

"Then why impute it to me; answer me that?" said she, crossing her hands behind her back, and staring haughtily at him.

"Just because I 'm clean at my wits' end,—just because I neither understand one word I hear, or what I say in reply. If you 'll just tell me what it is you propose, I 'll do my best, with God's blessing, to follow you; but don't ask me for advice, Dinah, and don't fly out because I 'm not as quick-witted and as clever as yourself."

There was something almost so abject in his misery that she seemed touched by it, and, in a voice of a very calm and kindly meaning, she said,—

"I have been thinking a good deal over that letter of Josephine's; she says she wants our consent to take the veil as a nun; that, by the rules of the order, when her novitiate is concluded, she must go into the world for at least some months,—a time meant to test her faithfulness to her vows, and the tranquillity with which she can renounce forever all the joys and attractions of life. We, it is true, have no means of surrounding her with such temptations; but we might try and supply their place by some less brilliant but not less attractive ones. We might offer her, what we ought to have offered her years ago,—a home! What do you say to this, Peter?"

"That I love you for it, sister Dinah, with all my heart," said he, kissing her on each cheek; "that it makes me happier than I knew I ever was to be again."

"Of course, to bring Josephine here, this must not be an inn, Peter."

"Certainly not, Dinah,—certainly not. But I can think of nothing but the joy of seeing her,—poor George's child I How I have yearned to know if she was like him,—if she had any of his ways, any traits of that quaint, dry humor he had, and, above all, of that disposition that made him so loved by every one."

"And cheated by every one too, brother Peter; don't forget that!"

"Who wants to think of it now?" said he, sorrowfully.

"I never reject a thought because it has unpleasant associations. It would be but a sorry asylum which only admitted the well-to-do and the happy."

"How are we to get the dear child here, Dinah? Let us consider the matter. It is a long journey off."

"I have thought of that too," said she, sententiously, "but not made up my mind."

"Let us ask M'Cormick about it, Dinah; he's coming up this evening to play his Saturday night's rubber with Dill. He knows the Continent well."

"There will be another saving that I did n't remember, Peter. The weekly bottle of whiskey, and the candles, not to speak of the four or five shillings your pleasant companions invariably carry away with them,—all may be very advantageously dispensed with."

"When Josephine 's here, I 'll not miss it," said he, good-humoredly. Then suddenly remembering that his sister might not deem the speech a gracious one to herself, he was about to add something; but she was gone.

CHAPTER III.

OUR NEXT NEIGHBORS

Should there be amongst my readers any one whose fortune it has been in life only to associate with the amiable, the interesting, and the agreeable, all whose experiences of mankind are rose-tinted, to him I would say, Skip over two people I am now about to introduce, and take up my story at some later stage, for I desire to be truthful, and, as is the misfortune of people in my situation, I may be very disagreeable.

After all, I may have made more excuses than were needful. The persons I would present are in that large category, the commonplace, and only as uninviting and as tiresome as we may any day meet in a second-class on the railroad. Flourish, therefore, penny trumpets, and announce Major M'Cormick. The Major, so confidently referred to by Barrington in our last chapter as a high authority on matters continental, was a very shattered remnant of the unhappy Walcheren expedition. He was a small, mean-looking, narrow-faced man, with a thin, bald head, and red whiskers. He walked very lame from an injury to his hip; "his wound," he called it, though his candor did not explain that it was incurred by being thrown down a hatchway by a brother officer in a drunken brawl. In character he was a saving, penurious creature, without one single sympathy outside his own immediate interests. When some sixteen or eighteen years before the Barringtons had settled in the neighborhood, the Major began to entertain thoughts of matrimony. Old soldiers are rather given to consider marriage as an institution especially intended to solace age and console rheumatism, and so M'Cormick debated with himself whether he had not arrived at the suitable time for this indulgence, and also whether Miss Dinah Barrington was not the individual destined to share his lot and season his gruel.

But a few years back and his ambition would as soon have aspired to an archduchess as to the sister of Barrington, of Barrington Hall, whose realms of social distinction separated them; but now, fallen from their high estate, forgotten by the world, and poor, they had come down—at least, he thought so—to a level in which there would be no presumption in his pretensions. Indeed, I half suspect that he thought there was something very high-minded and generous in his intentions with regard to them. At all events, there was a struggle of some sort in his mind which went on from year to year undecided. Now, there are men—for the most part old bachelors—to whom an unfinished project is a positive luxury, who like to add, day by day, a few threads to the web of fate, but no more. To the Major it was quite enough that "some fine day or other"—so he phrased it—he'd make his offer, just as he thought how, in the same propitious weather, he 'd put a new roof on his cottage, and fill up that quarry-hole near his gate, into which he had narrowly escaped tumbling some half-dozen times. But thanks to his caution and procrastination, the roof, and the project, and the quarry-hole were exactly, or very nearly, in the same state they had been eighteen years before.

Rumor said—as rumor will always say whatever has a tinge of ill-nature in it—that Miss Barrington would have accepted him; vulgar report declared that she would "jump at the offer." Whether this be, or not, the appropriate way of receiving a matrimonial proposal, the lady was not called upon to display her activity. He never told his love.

It is very hard to forgive that secretary, home or foreign, who in the day of his power and patronage could, but did not, make us easy for life with this mission or that com-missionership. It is not easy to believe that our uncle the bishop could not, without any undue strain upon his conscience, have made us something, albeit a clerical error, in his diocese, but infinitely more difficult is it to pardon him who, having suggested dreams of wedded happiness, still stands hesitating, doubting, and canvassing,—a timid bather, who shivers on the beach, and then puts on his clothes again.

It took a long time—it always does in such cases—ere Miss Barrington came to read this man aright. Indeed, the light of her own hopes had dazzled her, and she never saw him clearly till they were extinguished; but when the knowledge did come, it came trebled with compound interest, and she saw him in all that displayed his miserable selfishness; and although her brother, who found it hard to believe any one bad who had not been tried for a capital felony, would explain away many a meanness by saying, "It is just his way,—a way, and no more!" she spoke out fearlessly, if not very discreetly, and declared she detested him. Of course she averred it was his manners, his want of breeding, and his familiarity that displeased her. He might be an excellent creature,—perhaps he was; *that* was nothing to her. All his moral qualities might have an interest for his friends; she was a mere acquaintance, and was only concerned for what related to his bearing in society. Then Walcheren was positively odious to her. Some little solace she felt at the thought that the expedition was a failure and inglorious; but when she listened to the fiftieth time-told tale of fever and ague, she would sigh, not for those who suffered, but over the one that escaped. It is a great blessing to men of uneventful lives and scant imagination when there is any one incident to which memory can refer unceasingly. Like some bold headland last seen at sea, it lives in the mind throughout the voyage. Such was this ill-starred expedition to the Major. It dignified his existence to himself, though his memory never soared above the most ordinary details and vulgar incidents. Thus he would maunder on for hours, telling how the ships sailed and parted company, and joined again; how the old "Brennus" mistook a signal and put back to Hull, and how the "Sarah Reeves," his own transport, was sent after her. Then he grew picturesque about Flushing, as first seen through the dull fogs of the Scheldt, with village spires peeping through the heavy vapor, and the strange Dutch language, with its queer names for the vegetables and fruit brought by the boats alongside.

"You won't believe me, Miss Dinah, but, as I sit here, the peaches was like little melons, and the cherries as big as walnuts."

"They made cherry-bounce out of them, I hope, sir," said she, with a scornful smile.

"No, indeed, ma'am," replied he, dull to the sarcasm; "they ate them in a kind of sauce with roast-pig, and mighty good too!"

But enough of the Major; and now a word, and only a word, for his companion, already alluded to by Barrington.

Dr. Dill had been a poor "Dispensary Doctor" for some thirty years, with a small practice, and two or three grand patrons at some miles off, who employed him for the servants, or for the children in "mild cases," and who even extended to him a sort of contemptuous courtesy that serves to make a proud man a bear, and an humble man a sycophant.

Dill was the reverse of proud, and took to the other line with much kindliness. To have watched him in his daily round you would have said that he liked being trampled on, and actually enjoyed being crushed. He smiled so blandly, and looked so sweetly under it all, as though it was a kind of moral shampooing, from which he would come out all the fresher and more vigorous.

The world is certainly generous in its dealings with these temperaments; it indulges them to the top of their hearts, and gives them humiliations to their heart's content. Rumor—the same wicked goddess who libelled Miss Barrington—hinted that the doctor was not, within his own walls and under his own roof, the suffering angel the world saw him, and that he occasionally did a little trampling there on his own account. However, Mrs. Dill never complained; and though the children wore a tremulous terror and submissiveness in their looks, they were only suitable family traits, which all redounded to their credit, and made them "so like the doctor."

Such were the two worthies who slowly floated along on the current of the river of a calm summer's evening, to visit the Barringtons. As usual, the talk was of their host. They discussed his character and his habits and his debts, and the difficulty he had in raising that little loan; and in close juxtaposition with this fact, as though pinned on the back of it, his sister's overweening pride and pretension. It had been the Major's threat for years that he 'd "take her down a peg one of these days." But either he was mercifully unwilling to perform the act, or that the suitable hour for it had not come; but there she remained, and there he left her, not taken down one inch, but loftier and haughtier than ever. As the boat rounded the point from which the cottage was visible through the trees and some of the outhouses could be descried, they reverted to the ruinous state everything was falling into. "Straw is cheap enough, anyhow," said the Major. "He might put a new thatch on that cow-house, and I 'm sure a brush of paint would n't ruin any one." Oh, my dear reader! have you not often heard—I know that I have—such comments as these, such reflections on the indolence or indifference which only needed so very little to reform, done, too, without trouble or difficulty, habits that could be corrected, evil ways reformed, and ruinous tendencies arrested, all as it were by a "rush of paint," or something just as uncostly?

"There does n't seem to be much doing here, Dill," said M'Cormick, as they landed. "All the boats are drawn up ashore. And faith! I don't wonder, that old woman is enough to frighten the fish out of the river."

"Strangers do not always like that sort of thing," modestly remarked the doctor, — the "always" being peculiarly marked for emphasis. "Some will say, an inn should be an inn."

"That's my view of it. What I say is this: I want my bit of fish, and my beefsteak, and my pint of wine, and I don't want to know that the landlord's grandfather entertained the king, or that his aunt was a lady-in-waiting. 'Be' as high as you like,' says I, 'but don't make the bill so,' — eh, Dill?" And he cackled the harsh ungenial laugh which seems the birthright of all sorry jesters; and the doctor gave a little laugh too, more from habit, however, than enjoyment.

"Do you know, Dill," said the Major, disengaging himself from the arm which his lameness compelled him to lean on, and standing still in the pathway, — "do you know that I never reach thus far without having a sort of struggle with myself whether I won't turn back and go home again. Can you explain that, now?"

"It is the wound, perhaps, pains you, coming up the hill."

"It is not the wound. It's that woman!"

"Miss Barrington?"

"Just so. I have her before me now, sitting up behind the urn there, and saying, 'Have you had tea, Major M'Cormick?' when she knows well she did n't give it to me. Don't you feel that going up to the table for your cup is for all the world like doing homage?"

"Her manners are cold, — certainly cold."

"I wish they were. It's the fire that's in her I 'm afraid of! She has as wicked an eye in her head as ever I saw."

"She was greatly admired once, I 'm told; and she has many remains of beauty."

"Oh! for the matter of looks, there's worse. It's her nature, her temper, — herself, in fact, I can't endure."

"What is it you can't endure, M'Cormick?" cried Barrington, emerging from a side walk where he had just caught the last words. "If it be anything in this poor place of mine, let me hear, that I may have it amended."

"How are ye, — how are ye?" said the Major, with a very confused manner. "I was talking politics with Dill. I was telling him how I hated *them* Tories."

"I believe they are all pretty much alike," said Barring-ton; "at least, I knew they were in my day. And though we used to abuse him, and drink all kind of misfortunes to him every day of our lives, there was n't a truer gentleman nor a finer fellow in Ireland than Lord Castlereagh."

"I'm sure of it. I've often heard the same remark," chimed in Dill.

"It's a pity you didn't think so at the time of the Union," said M'Cormick, with a sneer.

"Many of us did; but it would not make us sell our country. But what need is there of going back to those times, and things that can't be helped now? Come in and have a cup of tea. I see my sister is waiting for us."

Why was it that Miss Barrington, on that evening, was grander and statelier than ever? Was it some anticipation of the meditated change in their station had impressed her manner with more of pride? I know not; but true it is she received her visitors with a reserve that was actually chilling. To no end did Barrington exert himself to conceal or counteract this frigidity. In all our moral chemistry we have never yet hit upon an antidote to a chilling reception.

WARM TEA AND COLD RECEPTION

The doctor was used to this freezing process, and did not suffer like his companion. To him, life was a huge ice-pail; but he defied frost-bite, and bore it. The

Major, however chafed and fidgeted under the treatment, and muttered to himself very vengeful sentiments about that peg he had determined to take her down from.

"I was hoping to be able to offer you a nosegay, dear lady," said Dill,—this was his customary mode of address to her, an ingenious blending of affection with deference, but in which the stronger accent on the last word showed the deference to predominate,—"but the rain has come so late, there's not a stock in the garden fit to present to you."

"It is just as well, sir. I detest gillyflowers."

The Major's eyes sparkled with a spiteful delight, for he was sorely jealous of the doctor's ease under difficulties.

"We have, indeed, a few moss-roses."

"None to be compared to our own, sir. Do not think of it."

The Major felt that his was not a giving disposition, and consequently it exempted him from rubs and rebuffs of this sort. Meanwhile, unabashed by failure, the doctor essayed once more: "Mrs. Dill is only waiting to have the car mended, to come over and pay her dutiful respects to you, Miss Dinah."

"Pray tell her not to mind it, Dr. Dill," replied she, sharply, "or to wait till the fourth of next month, which will make it exactly a year since her last visit; and her call can be then an annual one, like the tax-gatherer's."

"Bother them for taxes altogether," chimed in Barrington, whose ear only caught the last word. "You haven't done with the county cess when there's a fellow at you for tithes; and they're talking of a poor-rate."

"You may perceive, Dr. Dill, that your medicines have not achieved a great success against my brother's deafness."

"We were all so at Walcheren," broke in M'Cormick; "when we 'd come out of the trenches, we could n't hear for hours."

"My voice may be a shrill one, Major M'Cormick, but I'll have you to believe that it has not destroyed my brother's tympanum."

"It's not the tympanum is engaged, dear lady; it's the Eustachian tube is the cause here. There's a passage leads down from the internal ear—"

"I declare, sir, I have just as little taste for anatomy as for fortification; and though I sincerely wish you could cure my brother, as I also wish these gentlemen could have taken Walcheren, I have not the slightest desire to know how."

"I 'll beg a little more tea in this, ma'am," said the Major, holding out his cup.

"Do you mean water, sir? Did you say it was too strong?"

"With your leave, I 'll take it a trifle stronger," said he, with a malicious twinkle in his eye, for he knew all the offence his speech implied.

"I'm glad to hear you say so, Major M'Cormick. I'm happy to know that your nerves are stronger than at the time of that expedition you quote with such pleasure. Is yours to your liking, sir?"

"I 'll ask for some water, dear lady," broke in Dill, who began to think that the fire was hotter than usual. "As I said to Mrs. Dill, 'Molly,' says I, 'how is it that I never drink such tea anywhere as at the—'" He stopped, for he was going to say, the Harringtons', and he trembled at the liberty; and he dared not say the Fisherman's Home, lest it should be thought he was recalling their occupation; and so, after a pause and a cough, he stammered out—"'at the sweet cottage.'" Nor was his confusion the less at perceiving how she had appreciated his difficulty, and was smiling at it.

"Very few strangers in these parts lately, I believe," said M'Cormick, who knew that his remark was a dangerous one.

"I fancy none, sir," said she, calmly. "We, at least, have no customers, if that be the name for them."

"It's natural, indeed, dear lady, you shouldn't know how they are called," began the doctor, in a fawning tone, "reared and brought up as you were."

The cold, steady stare of Miss Barrington arrested his speech; and though he made immense efforts to recover himself, there was that in her look which totally overcame him. "Sit down to your rubber, sir," said she, in a whisper that seemed to thrill through his veins. "You will find yourself far more at home at the odd trick there, than attempting to console me about my lost honors." And with this fierce admonition, she gave a little nod, half in adieu, half in admonition, and swept haughtily out of the room.

M'Cormick heaved a sigh as the door closed after her, which very plainly bespoke how much he felt the relief.

"My poor sister is a bit out of spirits this evening," said Barrington, who merely saw a certain show of constraint over his company, and never guessed the cause. "We've had some unpleasant letters, and one thing or another to annoy us, and if she does n't join us at supper, you 'll excuse her, I know, M'Cormick."

"That we will, with—" He was going to add, "with a heart and a half," for he felt, what to him was a rare sentiment, "gratitude;" but Dill chimed in,—

"Of course, we couldn't expect she'd appear. I remarked she was nervous when we came in. I saw an expression in her eye—"

"So did I, faith," muttered M'Cormick, "and I'm not a doctor."

"And here's our whist-table," said Barrington, bustling about; "and there 's a bit of supper ready there for us in that room, and we 'll help ourselves, for I 've sent Darby to bed. And now give me a hand with these cards, for they 've all got mixed together."

Barrington's task was the very wearisome one of trying to sort out an available pack from some half-dozen of various sizes and colors.

"Is n't this for all the world like raising a regiment out of twenty volunteer corps?" said M'Cormick.

"Dill would call it an hospital of incurables," said Barrington. "Have you got a knave of spades and a seven? Oh dear, dear! the knave, with the head off him! I begin to suspect we must look up a new pack." There was a tone of misgiving in the way he said this; for it implied a reference to his sister, and all its consequences. Affecting to search for new cards in his own room, therefore, he arose and went out.

"I wouldn't live in a slavery like that," muttered the Major, "to be King of France."

"Something has occurred here. There is some latent source of irritation," said Dill, cautiously. "Barrington's own manner is fidgety and uneasy. I have my suspicion matters are going on but poorly with them."

While this sage diagnosis was being uttered, M'Cormick had taken a short excursion into the adjoining room, from which he returned, eating a pickled onion. "It's the old story; the cold roast loin and the dish of salad. Listen! Did you hear that shout?"

"I thought I heard one awhile back; but I fancied afterwards it was only the noise of the river over the stones."

"It is some fellows drawing the river; they poach under his very windows, and he never sees them."

"I 'm afraid we 're not to have our rubber this evening," said Dill, mournfully.

"There's a thing, now, I don't understand!" said M'Cormick, in a low but bitter voice. "No man is obliged to see company, but when he does do it, he oughtn't to be running about for a tumbler here and a mustard-pot there. There's the noise again; it's fellows robbing the salmon-weir!"

"No rubber to-night, I perceive that," reiterated the doctor, still intent upon the one theme.

"A thousand pardons I ask from each of you," cried Barrington, coming hurriedly in, with a somewhat flushed face; "but I 've had such a hunt for these cards. When I put a thing away nowadays, it's as good as gone to me, for I remember nothing. But here we are, now, all right."

The party, like men eager to retrieve lost time, were soon deep in their game, very little being uttered, save such remarks as the contest called for. The Major was of that order of players who firmly believe fortune will desert them if they don't whine and complain of their luck, and so everything from him was a lamentation. The doctor, who regarded whist pathologically, no more gave up a game than he would a patient. He had witnessed marvellous recoveries in the most hopeless cases, and he had been rescued by a "revoke" in the last hour. Unlike each, Barrington was one who liked to chat over his game, as he would over his wine. Not that he took little interest in it, but it had no power to absorb and engross him. If a man derive very great pleasure from a pastime in which, after years and years of practice, he can attain no eminence nor any mastery, you may be almost certain he is one of an amiable temperament Nothing short of real goodness of nature could go on deriving enjoyment from a pursuit associated with continual defeats. Such a one must be hopeful, he must be submissive, he must have no touch of ungenerous jealousy in his nature, and, withal, a zealous wish to do better. Now he who can be all these, in anything, is no bad fellow.

If Barrington, therefore, was beaten, he bore it well. Cards were often enough against him, his play was always so; and though the doctor had words of bland consolation for disaster, such as the habits of his craft taught him, the Major was a pitiless adversary, who never omitted the opportunity of disinterring all his opponents' blunders, and singing a song of triumph over them. But so it is, — *tot genera hominum*, — so many kinds of whist-players are there!

Hour after hour went over, and it was late in the night. None felt disposed to sup; at least, none proposed it. The stakes were small, it is true, but small things are great to little men, and Barrington's guests were always the winners.

"I believe if I was to be a good player, — which I know in my heart I never shall," said Barrington, — "that my luck would swamp me, after all. Look at that hand now, and say is there a trick in it?" As he said this, he spread out the cards of his "dummy" on the table, with the dis-consolation of one thoroughly beaten.

"Well, it might be worse," said Dill, consolingly. "There's a queen of diamonds; and I would n't say, if you could get an opportunity to trump the club—"

"Let him try it," broke in the merciless Major; "let him just try it! My name isn't Dan M'Cormick if he'll win one card in that hand. There, now, I lead the ace of clubs. Play!"

"Patience, Major, patience; let me look over my hand. I 'm bad enough at the best, but I 'll be worse if you hurry me. Is that a king or a knave I see there?"

"It's neither; it 's the queen!" barked out the Major.

"Doctor, you 'll have to look after my eyes as well as my ears. Indeed, I scarcely know which is the worst. Was not that a voice outside?"

"I should think it was; there have been fellows shouting there the whole evening. I suspect they don't leave you many fish in this part of the river."

"I beg your pardon," interposed Dill, blandly, "but you 've taken up my card by mistake."

While Barrington was excusing himself, and trying to recover his lost clew to the game, there came a violent knocking at the door, and a loud voice called out, "Holloa! Will some of ye open the door, or must I put my foot through it?"

"There *is* somebody there," said Barrington, quietly, for he had now caught the words correctly; and taking a candle, he hastened out.

"At last," cried a stranger, as the door opened, — "at last! Do you know that we've been full twenty minutes here, listening to your animated discussion over the odd trick? — I fainting with hunger, and my friend with pain." And so saying, he assisted another to limp forward, who leaned on his arm and moved with the greatest difficulty.

The mere sight of one in suffering repressed any notion of a rejoinder to his somewhat rude speech, and Barrington led the way into the room.

THE ACCIDENT

"Have you met with an accident?" asked he, as he placed the sufferer on a sofa.

"Yes," interposed the first speaker; "he slipped down one of those rocks into the river, and has sprained, if he has not broken, something."

"It is our good fortune to have advice here; this gentleman is a doctor."

"Of the Royal College, and an M.D. of Aberdeen, besides," said Dill, with a professional smile, while, turning back his cuffs, he proceeded to remove the shoe and stocking of his patient.

"Don't be afraid of hurting, but just tell me at once what's the matter," said the young fellow, down whose cheeks great drops were rolling in his agony.

"There is no pronouncing at once; there is great tumefaction here. It may be a mere sprain, or it may be a fracture of the fibula simple, or a fracture with luxation."

"Well, if you can't tell the injury, tell us what's to be done for it. Get him to bed, I suppose, first?" said the friend.

"By all means, to bed, and cold applications on the affected part."

"Here's a room all ready, and at hand," said Barrington, opening the door into a little chamber replete with comfort and propriety.

"Come," said the first speaker, "Fred, all this is very snug; one might have fallen upon worse quarters." And so saying, he assisted his friend forward, and deposited him upon the bed.

While the doctor busied himself with the medical cares for his patient, and arranged with due skill the appliances to relieve his present suffering, the other stranger related how they had lost their way, having first of all taken the wrong bank of the river, and been obliged to retrace their steps upwards of three miles to retrieve their mistake.

"Where were you going to?" asked Barringtou.

"We were in search of a little inn they had told us of, called the 'Fisherman's Home.' I conclude we have reached it at last, and you are the host, I take it?"

Barrington bowed assent.

"And these gentlemen are visitors here?" But without waiting for any reply,— difficult at all times, for he spoke with great rapidity and continual change of topic,—he now stooped down to whisper something to the sick man. "My friend thinks he'll do capitally now, and, if we leave him, that he'll soon drop asleep; so I vote we give him the chance." Thus saying, he made a gesture for the others to leave, following them up as they went, almost like one enforcing an order.

"If I am correct in my reading, you are a soldier, sir," said Barrington, when they reached the outer room, "and this gentleman here is a brother officer,—Major M'Cor-mick."

"Full pay, eh?"

"No, I am an old Walcheren man."

"Walcheren—Walcheren—why, that sounds like Malplaquet or Blenheim! Where the deuce was Walcheren? Did n't believe that there was an old tumbril of that affair to the fore still. You were all licked there, or you died of the ague, or jaundice? Oh, dummy whist, as I live! Who's the unlucky dog has got the dummy?—bad as Walcheren, by Jove! Is n't that a supper I see laid out there? Don't I smell Stilton from that room?"

"If you 'll do us the honor to join us—"

"That I will, and astonish you with an appetite too! We breakfasted at a beastly hole called Graigue, and tasted nothing since, except a few peaches I stole out of an old fellow's garden on the riverside,—'Old Dan the miser,' a country fellow called him."

"I have the honor to have afforded you the entertainment you speak of," said M'Cormick, smarting with anger.

"All right! The peaches were excellent,—would have been better if riper. I 'm afraid I smashed a window of yours; it was a stone I shied at a confounded dog,—a sort of terrier. Pickled onions and walnuts, by all that 's civilized! And so this is the 'Fisherman's Home,' and you the fisherman, eh? Well, why not show a light or a lantern over the door? Who the deuce is to know that this is a place of entertainment? We only guessed it at last."

"May I help you to some mutton?" said Barrington, more amused than put out by his guest's discursiveness.

"By all means. But don't carve it that way; cut it lengthwise, as if it were the saddle, which it ought to have been. You must tell me where you got this sherry. I have tasted nothing like it for many a day,—real brown sherry. I suppose you know how they brown it? It's not done by sugar,—that's a vulgar error. It's done by boiling; they boil down so many butts and reduce them to about a fourth or a fifth. You haven't got any currant-jelly, have you? it is just as good with cold mutton as hot. And then it is the wine thus reduced they use for coloring matter. I got up all my sherry experiences on the spot."

"The wine you approve of has been in my cellar about five-and-forty years."

"It would not if I 'd have been your neighbor, rely upon that. I'd have secured every bottle of it for our mess; and mind, whatever remains of it is mine."

"Might I make bold to remark," said Dill, interposing, "that we are the guests of my friend here on this occasion?"

"Eh, what,—guests?"

"I am proud enough to believe that you will not refuse me the honor of your company; for though an innkeeper, I write myself gentleman," said Barrington, blandly, though not without emotion.

"I should think you might," broke in the stranger, heartily; "and I'd say the man who had a doubt about your claims had very little of his own. And now a word of apology for the mode of our entrance here, and to introduce myself. I am Colonel Hunter, of the 21st Hussars; my friend is a young subaltern of the regiment."

A moment before, and all the awkwardness of his position was painful to Barrington. He felt that the traveller was there by a right, free to order, condemn, and criticise as he pleased. The few words of explanation, given in all the frankness of a soldier, and with the tact of a gentleman, relieved this embarrassment, and he was himself again. As for M'Cormick and Dill, the mere announcement of the regiment he commanded seemed to move and impress them. It was one of those corps especially known in the service for the rank and fortune of its officers. The Prince himself was their colonel, and they had acquired a wide notoriety for exclusiveness and pride, which, when treated by unfriendly critics, assumed a shape less favorable still.

Colonel Hunter, if he were to be taken as a type of his regiment, might have rebutted a good deal of this floating criticism; he had a fine honest countenance, a rich mellow voice, and a sort of easy jollity in manner, that spoke well both for his spirits and his temper. He did, it is true, occasionally chafe against some susceptible spot or other of those around him, but there was no malice prepense in it, any more than there is intentional offence in the passage of a strong man through a crowd; so he elbowed his way, and pushed on in conversation, never so much as suspecting that he jostled any one in his path.

Both Barrington and Hunter were inveterate sportsmen, and they ranged over hunting-fields and grouse mountains and partridge stubble and trout streams with all the zest of men who feel a sort of mesmeric brotherhood in the interchange of their experiences. Long after the Major and the doctor had taken their leave, they sat there recounting stories of their several adventures, and recalling incidents of flood and field.

In return for a cordial invitation to Hunter to stay and fish the river for some days, Barrington pledged himself to visit the Colonel the first time he should go up to Kilkenny.

"And I'll mount you. You shall have a horse I never lent in my life. I'll put you on Trumpeter,—sire Sir Hercules,—no mistake there; would carry sixteen stone with the fastest hounds in England."

Barrington shook his head, and smiled, as he said, "It's two-and-twenty years since I sat a fence. I'm afraid I'll not revive the fame of my horsemanship by appearing again in the saddle."

"Why, what age do you call yourself?"

"Eighty-three, if I live to August next."

"I'd not have guessed you within ten years of it. I've just passed fifty, and already I begin to look for a horse with more bone beneath the knee, and more substance across the loins."

"These are only premonitory symptoms, after all," said Barrington, laughing. "You've many a day before you come to a fourteen-hand cob and a kitchen chair to mount him."

Hunter laughed at the picture, and dashed away, in his own half-reckless way, to other topics. He talked of his regiment proudly, and told Barrington what a splendid set of young fellows were his officers. "I'll show you such a mess," said he, "as no corps in the service can match." While he talked of their high-hearted and generous natures, and with enthusiasm of the life of a soldier, Barrington could scarcely refrain from speaking of his own "boy," the son from whom he had hoped so much, and whose loss had been the death-blow to all his ambitions. There were, however, circumstances in that story which sealed his lips; and though the father never believed one syllable of the allegations against his son, though he had paid the penalty of a King's Bench mandamus and imprisonment for horsewhipping the editor who had aspersed his "boy," the world and the world's verdict were against him, and he did not dare to revive the memory of a name against which all the severities of the press had been directed, and public opinion had condemned with all its weight and power.

"I see that I am wearying you," said Hunter, as he remarked the grave and saddened expression that now stole over Barrington's face. "I ought to have remembered what an hour it was,—more than half-past two." And without waiting to hear a reply, he shook his host's hand cordially and hurried off to his room.

While Barrington busied himself in locking up the wine, and putting away half-finished decanters,—cares that his sister's watchfulness very imperatively exacted,—he heard, or fancied he heard, a voice from the room where the sick man lay. He opened the door very gently and looked in.

"All right," said the youth. "I'm not asleep, nor did I want to sleep, for I have been listening to you and the Colonel these two hours, and with rare pleasure, I can tell you. The Colonel would have gone a hundred miles to meet a man like yourself, so fond of the field and such a thorough sportsman."

"Yes, I was so once," sighed Barrington, for already had come a sort of reaction to the late excitement.

"Isn't the Colonel a fine fellow?" said the young man, as eager to relieve the awkwardness of a sad theme as to praise one he loved. "Don't you like him?"

"That I do!" said Barrington, heartily. "His fine genial spirit has put me in better temper with myself than I fancied was in my nature to be. We are to have some trout-fishing together, and I promise you it sha'n't be my fault if *he* doesn't like *me*."

"And may I be of the party?—may I go with you?"

"Only get well of your accident, and you shall do whatever you like. By the way, did not Colonel Hunter serve in India?"

"For fifteen years. He has only left Bengal within a few months."

"Then he can probably help me to some information. He may be able to tell me—Good-night, good-night," said he, hurriedly; "to-morrow will be time enough to think of this."

CHAPTER IV.

FRED CONYERS

Very soon after daybreak the Colonel was up and at the bedside of his young friend.

"Sorry to wake you, Fred," said he, gently; "but I have just got an urgent despatch, requiring me to set out at once for Dublin, and I did n't like to go without asking how you get on."

"Oh, much better, sir. I can move the foot a little, and I feel assured it 's only a severe sprain."

"That's all right. Take your own time, and don't attempt to move about too early. You are in capital quarters here, and will be well looked after. There is only one difficulty, and I don't exactly see how to deal with it. Our host is a reduced gentleman, brought down to keep an inn for support, but what benefit he can derive from it is not so very clear; for when I asked the man who fetched me hot water this morning for my bill, he replied that his master told him I was to be his guest here for a week, and not on any account to accept money from me. Ireland is a very strange place, and we are learning something new in it every day; but this is the strangest thing I have met yet."

"In *my* case this would be impossible. I must of necessity give a deal of trouble,—not to say that it would add unspeakably to my annoyance to feel that I could not ask freely for what I wanted."

"I have no reason to suppose, mind you, that you are to be dealt with as I have been, but it would be well to bear in mind who and what these people are."

"And get away from them as soon as possible," added the young fellow, half peevishly.

"Nay, nay, Fred; don't be impatient. You'll be delighted with the old fellow, who is a heart-and-soul sportsman. What station he once occupied I can't guess; but in the remarks he makes about horses and hounds, all his knowing hints on stable management and the treatment of young cattle, one would say that he must have had a large fortune and kept a large establishment."

In the half self-sufficient toss of the head which received this speech, it was plain that the young man thought his Colonel was easily imposed on, and that such pretensions as these would have very little success with *him*.

"I have no doubt some of your brother officers will take a run down to see how you get on, and, if so, I 'll send over a hamper of wine, or something of the kind, that you can manage to make him accept."

"It will not be very difficult, I opine," said the young man, laughingly.

"No, no," rejoined the other, misconstruing the drift of his words. "You have plenty of tact, Fred. You 'll do the thing with all due delicacy. And now, good-bye. Let me hear how you fare here." And with a hearty farewell they parted.

There was none astir in the cottage but Darby as the Colonel set out to gain the high-road, where the post-horses awaited him. From Darby, however, as he went along, he gathered much of his host's former history. It was with astonishment he learned that the splendid house of Barring-ton Hall, where he had been dining with an earl a few days ago, was the old family seat of that poor innkeeper; that the noble deer-park had once acknowledged him for master. "And will again, plase God!" burst in Darby, who thirsted for an opportunity to launch out into law, and all its bright hopes and prospects.

"We have a record on trial in Trinity Term, and an argument before the twelve Judges, and the case is as plain as the nose on your honor's face; for it was ruled by Chief Baron Medge, in the great cause of 'Peter against Todd, a widow,' that a settlement couldn't be broke by an estreat."

"You are quite a lawyer, I see," said the Colonel.

"I wish I was. I 'd rather be a judge on the bench than a king on his throne."

"And yet I am beginning to suspect law may have cost your master dearly."

"It is not ten, or twenty—no, nor thirty—thousand pounds would see him through it!" said Darby, with a triumph in his tone that seemed to proclaim a very proud declaration. "There 's families would be comfortable for life with just what we spent upon special juries."

"Well, as you tell me he has no family, the injury has been all his own."

"That's true. We're the last of the ould stock," said he, sorrowfully; and little more passed between them, till the Colonel, on parting, put a couple of guineas in his hand, and enjoined him to look after the young friend he had left behind him.

It is now my task to introduce this young gentleman to my readers. Frederick Conyers, a cornet in his Majesty's Hussars, was the only son of a very distinguished officer, Lieutenant-General Conyers, a man who had not alone served with great reputation in the field, but held offices of high political trust in India, the country where all his life had been passed. Holding a high station as a political resident at a native court, wielding great power, and surrounded by an undeviating homage, General Conyers saw his son growing up to manhood with everything that could foster pride and minister to self-exaltation around him. It was not alone the languor and indolence of an Eastern life that he had to dread for him, but the haughty temper and overbearing spirit so sure to come out of habits of domination in very early life.

Though he had done all that he could to educate his son, by masters brought at immense cost from Europe, the really important element of education,—the self-control and respect for other's rights,—only to be acquired by daily life and intercourse with equals, this he could not supply; and he saw, at last, that the project he had so long indulged, of keeping his son with him, must be abandoned. Perhaps the rough speech of an old comrade helped to dispel the illusion, as he asked, "Are you bringing up that boy to be a Rajah?" His first thought was to send him to one of the Universities, his great desire being that the young man should feel some ambition for public life and its distinctions. He bethought him, how-ever, that while the youth of Oxford and Cambridge enter upon a college career, trained by all the discipline of our public schools, Fred would approach the ordeal without any such preparation whatever. Without one to exert authority over him, little accustomed to the exercise of self-restraint, the experiment was too perilous.

To place him, therefore, where, from the very nature of his position, some guidance and control would be exercised, and where by the working of that model democracy—a mess—he would be taught to repress self-sufficiency and presump-tion, he determined on the army, and obtained a cornetcy in a regiment command-ed by one who had long served on his own staff. To most young fellows such an opening in life would have seemed all that was delightful and enjoyable. To be just twenty, gazetted to a splendid cavalry corps, with a father rich enough and generous enough to say, "Live like the men about you, and don't be afraid that your checks will come back to you," these are great aids to a very pleasant exis-tence. Whether the enervation of that life of Oriental indulgence had now become a nature to him, or whether he had no liking for the service itself, or whether the change from a condition of almost princely state to a position of mere equality with others, chafed and irritated him, but so is it, he did not "take to" the regiment, nor the regiment to him.

Now it is a fact, and not a very agreeable fact either, that a man with a mass of noble qualities may fail to attract the kindliness and good feeling towards him which a far less worthy individual, merely by certain traits, or by the semblance of them, of a yielding, passive nature is almost sure to acquire.

Conyers was generous, courageous, and loyal, in the most chivalrous sense of that word, to every obligation of friendship. He was eminently truthful and honorable; but he had two qualities whose baneful influence would disparage the very best of gifts. He was "imperious," and, in the phrase of his brother officers, "he never gave in." Some absurd impression had been made on him, as a child, that obstinacy and persistency were the noblest of attributes, and that, having said a thing, no event or circumstance could ever occur to induce a change of opinion.

Such a quality is singularly unfitted to youth, and marvellously out of place in a regiment; hence was it that the "Rajah," as he was generally called by his com-rades, had few intimates, and not one friend amongst them.

If I have dwelt somewhat lengthily on these traits, it is because their possessor is one destined to be much before us in this history. I will but chronicle one other feature. I am sorry it should be a disqualifying one. Owing in great measure, per-haps altogether, to his having been brought up in the East, where Hindoo craft and subtlety were familiarized to his mind from infancy, he was given to suspect that few things were ever done from the motives ascribed to them, and that under the open game of life was another concealed game, which was the real one. As yet, this dark and pernicious distrust had only gone the length of impressing him with a sense of his own consummate acuteness, an amount of self-satisfaction, which my reader may have seen tingeing the few words he exchanged with his Colonel before separating.

Let us see him now as he sits in a great easy-chair, his sprained ankle resting on another, in a little honeysuckle-covered arbor of the garden, a table covered with books and fresh flowers beside him, while Darby stands ready to serve him from the breakfast-table, where a very tempting meal is already spread out.

"So, then, I can't see your master, it seems," said Con-yers, half peevishly.

"Faix you can't; he's ten miles off by this. He got a letter by the post, and set out half an hour after for Kilkenny. He went to your honor's door, but seeing you was asleep he would n't wake you; 'but, Darby,' says he, 'take care of that young gentleman, and mind,' says he, 'that he wants for nothing.'"

"Very thoughtful of *him*,—very considerate indeed," said the youth; but in what precise spirit it is not easy to say.

"Who lives about here? What gentlemen's places are there, I mean?"

"There's Lord Carrackmore, and Sir Arthur Godfrey, and Moore of Ballyduff, and Mrs. Powerscroft of the Grove—"

"Do any of these great folks come down here?"

Darby would like to have given a ready assent,—he would have been charmed to say that they came daily, that they made the place a continual rendezvous; but as he saw no prospect of being able to give his fiction even twenty-four hours' currency, he merely changed from one leg to the other, and, in a tone of apology, said, "Betimes they does, when the sayson is fine."

"Who are the persons who are most frequently here?"

"Those two that you saw last night,—the Major and Dr. Dill. They 're up here every second day, fishing, and eating their dinner with the master."

"Is the fishing good?"

"The best in Ireland."

"And what shooting is there,—any partridges?"

"Partridges, be gorra! You could n't see the turnips for them."

"And woodcocks?"

"Is it woodcocks! The sky is black with the sight of them."

"Any lions?"

"Well, maybe an odd one now and then," said Darby, half apologizing for the scarcity.

There was an ineffable expression of self-satisfaction in Conyers's face at the subtlety with which he had drawn Darby into this admission; and the delight in his own acuteness led him to offer the poor fellow a cigar, which he took with very grateful thanks.

DARBY FEELINGLY APOLOGISES FOR THE SCARCITY OF IRISH LIONS

"From what you tell me, then, I shall find this place stupid enough till I am able to be up and about, eh? Is there any one who can play chess hereabout?"

"Sure there's Miss Dinah; she's a great hand at it, they tell me."

"And who is Miss Dinah? Is she young,—is she pretty?"

Darby gave a very cautious look all around him, and then closing one eye, so as to give his face a look of intense cunning, he nodded very significantly twice.

"What do you mean by that?"

"I mane that she'll never see sixty; and for the matter of beauty—"

"Oh, you have said quite enough; I 'm not curious about her looks. Now for another point. If I should want to get away from this, what other inn or hotel is there in the neighborhood?"

"There's Joe M'Cabe's, at Inistioge; but you are better where you are. Where will you see fresh butter like that? and look at the cream, the spoon will stand in it. Far and near it's given up to her that nobody can make coffee like Miss Dinah; and when you taste them trout, you 'll tell me if they are not fit for the king."

"Everything is excellent,—could not be better; but there's a difficulty. There's a matter which to me at least makes a stay here most unpleasant. My friend tells me that he could not get his bill,—that he was accepted as a guest. Now I can't permit this—"

"There it is, now," said Darby, approaching the table, and dropping his voice to a confidential whisper. "That's the master's way. If he gets a stranger to sit down with him to dinner or supper, he may eat and drink as long as he plases, and sorra sixpence he'll pay; and it's that same ruins us, nothing else, for it's then he 'll call for the best sherry, and that ould Maderia that's worth a guinea a bottle. What's the use, after all, of me inflaming the bill of the next traveller, and putting down everything maybe double? And worse than all," continued he, in a tone of horror, "let him only hear any one complain about his bill or saying, 'What's this?' or 'I didn't get that,' out he'll come, as mighty and as grand as the Lord-Liftinint, and say, 'I 'm sorry, sir, that we failed to make this place agreeable to you. Will you do me the favor not to mind the bill at all?' and with that he'd tear it up in little bits and walk away."

"To me that would only be additional offence. I 'd not endure it."

"What could you do? You'd maybe slip a five-pound note into my hand, and say, 'Darby my man, settle this little matter for me; you know the ways of the place.'"

"I 'll not risk such an annoyance, at all events; that I 'm determined on."

Darby began now to perceive that he had misconceived his brief, and must alter his pleadings as quickly as possible; in fact, he saw he was "stopping an earth" he had meant merely to mask. "Just leave it all to me, your honor,—leave it all to me, and I 'll have your bill for you every morning on the breakfast-table. And why would n't you? Why would a gentleman like your honor be behouldin' to any one for his meat and drink?" burst he in, with an eager rapidity. "Why would n't you say, 'Darby, bring me this, get me that, fetch me the other; expinse is no object in life tome'?"

There was a faint twinkle of humor in the eye of Conyers, and Darby stopped short, and with that half-lisping simplicity which a few Irishmen understand to perfection, and can exercise whenever the occasion requires, he said: "But sure is n't your honor laughing at me, is n't it just making fun of me you are? All because I'm a poor ignorant crayture that knows no better!"

"Nothing of that kind," said Conyers, frankly. "I was only smiling at thoughts that went through my head at the moment."

"Well, faix! there's one coming up the path now won't make you laugh," said

Darby, as he whispered, "It's Dr. Dill."

The doctor was early with his patient; if the case was not one of urgency, the sufferer was in a more elevated rank than usually fell to the chances of Dispensary practice. Then, it promised to be one of the nice chronic cases, in which tact and personal agreeability—the two great strongholds of Dr. Dill in his own estimation—were of far more importance than the materia medica. Now, if Dill's world was not a very big one, he knew it thoroughly. He was a chronicle of all the family incidents of the county, and could recount every disaster of every house for thirty miles round.

When the sprain had, therefore, been duly examined, and all the pangs of the patient sufficiently condoled with to establish the physician as a man of feeling, Dill proceeded to his task as a man of the world. Conyers, however, abruptly stopped him, by saying, "Tell me how I'm to get out of this place; some other inn, I mean."

"You are not comfortable here, then?" asked Dill.

"In one sense, perfectly so. I like the quietness, the delightful tranquillity, the scenery,—everything, in short, but one circumstance. I'm afraid these worthy people—whoever they are—want to regard me as a guest. Now I don't know them,—never saw them,—don't care to see them. My Colonel has a liking for all this sort of thing. It has to his mind a character of adventure that amuses him. It would n't in the least amuse me, and so I want to get away."

"Yes," repeated Dill, blandly, after him, "wants to get away; desires to change the air."

"Not at all," broke in Conyers, peevishly; "no question of air whatever. I don't want to be on a visit. I want an inn. What is this place they tell me of up the river,—Inis—something?"

"Inistioge. M'Cabe's house; the 'Spotted Duck;' very small, very poor, far from clean, besides."

"Is there nothing else? Can't you think of some other place? For I can't have my servant here, circumstanced as I am now."

The doctor paused to reply. The medical mind is eminently ready-witted, and Dill at a glance took in all the dangers of removing his patient. Should he transfer him to his own village, the visit which now had to be requited as a journey of three miles and upwards, would then be an affair of next door. Should he send him to Thomastown, it would be worse again, for then he would be within the precincts of a greater than Dill himself,—a practitioner who had a one-horse phaeton, and whose name was written on brass. "Would you dislike a comfortable lodging in a private family,—one of the first respectability, I may make bold to call it?"

"Abhor it!—couldn't endure it! I'm not essentially troublesome or exacting, but I like to be able to be either, whenever the humor takes me."

"I was thinking of a house where you might freely take these liberties—"

"Liberties! I call them rights, doctor, not liberties! Can't you imagine a man, not very wilful, not very capricious, but who, if the whim took him, would n't stand being thwarted by any habits of a so-called respectable family? There, don't throw up your eyes, and misunderstand me. All I mean is, that my hours of eating and sleeping have no rule. I smoke everywhere; I make as much noise as I please; and I never brook any impertinent curiosity about what I do, or what I leave undone."

"Under all the circumstances, you had, perhaps, better remain where you are," said Dill, thoughtfully.

"Of course, if these people will permit me to pay for my board and lodging. If they 'll condescend to let me be a stranger, I ask for nothing better than this place."

"Might I offer myself as a negotiator?" said Dill, insinuatingly; "for I opine that the case is not of the difficulty you suppose. Will you confide it to my hands?"

"With all my heart. I don't exactly see why there should be a negotiation at all; but if there must, pray be the special envoy."

When Dill arose and set out on his mission, the young fellow looked after him with an expression that seemed to say, "How you all imagine you are humbugging me, while I read every one of you like a book!"

Let us follow the doctor, and see how he acquitted himself in his diplomacy.

CHAPTER V.

DILL AS A DIPLOMATIST

Dr. Dill had knocked twice at the door of Miss Barrington's little sitting-room, and no answer was returned to his summons.

"Is the dear lady at home?" asked he, blandly. But, though he waited for some seconds, no reply came.

"Might Dr. Dill be permitted to make his compliments?"

"Yes, come in," said a sharp voice, very much with the expression of one wearied out by importunity. Miss Barrington gave a brief nod in return for the profound obeisance of her visitor, and then turned again to a large map which covered the table before her.

"I took the opportunity of my professional call here this morning—"

"How is that young man,—is anything broken?"

"I incline to say there is no fracture. The flexors, and perhaps, indeed, the annular ligament, are the seat of all the mischief."

"A common sprain, in fact; a thing to rest for one day, and hold under the pump the day after."

"The dear lady is always prompt, always energetic; but these sort of cases are often complicated, and require nice management."

"And frequent visits," said she, with a dry gravity.

"All the world must live, dear lady,—all the world must live."

"Your profession does not always sustain your theory, sir; at least, popular scandal says you kill as many as you cure." "I know the dear lady has little faith in physic."

"Say none, sir, and you will be nearer the mark; but, remember, I seek no converts; I ask nobody to deny himself the luxuries of senna and gamboge because I prefer beef and mutton. You wanted to see my brother, I presume," added she, sharply, "but he started early this morning for Kilkenny. The Solicitor-General wanted to say a few words to him on his way down to Cork."

"That weary law! that weary law!" ejaculated Dill, fervently; for he well knew with what little favor Miss Barrington regarded litigation.

"And why so, sir?" retorted she, sharply. "What greater absurdity is there in being hypochondriac about your property than your person? My brother's taste inclines to depletion by law; others prefer the lancet."

"Always witty, always smart, the dear lady," said Dill, with a sad attempt at a smile. The flattery passed without acknowledgment of any kind, and he resumed: "I dropped in this morning to you, dear lady, on a matter which, perhaps, might not be altogether pleasing to you."

"Then don't do it, sir."

"If the dear lady would let me finish—"

"I was warning you, sir, not even to begin."

"Yes, madam," said he, stung into something like resistance; "but I would have added, had I been permitted, without any due reason for displeasure on your part."

"And are *you* the fitting judge of that, sir? If you know, as you say you know, that you are about to give me pain, by what presumption do you assert that it must be for my benefit? What's it all about?"

"I come on the part of this young gentleman, dear lady, who, having learned—I cannot say where or how—that he is not to consider himself here at an inn, but, as a guest, feels, with all the gratitude that the occasion warrants, that he has no claim to the attention, and that it is one which would render his position here too painful to persist in."

"How did he come by this impression, sir? Be frank and tell me."

"I am really unable to say, Miss Dinah."

"Come, sir, be honest, and own that the delusion arose from yourself,—yes, from yourself. It was in perceiving the courteous delicacy with which you declined a fee that he conceived this flattering notion of us; but go back to him, doctor, and say it is a pure mistake; that his breakfast will cost him one shilling, and his dinner two; the price of a boat to fetch him up to Thomastown is half a crown, and that the earlier he orders one the better. Listen to me, sir," said she, and her lips trembled with passion,—"listen to me, while I speak of this for the first and last time. Whenever my brother, recurring to what he once was, has been emboldened to treat a passing stranger as his guest, the choice has been so judiciously exercised as to fall upon one who could respect the motive and not resent the liberty; but never till this moment has it befallen us to be told that the possibility—the bare possibility—of such a presumption should be met by a declaration of refusal. Go back, then, to your patient, sir; assure him that he is at an inn, and that he has the right to be all that his purse and his want of manners can insure him."

"Dear lady, I'm, maybe, a bad negotiator."

"I trust sincerely, sir, you are a better doctor."

"Nothing on earth was further from my mind than offence—"

"Very possibly, sir; but, as you are aware, blisters will occasionally act with all the violence of caustics, so an irritating theme may be pressed at a very inauspicious moment. My cares as a hostess are not in very good favor with me just now. Counsel your young charge to a change of air, and I 'll think no more of the matter."

Had it been a queen who had spoken, the doctor could not more palpably have felt that his audience had terminated, and his only duty was to withdraw.

And so he did retire, with much bowing and graciously smiling, and indicating, by all imaginable contortions, gratitude for the past and humility forever.

I rejoice that I am not obliged to record as history the low but fervent mutterings that fell from his lips as he closed the door after him, and by a gesture of menace showed his feelings towards her he had just quitted. "Insolent old woman!" he burst out as he went along, "how can she presume to forget a station that every incident of her daily life recalls? In the rank she once held, and can never return to, such manners would be an outrage; but I 'll not endure it again. It is your last triumph, Miss Dinah; make much of it." Thus sustained by a very Dutch courage, — for this national gift can come of passion as well as drink, — he made his way to his patient's presence, smoothing his brow, as he went, and recalling the medico-chirurgical serenity of his features.

"I have not done much, but I have accomplished something," said he, blandly. "I am at a loss to understand what they mean by introducing all these caprices into their means of life; but, assuredly, it will not attract strangers to the house."

"What are the caprices you allude to?"

"Well, it is not very easy to say; perhaps I have not expressed my meaning quite correctly; but one thing is clear, a stranger likes to feel that his only obligation in an inn is to discharge the bill."

"I say, doctor," broke in Conyers, "I have been thinking the matter over. Why should I not go back to my quarters? There might surely be some means contrived to convey me to the high-road; after that, there will be no difficulty whatever."

The doctor actually shuddered at the thought. The sportsman who sees the bird he has just winged flutter away to his neighbor's preserve may understand something, at least, of Dr. Dill's discomfiture as he saw his wealthy patient threatening a departure. He quickly, therefore, summoned to his aid all those terrors which had so often done good service on like occasions. He gave a little graphic sketch of every evil consequence that might come of an imprudent journey. The catalogue was a bulky one; it ranged over tetanus, mortification, and disease of the bones. It included every sort and description of pain as classified by science, into "dull, weary, and incessant," or "sharp lancinating agony." Now Conyers was as brave as a lion, but had, withal, one of those temperaments which are miserably sensitive under suffering, and to which the mere description of pain is itself an acute pang. When, therefore, the doctor drew the picture of a case very like the present one, where amputation came too late, Conyers burst in with, "For mercy's sake, will you stop! I can't sit here to be cut up piece-meal; there's not a nerve in my body you haven't set ajar." The doctor blandly took out his massive watch, and laid his fingers on the young man's pulse. "Ninety-eight, and slightly intermittent," said he, as though to himself.

"What does that mean?" asked Conyers, eagerly.

"The irregular action of the heart implies abnormal condition of the nervous system, and indicates, imperatively, rest, repose, and tranquillity."

"If lethargy itself be required, this is a capital place for it," sighed Conyers, drearily.

"You have n't turned your thoughts to what I said awhile ago, being domesticated, as one might call it, in a nice quiet family, with all the tender attentions of a home, and a little music in the evening."

Simple as these words were, Dill gave to each of them an almost honeyed utterance.

"No; it would bore me excessively. I detest to be looked after; I abhor what are called attentions."

"Unobtrusively offered,—tendered with a due delicacy and reserve?"

"Which means a sort of simpering civility that one has to smirk for in return. No, no; I was bred up in quite a different school, where we clapped our hands twice when we wanted a servant, and the fellow's head paid for it if he was slow in coming. Don't tell me any more about your pleasant family, for they 'd neither endure me, nor I them. Get me well as fast as you can, and out of this confounded place, and I 'll give you leave to make a vascular preparation of me if you catch me here again!"

The doctor smiled, as doctors know how to smile when patients think they have said a smartness, and now each was somewhat on better terms with the other.

"By the way, doctor," said Conyers, suddenly, "you have n't told me what the old woman said. What arrangement did you come to?"

"Your breakfast will cost one shilling, your dinner two. She made no mention of your rooms, but only hinted that, whenever you took your departure, the charge for the boat was half a crown."

"Come, all this is very business-like, and to the purpose; but where, in Heaven's name, did any man live in this fashion for so little? We have a breakfast-mess, but it's not to be compared with this,—such a variety of bread, such grilled trout, such a profusion of fruit. After all, doctor, it is very like being a guest, the nominal charge being to escape the sense of a favor. But perhaps one can do here as at one of those 'hospices' in the Alps, and make a present at parting to requite the hospitality."

"It is a graceful way to record gratitude," said the doctor, who liked to think that the practice could be extended to other reminiscences.

"I must have my servant and my books, my pipes and my Spitz terrier. I 'll get a target up, besides, on that cherry-tree, and practise pistol-shooting as I sit here. Could you find out some idle fellow who would play chess or *écarté* with me,—a curate or a priest,—I 'm not particular; and when my man Holt comes, I 'll make him string my grass-mat hammock between those two elms, so that I can fish with-out the bore of standing up for it. Holt is a rare clever fellow, and you 'll see how he'll get things in order here before he's a day in the place."

The doctor smiled again, for he saw that his patient desired to be deemed a marvel of resources and a mine of original thought. The doctor's smile was ap-portioned to his conversation, just as he added syrups in his prescriptions. It was, as he himself called it, the "vehicle," without special efficacy in itself, but it aided to get down the "active principle." But he did more than smile. He promised all possible assistance to carry out his patient's plans. He was almost certain that a friend of his, an old soldier, too, — a Major M'Cormick, — could play *écarté*, though, perhaps, it might be cribbage; and then Father Cody, he could answer for it, was wonderful at skittles, though, for the present, that game might not be practicable; and as for books, the library at Woodstay was full of them, if the key could only be come at, for the family was abroad; and, in fact, he displayed a most generous will-ingness to oblige, although, when brought to the rude test of reality, his pictures were only dissolving views of pleasures to come.

When he took his leave at last, he left Conyers in far better spirits than he found him. The young fellow had begun to castle-build about how he should pass his time, and in such architecture there is no room for ennui. And what a rare or-gan must constructiveness be, when even in its mockery it can yield such pleasure! We are very prone to envy the rich man, whose wealth sets no limit to his caprices; but is not a rich fancy, that wondrous imaginative power which unweariedly in-vents new incidents, new personages, new situations, a very covetable possession? And can we not, in the gratification of the very humblest exercise of this quality, rudely approximate to the ecstasy of him who wields it in all its force? Not that Fred Conyers was one of these; he was a mere tyro in the faculty, and could only carry himself into a region where he saw his Spitz terrier jump between the back rails of a chair, and himself sending bullet after bullet through the very centre of the bull's eye.

Be it so. Perhaps you and I, too, my reader, have our Spitz terrier and bull's-eye days, and, if so, let us be grateful for them.

CHAPTER VI.

THE DOCTOR'S DAUGHTER

Whether it was that Dr. Dill expended all the benevolence of his disposition in the course of his practice, and came home utterly exhausted, but so it was, that his family never saw him in those moods of blandness which he invariably appeared in to his patients. In fact, however loaded he went forth with these wares of a morning, he disposed of every item of his stock before he got back at night; and when poor Mrs. Dill heard, as she from time to time did hear, of the doctor's gentleness, his kindness in suffering, his beautiful and touching sympathy with sorrow, she listened with the same sort of semi-stupid astonishment she would have felt on hearing some one eulogizing the climate of Ireland, and going rapturous about the blue sky and the glorious sunshine. Unhappy little woman, she only saw him in his dark days of cloud and rain, and she never came into his presence except in a sort of moral mackintosh made for the worst weather.

The doctor's family consisted of seven children, but our concern is only with the two eldest,—a son and a daughter. Tom was two years younger than his sister, who, at this period of our story, was verging on nineteen. He was an awkward, ungainly youth, large-jointed, but weakly, with a sandy red head and much-freckled face, just such a disparaging counterpart of his sister as a coarse American piracy often presents of one of our well-printed, richly papered English editions. "It was all there," but all unseemly, ungraceful, undignified; for Polly Dill was pretty. Her hair was auburn, her eyes a deep hazel, and her skin a marvel of transparent whiteness. You would never have hesitated to call her a very pretty girl if you had not seen her brother, but, having seen him, all the traits of her good looks suffered in the same way that Grisi's "Norma" does from the horrid recollection of Paul Bedford's.

After all, the resemblance went very little further than this "travestie," for while he was a slow, heavy-witted, loutish creature, with low tastes and low ambitions, she was a clever, intelligent girl, very eagerly intent on making something of her advantages. Though the doctor was a general practitioner, and had a shop, which he called "Surgery," in the village, he was received at the great houses in a sort of half-intimate, half-patronizing fashion; as one, in short, with whom it was not necessary to be formal, but it might become very inconvenient to have a coldness. These were very sorry credentials for acceptance, but he made no objection to them.

A few, however, of the "neighbors"—it would be ungenerous to inquire the motive, for in this world of ours it is just as well to regard one's five-pound note as convertible into five gold sovereigns, and not speculate as to the kind of rags it is made of—were pleased to notice Miss Dill, and occasionally invite her to their larger gatherings, so that she not only gained opportunities of cultivating her social gifts, but, what is often a greater spur to ambition, of comparing them with those of others.

Now this same measuring process, if only conducted without any envy or ungenerous rivalry, is not without its advantage. Polly Dill made it really profitable. I will not presume to say that, in her heart of hearts, she did not envy the social accidents that gave others precedence before her, but into her heart of hearts neither you nor I have any claim to enter. Enough that we know nothing in her outward conduct or bearing revealed such a sentiment. As little did she maintain her position by flattery, which many in her ambiguous station would have relied upon as a stronghold. No; Polly followed a very simple policy, which was all the more successful that it never seemed to be a policy at all. She never in any way attracted towards her the attentions of those men who, in the marriageable market, were looked on as the choice lots; squires in possession, elder sons, and favorite nephews, she regarded as so much forbidden fruit. It was a lottery in which she never took a ticket It is incredible how much kindly notice and favorable recognition accrued to her from this line.

We all know how pleasant it is to be next to the man at a promiscuous dinner who never eats turtle nor cares for "Cliquot;" and in the world at large there are people who represent the calabash and the champagne.

Then Polly played well, but was quite as ready to play as to dance. She sang prettily, too, and had not the slightest objection that one of her simple ballads should be the foil to a grand performance of some young lady, whose artistic agonies rivalled Alboni's. So cleverly did Polly do all this, that even her father could not discover the secret of her success; and though he saw "his little girl" as he called her, more and more sought after and invited, he continued to be persuaded that all this favoritism was only the reflex of his own popularity. How, then, could mere acquaintances ever suspect what to the eye of those nearer and closer was so inscrutable?

Polly Dill rode very well and very fearlessly, and occasionally was assisted to "a mount" by some country gentleman, who combined gallantry with profit, and knew that the horse he lent could never be seen to greater advantage. Yet, even in this, she avoided display, quite satisfied, as it seemed, to enjoy herself thoroughly, and not attract any notice that could be avoided. Indeed, she never tried for "a place," but rather attached herself to some of the older and heavier weights, who grew to believe that they were especially in charge of her, and nothing was more common, at the end of a hard run, than to hear such self-gratulations as, "I think I took great care of you, Miss Dill?" "Eh, Miss Polly! you see I'm not such a bad leader!" and so on.

Such was the doctor's "little girl," whom I am about to present to my readers under another aspect. She is at home, dressed in a neatly fitting but very simple cotton dress, her hair in two plain bands, and she is seated at a table, at the opposite of which lounges her brother Tom with an air of dogged and sleepy indolence, which extends from his ill-trimmed hair to his ill-buttoned waistcoat.

"Never mind it to-day, Polly," said he, with a yawn. "I've been up all night, and have no head for work. There's a good girl, let's have a chat instead."

"Impossible, Tom," said she, calmly, but with decision. "To-day is the third. You have only three weeks now and two days before your examination. We have all the bones and ligaments to go over again, and the whole vascular system. You 've forgotten every word of Harrison."

"It does n't signify, Polly. They never take a fellow on anything but two arteries for the navy. Grove told me so."

"Grove is an ass, and got plucked twice. It is a perfect disgrace to quote him."

"Well, I only wish I may do as well. He's assistant-surgeon to the 'Taurus' gun-brig on the African station; and if I was there, it's little I 'd care for the whole lot of bones and balderdash."

"Come, don't be silly. Let us go on with the scapula. Describe the glenoid cavity."

"If you were the girl you might be, I'd not be bored with all this stupid trash, Polly."

"What do you mean? I don't understand you."

"It's easy enough to understand me. You are as thick as thieves, you and that old Admiral,—that Sir Charles Cobham. I saw you talking to the old fellow at the meet the other morning. You 've only to say, 'There's Tom—my brother Tom—wants a navy appointment; he's not passed yet, but if the fellows at the Board got a hint, just as much as, "Don't be hard on him—"'"

"I 'd not do it to make you a post-captain, sir," said she, severely. "You very much overrate my influence, and very much underrate my integrity, when you ask it."

"Hoity-toity! ain't we dignified! So you'd rather see me plucked, eh?"

"Yes, if that should be the only alternative."

"Thank you, Polly, that's all! thank you," said he; and he drew his sleeve across his eyes.

"My dear Tom," said she, laying her white soft hand on his coarse brown fingers, "can you not see that if I even stooped to anything so unworthy, that it would compromise your whole prospects in life? You'd obtain an assistant-surgeoncy, and never rise above it."

"And do I ask to rise above it? Do I ask anything beyond getting out of this house, and earning bread that is not grudged me?"

"Nay, nay; if you talk that way, I've done."

"Well, I do talk that way. He sent me off to Kilkenny last week—you saw it yourself—to bring out that trash for the shop, and he would n't pay the car hire, and made me carry two stone of carbonate of magnesia and a jar of leeches fourteen miles. You were just taking that post and rail out of Nixon's lawn as I came by. You saw me well enough."

"I am glad to say I did not," said she, sighing.

"I saw you, then, and how that gray carried you! You were waving a handkerchief in your hand; what was that for?"

"It was to show Ambrose Bushe that the ground was good; he was afraid of being staked!"

POLLY DILL

"That's exactly what I am. I 'm afraid of being 'staked up' at the Hall, and if *you* 'd take as much trouble about your brother as you did for Ambrose Bushe—"

"Tom, Tom, I have taken it for eight weary months. I believe I know Bell on the bones, and Harrison on the arteries, by heart!"

"Who thanks you?" said he, doggedly. "When you read a thing twice, you never forget it; but it's not so with me."

"Try what a little work will do, Tom; be assured there is not half as much disparity between people's brains as there is between their industry."

"I'd rather have luck than either, I know that. It's the only thing, after all."

She gave a very deep sigh, and leaned her head on her hand.

"Work and toil as hard as you may," continued he, with all the fervor of one on a favorite theme, "if you haven't luck you 'll be beaten. Can you deny that, Polly?"

"If you allow me to call merit what you call luck, I'll agree with you. But I 'd much rather go on with our work. What is the insertion of the deltoid? I'm sure you know *that!*"

"The deltoid! the deltoid!" muttered he. "I forget all about the deltoid, but, of course, it's like the rest of them. It's inserted into a ridge or a process, or whatever you call it—"

"Oh, Tom, this is very hopeless. How can you presume to face your examiners with such ignorance as this?"

"I'll tell you what I'll do, Polly; Grove told me he did it,—if I find my pluck failing me, I 'll have a go of brandy before I go in."

She found it very hard not to laugh at the solemn gravity of this speech, and just as hard not to cry as she looked at him who spoke it At the same moment Dr. Dill opened the door, calling out sharply, "Where's that fellow, Tom? Who has seen him this morning?"

"He's here, papa," said Polly. "We are brushing up the anatomy for the last time."

"His head must be in capital order for it, after his night's exploit. I heard of you, sir, and your reputable wager. Noonan was up here this morning with the whole story!"

"I 'd have won if they 'd not put snuff in the punch—"

"You are a shameless hound—"

"Oh, papa! If you knew how he was working,—how eager he is to pass his examination, and be a credit to us all, and owe his independence to himself—"

"I know more of him than you do, miss,—far more, too, than he is aware of,—and I know something of myself also; and I tell him now, that if he's rejected at the examination, he need not come back here with the news."

"And where am I to go, then?" asked the young fellow, half insolently.

"You may go—" Where to, the doctor was not suffered to indicate, for already Polly had thrown herself into his arms and arrested the speech.

"Well, I suppose I can 'list; a fellow need not know much about gallipots for that." As he said this, he snatched up his tattered old cap and made for the door.

"Stay, sir! I have business for you to do," cried Dill, sternly. "There's a young gentleman at the 'Fisherman's Home' laid up with a bad sprain. I have prescribed twenty leeches on the part. Go down and apply them."

"That's what old Molly Day used to do," said Tom, angrily.'

"Yes, sir, and knew more of the occasion that required it than you will ever do. See that you apply them all to the outer ankle, and attend well to the bleeding; the patient is a young man of rank, with whom you had better take no liberties."

"If I go at all—"

"Tom, Tom, none of this!" said Polly, who drew very close to him, and looked up at him with eyes full of tears.

"Am I going as your son this time? or did you tell him—as you told Mr. Nixon—that you 'd send your young man?"

"There! listen to that!" cried the doctor, turning to Polly. "I hope you are proud of your pupil."

She made no answer, but whispering some hurried words in her brother's ear, and pressing at the same time something into his hand, she shuffled him out of the room and closed the door.

The doctor now paced the room, so engrossed by passion that he forgot he was not alone, and uttered threats and mumbled out dark predictions with a fearful energy. Meanwhile Polly put by the books and drawings, and removed everything which might recall the late misadventure.

"What's your letter about, papa?" said she, pointing to a square-shaped envelope which he still held in his hand.

"Oh, by the way," said he, quietly, "this is from Cob-ham. They ask us up there to dinner to-day, and to stop the night." The doctor tried very hard to utter this speech with the unconcern of one alluding to some every-day occurrence. Nay, he did more; he endeavored to throw into it a certain air of fastidious weariness, as though to say, "See how these people will have me; mark how they persecute me with their attentions!"

Polly understood the "situation" perfectly, and it was with actual curiosity in her tone she asked, "Do you mean to go, sir?"

"I suppose we must, dear," he said, with a deep sigh. "A professional man is no more the arbiter of his social hours than of his business ones. Cooper always said dining at home costs a thousand a year."

"So much, papa?" asked she, with much semblance of innocence.

"I don't mean to myself," said he, reddening, "nor to any physician in country practice; but we all lose by it, more or less."

Polly, meanwhile, had taken the letter, and was reading it over. It was very brief. It had been originally begun, "Lady Cobham presents," but a pen was run through the words, and it ran,—

"Dear Dr. Dill,—If a short notice will not inconvenience you, will you and your daughter dine here to-day at seven? There is no moon, and we shall expect you to stay the night.

"Truly yours,
"Georgiana Cobham.

"The Admiral hopes Miss D. will not forget to bring her music."

"Then we go, sir?" asked she, with eagerness; for it was a house to which she had never yet been invited, though she had long wished for the entrée.

"I shall go, certainly," said he. "As to you, there will be the old discussion with your mother as to clothes, and the usual declaration that you have really nothing to put on."

"Oh! but I have, papa. My wonderful-worked muslin, that was to have astonished the world at the race ball, but which arrived too late, is now quite ready to captivate all beholders; and I have just learned that new song, 'Where's the slave so lowly?' which I mean to give with a most rebellious fervor; and, in fact, I am dying to assault this same fortress of Cobham, and see what it is like inside the citadel."

"Pretty much like Woodstay, and the Grove, and Mount Kelly, and the other places we go to," said Dill, pompously.

"The same sort of rooms, the same sort of dinner, the same company; nothing different but the liveries."

"Very true, papa; but there is always an interest in seeing how people behave in their own house, whom you have never seen except in strangers'. I have met Lady Cobham at the Beachers', where she scarcely noticed me. I am curious to see what sort of reception she will vouchsafe me at home."

"Well, go and look after your things, for we have eight miles to drive, and Billy has already been at Dangan and over to Mooney's Mills, and he 's not the fresher for it."

"I suppose I 'd better take my hat and habit, papa?"

"What for, child?"

"Just as you always carry your lancets, papa,—you don't know what may turn up." And she was off before he could answer her.

CHAPTER VII.

TOM DILL'S FIRST PATIENT

Before Tom Dill had set out on his errand he had learned all about his father and sister's dinner engagement; nor did the contrast with the way in which his own time was to be passed at all improve his temper. Indeed, he took the opportunity of intimating to his mother how few favors fell to her share or his own,—a piece of information she very philosophically received, all her sympathies being far more interested for the sorrows of "Clarissa Harlowe" than for any incident that occurred around her. Poor old lady! she had read that story over and over again, till it might seem that every word and every comma in it had become her own; but she was blessed with a memory that retained nothing, and she could cry over the sorrowful bits, and pant with eagerness at the critical ones, just as passionately, just as fervently, as she had done for years and years before. Dim, vague perceptions she might have retained of the personages, but these only gave them a stronger truthfulness, and made them more like the people of the real world, whom she had seen, passingly, once, and was now to learn more about. I doubt if Mezzofanti ever derived one tenth of the pleasure from all his marvellous memory that she did from the want of one.

Blessed with that one book, she was proof against all the common accidents of life. It was her sanctuary against duns, and difficulties, and the doctor's temper. As the miser feels a sort of ecstasy in the secret of his hoarded wealth, so had she an intense enjoyment in thinking that all dear Clarissa's trials and sufferings were only known to her. Neither the doctor, nor Polly, nor Tom, so much as suspected them. It was like a confidence between Mr. Richardson and herself, and for nothing on earth would she have betrayed it.

Tom had no such resources, and he set out on his mission with no very remarkable good feeling towards the world at large. Still, Polly had pressed into his hand a gold half-guinea,—some very long-treasured keepsake, the birthday gift of a godmother in times remote, and now to be converted into tobacco and beer, and some articles of fishing-gear which he greatly needed.

Seated in one of those light canoe-shaped skiffs,—"cots," as they are called on these rivers,—he suffered himself to be carried lazily along by the stream, while he tied his flies and adjusted his tackle. There is, sometimes, a stronger sense of unhappiness attached to what is called being "hardly used" by the world, than to a direct palpable misfortune; for though the sufferer may not be able, even to his own heart, to set out, with clearness, one single count in the indictment, yet a general sense of hard treatment, unfairness, and so forth, brings with it great depression, and a feeling of desolation.

Like all young fellows of his stamp, Tom only saw his inflictions, not one of his transgressions. He knew that his father made a common drudge of him, employed him in all that was wearisome and even menial in his craft, admitted him to no confidences, gave him no counsels, and treated him in every way like one who was never destined to rise above the meanest cares and lowest duties. Even those little fleeting glances at a brighter future which Polly would now and then open to his ambition, never came from his father, who would actually ridicule the notion of his obtaining a degree, and make the thought of a commission in the service a subject for mockery.

He was low in heart as he thought over these things. "If it were not for Polly," so he said to himself, "he 'd go and enlist;" or, as his boat slowly floated into a dark angle of the stream where the water was still and the shadow deep, he even felt he could do worse. "Poor Polly!" said he, as he moved his hand to and fro in the cold clear water, "you 'd be very, very sorry for me. You, at least, knew that I was not all bad, and that I wanted to be better. It was no fault of mine to have a head that could n't learn. I 'd be clever if I could, and do everything as well as she does; but when they see that I have no talents, that if they put the task before me I cannot master it, sure they ought to pity me, not blame me." And then he bent over the boat and looked down eagerly into the water, till, by long dint of gazing, he saw, or he thought he saw, the gravelly bed beneath; and again he swept his hand through it, — it was cold, and caused a slight shudder. Then, suddenly, with some fresh impulse, he threw off his cap, and kicked his shoes from him. His trembling hands buttoned and unbuttoned his coat with some infirm, uncertain purpose. He stopped and listened; he heard a sound; there was some one near, — quite near. He bent down and peered under the branches that hung over the stream, and there he saw a very old and infirm man, so old and infirm that he could barely creep. He had been carrying a little bundle of fagots for firewood, and the cord had given way, and his burden fallen, scattered, to the ground. This was the noise Tom had heard. For a few minutes the old man seemed overwhelmed with his disaster, and stood motionless, contemplating it; then, as it were, taking courage, he laid down his staff, and bending on his knees, set slowly to work to gather up his fagots.

There are minutes in the lives of all of us when some simple incident will speak to our hearts with a force that human words never carried, — when the most trivial event will teach a lesson that all our wisdom never gave us. "Poor old fellow," said Tom, "he has a stout heart left to him still, and he 'll not leave his load behind him!" And then his own craven spirit flashed across him, and he hid his face in his hand and cried bitterly.

Suddenly rousing himself with a sort of convulsive shake, he sent the skiff with a strong shove in shore, and gave the old fellow what remained to him of Polly's present; and then, with a lighter spirit than he had known for many a day, rowed manfully on his way.

The evening—a soft, mellow, summer evening—was just falling as Tom reached the little boat quay at the "Fisherman's Home," — a spot it was seldom his fortune to visit, but one for whose woodland beauty and trim comfort he had a deep admiration. He would have liked to have lingered a little to inspect the boat-house, and the little aviary over it, and the small cottage on the island, and the little terrace made to fish from; but Darby had caught sight of him as he landed, and came hurriedly down to say that the young gentleman was growing very impatient for his coming, and was even hinting at sending for another doctor if he should not soon appear.

If Conyers was as impatient as Darby represented, he had, at least, surrounded himself with every appliance to allay the fervor of that spirit He had dined under a spreading sycamore-tree, and now sat with a table richly covered before him. Fruit, flowers, and wine abounded, with a profusion that might have satisfied several guests; for, as he understood that he was to consider himself at an inn, he resolved, by ordering the most costly things, to give the house all the advantage of his presence. The most delicious hothouse fruit had been procured from the gardener of an absent proprietor in the neighborhood, and several kinds of wine figured on the table, over which, and half shadowed by the leaves, a lamp had been suspended, throwing a fitful light over all, that imparted a most picturesque effect to the scene.

And yet, amidst all these luxuries and delights, Bal-shazzar was discontented; his ankle pained him; he had been hobbling about on it all day, and increased the inflammation considerably; and, besides this, he was lonely; he had no one but Darby to talk to, and had grown to feel for that sapient functionary a perfect abhorrence, — his everlasting compliance, his eternal coincidence with everything, being a torment infinitely worse than the most dogged and mulish opposition. When, therefore, he heard at last the doctor's son had come with the leeches, he hailed him as a welcome guest.

"What a time you have kept me waiting!" said he, as the loutish young man came forward, so astounded by the scene before him that he lost all presence of mind. "I have been looking out for you since three o'clock, and pottering down the river and back so often, that I have made the leg twice as thick again."

"Why didn't you sit quiet?" said Tom, in a hoarse, husky tone.

"Sit quiet!" replied Conyers, staring half angrily at him; and then as quickly perceiving that no impertinence had been intended, which the other's changing color and evident confusion attested, he begged him to take a chair and fill his glass. "That next you is some sort of Rhine wine: this is sherry; and here is the very best claret I ever tasted."

"Well, I'll take that," said Tom, who, accepting the recommendation amidst luxuries all new and strange to him, proceeded to fill his glass, but so tremblingly that he spilled the wine all about the table, and then hurriedly wiped it up with his handkerchief.

Conyers did his utmost to set his guest at his ease. He passed his cigar-case across the table, and led him on, as well as he might, to talk. But Tom was awestruck, not alone by the splendors around him, but by the condescension of his host; and he could not divest himself of the notion that he must have been mistaken for somebody else, to whom all these blandishments might be rightfully due.

"Are you fond of shooting?" asked Conyers, trying to engage a conversation.

"Yes," was the curt reply.

"There must be good sport hereabouts, I should say. Is the game well preserved?"

"Too well for such as me. I never get a shot without the risk of a jail, and it would be cheaper for me to kill a cow than a woodcock!" There was a stern gravity in the way he said this that made it irresistibly comic, and Conyers laughed out in spite of himself.

"Have n't you a game license?" asked he.

"Haven't I a coach-and-six? Where would I get four pounds seven and ten to pay for it?"

The appeal was awkward, and for a moment Conyers was silent At last he said, "You fish, I suppose?"

"Yes; I kill a salmon whenever I get a quiet spot that nobody sees me, and I draw the river now and then with a net at night."

"That's poaching, I take it."

"It 's not the worse for that!" said Tom, whose pluck was by this time considerably assisted by the claret.

"Well, it's an unfair way, at all events, and destroys real sport"

"Real sport is filling your basket."

"No, no; there's no real sport in doing anything that's unfair, —anything that's un— —" He stopped short, and swallowed off a glass of wine to cover his confusion.

"That's all mighty fine for you, who can not only pay for a license, but you 're just as sure to be invited here, there, and everywhere there's game to be killed. But think of me, that never snaps a cap, never throws a line, but he knows it's worse than robbing a hen-roost, and often, maybe, just as fond of it as yourself!"

Whether it was that, coming after Darby's mawkish and servile agreement with everything, this rugged nature seemed more palatable, I cannot say; but so it was, Con-yers felt pleasure in talking to this rough unpolished creature, and hearing his opinions in turn. Had there been in Tom Dill's manner the slightest shade of any pretence, was there any element of that which, for want of a better word, we call "snobbery," Conyers would not have endured him for a moment, but Tom was perfectly devoid of this vulgarity. He was often coarse in his remarks, his expressions were rarely measured by any rule of good manners; but it was easy to see that he never intended offence, nor did he so much as suspect that he could give that weight to any opinion which he uttered to make it of moment.

Besides these points in Tom's favor, there was another, which also led Conyers to converse with him. There is some very subtle self-flattery in the condescension of one well to do in all the gifts of fortune associating, in an assumed equality, with some poor fellow to whom fate has assigned the shady side of the highway. Scarcely a subject can be touched without suggesting something for self-gratulation; every comparison, every contrast is in his favor, and Conyers, without being more of a puppy than the majority of his order, constantly felt how immeasurably above all his guest's views of his life and the world were his own,—not alone that he was more moderate in language and less prone to attribute evil, but with a finer sense of honor and a wider feeling of liberality.

When Tom at last, with some shame, remembered that he had forgotten all about the real object of his mission, and had never so much as alluded to the leeches, Conyers only laughed and said, "Never mind them to-night. Come back to-morrow and put them on; and mind,—come to breakfast at ten or eleven o'clock."

"What am I to say to my father?"

"Say it was a whim of mine, which it is. You are quite ready to do this matter now. I see it; but I say no. Is n't that enough?"

"I suppose so!" muttered Tom, with a sort of dogged misgiving.

"It strikes me that you have a very respectable fear of your governor. Am I right?"

"Ain't you afraid of yours?" bluntly asked the other.

"Afraid of mine!" cried Conyers, with a loud laugh; "I should think not. Why, my father and myself are as thick as two thieves. I never was in a scrape that I did n't tell him. I 'd sit down this minute and write to him just as I would to any fellow in the regiment."

"Well, there 's only one in all the world I 'd tell a secret to, and it is n't My father!"

"Who is it, then?"

"My sister Polly!" It was impossible to have uttered these words with a stronger sense of pride. He dwelt slowly upon each of them, and, when he had finished, looked as though he had said something utterly undeniable.

"Here's her health,—in a bumper too!" cried Conyers.

"Hurray, hurray!" shouted out Tom, as he tossed off his full glass, and set it on the table with a bang that smashed it. "Oh, I beg pardon! I didn't mean to break the tumbler."

"Never mind it, Dill; it's a trifle. I half hoped you had done it on purpose, so that the glass should never be drained to a less honored toast. Is she like *you*?"

"Like me,—like me?" asked he, coloring deeply. "Polly like me?"

"I mean is there a family resemblance? Could you be easily known as brother and sister?"

"Not a bit of it. Polly is the prettiest girl in this county, and she 's better than she 's handsome. There's nothing she can't do. I taught her to tie flies, and she can put wings on a green-drake now that would take in any salmon that ever swam. Martin Keene sent her a pound-note for a book of 'brown hackles,' and, by the way, she gave it to *me*. And if you saw her on the back of a horse!—Ambrose Bushe's gray mare, the wickedest devil that ever was bridled, one buck jump after another the length of a field, and the mare trying to get her head between her fore-legs, and Polly handling her so quiet, never out of temper, never hot, but always saying, 'Ain't you ashamed of yourself, Dido? Don't you see them all laughing at us?'"

"I am quite curious to see her. Will you present me one of these days?"

Tom mumbled out something perfectly unintelligible.

"I hope that I may be permitted to make her acquaintance," repeated he, not feeling very certain that his former speech was quite understood.

"Maybe so," grumbled he out at last, and sank back in his chair with a look of sulky ill-humor; for so it was that poor Tom, in his ignorance of life and its ways, deemed the proposal one of those free-and-easy suggestions which might be made to persons of very inferior station, and to whom the fact of acquaintance-ship should be accounted as a great honor.

Conyers was provoked at the little willingness shown to meet his offer,—an offer he felt to be a very courteous piece of condescension on his part,—and now both sat in silence. At last Tom Dill, long struggling with some secret impulse, gave way, and in a tone far more decided and firm than heretofore, said, "Maybe you think, from seeing what sort of a fellow I am, that my sister ought to be like me; and because *I* have neither manners nor education, that she 's the same? But listen to me now; she 's just as little like me as you are yourself. You 're not more of a gentleman than she's a lady!"

"I never imagined anything else."

"And what made you talk of bringing her up here to present her to you, as you called it? Was she to be trotted out in a cavasin, like a filly?"

"My dear fellow," said Conyers, good-humoredly, "you never made a greater mistake. I begged that you would present *me* to your sister. I asked the sort of fa-vor which is very common in the world, and in the language usually employed to convey such a request. I observed the recognized etiquette—"

"What do I know about etiquette? If you'd have said, 'Tom Dill, I want to be introduced to your sister,' I 'd have guessed what you were at, and I 'd have said, 'Come back in the boat with me to-morrow, and so you shall.'"

"It's a bargain, then, Dill. I want two or three things in the village, and I accept your offer gladly."

Not only was peace now ratified between them, but a closer feeling of inti-macy established; for poor Tom, not much spoiled by any excess of the world's sympathy, was so delighted by the kindly interest shown him, that he launched out freely to tell all about himself and his fortunes, how hardly treated he was at home, and how ill usage had made him despondent, and despondency made him dissolute. "It's all very well to rate a fellow about his taste for low pleasures and low companions; but what if he's not rich enough for better? He takes them just as he smokes cheap tobacco, because he can afford no other. And do you know," continued he, "you are the first real gentleman that ever said a kind word to me, or asked me to sit down in his company. It's even so strange to me yet, that maybe when I 'm rowing home to-night I 'll think it's all a dream,—that it was the wine got into my head."

"Is not some of this your own fault?" broke in Conyers. "What if you had held your head higher—"

"Hold my head higher!" interrupted Tom. "With this on it, eh?" And he took up his ragged and worn cap from the ground, and showed it. "Pride is a very fine thing when you can live up to it; but if you can't it's only ridiculous. I don't say," added he, after a few minutes of silence, "but if I was far away from this, where nobody knew me, where I did n't owe little debts on every side, and was n't obliged to be intimate with every idle vagabond about—I don't say but I'd try to be something better. If, for instance, I could get into the navy—"

"Why not the army? You 'd like it better."

"Ay! but it 's far harder to get into. There's many a rough fellow like myself aboard ship that they would n't take in a regiment. Besides, how could I get in without interest?"

"My father is a Lieutenant-General. I don't know whether he could be of service to you."

"A Lieutenant-General!" repeated Tom, with the reverential awe of one alluding to an actual potentate.

"Yes. He has a command out in India, where I feel full sure he could give you something. Suppose you were to go out there? I 'd write a letter to my father and ask him to befriend you."

"It would take a fortune to pay the journey," said Tom, despondingly.

"Not if you went out on service; the Government would send you free of cost. And even if you were not, I think we might manage it. Speak to your father about it."

"No," said he, slowly. "No; but I 'll talk it over with Polly. Not but I know well she'll say, 'There you are, castle-building and romancing. It's all moonshine! Nobody ever took notice of you,—nobody said he 'd interest himself about you.'"

"That's easily remedied. If you like it, I 'll tell your sister all about it myself. I 'll tell her it's my plan, and I 'll show her what I think are good reasons to believe it will be successful."

"Oh! would you—would you!" cried he, with a choking sensation in the throat; for his gratitude had made him almost hysterical.

"Yes," resumed Conyers. "When you come up here tomorrow, we 'll arrange it all. I 'll turn the matter all over in my mind, too, and I have little doubt of our being able to carry it through."

"You 'll not tell my father, though?"

"Not a word, if you forbid it. At the same time, you must see that he'll have to hear it all later on."

"I suppose so," muttered Tom, moodily, and leaned his head thoughtfully on his hand. But one half-hour back and he would have told Conyers why he desired this concealment; he would have declared that his father, caring more for his services than his future good, would have thrown every obstacle to his promotion, and would even, if need were, have so represented him to Conyers that he would have appeared utterly unworthy of his interest and kindness; but now not one word of all this escaped him. He never hinted another reproach against his father, for already a purer spring had opened in his nature, the rocky heart had been smitten by words of gentleness, and he would have revolted against that which should degrade him in his own esteem.

"Good night," said Conyers, with a hearty shake of the hand, "and don't forget your breakfast engagement tomorrow."

"What 's this?" said Tom, blushing deeply, as he found a crumpled bank-note in his palm.

"It's your fee, my good fellow, that's all," said the other, laughingly.

"But I can't take a fee. I have never done so. I have no right to one. I am not a doctor yet."

"The very first lesson in your profession is not to anger your patient; and if you would not provoke me, say no more on this matter." There was a half-semblance of haughtiness in these words that perhaps the speaker never intended; at all events, he was quick enough to remedy the effect, for he laid his hand good-naturedly on the other's shoulder and said, "For my sake, Dill,—for my sake."

"I wish I knew what I ought to do," said Tom, whose pale cheek actually trembled with agitation. "I mean," said he, in a shaken voice, "I wish I knew what would make *you* think best of me."

"Do you attach so much value to my good opinion, then?"

"Don't you think I might? When did I ever meet any one that treated me this way before?"

The agitation in which he uttered these few words imparted such a semblance of weakness to him that Conyers pressed him down into a chair, and filled up his glass with wine.

"Take that off, and you 'll be all right presently," said he, in a kind tone.

Tom tried to carry the glass to his lips, but his hand trembled so that he had to set it down on the table.

"I don't know how to say it," began he, "and I don't know whether I ought to say it, but somehow I feel as if I could give my heart's blood if everybody would behave to me the way you do. I don't mean, mind you, so generously, but treating me as if—as if—as if—" gulped he out at last, "as if I was a gentleman."

"And why not? As there is nothing in your station that should deny that claim, why should any presume to treat you otherwise?"

"Because I'm not one!" blurted he out; and covering his face with his hands, he sobbed bitterly.

"Come, come, my poor fellow, don't be down-hearted. I 'm not much older than yourself, but I 've seen a good deal of life; and, mark *my* words, the price a man puts on himself is the very highest penny the world will ever bid for him; he 'll not always get *that*, but he 'll never—no, never, get a farthing beyond it!"

Tom stared vacantly at the speaker, not very sure whether he understood the speech, or that it had any special application to him.

"When you come to know life as well as I do," continued Conyers, who had now launched into a very favorite theme, "you'll learn the truth of what I say. Hold your head high; and if the world desires to see you, it must at least look up!"

"Ay, but it might laugh too!" said Tom, with a bitter gravity, which considerably disconcerted the moralist, who pitched away his cigar impatiently, and set about selecting another.

"I suspect I understand *your* nature. For," said he, after a moment or two, "I have rather a knack in reading people. Just answer me frankly a few questions."

"Whatever you like," said the other, in a half-sulky sort of manner.

"Mind," said Conyers, eagerly, "as there can be no offence intended, you'll not feel any by whatever I may say."

"Go on," said Tom, in the same dry tone.

"Ain't you obstinate?"

"I am."

"I knew it. We had not talked half an hour together when I detected it, and I said to myself, 'That fellow is one so rooted in his own convictions, it is scarcely possible to shake him.'"

"What next?" asked Tom.

"You can't readily forgive an injury; you find it very hard to pardon the man who has wronged you."

"I do not; if he did n't go on persecuting me, I would n't think of him at all."

"Ah, that's a mistake. Well, I know you better than you know yourself; you *do* keep up the memory of an old grudge,—you can't help it."

"Maybe so, but I never knew it."

"You have, however, just as strong a sentiment of gratitude."

"I never knew that, either," muttered he; "perhaps because it has had so little provocation!"

"Bear in mind," said Conyers, who was rather disconcerted by the want of concurrence he had met with, "that I am in a great measure referring to latent qualities,—things which probably require time and circumstances to develop."

"Oh, if that's it," said Dili, "I can no more object than I could if you talked to me about what is down a dozen fathoms in the earth under our feet. It may be granite or it may be gold, for what I know; the only thing that I see is the gravel before me."

"I 'll tell you a trait of your character you can't gainsay," said Conyers, who was growing more irritated by the opposition so unexpectedly met with, "and it's one you need not dig a dozen fathoms down to discover,—you are very reckless."

"Reckless—reckless,—you call a fellow reckless that throws away his chance, I suppose?"

"Just so."

"But what if he never had one?"

"Every man has a destiny; every man has that in his fate which he may help to make or to mar as he inclines to. I suppose you admit that?"

"I don't know," was the sullen reply.

"Not know? Surely you needn't be told such a fact to recognize it!"

"All I know is this," said Tom, resolutely, "that I scarcely ever did anything in my life that it was n't found out to be wrong, so that at last I 've come to be pretty careless what I do; and if it was n't for Polly,—if it was n't for Polly—" He stopped, drew his sleeve across his eyes, and turned away, unable to finish.

"Come, then," said Conyers, laying his hand affectionately on the other's shoulder, "add my friendship to *her* love for you, and see if the two will not give you encouragement; for I mean to be your friend, Dill."

"Do you?" said Tom, with the tears in his eyes.

"There 's my hand on it."

CHAPTER VIII.

FINE ACQUAINTANCES

There is a law of compensation even for the small things of this life, and by the wise enactments of that law, human happiness, on the whole, is pretty equally distributed. The rich man, probably, never felt one tithe of the enjoyment in his noble demesne that it yielded to some poor artisan who strolled through it on a holiday, and tasted at once the charms of a woodland scene with all the rapturous delight of a day of rest.

Arguing from these premises, I greatly doubt if Lady Cobham, at the head of her great household, with her house crowded with distinguished visitors, surrounded by every accessory of luxury and splendor, tasted anything approaching to the delight felt by one, the very humblest of her guests, and who for a brief twenty-four hours partook of her hospitality.

Polly Dill, with all her desire and ambition for notice amongst the great people of the county, had gone to this dinner-party with considerable misgivings. She only knew the Admiral in the hunting-field; of her Ladyship she had no knowledge whatever, save in a few dry sentences uttered to her from a carriage one day at "the meet," when the Admiral, with more sailor-like frankness than politeness, presented her by saying, "This is the heroine of the day's run, Dr. Dill's daughter." And to this was responded a stare through a double eye-glass, and a cold smile and a few still colder words, affecting to be compliment, but sounding far more like a correction and a rebuke.

No wonder, then, if Polly's heart was somewhat faint about approaching as a hostess one who could be so repelling as a mere acquaintance. Indeed, one less resolutely bent on her object would not have encountered all the mortification and misery her anticipation pictured; but Polly fortified herself by the philosophy that said, "There is but one road to this goal; I must either take that one, or abandon the journey." And so she did take it.

Either, however, that she had exaggerated the grievance to her own mind, or that her Ladyship was more courteous at home than abroad; but Polly was charmed with the kindness of her reception. Lady Cobham had shaken hands with her, asked her had she been hunting lately, and was about to speak of her horsemanship to a grim old lady beside her, when the arrival of other guests cut short the compliment, and Polly passed on—her heart lightened of a great load—to mix with the general company.

I have no doubt it was a pleasant country-house; it was called the pleasantest in the county. On the present occasion it counted amongst its guests not only the great families of the neighborhood, but several distinguished visitors from a distance, of whom two, at least, are noteworthy,—one, the great lyric poet; the other, the first tragic actress of her age and country. The occasion which assembled them was a project originally broached at the Admiral's table, and so frequently discussed afterwards that it matured itself into a congress. The plan was to get up theatricals for the winter season at Kilkenny, in which all the native dramatic ability should be aided by the first professional talent. Scarcely a country-house that could not boast of, at least, one promising performer. Ruthven and Campion and Probart had in their several walks been applauded by the great in art, and there were many others who in the estimation of friends were just as certain of a high success.

Some passing remark on Polly's good looks, and the suitability of her face and style for certain small characters in comedy,—the pink ribboned damsels who are made love to by smart valets,—induced Lady Cobham to include her in her list; and thus, on these meagre credentials, was she present. She did not want notice or desire recognition; she was far too happy to be there, to hear and see and mark and observe all around her, to care for any especial attention. If the haughty Arabellas and Georgianas who swept past her without so much as a glance, were not, in her own estimation, superior in personal attractions, she knew well that they were so in all the accidents of station and the advantages of dress; and perhaps—who knows?—the reflection was not such a discouraging one.

No memorable event, no incident worth recording, marked her visit. In the world of such society the machinery moves with regularity and little friction. The comedy of real life is admirably played out by the well-bred, and Polly was charmed to see with what courtesy, what consideration, what deference people behaved to each other; and all without an effort,—perhaps without even a thought.

It was on the following day, when she got home and sat beside her mother's chair, that she related all she had seen. Her heart was filled with joy; for, just as she was taking her leave, Lady Cobham had said, "You have been promised to us for Tuesday next, Miss Dill. Pray don't forget it!" And now she was busily engaged in the cares of toilette; and though it was a mere question of putting bows of a sky-blue ribbon on a muslin dress,—one of those little travesties by which rustic beauty emulates ball-room splendor,—to her eyes it assumed all the importance of a grand preparation, and one which she could not help occasionally rising to contemplate at a little distance.

"Won't it be lovely, mamma," she said, "with a moss-rose—a mere bud—on each of those bows? But I have n't told you of how he sang. He was the smallest little creature in the world, and he tripped across the room with his tiny feet like a bird, and he kissed Lady Cobham's hand with a sort of old-world gallantry, and pressed a little sprig of jasmine she gave him to his heart,—this way,—and then he sat down to the piano. I thought it strange to see a man play!"

"Effeminate,—very," muttered the old lady, as she wiped her spectacles.

"Well, I don't know, mamma,—at least, after a moment, I lost all thought of it, for I never heard anything like his singing before. He had not much voice, nor, perhaps, great skill, but there was an expression in the words, a rippling melody with which the verses ran from his lips, while the accompaniment tinkled on beside them, perfectly rapturous. It all seemed as if words and air were begotten of the moment, as if, inspired on the instant, he poured forth the verses, on which he half dwelt, while thinking over what was to follow, imparting an actual anxiety as you listened, lest he should not be ready with his rhyme; and through all there was a triumphant joy that lighted up his face and made his eyes sparkle with a fearless lustre, as of one who felt the genius that was within him, and could trust it." And then he had been so complimentary to herself, called her that charming little "rebel," after she had sung "Where 's the Slave," and told her that until he had heard the words from her lips he did not know they were half so treasonable. "But, mamma dearest, I have made a conquest; and such a conquest, — the hero of the whole society, — a Captain Stapylton, who did something or captured somebody at Waterloo, — a bold dragoon, with a gorgeous pelisse all slashed with gold, and such a mass of splendor that he was quite dazzling to look upon." She went on, still very rapturously, to picture him. "Not very young; that is to say, he might be thirty-five, or perhaps a little more, — tall, stately, even dignified in appearance, with a beard and moustache almost white, — for he had served much in India, and he was dark-skinned as a native." And this fine soldier, so sought after and so courted, had been markedly attentive to her, danced with her twice, and promised she should have his Arab, "Mahmoud," at her next visit to Cobham. It was very evident that his notice of her had called forth certain jealousies from young ladies of higher social pretensions, nor was she at all indifferent to the peril of such sentiments, though she did not speak of them to her mother, for, in good truth, that worthy woman was not one to investigate a subtle problem, or suggest a wise counsel; not to say that her interests were far more deeply engaged for Miss Harlowe than for her daughter Polly, seeing that in the one case every motive, and the spring to every motive, was familiar to her, while in the other she possessed but some vague and very strange notions of what was told her. Clarissa had made a full confidence to her: she had wept out her sorrows on her bosom, and sat sobbing on her shoulder. Polly came to her with the frivolous narrative of a ball-room flirtation, which threatened no despair nor ruin to any one. Here were no heart-consuming miseries, no agonizing terrors, no dreadful casualties that might darken a whole existence; and so Mrs. Dill scarcely followed Polly's story at all, and never with any interest.

Polly went in search of her brother, but he had left home early that morning with the boat, no one knew whither, and the doctor was in a towering rage at his absence. Tom, indeed, was so full of his success with young Conyers that he never so much as condescended to explain his plans, and simply left a message to say, "It was likely he 'd be back by dinner-time." Now Dr. Dill was not in one of his blandest humors. Amongst the company at Cobham, he had found a great physician from Kilkenny, plainly showing him that all his social sacrifices were not to his professional benefit, and that if colds and catarrhs were going, his own services would never be called in. Captain Stapylton, too, to whom Polly had presented him, told him that he "feared a young brother officer of his, Lieutenant Conyers, had fallen into the hands of some small village practitioner, and that he would take immediate measures to get him back to headquarters," and then moved off, without giving him the time for a correction of the mistake.

He took no note of his daughter's little triumphs, the admiration that she excited, or the flatteries that greeted her. It is true he did not possess the same means of measuring these that she had, and in all that dreary leisure which besets an unhonored guest, he had ample time to mope and fret and moralize, as gloomily as might be. If, then, he did not enjoy himself on his visit, he came away from it soured and ill-humored.

He denounced "junketings"—by which unseemly title he designated the late entertainment—as amusements too costly for persons of his means. He made a rough calculation—a very rough one—of all that the "precious tomfoolery" had cost: the turnpike which he had paid, and the perquisites to servants—which he had not; the expense of Polly's finery,—a hazarded guess she would have been charmed to have had confirmed; and, ending the whole with a startling total, declared that a reign of rigid domestic economy must commence from that hour. The edict was something like what one reads from the French Government, when about to protest against some license of the press, and which opens by proclaiming that "the latitude hitherto conceded to public discussion has not been attended with those gratifying results so eagerly anticipated by the Imperial administration." Poor Mrs. Dill—like a mere journalist—never knew she had been enjoying blessings till she was told she had forfeited them forever, and she heard with a confused astonishment that the household charges would be still further reduced, and yet food and fuel and light be not excluded from the supplies. He denounced Polly's equestrianism as a most ruinous and extravagant pursuit. Poor Polly, whose field achievements had always been on a borrowed mount! Tom was a scapegrace, whose debts would have beggared half-a-dozen families,—wretched dog, to whom a guinea was a gold-mine; and Mrs. Dill, unhappy Mrs. Dill, who neither hunted, nor smoked, nor played skittles, after a moment's pause, he told her that his hard-earned pence should not be wasted in maintaining a "circulating library." Was there ever injustice like this? Talk to a man with one meal a day about gluttony, lecture the castaway at sea about not giving way to his appetites, you might just as well do so as to preach to Mrs. Dill—with her one book, and who never wanted another—about the discursive costliness of her readings.

Could it be that, like the cruel jailer, who killed the spider the prisoner had learned to love, he had resolved to rob her of Clarissa? The thought was so overwhelming that it stunned her; and thus stupefied, she saw the doctor issue forth on his daily round, without venturing one word in answer. And he rode on his way,—on that strange mission of mercy, meanness, of honest sympathy, or mock philanthropy, as men's hearts and natures make of it,—and set out for the "Fisherman's Home."

CHAPTER IX.

A COUNTRY DOCTOR

In a story, as in a voyage, one must occasionally travel with uncongenial companions. Now I have no reason for hoping that any of my readers care to keep Dr. Dill's company, and yet it is with Dr. Dill we must now for a brief space foregather. He was on his way to visit his patient at the "Fisherman's Home," having started, intentionally very early, to be there before Stapylton could have interposed with any counsels of removing him to Kilkenny.

The world, in its blind confidence in medical skill, and its unbounded belief in certain practitioners of medicine, is but scantily just to the humbler members of the craft in regard to the sensitiveness with which they feel the withdrawal of a patient from their care, and the substitution of another physician. The doctor who has not only heard, but felt Babington's adage, that the difference between a good physician and a bad one is only "the difference between a pound and a guinea," naturally thinks it a hard thing that his interests are to be sacrificed for a mere question of five per cent. He knows, besides, that they can each work on the same materials with the same tools, and it can be only through some defect in his self-confidence that he can bring himself to believe that the patient's chances are not pretty much alike in *his* hands or his rival's. Now Dr. Dill had no feelings of this sort; no undervaluing of himself found a place in his nature. He regarded medical men as tax-gatherers, and naturally thought it mattered but little which received the impost; and, thus reflecting, he bore no good will towards that gallant Captain, who, as we have seen, stood so well in his daughter's favor. Even hardened men of the world—old footsore pilgrims of life—have their prejudices, and one of these is to be pleased at thinking they had augured unfavorably of any one they had afterwards learned to dislike. It smacks so much of acuteness to be able to say, "I was scarcely presented to him; we had not exchanged a dozen sentences when I saw this, that, and t' other." Dill knew this man was overbearing, insolent, and oppressive, that he was meddlesome and interfering, giving advice unasked for, and presuming to direct where no guidance was required. He suspected he was not a man of much fortune; he doubted he was a man of good family. All his airs of pretensions—very high and mighty they were—did not satisfy the doctor. As he said himself, he was a very old bird, but he forgot to add that he had always lived in an extremely small cage.

The doctor had to leave his horse on the high-road and take a small footpath, which led through some meadows till it reached the little copse of beech and ilex that sheltered the cottage and effectually hid it from all view from the road. The doctor had just gained the last stile, when he suddenly came upon a man repairing a fence, and whose labors were being overlooked by Miss Barrington. He had scarcely uttered his most respectful salutations, when she said, "It is, perhaps, the last time you will take that path through the Lock Meadow, Dr. Dill. We mean to close it up after this week."

"Close it up, dear lady!—a right of way that has existed Heaven knows how long. I remember it as a boy myself."

"Very probably, sir, and what you say vouches for great antiquity; but things may be old and yet not respectable. Besides, it never was what you have called it,—a right of way. If it was, where did it go to?"

"It went to the cottage, dear lady. The 'Home' was a mill in those days."

"Well, sir, it is no longer a mill, and it will soon cease to be an inn."

"Indeed, dear lady! And am I to hope that I may congratulate such kind friends as you have ever been to me on a change of fortune?"

"Yes, sir; we have grown so poor that, to prevent utter destitution, we have determined to keep a private station; and with reference to that, may I ask you when this young gentleman could bear removal without injury?"

"I have not seen him to-day, dear lady; but judging from the inflammatory symptoms I remarked yesterday, and the great nervous depression—"

"I know nothing about medicine, sir; but if the nervous depression be indicated by a great appetite and a most noisy disposition, his case must be critical."

"Noise, dear lady!"

"Yes, sir; assisted by your son, he sat over his wine till past midnight, talking extremely loudly, and occasionally singing. They have now been at breakfast since ten o'clock, and you will very soon be able to judge by your own ears of the well-regulated pitch of the conversation."

"My son, Miss Dinah! Tom Dill at breakfast here?"

"I don't know whether his name be Tom or Harry, sir, nor is it to the purpose; but he is a red-haired youth, with a stoop in the shoulders, and a much-abused cap."

Dill groaned over a portrait which to him was a photograph.

"I 'll see to this, dear lady. This shall be looked into," muttered he, with the purpose of a man who pledged himself to a course of action; and with this he moved on. Nor had he gone many paces from the spot when he heard the sound of voices, at first in some confusion, but afterwards clearly and distinctly.

"I 'll be hanged if I 'd do it, Tom," cried the loud voice of Conyers. "It's all very fine talking about paternal authority and all that, and so long as one is a boy there's no help for it; but you and I are men. We have a right to be treated like men, have n't we?"

"I suppose so," muttered the other, half sulkily, and not exactly seeing what was gained by the admission.

"Well, that being so," resumed Conyers, "I'd say to the governor, 'What allowance are you going to make me?'"

"Did you do that with your father?" asked Tom, earnestly.

"No, not exactly," stammered out the other. "There was not, in fact, any need for it, for my governor is a rare jolly fellow,—such a trump! What he said to me was, 'There's a check-book, George; don't spare it.'"

"Which was as much as to say, 'Draw what you like.'"

"Yes, of course. He knew, in leaving it to my honor, there was no risk of my committing any excess; so you see there was no necessity to make my governor 'book up.' But if I was in your place I'd do it. I pledge you my word I would."

Tom only shook his head very mournfully, and made no answer. He felt, and felt truly, that there is a worldly wisdom learned only in poverty and in the struggles of narrow fortune, of which the well-to-do know absolutely nothing. Of what avail to talk to him of an unlimited credit, or a credit to be bounded only by a sense of honor? It presupposed so much that was impossible, that he would have laughed if his heart had been but light enough.

"Well, then," said Conyers, "if you have n't courage for this, let me do it; let me speak to your father."

"What could you say to him?" asked Tom, doggedly.

"Say to him?—what could I say to him?" repeated he, as he lighted a fresh cigar, and affected to be eagerly interested in the process. "It's clear enough what I'd say to him."

"Let us hear it, then," growled out Tom, for he had a sort of coarse enjoyment at the other's embarrassment. "I'll be the doctor now, and listen to you." And with this he squared his chair full in front of Conyers, and crossed his arms imposingly on his chest "You said you wanted to speak to me about my son Tom, Mr. Conyers; what is it you have to say?"

"Well, I suppose I'd open the matter delicately, and, perhaps, adroitly. I'd say, 'I have remarked, doctor, that your son is a young fellow of very considerable abilities—'"

"For what?" broke in Tom, huskily.

"Come, you 're not to interrupt in this fashion, or I can't continue. I'd say something about your natural cleverness; and what a pity it would be if, with very promising talents, you should not have those fair advantages which lead a man to success in life."

"And do you know what *he* 'd say to all that?"

"No."

"Well, I'll tell you. He'd say 'Bother!' Just 'bother.'"

"What do you mean by 'bother'?"

"That what you were saying was all nonsense. That you did n't know, nor you never could know, the struggles of a man like himself, just to make the two ends meet; not to be rich, mind you, or lay by money, or have shares in this, or stocks in that, but just to live, and no more."

"Well, I'd say, 'Give him a few hundred pounds, and start him.'"

"Why don't you say a few thousands? It would sound grander, and be just as likely. Can't you see that everybody hasn't a Lieutenant-General for a father? and that what you 'd give for a horse—that would, maybe, be staked to-morrow—would perhaps be a fortune for a fellow like me? What's that I hear coming up the river? That's the doctor, I 'm sure. I 'll be off till he's gone." And without waiting to hear a word, he sprang from his chair and disappeared in the wood.

Dr. Dill only waited a few seconds to compose his features, somewhat excited by what he had overheard; and then coughing loudly, to announce his approach, moved gravely along the gravel path.

"And how is my respected patient?" asked he, blandly. "Is the inflammation subsiding, and are our pains diminished?"

"My ankle is easier, if you mean that," said Conyers, bluntly.

"Yes, much easier,—much easier," said the doctor, examining the limb; "and our cellular tissue has less effusion, the sheaths of the tendons freer, and we are generally better. I perceive you have had the leeches applied. Did Tom—my son—give you satisfaction? Was he as attentive and as careful as you wished?"

"Yes, I liked him. I wish he 'd come up every day while I remain. Is there any objection to that arrangement?"

"None, dear sir,—none. His time is fully at your service; he ought to be working hard. It is true he should be reading eight or ten hours a day, for his examination; but it is hard to persuade him to it. Young men will be young men!"

"I hope so, with all my heart. At least, I, for one, don't want to be an old one. Will you do me a favor, doctor? and will you forgive me if I don't know how to ask it with all becoming delicacy? I'd like to give Tom a helping hand. He's a good fellow,—I 'm certain he is. Will you let me send him out to India, to my father? He has lots of places to give away, and he 'd be sure to find something to suit him. You have heard of General Conyers, perhaps, the political resident at Delhi? That's my governor." In the hurry and rapidity with which he spoke, it was easy to see how he struggled with a sense of shame and confusion.

Dr. Dill was profuse of acknowledgments; he was even moved as he expressed his gratitude. "It was true," he remarked, "that his life had been signalled by these sort of graceful services, or rather offers of services; for we are proud if we are poor, sir. 'Dill aut nil' is the legend of our crest, which means that we are ourselves or nothing."

"I conclude everybody else is in the same predicament," broke in Conyers, bluntly.

"Not exactly, young gentleman,—not exactly. I think I could, perhaps, explain—"

"No, no; never mind it. I 'm the stupidest fellow in the world at a nice distinction; besides, I'll take your word for the fact. You have heard of my father, have n't you?"

"I heard of him so late as last night, from a brother officer of yours, Captain Stapylton."

"Where did you meet Stapylton?" asked Conyers, quickly.

"At Sir Charles Cobham's. I was presented to him by my daughter, and he made the most kindly inquiries after you, and said that, if possible, he'd come over here to-day to see you."

"I hope he won't; that's all," muttered Conyers. Then, correcting himself suddenly, he said: "I mean, I scarcely know him; he has only joined us a few months back, and is a stranger to every one in the regiment. I hope you did n't tell him where I was."

"I'm afraid that I did, for I remember his adding, 'Oh! I must carry him off. I must get him back to headquarters.'"

"Indeed! Let us see if he will. That's the style of these 'Company's' officers,— he was in some Native corps or other,—they always fancy they can bully a subaltern; but Black Stapylton will find himself mistaken this time."

"He was afraid that you had not fallen into skilful hands; and, of course, it would not have come well from me to assure him of the opposite."

"Well, but what of Tom, doctor? You have given me no answer."

"It is a case for reflection, my dear young friend, if I may be emboldened to call you so. It is not a matter I can say yes or no to on the instant. I have only two grown-up children: my daughter, the most affectionate, the most thoughtful of girls, educated, too, in a way to grace any sphere—"

"You need n't tell me that Tom is a wild fellow," broke in Conyers,—for he well understood the antithesis that was coming; "he owned it all to me, himself. I have no doubt, too, that he made the worst of it; for, after all, what signifies a dash of extravagance, or a mad freak or two? You can't expect that we should all be as wise and as prudent and as cool-headed as Black Stapylton."

"You plead very ably, young gentleman," said Dill, with his smoothest accent, "but you must give me a little time."

"Well, I'll give you till to-morrow,—to-morrow, at this hour; for it wouldn't be fair to the poor fellow to keep him in a state of uncertainty. His heart is set on the plan; he told me so."

"I 'll do my best to meet your wishes, my dear young gentleman; but please to bear in mind that it is the whole future fate of my son I am about to decide. Your father may not, possibly, prove so deeply interested as you are; he may—not unreasonably, either—take a colder view of this project; he may chance to form a lower estimate of my poor boy than it is your good nature to have done."

"Look here, doctor; I know my governor something better than you do, and if I wrote to him, and said, 'I want this fellow to come home with a lac of rupees,' he 'd start him to-morrow with half the money. If I were to say, 'You are to give him the best thing in your gift,' there's nothing he 'd stop at; he 'd make him a judge, or a receiver, or some one of those fat things that send a man back to England with a fortune. What's that fellow whispering to you about? It's something that concerns me."

This sudden interruption was caused by the approach of Darby, who had come to whisper something in the doctor's ear.

"It is a message he has brought me; a matter of little consequence. I 'll look to it, Darby. Tell your mistress it shall be attended to." Darby lingered for a moment, but the doctor motioned him away, and did not speak again till he had quitted the spot. "How these fellows will wait to pick up what passes between their betters," said Dill, while he continued to follow him with his eyes. "I think I mentioned to you once, already, that the persons who keep this house here are reduced gentry, and it is now my task to add that, either from some change of fortune or from caprice, they are thinking of abandoning the inn, and resuming—so far as may be possible for them—their former standing. This project dates before your arrival here; and now, it would seem, they are growing impatient to effect it; at least, a very fussy old lady—Miss Barrington—has sent me word by Darby to say her brother will be back here tomorrow or next day, with some friends from Kilkenny, and she asks at what time your convalescence is likely to permit removal."

"Turned out, in fact, doctor,—ordered to decamp! You must say, I 'm ready, of course; that is to say, that I 'll go at once. I don't exactly see how I 'm to be moved in this helpless state, as no carriage can come here; but you 'll look to all that for me. At all events, go immediately, and say I shall be off within an hour or so."

"Leave it all to me,—leave it in my hands. I think I see what is to be done," said the doctor, with one of his confident little smiles, and moved away.

There was a spice of irritation in Conyers's manner as he spoke. He was very little accustomed to be thwarted in anything, and scarcely knew the sensation of having a wish opposed, or an obstacle set against him, but simply because there was a reason for his quitting the place, grew all the stronger his desire to remain there. He looked around him, and never before had the foliage seemed so graceful; never had the tints of the copper-beech blended so harmoniously with the stone-pine and the larch; never had the eddies of the river laughed more joyously, nor the blackbirds sung with a more impetuous richness of melody. "And to say that I must leave all this, just when I feel myself actually clinging to it. I could spend my whole life here. I glory in this quiet, unbroken ease; this life, that slips along as waveless as the stream there! Why should n't I buy it; have it all my own, to come down to whenever I was sick and weary of the world and its dissipations? The spot is small; it couldn't be very costly; it would take a mere nothing to main-tain. And to have it all one's own!" There was an actual ecstasy in the thought; for in that same sense of possession there is a something that resembles the sense of identity. The little child with his toy, the aged man with his proud demesne, are tasters of the same pleasure.

"You are to use your own discretion, my dear young gentleman, and go when it suits you, and not before," said the doctor, returning triumphantly, for he felt like a successful envoy. "And now I will leave you. To-morrow you shall have my answer about Tom."

Conyers nodded vaguely; for, alas! Tom, and all about him, had completely lapsed from his memory.

CHAPTER X.

BEING "BORED"

It is a high testimony to that order of architecture which we call castle-building, that no man ever lived in a house so fine he could not build one more stately still out of his imagination. Nor is it only to grandeur and splendor this superiority extends, but it can invest lowly situations and homely places with a charm which, alas! no reality can rival.

Conyers was a fortunate fellow in a number of ways; he was young, good-looking, healthy, and rich. Fate had made place for him on the very sunniest side of the causeway, and, with all that, he was happier on that day, through the mere play of his fancy, than all his wealth could have made him. He had fashioned out a life for himself in that cottage, very charming, and very enjoyable in its way. He would make it such a spot that it would have resources for him on every hand, and he hugged himself in the thought of coming down here with a friend, or, perhaps, two friends, to pass days of that luxurious indolence so fascinating to those who are, or fancy they are, wearied of life's pomps and vanities.

Now there are no such scoffers at the frivolity and emptiness of human wishes as the well-to-do young fellows of two or three-and-twenty. They know the "whole thing," and its utter rottenness. They smile compassionately at the eagerness of all around them; they look with bland pity at the race, and contemptuously ask, of what value the prize when it is won? They do their very best to be gloomy moralists, but they cannot. They might as well try to shiver when they sit in the sunshine. The vigorous beat of young hearts, and the full tide of young pulses, will tell against all the mock misanthropy that ever was fabricated! It would not be exactly fair to rank Conyers in this school, and yet he was not totally exempt from some of its teachings. Who knows if these little imaginary glooms, these brain-created miseries, are not a kind of moral "alterative" which, though depressing at the instant, render the constitution only more vigorous after?

At all events, he had resolved to have the cottage, and, going practically to work, he called Darby to his counsels to tell him the extent of the place, its boundaries, and whatever information he could afford as to the tenure and its rent.

"You 'd be for buying it, your honor!" said Darby, with the keen quick-sightedness of his order.

"Perhaps I had some thoughts of the kind; and, if so, I should keep you on."

Darby bowed his gratitude very respectfully. It was too long a vista for him to strain his eyes at, and so he made no profuse display of thankfulness. With all their imaginative tendencies, the lower Irish are a very bird-in-the-hand sort of people.

"Not more than seventeen acres!" cried Conyers, in astonishment. "Why, I should have guessed about forty, at least. Isn't that wood there part of it?"

"Yes, but it's only a strip, and the trees that you see yonder is in Carriclough; and them two meadows below the salmon weir is n't ours at all; and the island itself we have only a lease of it."

"It's all in capital repair, well kept, well looked after?"

"Well, it is, and isn't!" said he, with a look of disagreement. "He'd have one thing, and she'd have another; *he* 'd spend every shilling he could get on the place, and *she* 'd grudge a brush of paint, or a coat of whitewash, just to keep things together."

"I see nothing amiss here," said Conyers, looking around him. "Nobody could ask or wish a cottage to be neater, better furnished, or more comfortable. I confess I do not perceive anything wanting."

"Oh, to be sure, it's very nate, as your honor says; but then—" And he scratched his head, and looked confused.

"But then, what—out with it?"

"The earwigs is dreadful; wherever there 's roses and sweetbrier there's no livin' with them. Open the window and the place is full of them."

Mistaking the surprise he saw depicted in his hearer's face for terror, Darby launched forth into a description of insect and reptile tortures that might have suited the tropics; to hear him, all the stories of the white ant of India, or the gallinipper of Demerara, were nothing to the destructive powers of the Irish earwig. The place was known for them all over the country, and it was years and years lying empty, "by rayson of thim plagues."

Now, if Conyers was not intimidated to the full extent Darby intended by this account, he was just as far from guessing the secret cause of this representation, which was simply a long-settled plan of succeeding himself to the ownership of the "Fisherman's Home," when, either from the course of nature or an accident, a vacancy would occur. It was the grand dream of Darby's life, the island of his Government, his seat in the Cabinet, his Judgeship, his Garter, his everything, in short, that makes human ambition like a cup brimful and overflowing; and what a terrible reverse would it be if all these hopes were to be dashed just to gratify the passing caprice of a mere traveller!

"I don't suppose your honor cares for money, and, maybe, you 'd as soon pay twice over the worth of anything; but here, between our two selves, I can tell you, you 'd buy an estate in the county cheaper than this little place. They think, because they planted most of the trees and made the fences themselves, that it's like the King's Park. It's a fancy spot, and a fancy price, they'll ask for it But I know of another worth ten of it,—a real, elegant place; to be sure, it's a trifle out of repair, for the ould naygur that has it won't lay out a sixpence, but there 's every con-vaniency in life about it. There's the finest cup potatoes, the biggest turnips ever I see on it, and fish jumpin' into the parlor-window, and hares runnin' about like rats."

"I don't care for all that; this cottage and these grounds here have taken my fancy."

"And why would n't the other, when you seen it? The ould Major that lives there wants to sell it, and you 'd get it a raal bargain. Let me row your honor up there this evening. It's not two miles off, and the river beautiful all the way."

Conyers rejected the proposal abruptly, haughtily. Darby had dared to throw down a very imposing card-edifice, and for the moment the fellow was odious to him. All the golden visions of his early morning, that poetized life he was to lead, that elegant pastoralism, which was to blend the splendor of Lucullus with the simplicity of a Tityrus, all rent, torn, and scattered by a vile hind, who had not even a conception of the ruin he had caused.

And yet Darby had a misty consciousness of some success. He did not, indeed, know that his shell had exploded in a magazine; but he saw, from the confusion in the garrison, that his shot had told severely somewhere.

"Maybe your honor would rather go to-morrow? or maybe you 'd like the Major to come up here himself, and speak to you?"

"Once for all, I tell you, No! Is that plain? No! And I may add, my good fellow, that if you knew me a little better, you 'd not tender me any advice I did not ask for."

"And why would I? Would n't I be a baste if I did?"

"I think so," said Conyers, dryly, and turned away. He was out of temper with everything and everybody,—the doctor, and his abject manner; Tom, and his roughness; Darby, and his roguish air of self-satisfied craftiness; all, for the moment, displeased and offended him. "I 'll leave the place to-morrow; I 'm not sure I shall not go to-night D'ye hear?"

Darby bowed respectfully.

"I suppose I can reach some spot, by boat, where a carriage can be had?"

"By coorse, your honor. At Hunt's Mills, or Shibna-brack, you 'll get a car easy enough. I won't say it will be an elegant convaniency, but a good horse will rowl you along into Thomastown, where you can change for a shay."

Strange enough, this very facility of escape annoyed him. Had Darby only told him that there were all manner of difficulties to getting away,—that there were shallows in the river, or a landslip across the road,—he would have addressed himself to overcome the obstacles like a man; but to hear that the course was open, that any one might take it, was intolerable.

"I suppose, your honor, I 'd better get the boat ready, at all events?"

"Yes, certainly,—that is, not till I give further orders. I 'm the only stranger here, and I can't imagine there can be much difficulty in having a boat at any hour. Leave me, my good fellow; you only worry me. Go!"

And Darby moved away, revolving within himself the curious problem, that if, having plenty of money enlarged a man's means of enjoyment, it was strange how little effect it produced upon his manners. As for Conyers, he stood moodily gazing on the river, over whose placid surface a few heavy raindrops were just falling; great clouds, too, rolled heavily over the hillsides, and gathered into ominous-looking masses over the stream, while a low moaning sound of very far-off thunder foretold a storm.

Here, at least, was a good tangible grievance, and he hugged it to his heart. He was weather-bound! The tree-tops were already shaking wildly, and dark scuds flying fast over the mottled sky. It was clear that a severe storm was near. "No help for it now," muttered he, "if I must remain here till to-morrow." And hobbling as well as he could into the house, he seated himself at the window to watch the hurricane. Too closely pent up between the steep sides of the river for anything like destructive power, the wind only shook the trees violently, or swept along the stream with tiny waves, which warred against the current; but even these were soon beaten down by the rain,—that heavy, swooping, splashing rain, that seems to come from the overflowing of a lake in the clouds. Darker and darker grew the atmosphere as it fell, till the banks of the opposite side were gradually lost to view, while the river itself became a yellow flood, surging up amongst the willows that lined the banks. It was not one of those storms whose grand effects of lightning, aided by pealing thunder, create a sense of sublime terror, that has its own ecstasy; but it was one of those dreary evenings when the dull sky shows no streak of light, and when the moist earth gives up no perfume, when foliage and hillside and rock and stream are leaden-colored and sad, and one wishes for winter, to close the shutter and draw the curtain, and creep close to the chimney-corner as to a refuge.

Oh, what comfortless things are these summer storms! They come upon us like some dire disaster in a time of festivity. They swoop down upon our days of sunshine like a pestilence, and turn our joy into gloom, and all our gladness to despondency, bringing back to our minds memories of comfortless journeys, weariful ploddings, long nights of suffering.

I am but telling what Conyers felt at this sudden change of weather. You and I, my good reader, know better. We feel how gladly the parched earth drinks up the refreshing draught, how the seared grass bends gratefully to the skimming rain, and the fresh buds open with joy to catch the pearly drops. We know, too, how the atmosphere, long imprisoned, bursts forth into a joyous freedom, and comes back to us fresh from the sea and the mountain rich in odor and redolent of health, making the very air breathe an exquisite luxury. We know all this, and much more that he did not care for.

Now Conyers was only "bored," as if anything could be much worse; that is to say, he was in that state of mind in which resources yield no distraction, and nothing is invested with an interest sufficient to make it even passingly amusing. He wanted to do something, though the precise something did not occur to him. Had he been well, and in full enjoyment of his strength, he 'd have sallied out into the storm and walked off his ennui by a wetting. Even a cold would be a good exchange for the dreary blue-devilism of his depression; but this escape was denied him, and he was left to fret, and chafe, and fever himself, moving from window to chimney-corner, and from chimney-corner to sofa, till at last, baited by self-tormentings, he opened his door and sallied forth to wander through the rooms, taking his chance where his steps might lead him.

Between the gloomy influences of the storm and the shadows of a declining day he could mark but indistinctly the details of the rooms he was exploring. They presented little that was remarkable; they were modestly furnished, nothing costly nor expensive anywhere, but a degree of homely comfort rare to find in an inn. They had, above all, that habitable look which so seldom pertains to a house of entertainment, and, in the loosely scattered books, prints, and maps showed a sort of flattering trustfulness in the stranger who might sojourn there. His wanderings led him, at length, into a somewhat more pretentious room, with a piano and a harp, at one angle of which a little octangular tower opened, with windows in every face, and the spaces between them completely covered by miniatures in oil, or small cabinet pictures. A small table with a chess-board stood here, and an unfinished game yet remained on the board. As Conyers bent over to look, he perceived that a book, whose leaves were held open by a smelling-bottle, lay on the chair next the table. He took this up, and saw that it was a little volume treating of the game, and that the pieces on the board represented a problem. With the eagerness of a man thirsting for some occupation, he seated himself at the table, and set to work at the question. "A Mate in Six Moves" it was headed, but the pieces had been already disturbed by some one attempting the solution. He replaced them by the directions of the volume, and devoted himself earnestly to the task. He was not a good player, and the problem posed him. He tried it again and again, but ever unsuccessfully. He fancied that up to a certain point he had followed the right track, and repeated the same opening moves each time. Meanwhile the evening was fast closing in, and it was only with difficulty he could see the pieces on the board.

Bending low over the table, he was straining his eyes at the game, when a low, gentle voice from behind his chair said, "Would you not wish candles, sir? It is too dark to see here."

Conyers turned hastily, and as hastily recognized that the person who addressed him was a gentlewoman. He arose at once, and made a sort of apology for his intruding.

"Had I known you were a chess-player, sir," said she, with the demure gravity of a composed manner, "I believe I should have sent you a challenge; for my brother, who is my usual adversary, is from home."

"If I should prove a very unworthy enemy, madam, you will find me a very grateful one, for I am sorely tired of my own company."

"In that case, sir, I beg to offer you mine, and a cup of tea along with it."

Conyers accepted the invitation joyfully, and followed Miss Barrington to a small but most comfortable little room, where a tea equipage of exquisite old china was already prepared.

THE PROBLEM

"I see you are in admiration of my teacups; they are the rare Canton blue, for we tea-drinkers have as much epicurism in the form and color of a cup as wine-bibbers profess to have in a hock or a claret glass. Pray take the sofa; you will find it more comfortable than a chair. I am aware you have had an accident."

Very few and simple as were her words, she threw into her manner a degree of courtesy that seemed actual kindness; and coming, as this did, after his late solitude and gloom, no wonder was it that Conyers was charmed with it. There was, besides, a quaint formality—a sort of old-world politeness in her breeding—which relieved the interview of awkwardness by taking it out of the common category of such events.

When tea was over, they sat down to chess, at which Conyers had merely proficiency enough to be worth beating. Perhaps the quality stood him in good stead; perhaps certain others, such as his good looks and his pleasing manners, were even better aids to him; but certain it is, Miss Barrington liked her guest, and when, on arising to say good-night, he made a bungling attempt to apologize for having prolonged his stay at the cottage beyond the period which suited their plans, she stopped him by saying, with much courtesy, "It is true, sir, we are about to relinquish the inn, but pray do not deprive us of the great pleasure we should feel in associating its last day or two with a most agreeable guest. I hope you will remain till my brother comes back and makes your acquaintance."

Conyers very cordially accepted the proposal, and went off to his bed far better pleased with himself and with all the world than he well believed it possible he could be a couple of hours before.

CHAPTER XI.

A NOTE TO BE ANSWERED

While Conyers was yet in bed the following morning, a messenger arrived at the house with a note for him, and waited for the answer. It was from Stapylton, and ran thus:—

"Cobham Hall, Tuesday morning.

"Dear Con.,—The world here—and part of it is a very pretty world, with silky tresses and trim ankles—has declared that you have had some sort of slight accident, and are laid up at a miserable wayside inn, to be blue-devilled and doctored à *discrétion*. I strained my shoulder yesterday hunting,—my horse swerved against a tree,—or I should ascertain all the particulars of your disaster in person; so there is nothing left for it but a note.

"I am here domesticated at a charming country-house, the host an old Admiral, the hostess a *ci-devant* belle of London,—in times not very recent,—and more lately what is called in newspapers 'one of the ornaments of the Irish Court.' We have abundance of guests,—county dons and native celebrities, clerical, lyrical, and quizzical, several pretty women, a first-rate cellar, and a very tolerable cook. I give you the catalogue of our attractions, for I am commissioned by Sir Charles and my Lady to ask you to partake of them. The invitation is given in all cordiality, and I hope you will not decline it, for it is, amongst other matters, a good opportunity of seeing an Irish 'interior,' a thing of which I have always had my doubts and misgivings, some of which are now solved; others I should like to investigate with your assistance. In a word, the whole is worth seeing, and it is, besides, one of those experiences which can be had on very pleasant terms. There is perfect liberty; always something going on, and always a way to be out of it if you like. The people are, perhaps, not more friendly than in England, but they are far more familiar; and if not more disposed to be pleased, they tell you they are, which amounts to the same. There is a good deal of splendor, a wide hospitality, and, I need scarcely add, a considerable share of bad taste. There is, too, a costly attention to the wishes of a guest, which will remind you of India, though I must own the Irish Brahmin has not the grand, high-bred air of the Bengalee. But again I say, come and see.

"I have been told to explain to you why they don't send their boat. There is something about draught of water, and something about a 'gash,' whatever that is: I opine it to be a rapid. And then I am directed to say, that if you will have yourself paddled up to Brown's Barn, the Cobham barge will be there to meet you.

"I write this with some difficulty, lying on my back on a sofa, while a very pretty girl is impatiently waiting to continue her reading to me of a new novel called 'The Antiquary.' a capital story, but strangely disfigured by whole scenes in a Scottish dialect. You must read it when you come over.

"You have heard of Hunter, of course. I am sure you will be sorry at his leaving us. For myself, I knew him very slightly, and shall not have to regret him like older friends; not to say that I have been so long in the service that I never believe in a Colonel. Would you go with him if he gave you the offer? There is such a row and uproar all around me, that I must leave off. Have I forgotten to say that if you stand upon the 'dignities,' the Admiral will go in person to invite you, though he has a foot in the gout. I conclude you will not exact this, and I *know* they will take your acceptance of this mode of invitation as a great favor. Say the hour and the day, and believe me yours always,

"Horace Stapylton.

"Sir Charles is come to say that if your accident does not interfere with riding, he hopes you will send for your horses. He has ample stabling, and is vainglorious about his beans. That short-legged chestnut you brought from Norris would cut a good figure here, as the fences lie very close, and you must be always 'in hand.' If you saw how the women ride! There is one here now — a 'half-bred 'un' — that pounded us all — a whole field of us — last Saturday. You shall see her. I won't promise you 'll follow her across her country."

The first impression made on the mind of Conyers by this letter was surprise that Stapylton, with whom he had so little acquaintance, should write to him in this tone of intimacy; Stapylton, whose cold, almost stern manner seemed to repel any approach, and now he assumed all the free-and-easy air of a comrade of his own years and standing. Had he mistaken the man, or had he been misled by inferring from his bearing in the regiment what he must be at heart?

This, however, was but a passing thought; the passage which interested him most of all was about Hunter. Where and for what could he have left, then? It was a regiment he had served in since he entered the army. What could have led him to exchange? and why, when he did so, had he not written him one line — even one — to say as much? It was to serve under Hunter, his father's old aide-de-camp in times back, that he had entered that regiment; to be with him, to have his friendship, his counsels, his guidance. Colonel Hunter had treated him like a son in every respect, and Conyers felt in his heart that this same affection and interest it was which formed his strongest tie to the service. The question, "Would you go with him if he gave you the offer?" was like a reflection on him, while no such option had been extended to him. What more natural, after all, than such an offer? so Stapylton thought,—so all the world would think. How he thought over the constantly recurring questions of his brother-officers: "Why didn't you go with Hunter?" "How came it that Hunter did not name you on his staff?" "Was it fair—was it generous in one who owed all his advancement to his father—to treat him in this fashion?" "Were the ties of old friendship so lax as all this?" "Was distance such an enemy to every obligation of affection?" "Would his father believe that such a slight had been passed upon him undeservedly? Would not the ready inference be, 'Hunter knew you to be incapable,—unequal to the duties he required. Hunter must have his reasons for passing you over'?" and such like. These reflections, very bitter in their way, were broken in upon by a request from Miss Barrington for his company at breakfast. Strange enough, he had half forgotten that there was such a person in the world, or that he had spent the preceding evening very pleasantly in her society.

"I hope you have had a pleasant letter," said she, as he entered, with Stapylton's note still in his hand.

"I can scarcely call it so, for it brings me news that our Colonel—a very dear and kind friend to me—is about to leave us."

"Are these not the usual chances of a soldier's life? I used to be very familiar once on a time with such topics."

"I have learned the tidings so vaguely, too, that I can make nothing of them. My correspondent is a mere acquaintance,—a brother officer, who has lately joined us, and cannot feel how deeply his news has affected me; in fact, the chief burden of his letter is to convey an invitation to me, and he is full of country-house people and pleasures. He writes from a place called Cobham."

"Sir Charles Cobham's. One of the best houses in the county."

"Do you know them?" asked Conyers, who did not, till the words were out, remember how awkward they might prove.

She flushed slightly for a moment, but, speedily recovering herself, said: "Yes, we knew them once. They had just come to the country, and purchased that estate, when our misfortunes overtook us. They showed us much attention, and such kindness as strangers could show, and they evinced a disposition to continue it; but, of course, our relative positions made intercourse impossible. I am afraid," said she, hastily, "I am talking in riddles all this time. I ought to have told you that my brother once owned a good estate here. We Barringtons thought a deal of ourselves in those days." She tried to say these words with a playful levity, but her voice shook, and her lip trembled in spite of her.

Conyers muttered something unintelligible about "his having heard before," and his sorrow to have awakened a painful theme; but she stopped him hastily, saying, "These are all such old stories now, one should be able to talk them over unconcernedly; indeed, it is easier to do so than to avoid the subject altogether, for there is no such egotist as your reduced gentleman." She made a pretext of giving him his tea, and helping him to something, to cover the awkward pause that followed, and then asked if he intended to accept the invitation to Cobham.

"Not if you will allow me to remain here. The doctor says three days more will see me able to go back to my quarters."

"I hope you will stay for a week, at least, for I scarcely expect my brother before Saturday. Meanwhile, if you have any fancy to visit Cobham, and make your acquaintance with the family there, remember you have all the privileges of an inn here, to come and go, and stay at your pleasure."

"I do not want to leave this. I wish I was never to leave it," muttered he below his breath.

"Perhaps I guess what it is that attaches you to this place," said she, gently. "Shall I say it? There is something quiet, something domestic here, that recalls 'Home.'"

"But I never knew a home," said Conyers, falteringly. "My mother died when I was a mere infant, and I knew none of that watchful love that first gives the sense of home. You may be right, however, in supposing that I cling to this spot as what should seem to me like a home, for I own to you I feel very happy here."

"Stay then, and be happy," said she, holding out her hand, which he clasped warmly, and then pressed to his lips.

"Tell your friend to come over and dine with you any day that he can tear himself from gay company and a great house, and I will do my best to entertain him suitably."

"No. I don't care to do that; he is a mere acquaintance; there is no friendship between us, and, as he is several years older than me, and far wiser, and more man of the world, I am more chilled than cheered by his company. But you shall read his letter, and I 'm certain you 'll make a better guess at his nature than if I were to give you my own version of him at any length." So saying, he handed Stapyl-ton's note across the table; and Miss Dinah, having deliberately put on her spectacles, began to read it.

"It's a fine manly hand,—very bold and very legible, and says something for the writer's frankness. Eh? 'a miserable wayside inn!' This is less than just to the poor 'Fisherman's Home.' Positively, you must make him come to dinner, if it be only for the sake of our character. This man is not amiable, sir," said she, as she read on, "though I could swear he is pleasant company, and sometimes witty. But there is little of genial in his pleasantry, and less of good nature in his wit."

"Go on," cried Conyers; "I 'm quite with you."

"Is he a person of family?" asked she, as she read on some few lines further.

"We know nothing about him; he joined us from a native corps, in India; but he has a good name and, apparently, ample means. His appearance and manner are equal to any station."

"For all that, I don't like him, nor do I desire that you should like him. There is no wiser caution than that of the Psalmist against 'sitting in the seat of the scornful.' This man is a scoffer."

"And yet it is not his usual tone. He is cold, retiring, almost shy. This letter is not a bit like anything I ever saw in his character."

"Another reason to distrust him. Set my mind at ease by saying 'No' to his invitation, and let me try if I cannot recompense you by homeliness in lieu of splendor. The young lady," added she, as she folded the letter, "whose horsemanship is commemorated at the expense of her breeding, must be our doctor's daughter. She is a very pretty girl, and rides admirably. Her good looks and her courage might have saved her the sarcasm. I have my doubts if the man that uttered it be thorough-bred."

"Well, I 'll go and write my answer," said Conyers, rising. "I have been keeping his messenger waiting all this time. I will show it to you before I send it off."

CHAPTER XII.

THE ANSWER

"Will this do?" said Conyers, shortly after, entering the room with a very brief note, but which, let it be owned, cost him fully as much labor as more practised hands occasionally bestow on a more lengthy despatch. "I suppose it's all that's civil and proper, and I don't care to make any needless professions. Pray read it, and give me your opinion." It was so brief that I may quote it:—

> "Dear Captain Stapylton,—Don't feel any apprehensions about me. I am in better quarters than I ever fell into in my life, and my accident is not worth speaking of. I wish you had told me more of our Colonel, of whose movements I am entirely ignorant. I am sincerely grateful to your friends for thinking of me, and hope, ere I leave the neighborhood, to express to Sir Charles and Lady Cobham how sensible I am of their kind intentions towards me.
>
> "I am, most faithfully yours,
"F. CONYERS."

"It is very well, and tolerably legible," said Miss Barrington, dryly; "at least I can make out everything but the name at the end."

"I own I do not shine in penmanship; the strange characters at the foot were meant to represent 'Conyers.'"

"Conyers! Conyers! How long is it since I heard that name last, and how familiar I was with it once! My nephew's dearest friend was a Conyers."

"He must have been a relative of mine in some degree; at least, we are in the habit of saying that all of the name are of one family."

Not heeding what he said, the old lady had fallen back in her meditations to a very remote "long ago," and was thinking of a time when every letter from India bore the high-wrought interest of a romance, of which her nephew was the hero,—times of intense anxiety, indeed, but full of hope withal, and glowing with all the coloring with which love and an exalted imagination can invest the incidents of an adventurous life.

"It was a great heart he had, a splendidly generous nature, far too high-souled and too exacting for common friendships, and so it was that he had few friends. I am talking of my nephew," said she, correcting herself suddenly. "What a boon for a young man to have met him, and formed an attachment to him. I wish you could have known him. George would have been a noble example for you!" She paused for some minutes, and then suddenly, as it were remembering herself, said, "Did you tell me just now, or was I only dreaming, that you knew Ormsby Conyers?"

"Ormsby Conyers is my father's name," said he, quickly.

"Captain in the 25th Dragoons?" asked she, eagerly.

"He was so, some eighteen or twenty years ago."

"Oh, then, my heart did not deceive me," cried she, taking his hand with both her own, "when I felt towards you like an old friend. After we parted last night, I asked myself, again and again, how was it that I already felt an interest in you? What subtle instinct was it that whispered this is the son of poor George's dearest friend,—this is the son of that dear Ormsby Conyers of whom every letter is full? Oh, the happiness of seeing you under this roof! And what a surprise for my poor brother, who clings only the closer, with every year, to all that reminds him of his boy!"

"And you knew my father, then?" asked Conyers, proudly.

"Never met him; but I believe I knew him better than many who were his daily intimates: for years my nephew's letters were journals of their joint lives—they seemed never separate. But you shall read them yourself. They go back to the time when they both landed at Calcutta, young and ardent spirits, eager for adventure, and urged by a bold ambition to win distinction. From that day they were insepa- rable. They hunted, travelled, lived together; and so attached had they become to each other, that George writes in one letter: 'They have offered me an appointment on the staff, but as this would separate me from Ormsby, it is not to be thought of.' It was to me George always wrote, for my brother never liked letter-writing, and thus I was my nephew's confidante, and intrusted with all his secrets. Nor was there one in which your father's name did not figure. It was, how Ormsby got him out of this scrape, or took his duty for him, or made this explanation, or raised that sum of money, that filled all these. At last—I never knew why or how—George ceased to write to me, and addressed all his letters to his father, marked 'Strictly private' too, so that I never saw what they contained. My brother, I believe, suf- fered deeply from the concealment, and there must have been what to him seemed a sufficient reason for it, or he would never have excluded me from that share in his confidence I had always possessed. At all events, it led to a sort of estrange- ment between us,—the only one of our lives. He would tell me at intervals that George was on leave; George was at the Hills; he was expecting his troop; he had been sent here or there; but nothing more, till one morning, as if unable to bear the burden longer, he said, 'George has made up his mind to leave his regiment and take service with one of the native princes. It is an arrangement sanctioned by the Government, but it is one I grieve over and regret greatly.' I asked eagerly to hear further about this step, but he said he knew nothing beyond the bare fact. I then said, 'What does his friend Conyers think of it?' and my brother dryly replied, 'I am not aware that he has been consulted.' Our own misfortunes were fast closing around us, so that really we had little time to think of anything but the difficulties that each day brought forth. George's letters grew rarer and rarer; rumors of him reached us; stories of his gorgeous mode of living, his princely state and splendid retinue, of the high favor he enjoyed with the Rajah, and the influence he wielded over neighboring chiefs; and then we heard, still only by rumor, that he had married a native princess, who had some time before been converted to Christianity. The first intimation of the fact from himself came, when, announcing that he had sent his daughter, a child of about five years old, to Europe to be educated—" She paused here, and seemed to have fallen into a revery over the past; when Conyers suddenly asked,—

"And what of my father all this time? Was the old intercourse kept up between them?"

"I cannot tell you. I do not remember that his name occurred till the memorable case came on before the House of Commons—the inquiry, as it was called, into Colonel Barrington's conduct in the case of Edwardes, a British-born subject of his Majesty, serving in the army of the Rajah of Luckerabad. You have, perhaps, heard of it?"

"Was that the celebrated charge of torturing a British subject?"

"The same; the vilest conspiracy that ever was hatched, and the cruellest persecution that ever broke a noble heart. And yet there were men of honor, men of purest fame and most unblemished character, who harkened in to that infamous cry, and actually sent out emissaries to India to collect evidence against my poor nephew. For a while the whole country rang with the case. The low papers, which assailed the Government, made it matter of attack on the nature of the British rule in India, and the ministry only sought to make George the victim to screen themselves from public indignation. It was Admiral Byng's case once more. But I have no temper to speak of it, even after this lapse of years; my blood boils now at the bare memory of that foul and perjured association. If you would follow the story, I will send you the little published narrative to your room, but, I beseech you, do not again revert to it. How I have betrayed myself to speak of it I know not. For many a long year I have prayed to be able to forgive one man, who has been the bitterest enemy of our name and race. I have asked for strength to bear the burden of our calamity, but more earnestly a hundred-fold I have entreated that forgiveness might enter my heart, and that if vengeance for this cruel wrong was at hand, I could be able to say, 'No, the time for such feeling is gone by.' Let me not, then, be tempted by any revival of this theme to recall all the sorrow and all the indignation it once caused me. This infamous book contains the whole story as the world then believed it. You will read it with interest, for it concerned one whom your father dearly loved. But, again. I say, when we meet again let us not return to it. These letters, too, will amuse you; they are the diaries of your father's early life in India as much as George's, but of them we can talk freely."

It was so evident that she was speaking with a forced calm, and that all her self-restraint might at any moment prove unequal to the effort she was making, that Conyers, affecting to have a few words to say to Stapylton's messenger, stole away, and hastened to his room to look over the letters and the volume she had given him.

He had scarcely addressed himself to his task when a knock came to the door, and at the same instant it was opened in a slow, half-hesitating way, and Tom Dill stood before him. Though evidently dressed for the occasion, and intending to present himself in a most favorable guise, Tom looked far more vulgar and unprepossessing than in the worn costume of his every-day life, his bright-but-toned blue coat and yellow waistcoat being only aggravations of the low-bred air that unhappily beset him. Worse even than this, however, was the fact that, being somewhat nervous about the interview before him, Tom had taken what his father would have called a diffusible stimulant, in the shape of "a dandy of punch," and bore the evidences of it in a heightened color and a very lustrous but wandering eye.

TOM DILL IN HIS BEST

"Here I am," said he, entering with a sort of easy swagger, but far more affected than real, notwithstanding the "dandy."

"Well, and what then?" asked Conyers, haughtily, for the vulgar presumption of his manner was but a sorry advocate in his favor. "I don't remember, that I sent for you."

"No; but my father told me what you said to him, and I was to come up and thank you, and say, 'Done!' to it all."

Conyers turned a look—not a very pleased or very flattering look—at the loutish figure before him, and in his changing color might be seen the conflict it cost him to keep down his rising temper. He was, indeed, sorely tried, and his hand shook as he tossed over the books on his table, and endeavored to seem occupied in other matters.

"Maybe you forget all about it," began Tom. "Perhaps you don't remember that you offered to fit me out for India, and send me over with a letter to your father—"

"No, no, I forget nothing of it; I remember it all." He had almost said "only too well," but he coughed down the cruel speech, and went on hurriedly: "You have come, however, when I am engaged,—when I have other things to attend to. These letters here—In fact, this is not a moment when I can attend to you. Do you understand me?"

"I believe I do," said Tom, growing very pale.

"To-morrow, then, or the day after, or next week, will be time enough for all this. I must think over the matter again."

"I see," said Tom, moodily, as he changed from one foot to the other, and cracked the joints of his fingers, till they seemed dislocated. "I see it all."

"What do you mean by that?—what do you see?" asked Conyers, angrily.

"I see that Polly, my sister, was right; that she knew you better than any of us," said Tom, boldly, for a sudden rush of courage had now filled his heart. "She said, 'Don't let him turn your head, Tom, with his fine promises. He was in good humor and good spirits when he made them, and perhaps meant to keep them too; but he little knows what misery disappointment brings, and he'll never fret himself over the heavy heart he's giving you, when he wakes in the morning with a change of mind.' And then, she said another thing," added he, after a pause.

"And what was the other thing?"

"She said, 'If you go up there, Tom,' says she, 'dressed out like a shopboy in his Sunday suit, he'll be actually shocked at his having taken an interest in you. He 'll forget all about your hard lot and your struggling fortune, and only see your vulgarity.' 'Your vulgarity,'—that was the word." As he said this, his lip trembled, and the chair he leaned on shook under his grasp.

"Go back, and tell her, then, that she was mistaken," said Conyers, whose own voice now quavered. "Tell her that when I give my word I keep it; that I will maintain everything I said to you or to your father; and that when she imputed to me an indifference as to the feelings of others, she might have remembered whether she was not unjust to mine. Tell her that also."

"I will," said Tom, gravely. "Is there anything more?" "No, nothing more," said Conyers, who with difficulty suppressed a smile at the words and the manner of his questioner. "Good-bye, then. You 'll send for me when you want me," said Tom; and he was out of the room, and half-way across the lawn, ere Conyers could recover himself to reply.

Conyers, however, flung open the window, and cried to him to come back.

"I was nigh forgetting a most important part of the matter, Tom," said he, as the other entered, somewhat pale and anxious-looking. "You told me, t' other day, that there was some payment to be made,—some sum to be lodged before you could present yourself for examination. What about this? When must it be done?"

"A month before I go in," said Tom, to whom the very thought of the ordeal seemed full of terror and heart-sinking.

"And how soon do you reckon that may be?"

"Polly says not before eight weeks at the earliest. She says we 'll have to go over Bell on the Bones all again, and brush up the Ligaments, besides. If it was the Navy, they 'd not mind the nerves; but they tell me the Army fellows often take a man on the fifth pair, and I know if they do me, it's mighty little of India I 'll see."

"Plucked, eh?"

"I don't know what you mean by 'plucked,' but I 'd be turned back, which is, perhaps, the same. And no great disgrace, either," added he, with more of courage in his voice; "Polly herself says there's days she could n't remember all the branches of the fifth, and the third is almost as bad."

"I suppose if your sister could go up in your place, Tom, you 'd be quite sure of your diploma?"

"It's many and many a day I wished that same," sighed he, heavily. "If you heard her going over the 'Subclavian,' you 'd swear she had the book in her hand."

Conyers could not repress a smile at this strange piece of feminine accomplishment, but he was careful not to let Tom perceive it. Not, indeed, that the poor fellow was in a very observant mood; Polly's perfections, her memory, and her quickness were the themes that filled up his mind.

"What a rare piece of luck for you to have had such a sister, Tom!"

"Don't I say it to myself?—don't I repeat the very same words every morning when I awake? Maybe I 'll never come to any good; maybe my father is right, and that I 'll only be a disgrace as long as I live; but I hope one thing, at least, I 'll never be so bad that I 'll forget Polly, and all she done for me. And I'll tell you more," said he, with a choking fulness in his throat; "if they turn me back at my examination, my heart will be heavier for *her* than for myself."

"Come, cheer up, Tom; don't look on the gloomy side. You 'll pass, I 'm certain, and with credit too. Here 's the thirty pounds you 'll have to lodge—"

"It is only twenty they require. And, besides, I could n't take it; it's my father must pay." He stammered, and hesitated, and grew pale and then crimson, while his lips trembled and his chest heaved and fell almost convulsively.

"Nothing of the kind, Tom," said Conyers, who had to subdue his own emotion by an assumed sternness. "The plan is all my own, and I will stand no interference with it. I mean that you should pass your examination without your father knowing one word about it. You shall come back to him with your diploma, or whatever it is, in your hand, and say, 'There, sir, the men who have signed their names to that do not think so meanly of me as you do.'"

"And he'd say, the more fools they!" said Tom, with a grim smile.

"At all events," resumed Conyers, "I 'll have my own way. Put that note in your pocket, and whenever you are gazetted Surgeon-Major to the Guards, or Inspector-General of all the Hospitals in Great Britain, you can repay me, and with interest, besides, if you like it."

"You 've given me a good long day to be in your debt," said Tom; and he hurried out of the room before his overfull heart should betray his emotion.

It is marvellous how quickly a kind action done to another reconciles a man to himself. Doubtless conscience at such times condescends to play the courtier, and whispers, "What a good fellow you are! and how unjust the world is when it calls you cold and haughty and ungenial!" Not that I would assert higher and better thoughts than these do not reward him who, Samaritan-like, binds up the wounds of misery; but I fear me much that few of us resist self-flattery, or those little delicate adulations one can offer to his own heart when nobody overhears him.

At all events, Conyers was not averse to this pleasure, and grew actually to feel a strong interest for Tom Dill, all because that poor fellow had been the recipient of his bounty; for so is it the waters of our nature must be stirred by some act of charity or kindness, else their healing virtues have small efficacy, and cure not.

And then he wondered and questioned himself whether Polly might not possibly be right, and that his "governor" would marvel where and how he had picked up so strange a specimen as Tom. That poor fellow, too, like many an humble flower, seen not disadvantageously in its native wilds, would look strangely out of place when transplanted and treated as an exotic. Still he could trust to the wide and generous nature of his father to overlook small defects of manner and breeding, and take the humble fellow kindly.

Must I own that a considerable share of his hopefulness was derived from thinking that the odious blue coat and brass buttons could scarcely make part of Tom's kit for India, and that in no other costume known to civilized man could his *protégé* look so unprepossessingly?

CHAPTER XIII.

A FEW LEAVES FROM A BLUE-BOOK

The journal which Miss Barrington had placed in Conyers's hands was little else than the record of the sporting adventures of two young and very dashing fellows. There were lion and tiger hunts, so little varied in detail that one might serve for all, though doubtless to the narrator each was marked with its own especial interest. There were travelling incidents and accidents, and straits for money, and mishaps and arrests, and stories of steeple-chases and balls all mixed up together, and recounted so very much in the same spirit as to show how very little shadow mere misadventure could throw across the sunshine of their every-day life. But every now and then Conyers came upon some entry which closely touched his heart. It was how nobly Ormsby behaved. What a splendid fellow he was! so frank, so generous, such a horseman! "I wish you saw the astonishment of the Mahratta fellows as Ormsby lifted the tent-pegs in full career; he never missed one. Ormsby won the rifle-match; we all knew he would. Sir Peregrine invited Ormsby to go with him to the Hills, but he refused, mainly because I was not asked." Ormsby has been offered this, that, or t'other; in fact, that one name recurred in every second sentence, and always with the same marks of affection. How proud, too, did Barrington seem of his friend. "They have found out that no country-house is perfect without Ormsby, and he is positively persecuted with invitations. I hear the 'G.-G.' is provoked at Ormsby's refusal of a staff appointment. I'm in rare luck; the old Rajah of Tannanoohr has asked Ormsby to a grand elephant-hunt next week, and I'm to go with him. I'm to have a leave in October. Ormsby managed it somehow; he never fails, whatever he takes in hand. Such a fright as I got yesterday! There was a report in the camp Ormsby was going to England with despatches; it's all a mistake, however, he says. He believes he might have had the opportunity, had he cared for it."

If there was not much in these passing notices of his father, there was quite enough to impart to them an intense degree of interest. There is a wondrous charm, besides, in reading of the young days of those we have only known in maturer life, in hearing of them when they were fresh, ardent, and impetuous; in knowing, besides, how they were regarded by contemporaries, how loved and valued. It was not merely that Ormsby recurred in almost every page of this journal, but the record bore testimony to his superiority and the undisputed sway he exercised over his companions. This same power of dominating and directing had been the distinguishing feature of his after-life, and many an unruly and turbulent spirit had been reclaimed under Ormsby Conyers's hands.

As he read on, he grew also to feel a strong interest for the writer himself; the very heartiness of the affection he bestowed on his father, and the noble generosity with which he welcomed every success of that "dear fellow Ormsby," were more than enough to secure his interest for him. There was a bold, almost reckless dash, too, about Barrington which has a great charm occasionally for very young men. He adventured upon life pretty much as he would try to cross a river; he never looked for a shallow nor inquired for a ford, but plunged boldly in, and trusted to his brave heart and his strong arms for the rest. No one, indeed, reading even these rough notes, could hesitate to pronounce which of the two would "make the spoon," and which "spoil the horn." Young Conyers was eager to find some mention of the incident to which Miss Barrington had vaguely alluded. He wanted to read George Barrington's own account before he opened the little pamphlet she gave him, but the journal closed years before this event; and although some of the letters came down to a later date, none approached the period he wanted.

It was not till after some time that he remarked how much more unfrequently his father's name occurred in the latter portion of the correspondence. Entire pages would contain no reference to him, and in the last letter of all there was this towards the end: "After all, I am almost sorry that I am first for purchase, for I believe Ormsby is most anxious for his troop. I say 'I believe,' for he has not told me so, and when I offered to give way to him, he seemed half offended with me. You know what a bungler I am where a matter of any delicacy is to be treated, and you may easily fancy either that *I* mismanage the affair grossly, or that I am as grossly mistaken. One thing is certain, I 'd see promotion far enough, rather than let it make a coldness beween us, which could never occur if he were as frank as he used to be. My dear aunt, I wish I had your wise head to counsel me, for I have a scheme in my mind which I have scarcely courage for without some advice, and for many reasons I cannot ask O.'s opinion. Between this and the next mail I 'll think it over carefully, and tell you what I intend.

"I told you that Ormsby was going to marry one of the Gpvernor-General's daughters. It is all off,—at least, I hear so,—and O. has asked for leave to go home. I suspect he is sorely cut up about this, but he is too proud a fellow to let the world see it. Report says that Sir Peregrine heard that he played. So he does, because he does everything, and everything well. If he does go to England, he will certainly pay you a visit. Make much of him for my sake; you could not make too much for his own."

This was the last mention of his father, and he pondered long and thoughtfully over it. He saw, or fancied he saw, the first faint glimmerings of a coldness between them, and he hastily turned to the printed report of the House of Commons inquiry, to see what part his father had taken. His name occurred but once; it was appended to an extract of a letter, addressed to him by the Governor-General. It was a confidential report, and much of it omitted in publication. It was throughout, however, a warm and generous testimony to Barrington's character. "I never knew a man," said he, "less capable of anything mean or unworthy; nor am I able to imagine any temptation strong enough to warp him from what he believed to be right. That on a question of policy his judgment might be wrong, I am quite ready to admit, but I will maintain that, on a point of honor, he would, and must, be infallible." Underneath this passage there was written, in Miss Barrington's hand, "Poor George never saw this; it was not published till after his death." So interested did young Conyers feel as to the friendship between these two men, and what it could have been that made a breach between them,—if breach there were,—that he sat a long time without opening the little volume that related to the charge against Colonel Barrington. He had but to open it, however, to guess the spirit in which it was written. Its title was, "The Story of Samuel Ed-wardes, with an Account of the Persecutions and Tortures inflicted on him by Colonel George Barrington, when serving in command of the Forces of the Meer Nagheer Assahr, Rajah of Luckerabad, based on the documents produced before the Committee of the House, and private authentic information." Opposite to this lengthy title was an ill-executed wood-cut of a young fellow tied up to a tree, and being flogged by two native Indians, with the inscription at foot: "Mode of celebrating His Majesty's Birthday, 4th of June, 18—, at the Residence of Luckerabad."

In the writhing figure of the youth, and the ferocious glee of his executioners, the artist had displayed all his skill in expression, and very unmistakably shown, besides, the spirit of the publication. I have no intention to inflict this upon my reader. I will simply give him—and as briefly as I am able—its substance.

The Rajah of Luckerabad, an independent sovereign, living on the best of terms with the Government of the Company, had obtained permission to employ an English officer in the chief command of his army, a force of some twenty-odd thousand, of all arms. It was essential that he should be one not only well acquaint-ed with the details of command, but fully equal to the charge of organization of a force; a man of energy and decision, well versed in Hindostanee, and not alto-gether ignorant of Persian, in which, occasionally, correspondence was carried on. Amongst the many candidates for an employment so certain to insure the fortune of its possessor, Major Barrington, then a brevet Lieutenant-Colonel, was chosen.

It is not improbable that, in mere technical details of his art, he might have had many equal and some superior to him; it was well known that his personal req-uisites were above all rivalry. He was a man of great size and strength, of a most commanding presence, an accomplished linguist in the various dialects of Central India and a great master of all manly exercises. To these qualities he added an Oriental taste for splendor and pomp. It had always been his habit to live in a style of costly extravagance, with the retinue of a petty prince, and when he travelled it was with the following of a native chief.

Though, naturally enough, such a station as a separate command gave might be regarded as a great object of ambition by many, there was a good deal of sur-prise felt at the time that Barrington, reputedly a man of large fortune, should have accepted it; the more so since, by his contract, he bound himself for ten years to the Rajah, and thus forever extinguished all prospect of advancement in his own ser-vice. There were all manner of guesses afloat as to his reasons. Some said that he was already so embarrassed by his extravagance that it was his only exit out of dif-ficulty; others pretended that he was captivated by the gorgeous splendor of that Eastern life he loved so well; that pomp, display, and magnificence were bribes he could not resist; and a few, who affected to see more nearly, whispered that he was unhappy of late, had grown peevish and uncompanionable, and sought any change, so that it took him out of his regiment. Whatever the cause, he bade his brother-officers farewell without revealing it, and set out for his new destination. He had never anticipated a life of ease or inaction, but he was equally far from imagining anything like what now awaited him. Corruption, falsehood, robbery, on every hand! The army was little else than a brigand establishment, living on the peasants, and exacting, at the sword point, whatever they wanted. There was no obedience to discipline. The Rajah troubled himself about nothing but his plea-sures, and, indeed, passed his days so drugged with opium as to be almost insensi-ble to all around him. In the tribunals there was nothing but bribery, and the object of every one seemed to be to amass fortunes as rapidly as possible, and then hasten away from a country so insecure and dangerous.

For some days after his arrival, Barrington hesitated whether he would accept a charge so apparently hopeless; his bold heart, however, decided the doubt, and he resolved to remain. His first care was to look about him for one or two more trustworthy than the masses, if such there should be, to assist him, and the Rajah referred him to his secretary for that purpose. It was with sincere pleasure Bar-ring-ton discovered that this man was English,—that is, his father had been an Englishman, and his mother was a Malabar slave in the Rajah's household: his name was Edwardes, but called by the natives Ali Edwardes. He looked about six-ty, but his real age was about forty-six when Barrington came to the Residence. He was a man of considerable ability, uniting all the craft and subtlety of the Oriental with the dogged perseverance of the Briton. He had enjoyed the full favor of the Rajah for nigh twenty years, and was strongly averse to the appointment of an En-glish officer to the command of the army, knowing full well the influence it would have over his own fortunes. He represented to the Rajah that the Company was only intriguing to absorb his dominions with their own; that the new Command-er-in-chief would be their servant and not his; that it was by such machinery as this they secretly possessed themselves of all knowledge of the native sovereigns, learned their weakness and their strength, and through such agencies hatched those plots and schemes by which many a chief had been despoiled of his state.

The Rajah, however, saw that if he had a grasping Government on one side, he had an insolent and rebellious army on the other. There was not much to choose between them, but he took the side that he thought the least bad, and left the rest to Fate.

Having failed with the Rajah, Edwardes tried what he could do with Bar-rington; and certainly, if but a tithe of what he told him were true, the most natural thing in the world would have been that he should give up his appointment, and quit forever a land so hopelessly sunk in vice and corruption. Cunning and crafty as he was, however, he made one mistake, and that an irreparable one. When di-lating on the insubordination of the army, its lawless ways and libertine habits, he declared that nothing short of a superior force in the field could have any chance of enforcing discipline. "As to a command," said he, "it is simply ludicrous. Let any man try it and they will cut him down in the very midst of his staff."

That unlucky speech decided the question; and Barring-ton simply said,—

"I have heard plenty of this sort of thing in India; I never saw it,—I 'll stay."

Stay he did; and he did more: he reformed that rabble, and made of them a splendid force, able, disciplined, and obedient. With the influence of his success, added to that derived from the confidence reposed in him by the Rajah, he introduced many and beneficial changes into the administration; he punished peculators by military law, and brought knavish sutlers to the drum-head. In fact, by the exercise of a salutary despotism, he rescued the state from an impending bankruptcy and ruin, placed its finances in a healthy condition, and rendered the country a model of prosperity and contentment. The Rajah had, like most of his rank and class, been in litigation, occasionally in armed contention, with some of his neighbors,—one especially, an uncle, whom he accused of having robbed him, when his guardian, of a large share of his heritage. This suit had gone on for years, varied at times by little raids into each other's territories, to burn villages and carry away cattle. Though with a force more than sufficient to have carried the question with a strong hand, Barrington preferred the more civilized mode of leaving the matter in dispute to others, and suggested the Company as arbitrator. The negotiations led to a lengthy correspondence, in which Edwardes and his son, a youth of seventeen or eighteen, were actively occupied; and although Barrington was not without certain misgivings as to their trustworthiness and honesty, he knew their capacity, and had not, besides, any one at all capable of replacing them. While these affairs were yet pending, Barrington married the daughter of the Meer, a young girl whose mother had been a convert to Christianity, and who had herself been educated by a Catholic missionary. She died in the second year of her marriage, giving birth to a daughter; but Barrington had now become so completely the centre of all action in the state, that the Rajah interfered in nothing, leaving in his hands the undisputed control of the Government; nay, more, he made him his son by adoption, leaving to him not alone all his immense personal property, but the inheritance to his throne. Though Barrington was advised by all the great legal authorities he consulted in England that such a bequest could not be good in law, nor a British subject be permitted to succeed to the rights of an Eastern sovereignty, he obstinately declared that the point was yet untried; that, however theoretically the opinion might be correct, practically the question had not been determined, nor had any case yet occurred to rule as a precedent on it. If he was not much of a lawyer, he was of a temperament that could not brook opposition. In fact, to make him take any particular road in life, you had only to erect a barricade on it. When, therefore, he was told the matter could not be, his answer was, "It shall!" Calcutta lawyers, men deep in knowledge of Oriental law and custom, learned Moonshees and Pundits, were despatched by him at enormous cost, to England, to confer with the great authorities at home. Agents were sent over to procure the influence of great Parliamentary speakers and the leaders in the press to the cause. For a matter which, in the beginning, he cared scarcely anything, if at all, he had now grown to feel the most intense and absorbing interest. Half persuading himself that the personal question was less to him than the great privilege and right of an Englishman, he declared that he would rather die a beggar in the defence of the cause than abandon it. So possessed was he, indeed, of his rights, and so resolved to maintain them, supported by a firm belief that they would and must be ultimately conceded to him, that in the correspondence with the other chiefs every reference which spoke of the future sovereignty of Luckerabad included his own name and title, and this with an ostentation quite Oriental.

Whether Edwardes had been less warm and energetic in the cause than Barrington expected, or whether his counsels were less palatable, certain it is he grew daily more and more distrustful of him; but an event soon occurred to make this suspicion a certainty.

The negotiations between the Meer and his uncle had been so successfully conducted by Barrington, that the latter agreed to give up three "Pegunnahs," or villages he had unrightfully seized upon, and to pay a heavy mulct, besides, for the unjust occupation of them. This settlement had been, as may be imagined, a work of much time and labor, and requiring not only immense forbearance and patience, but intense watchfulness and unceasing skill and craft. Edwardes, of course, was constantly engaged in the affair, with the details of which he had been for years familiar. Now, although Barrington was satisfied with the zeal he displayed, he was less so with his counsels, Edwardes always insisting that in every dealing with an Oriental you must inevitably be beaten if you would not make use of all the stratagem and deceit he is sure to employ against you. There was not a day on which the wily secretary did not suggest some cunning expedient, some clever trick; and Barrington's abrupt rejection of them only impressed him with a notion of his weakness and deficiency.

One morning—it was after many defeats—Edwardes appeared with the draft of a document he had been ordered to draw out, and in which, of his own accord, he had made a large use of threats to the neighboring chief, should he continue to protract these proceedings. These threats very unmistakably pointed to the dire consequences of opposing the great Government of the Company; for, as the writer argued, the succession to the Ameer being already vested in an Englishman, it is perfectly clear the powerful nation he belongs to will take a very summary mode of dealing with this question, if not settled before he comes to the throne. He pressed, therefore, for an immediate settlement, as the best possible escape from difficulty.

Barrington scouted the suggestion indignantly; he would not hear of it.

"What," said he, "is it while these very rights are in litigation that I am to employ them as a menace? Who is to secure me being one day Rajah of Luckerabad? Not you, certainly, who have never ceased to speak coldly of my claims. Throw that draft into the fire, and never propose a like one to me again!"

The rebuke was not forgotten. Another draft was, however, prepared, and in due time the long-pending negotiations were concluded, the Meer's uncle having himself come to Luckerabad to ratify the contract, which, being engrossed on a leaf of the Rajah's Koran, was duly signed and sealed by both.

It was during the festivities incidental to this visit that Edwardes, who had of late made a display of wealth and splendor quite unaccountable, made a proposal to the Rajah for the hand of his only unmarried daughter, sister to Barrington's wife. The Rajah, long enervated by excess and opium, probably cared little about the matter; there were, indeed, but a few moments in each day when he could be fairly pronounced awake. He referred the question to Barrington. Not satisfied with an insulting rejection of the proposal, Barrington, whose passionate moments were almost madness, tauntingly asked by what means Edwardes had so suddenly acquired the wealth which had prompted this demand. He hinted that the sources of his fortune were more than suspected, and at last, carried away by anger, for the discussion grew violent, he drew from his desk a slip of paper, and held it up. "When your father was drummed out of the 4th Bengal Fusiliers for theft, of which this is the record, the family was scarcely so ambitious." For an instant Edwardes seemed overcome almost to fainting; but he rallied, and, with a menace of his clenched hand, but without one word, he hurried away before Barrington could resent the insult. It was said that he did not return to his house, but, taking the horse of an orderly that he found at the door, rode away from the palace, and on the same night crossed the frontier into a neighboring state.

It was on the following morning, as Barrington was passing a cavalry regiment in review, that young Edwardes, forcing his way through the staff, insolently asked, "What had become of his father?" and at the same instant levelling a pistol, he fired. The ball passed through Barrington's shako, and so close to the head that it grazed it. It was only with a loud shout to abstain that Barrington arrested the gleaming sabres that now flourished over his head. "Your father has fled, youngster!" cried he. "When you show him *that*," — and he struck him across the face with his horsewhip, — "tell him how near you were to have been an assassin!" With this savage taunt, he gave orders that the young fellow should be conducted to the nearest frontier, and turned adrift. Neither father nor son ever were seen there again.

Little did George Barrington suspect what was to come of that morning's work. Through what channel Edwardes worked at first was not known, but that he succeeded in raising up for himself friends in England is certain; by their means the very gravest charges were made against Barrington. One allegation was that by a forged document, claiming to be the assent of the English Government to his succession, he had obtained the submission of several native chiefs to his rule and a cession of territory to the Rajah of Luckerabad; and another charged him with having cruelly tortured a British subject named Samuel Edwardes, — an investigation entered into by a Committee of the House, and becoming, while it lasted, one of the most exciting subjects of public interest. Nor was the anxiety lessened by the death of the elder Edwardes, which occurred during the inquiry, and which Barrington's enemies declared to be caused by a broken heart; and the martyred or murdered Edwardes was no uncommon heading to a paragraph of the time.

Conyers turned to the massive Blue-book that contained the proceedings "in Committee," but only to glance at the examination of witnesses, whose very names were unfamiliar to him. He could perceive, however, that the inquiry was a long one, and, from the tone of the member at whose motion it was instituted, angry and vindictive.

Edwardes appeared to have preferred charges of long continued persecution and oppression, and there was native testimony in abundance to sustain the allegation; while the British Commissioner sent to Luckerabad came back so prejudiced against Barrington, from his proud and haughty bearing, that his report was unfavorable to him in all respects. There was, it is true, letters from various high quarters, all speaking of Barrington's early career as both honorable and distinguished; and, lastly, there was one signed Ormsby Conyers, a warm-hearted testimony "to the most straightforward gentleman and truest friend I have ever known." These were words the young man read and re-read a dozen times.

Conyers turned eagerly to read what decision had been come to by the Committee, but the proceedings had come abruptly to an end by George Barrington's death. A few lines at the close of the pamphlet mentioned that, being summoned to appear before the Governor-General in Council at Calcutta, Barrington refused. An armed force was despatched to occupy Luckerabad, on the approach of which Barrington rode forth to meet them, attended by a brilliant staff,—with what precise object none knew; but the sight of a considerable force, drawn up at a distance in what seemed order of battle, implied at least an intention to resist. Coming on towards the advanced pickets at a fast gallop, and not slackening speed when challenged, the men, who were Bengal infantry, fired, and Barrington fell, pierced by four bullets. He never uttered a word after, though he lingered on till evening. The force was commanded by Lieutenant-General Conyers.

There was little more to tell. The Rajah, implicated in the charges brought against Barrington, and totally unable to defend himself, despatched a confidential minister, Meer Mozarjah, to Europe to do what he might by bribery. This unhappy blunder filled the measure of his ruin, and after a very brief inquiry the Rajah was declared to have forfeited his throne and all his rights of succession. The Company took possession of Luckerabad, as a portion of British India, but from a generous compassion towards the deposed chief, graciously accorded him a pension of ten thousand rupees a month during his life.

My reader will bear in mind that I have given him this recital, not as it came before Conyers, distorted by falsehood and disfigured by misstatements, but have presented the facts as nearly as they might be derived from a candid examination of all the testimony adduced. Ere I return to my own tale, I ought to add that Edwardes, discredited and despised by some, upheld and maintained by others, left Calcutta with the proceeds of a handsome subscription raised in his behalf. Whether he went to reside in Europe, or retired to some other part of India, is not known. He was heard of no more.

As for the Rajah, his efforts still continued to obtain a revision of the sentence pronounced upon him, and his case was one of those which newspapers slur over and privy councils try to escape from, leaving to Time to solve what Justice has no taste for.

But every now and then a Blue-book would appear, headed "East India (the deposed Rajah of Luckerabad)," while a line in an evening paper would intimate that the Envoy of Meer Nagheer Assahr had arrived at a certain West-end hotel to prosecute the suit of his Highness before the Judicial Committee of the Lords. How pleasantly does a paragraph dispose of a whole life-load of sorrows and of wrongs that, perhaps, are breaking the hearts that carry them!

While I once more apologize to my reader for the length to which this narrative has run, I owe it to myself to state that, had I presented it in the garbled and incorrect version which came before Conyers, and had I interpolated all the misconceptions he incurred, the mistakes he first fell into and then corrected, I should have been far more tedious and intolerable still; and now I am again under weigh, with easy canvas, but over a calm sea, and under a sky but slightly clouded.

CHAPTER XIV.

BARRINGTON'S FORD

Conyers had scarcely finished his reading when he was startled by the galloping of horses under his window; so close, indeed, did they come that they seemed to shake the little cottage with their tramp. He looked out, but they had already swept past, and were hidden from his view by the copse that shut out the river. At the same instant he heard the confused sound of many voices, and what sounded to him like the plash of horses in the stream.

Urged by a strong curiosity, he hurried downstairs and made straight for the river by a path that led through the trees; but before he could emerge from the cover he heard cries of "Not there! not there! Lower down!" "No, no! up higher! up higher! Head up the stream, or you 'll be caught in the gash!" "Don't hurry; you've time enough!"

When he gained the bank, it was to see three horsemen, who seemed to be cheering, or, as it might be, warning a young girl who, mounted on a powerful black horse, was deep in the stream, and evidently endeavoring to cross it. Her hat hung on the back of her neck by its ribbon, and her hair had also fallen down; but one glance was enough to show that she was a consummate horsewoman, and whose courage was equal to her skill; for while steadily keeping her horse's head to the swift current, she was careful not to control him overmuch, or impede the free action of his powers. Heeding, as it seemed, very little the counsels or warnings showered on her by the bystanders, not one of whom, to Conyers's intense amazement, had ventured to accompany her, she urged her horse steadily forward.

"Don't hurry,—take it easy!" called out one of the horsemen, as he looked at his watch. "You have fifty-three minutes left, and it's all turf."

"She 'll do it,—I know she will!" "She 'll lose,—she must lose!" "It's ten miles to Foynes Gap!" "It's more!" "It's less!" "There!—see!—she's in, by Jove! she's in!" These varying comments were now arrested by the intense interest of the moment, the horse having impatiently plunged into a deep pool, and struck out to swim with all the violent exertion of an affrighted animal. "Keep his head up!" "Let him free, quite free!" "Get your foot clear of the stirrup!" cried out the bystanders, while in lower tones they muttered, "She would cross here!" "It's all her own fault!" Just at this instant she turned in her saddle, and called out something which, drowned in the rush of the river, did not reach them.

"Don't you see," cried Conyers, passionately, for his temper could no longer endure the impassive attitude of this on-looking, "one of the reins is broken, her bridle is smashed?"

And, without another word, he sprang into the river, partly wading, partly swimming, and soon reached the place where the horse, restrained by one rein alone, swam in a small circle, fretted by restraint and maddened by inability to resist.

"Leave him to me,—let go your rein," said Conyers, as he grasped the bridle close to the bit; and the animal, accepting the guidance, suffered himself to be led quietly till he reached the shallow. Once there, he bounded wildly forward, and, splashing through the current, leaped up the bank, where he was immediately caught by the others.

By the time Conyers had gained the land, the girl had quitted her saddle and entered the cottage, never so much as once turning a look on him who had rescued her. If he could not help feeling mortified at this show of indifference, he was not less puzzled by the manner of the others, who, perfectly careless of his dripping condition, discussed amongst themselves how the bridle broke, and what might have happened if the leather had proved tougher.

"It's always the way with her," muttered one, sulkily.

"I told her to ride the match in a ring-snaffle, but she's a mule in obstinacy! She 'd have won easily—ay, with five minutes to spare—if she'd have crossed at Nunsford. I passed there last week without wetting a girth."

"She 'll not thank *you* young gentleman, whoever you are," said the oldest of the party, turning to Conyers, "for your gallantry. She 'll only remember you as having helped her to lose a wager!"

"That's true!" cried another. "I never got as much as thank you for catching her horse one day at Lyrath, though it threw me out of the whole run afterwards."

"And this was a wager, then?" said Conyers.

"Yes. An English officer that is stopping at Sir Charles's said yesterday that nobody could ride from Lowe's Folly to Foynes as the crow flies; and four of us took him up—twenty-five pounds apiece—that Polly Dill would do it,—and against time, too,—an hour and forty."

"On a horse of mine," chimed in another,—"Bayther-shini"

"I must say it does not tell very well for your chivalry in these parts," said Conyers, angrily. "Could no one be found to do the match without risking a young girl's life on it?"

A very hearty burst of merriment met this speech, and the elder of the party rejoined,—

"You must be very new to this country, or you'd not have said that, sir. There's not a man in the hunt could get as much out of a horse as that girl."

"Not to say," added another, with a sly laugh, "that the Englishman gave five to one against her when he heard she was going to ride."

Disgusted by what he could not but regard as a most disgraceful wager, Conyers turned away, and walked into the house.

"Go and change your clothes as fast as you can," said Miss Barrington, as she met him in the porch. "I am quite provoked you should have wetted your feet in such a cause."

It was no time to ask for explanations; and Conyers hurried away to his room, marvelling much at what he had heard, but even more astonished by the attitude of cool and easy indifference as to what might have imperilled a human life. He had often heard of the reckless habits and absurd extravagances of Irish life, but he fancied that they appertained to a time long past, and that society had gradually assumed the tone and the temper of the English. Then he began to wonder to what class in life these persons belonged. The girl, so well as he could see, was certainly handsome, and appeared ladylike; and yet, why had she not even by a word acknowledged the service he rendered her? And lastly, what could old Miss Barrington mean by that scornful speech? These were all great puzzles to him, and like many great puzzles only the more embarrassing the more they were thought over.

The sound of voices drew him now to the window, and he saw one of the riding-party in converse with Darby at the door. They talked in a low tone together, and laughed; and then the horseman, chucking a half-crown towards Darby, said aloud,—

"And tell her that we 'll send the boat down for her as soon as we get back."

Darby touched his hat gratefully, and was about to retire within the house when he caught sight of Conyers at the window. He waited till the rider had turned the angle of the road, and then said,—

"That's Mr. St. George. They used to call him the Slasher, he killed so many in duels long ago; but he 's like a lamb now."

"And the young lady?"

"The young lady is it!" said Darby, with the air of one not exactly concurring in the designation. "She's old Dill's daughter, the doctor that attends you."

"What was it all about?"

"It was a bet they made with an English captain this morning that she 'd ride from Lowe's Folly to the Gap in an hour and a half. The Captain took a hundred on it, because he thought she 'd have to go round by the bridge; and they pretended the same, for they gave all kinds of directions about clearing the carts out of the road, for it's market-day at Thomastown; and away went the Captain as hard as he could, to be at the bridge first, to 'time her,' as she passed. But he has won the money!" sighed he, for the thought of so much Irish coin going into a Saxon pocket completely overcame him; "and what's more," added he, "the gentleman says it was all your fault!"

"All my fault!" cried Conyers, indignantly. "All my fault! Do they imagine that I either knew or cared for their trumpery wager! I saw a girl struggling in a danger from which not one of them had the manliness to rescue her!"

"Oh, take my word for it," burst in Darby, "it's not courage they want!"

"Then it is something far better than even courage, and I'd like to tell them so."

And he turned away as much disgusted with Darby as with the rest of his countrymen. Now, all the anger that filled his breast was not in reality provoked by the want of gallantry that he condemned; a portion, at least, was owing to the marvellous indifference the young lady had manifested to her preserver. Was peril such an every-day incident of Irish life that no one cared for it, or was gratitude a quality not cultivated in this strange land? Such were the puzzles that tormented him as he descended to the drawing-room.

As he opened the door, he heard Miss Barrington's voice, in a tone which he rightly guessed to be reproof, and caught the words, "Just as unwise as it is unbecoming," when he entered.

"Mr. Conyers, Miss Dill," said the old lady, stiffly; "the young gentleman who saved you, the heroine you rescued!" The two allocutions were delivered with a gesture towards each. To cover a moment of extreme awkwardness, Conyers blundered out something about being too happy, and a slight service, and a hope of no ill consequences to herself.

"Have no fears on that score, sir," broke in Miss Dinah. "Manly young ladies are the hardiest things in nature. They are as insensible to danger as they are to—" She stopped, and grew crimson, partly from anger and partly from the unspoken word that had almost escaped her.

"Nay, madam," said Polly, quietly, "I am really very much 'ashamed.'" And, simple as the words were, Miss Barrington felt the poignancy of their application to herself, and her hand trembled over the embroidery she was working.

She tried to appear calm, but in vain; her color came and went, and the stitches, in spite of her, grew irregular; so that, after a moment's struggle, she pushed the frame away, and left the room. While this very brief and painful incident was passing, Conyers was wondering to himself how the dashing horsewoman, with flushed cheek, flashing eye, and dishevelled hair, could possibly be the quiet, demure girl, with a downcast look, and almost Quaker-like simplicity of demeanor. It is but fair to add, though he himself did not discover it, that the contributions of Miss Dinah's wardrobe, to which poor Polly was reduced for dress, were not exactly of a nature to heighten her personal attractions; nor did a sort of short jacket, and a very much beflounced petticoat, set off the girl's figure to advantage. Polly never raised her eyes from the work she was sewing as Miss Barrington withdrew, but, in a low, gentle voice, said, "It was very good of you, sir, to come to my rescue, but you mustn't think ill of my countrymen for not having done so; they had given their word of honor not to lead a fence, nor open a gate, nor, in fact, aid me in any way."

"So that, if they could win their wager, your peril was of little matter," broke he in.

She gave a little low, quiet laugh, perhaps as much at the energy as at the words of his speech. "After all," said she, "a wetting is no great misfortune; the worst punishment of my offence was one that I never contemplated."

"What do you mean?" asked he.

"Doing penance for it in this costume," said she, drawing out the stiff folds of an old brocaded silk, and displaying a splendor of flowers that might have graced a peacock's tail; "I never so much as dreamed of this!"

There was something so comic in the way she conveyed her distress that he laughed outright. She joined him; and they were at once at their ease together.

"I think Miss Barrington called you Mr. Conyers," said she; "and if so, I have the happiness of feeling that my gratitude is bestowed where already there has been a large instalment of the sentiment. It is you who have been so generous and so kind to my poor brother."

"Has he told you, then, what we have been planning together?"

"He has told me all that *you* had planned out for him," said she, with a very gracious smile, which very slightly colored her cheek, and gave great softness to her expression. "My only fear was that the poor boy should have lost his head completely, and perhaps exaggerated to himself your intentions towards him; for, after all, I can scarcely think—"

"What is it that you can scarcely think?" asked he, after a long pause.

"Not to say," resumed she, unheeding his question, "that I cannot imagine how this came about. What could have led him to tell *you*—a perfect stranger to him—his hopes and fears, his struggles and his sorrows? How could you—by what magic did you inspire him with that trustful confidence which made him open his whole heart before you? Poor Tom, who never before had any confessor than myself!"

"Shall I tell you how it came about? It was talking of *you!*"

"Of me! talking of me!" and her cheek now flushed more deeply.

"Yes, we had rambled on over fifty themes, not one of which seemed to attach him strongly, till, in some passing allusion to his own cares and difficulties, he mentioned one who has never ceased to guide and comfort him; who shared not alone his sorrows, but his hard hours of labor, and turned away from her own pleasant paths to tread the dreary road of toil beside him."

"I think he might have kept all this to himself," said she, with a tone of almost severity.

"How could he? How was it possible to tell me his story, and not touch upon what imparted the few tints of better fortune that lighted it? I'm certain, besides, that there is a sort of pride in revealing how much of sympathy and affection we have derived from those better than ourselves, and I could see that he was actually vain of what you had done for him."

"I repeat, he might have kept this to himself. But let us leave this matter; and now tell me,—for I own I can hardly trust my poor brother's triumphant tale,—tell me seriously what the plan is?"

Conyers hesitated for a few seconds, embarrassed how to avoid mention of himself, or to allude but passingly to his own share in the project. At last, as though deciding to dash boldly into the question, he said, "I told him, if he 'd go out to India, I 'd give him such a letter to my father that his fortune would be secure. My governor is something of a swell out there," —and he reddened, partly in shame, partly in pride, as he tried to disguise his feeling by an affectation of ease, —"and that with *him* for a friend, Tom would be certain of success. You smile at my confidence, but you don't know India, and what scores of fine things are—so to say—to be had for asking; and although doctoring is all very well, there are fifty other ways to make a fortune faster. Tom could be a Receiver of Revenue; he might be a Political Resident. You don't know what they get. There's a fellow at Baroda has four thousand rupees a month, and I don't know how much more for dâk-money."

"I can't help smiling," said she, "at the notion of poor Tom in a palanquin. But, seriously, sir, is all this possible? or might it not be feared that your father, when he came to see my brother—who, with many a worthy quality, has not much to prepossess in his favor,—when, I say, he came to see your *protégé* is it not likely that he might—might—hold him more cheaply than you do?"

"Not when he presents a letter from me; not when it's I that have taken him up. You 'll believe me, perhaps, when I tell you what happened when I was but ten years old. We were up at Rangoon, in the Hills, when a dreadful hurricane swept over the country, destroying everything before it; rice, paddy, the indigo-crop, all were carried away, and the poor people left totally destitute. A subscription-list was handed about amongst the British residents, to afford some aid in the calamity, and it was my tutor, a native Moonshee, who went about to collect the sums. One morning he came back somewhat disconsolate at his want of success. A payment of eight thousand rupees had to be made for grain on that day, and he had not, as he hoped and expected, the money ready. He talked freely to me of his disappointment, so that, at last, my feelings being worked upon, I took up my pen and wrote down my name on the list, with the sum of eight thousand rupees to it Shocked at what he regarded as an act of levity, he carried the paper to my father, who at once said, 'Fred wrote it; his name shall not be dishonored;' and the money was paid. I ask you, now, am I reckoning too much on one who could do that, and for a mere child too?"

"That was nobly done," said she, with enthusiasm; and though Conyers went on, with warmth, to tell more of his father's generous nature, she seemed less to listen than to follow out some thread of her own reflections. Was it some speculation as to the temperament the son of such a father might possess? or was it some pleasurable revery regarding one who might do any extravagance and yet be forgiven? My reader may guess this, perhaps,—I cannot. Whatever her speculation, it lent a very charming expression to her features,—that air of gentle, tranquil happiness we like to believe the lot of guileless, simple natures.

Conyers, like many young men of his order, was very fond of talking of himself, of his ways, his habits, and his temper, and she listened to him very prettily,—so prettily, indeed, that when Darby, slyly peeping in at the half-opened door, announced that the boat had come, he felt well inclined to pitch the messenger into the stream.

"I must go and say good-bye to Miss Barrington," said Polly, rising. "I hope that this rustling finery will impart some dignity to my demeanor." And drawing wide the massive folds, she made a very deep courtesy, throwing back her head haughtily as she resumed her height in admirable imitation of a bygone school of manners.

POLLY DILL TAKES LEAVE OF CONYERS

"Very well,—very well, indeed! Quite as like what it is meant for as is Miss Polly Dill for the station she counterfeits!" said Miss Dinah, as, throwing wide the door, she stood before them.

"I am overwhelmed by your flattery, madam," said Polly, who, though very red, lost none of her self-possession; "but I feel that, like the traveller who tried on Charlemagne's armor, I am far more equal to combat in my every-day clothes."

"Do not enter the lists with me in either," said Miss Dinah, with a look of the haughtiest insolence. "Mr. Conyers, will you let me show you my flower-garden?"

"Delighted! But I will first see Miss Dill to her boat." "As you please, sir," said the old lady; and she withdrew with a proud toss of her head that was very unmistakable in its import.

"What a severe correction that was!" said Polly, half gayly, as she went along, leaning on his arm. "And *you* know that, whatever my offending, there was no mimicry in it. I was simply thinking of some great-grandmother who had, perhaps, captivated the heroes of Dettingen; and, talking of heroes, how courageous of you to come to my rescue!"

Was it that her arm only trembled slightly, or did it really press gently on his own as she said this? Certainly Conyers inclined to the latter hypothesis, for he drew her more closely to his side, and said, "Of course I stood by you. She was all in the wrong, and I mean to tell her so."

"Not if you would serve me," said she, eagerly. "I have paid the penalty, and I strongly object to be sentenced again. Oh, here's the boat!"

"Why it's a mere skiff. Are you safe to trust yourself in such a thing?" asked he, for the canoe-shaped "cot" was new to him.

"Of course!" said she, lightly stepping in. "There is even room for another." Then, hastily changing her theme, she asked, "May I tell poor Tom what you have said to me, or is it just possible that you will come up one of these days and see us?"

"If I might be permitted—"

"Too much honor for us!" said she, with such a capital imitation of his voice and manner that he burst into a laugh in spite of himself.

"Mayhap Miss Bamngton was not so far wrong: after all, you *are* a terrible mimic."

"Is it a promise, then? Am I to say to my brother you will come?" said she, seriously.

"Faithfully!" said he, waving his hand, for the boatmen had already got the skiff under weigh, and were sending her along like an arrow from a bow.

Polly turned and kissed her hand to him, and Conyers muttered something over his own stupidity for not being beside her, and then turned sulkily towards the cottage. A few hours ago and he had thought he could have passed his life here; there was a charm in the unbroken tranquillity that seemed to satisfy the longings of his heart, and now, all of a sudden, the place appeared desolate. Have you never, dear reader, felt, in gazing on some fair landscape, with mountain and stream and forest before you, that the scene was perfect, wanting nothing in form or tone or color, till suddenly a flash of strong sunlight from behind a cloud lit up some spot with a glorious lustre, to fade away as quickly into the cold tint it had worn before? Have you not felt then, I say, that the picture had lost its marvellous attraction, and that the very soul of its beauty had departed? In vain you try to recall the past impression; your memory will mourn over the lost, and refuse to be comforted. And so it is often in life: the momentary charm that came unexpectedly can become all in all to our imaginations, and its departure leave a blank, like a death, behind it.

Nor was he altogether satisfied with Miss Barrington. The "old woman"— alas! for his gallantry, it was so that he called her to himself—was needlessly severe. Why should a mere piece of harmless levity be so visited? At all events, he felt certain that he himself would have shown a more generous spirit. Indeed, when Polly had quizzed him, he took it all good-naturedly, and by thus turning his thoughts to his natural goodness and the merits of his character, he at length grew somewhat more well-disposed to the world at large. He knew he was naturally forgiving, and he felt he was very generous. Scores of fellows, bred up as he was, would have been perfectly unendurable; they would have presumed on their position, and done this, that, and t' other. Not one of them would have dreamed of taking up a poor ungainly bumpkin, a country doctor's cub, and making a man of him; not one of them would have had the heart to conceive or the energy to carry out such a project. And yet this he would do. Polly herself, sceptical as she was, should be brought to admit that he had kept his word. Selfish fellows would limit their plans to their own engagements, and weak fellows could be laughed out of their intentions; but *he* flattered himself that he was neither of these, and it was really fortunate that the world should see how little spoiled a fine nature could be, though surrounded with all the temptations that are supposed to be dangerous.

In this happy frame—for he was now happy—he reentered the cottage. "What a coxcomb!" will say my reader. Be it so. But it was a coxcomb who wanted to be something better.

Miss Barrington met him in the porch, not a trace of her late displeasure on her face, but with a pleasant smile she said, "I have just got a few lines from my brother. He writes in excellent spirits, for he has gained a lawsuit; not a very important case, but it puts us in a position to carry out a little project we are full of. He will be here by Saturday, and hopes to bring with him an old and valued friend, the Attorney-General, to spend a few days with us. I am, therefore, able to promise you an ample recompense for all the loneliness of your present life. I have cautiously abstained from telling my brother who you are; I keep the delightful surprise for the moment of your meeting. Your name, though associated with some sad memories, will bring him back to the happiest period of his life."

Conyers made some not very intelligible reply about his reluctance to impose himself on them at such a time, but she stopped him with a good-humored smile, and said,—

"Your father's son should know that where a Barrington lived he had a home,—not to say you have already paid some of the tribute of this homeliness, and seen me very cross and ill-tempered. Well, let us not speak of that now. I have your word to remain here." And she left him to attend to her household cares, while he strolled into the garden, half amused, half embarrassed by all the strange and new interests that had grown up so suddenly around him.

CHAPTER XV.

AN EXPLORING EXPEDITION

Whether from simple caprice, or that Lady Cobham desired to mark her disapprobation of Polly Dill's share in the late wager, is not open to me to say, but the festivities at Cob-ham were not, on that day, graced or enlivened by her presence. If the comments on her absence were brief, they were pungent, and some wise reflections, too, were uttered as to the dangers that must inevitably attend all attempts to lift people into a sphere above their own. Poor human nature! that unlucky culprit who is flogged for everything and for everybody, bore the brunt of these severities, and it was declared that Polly had done what any other girl "in her rank of life" might have done; and this being settled, the company went to luncheon, their appetites none the worse for the small *auto-da-fé* they had just celebrated.

"You'd have lost your money, Captain," whispered Ambrose Bushe to Stapylton, as they stood talking together in a window recess, "if that girl had only taken the river three hundred yards higher up. Even as it was, she 'd have breasted her horse at the bank if the bridle had not given way. I suppose you have seen the place?"

"I regret to say I have not. They tell me it's one of the strongest rapids in the river."

"Let me describe it to you," replied he; and at once set about a picture in which certainly no elements of peril were forgotten, and all the dangers of rocks and rapids were given with due emphasis. Stapylton seemed to listen with fitting attention, throwing out the suitable "Indeed! is it possible!" and such-like interjections, his mind, however, by no means absorbed by the narrative, but dwelling solely on a chance name that had dropped from the narrator.

"You called the place 'Barrington's Ford,'" said he, at last. "Who is Barrington?"

"As good a gentleman by blood and descent as any in this room, but now reduced to keep a little wayside inn,—the 'Fisherman's Home,' it is called. All come of a spendthrift son, who went out to India, and ran through every acre of the property before he died."

"What a strange vicissitude! And is the old man much broken by it?"

"Some would say he was; my opinion is, that he bears up wonderfully. Of course, to me, he never makes any mention of the past; but while my father lived, he would frequently talk to him over bygones, and liked nothing better than to speak of his son, Mad George as they called him, and tell all his wildest exploits and most harebrained achievements. But you have served yourself in India. Have you never heard of George Barrington?"

Stapylton shook his head, and dryly added that India was very large, and that even in one Presidency a man might never hear what went on in another.

"Well, this fellow made noise enough to be heard even over here. He married a native woman, and he either shook off his English allegiance, or was suspected of doing so. At all events, he got himself into trouble that finished him. It's a long complicated story, that I have never heard correctly. The upshot was, however, old Barrington was sold out stick and stone, and if it was n't for the ale-house he might starve."

"And his former friends and associates, do they rally round him and cheer him?"

"Not a great deal. Perhaps, however, that's as much his fault as theirs. He is very proud, and very quick to resent anything like consideration for his changed condition. Sir Charles would have him up here,—he has tried it scores of times, but all in vain; and now he is left to two or three of his neighbors, the doctor and an old half-pay major, who lives on the river, and I believe really he never sees any one else. Old M'Cormick knew George Barrington well; not that they were friends,—two men less alike never lived; but that's enough to make poor Peter fond of talking to him, and telling all about some lawsuits George left him for a legacy."

"This Major that you speak of, does he visit here? I don't remember to have seen him."

"M'Cormick!" said the other, laughing. "No, he 's a miserly old fellow that has n't a coat fit to go out in, and he's no loss to any one. It's as much as old Peter Barrington can do to bear his shabby ways, and his cranky temper, but he puts up with everything because he knew his son George. That's quite enough for old Peter; and if you were to go over to the cottage, and say, 'I met your son up in Bombay or Madras; we were quartered together at Ram-something-or-other,' he 'd tell you the place was your own, to stop at as long as you liked, and your home for life."

"Indeed!" said Stapylton, affecting to feel interested, while he followed out the course of his own thoughts.

"Not that the Major could do even that much!" continued Bushe, who now believed that he had found an eager listener. "There was only one thing in this world he'd like to talk about,—Walcheren. Go how or when you liked, or where or for what,—no matter, it was Walcheren you 'd get, and nothing else."

"Somewhat tiresome this, I take it!"

"Tiresome is no name for it! And I don't know a stronger proof of old Peter's love for his son's memory, than that, for the sake of hearing about him, he can sit and listen to the 'expedition.'"

There was a half-unconscious mimicry in the way he gave the last word that showed how the Major's accents had eaten their way into his sensibilities.

"Your portrait of this Major is not tempting," said Stapylton, smiling.

"Why would it? He's eighteen or twenty years in the neighborhood, and I never heard that he said a kind word or did a generous act by any one. But I get cross if I talk of him. Where are you going this morning? Will you come up to the Long Callows and look at the yearlings? The Admiral is very proud of his young stock, and he thinks he has some of the best bone and blood in Ireland there at this moment."

"Thanks, no; I have some notion of a long walk this morning. I take shame to myself for having seen so little of the country here since I came that I mean to repair my fault and go off on a sort of voyage of discovery."

"Follow the river from Brown's Barn down to Inistioge, and if you ever saw anything prettier I'm a Scotchman." And with this appalling alternative, Mr. Bushe walked away, and left the other to his own guidance.

Perhaps Stapylton is not the companion my reader would care to stroll with, even along the grassy path beside that laughing river, with spray-like larches bending overhead, and tender water-lilies streaming, like pennants, in the fast-running current. It may be that he or she would prefer some one more impressionable to the woodland beauty of the spot, and more disposed to enjoy the tranquil loveliness around him; for it is true the swarthy soldier strode on, little heeding the picturesque effects which made every succeeding reach of the river a subject for a painter. He was bent on finding out where M'Cormick lived, and on making the acquaintance of that bland individual.

"That's the Major's, and there's himself," said a countryman, as he pointed to a very shabbily dressed old man hoeing his cabbages in a dilapidated bit of garden-ground, but who was so absorbed in his occupation as not to notice the approach of a stranger.

"Am I taking too great a liberty," said Stapylton, as he raised his hat, "if I ask leave to follow the river path through this lovely spot?"

"Eh—what?—how did you come? You didn't pass round by the young wheat, eh?" asked M'Cormick, in his most querulous voice.

"I came along by the margin of the river."

"That's just it!" broke in the other. "There's no keeping them out that way. But I 'll have a dog as sure as my name is Dan. I'll have a bull-terrier that'll tackle the first of you that's trespassing there."

"I fancy I'm addressing Major M'Cormick," said Stapylton, never noticing this rude speech; "and if so, I will ask him to accord me the privilege of a brother-soldier, and let me make myself known to him,—Captain Stapylton, of the Prince's Hussars."

"By the wars!" muttered old Dan; the exclamation being a favorite one with him to express astonishment at any startling event. Then recovering himself, he added, "I think I heard there were three or four of ye stopping up there at Cobham; but I never go out myself anywhere. I live very retired down here."

"I am not surprised at that. When an old soldier can nestle down in a lovely nook like this, he has very little to regret of what the world is busy about outside it."

"And they are all ruining themselves, besides," said M'Cormick, with one of his malicious grins. "There's not a man in this county is n't mortgaged over head and ears. I can count them all on my fingers for you, and tell what they have to live on."

"You amaze me," said Stapylton, with a show of interest

"And the women are as bad as the men: nothing fine enough for them to wear; no jewels rich enough to put on! Did you ever hear them mention *me?*" asked he, suddenly, as though the thought flashed upon him that he had himself been exposed to comment of a very different kind.

"They told me of an old retired officer, who owned a most picturesque cottage, and said, if I remember aright, that the view from one of the windows was accounted one of the most perfect bits of river landscape in the kingdom."

"Just the same as where you 're standing,—no difference in life," said M'Cormick, who was not to be seduced by the flattery into any demonstration of hospitality.

"I cannot imagine anything finer," said Stapylton, as he threw himself at the foot of a tree, and seemed really to revel in enjoyment of the scene. "One might, perhaps, if disposed to be critical, ask for a little opening in that copse yonder. I suspect we should get a peep at the bold cliff whose summit peers above the tree-tops."

"You'd see the quarry, to be sure," croaked out the Major, "if that's what you mean."

"May I offer you a cigar?" said Stapylton, whose self-possession was pushed somewhat hard by the other. "An old campaigner is sure to be a smoker."

"I am not. I never had a pipe in my mouth since Walcheren."

"Since Walcheren! You don't say that you are an old Walcheren man?"

"I am, indeed. I was in the second battalion of the 103d,—the Duke's Fusiliers, if ever you heard of them."

"Heard of them! The whole world has heard of them; but I did n't know there was a man of that splendid corps surviving. Why, they lost—let me see—they lost every officer but—" Here a vigorous effort to keep his cigar alight interposed, and kept him occupied for a few seconds. "How many did you bring out of action,—four was it, or five? I'm certain you had n't six!"

"We were the same as the Buffs, man for man," said M'Cormick.

"The poor Buffs!—very gallant fellows too!" sighed Stapylton. "I have always maintained, and I always will maintain, that the Walcheren expedition, though not a success, was the proudest achievement of the British arms."

"The shakes always began after sunrise, and in less than ten minutes you 'd see your nails growing blue."

"How dreadful!"

"And if you felt your nose, you would n't know it was your nose; you 'd think it was a bit of a cold carrot."

"Why was that?"

"Because there was no circulation; the blood would stop going round; and you 'd be that way for four hours, — till the sweating took you, — just the same as dead."

"There, don't go on, — I can't stand it, — my nerves are all ajar already."

"And then the cramps came on," continued M'Cormick, in an ecstasy over a listener whose feelings he could harrow; "first in the calves of the legs, and then all along the spine, so that you 'd be bent like a fish."

"For Heaven's sake, spare me! I've seen some rough work, but that description of yours is perfectly horrifying! And when one thinks it was the glorious old 105th —"

"No, the 103d; the 105th was at Barbadoes," broke in the Major, testily.

"So they were, and got their share of the yellow fever at that very time too," said Stapylton, hazarding a not very rash conjecture.

"Maybe they did, and maybe they didn't," was the dry rejoinder.

It required all Stapylton's nice tact to get the Major once more full swing at the expedition, but he at last accomplished the feat, and with such success that M'Cormick suggested an adjournment within doors, and faintly hinted at a possible something to drink. The wily guest, however, declined this. "He liked," he said, "that nice breezy spot under those fine old trees, and with that glorious reach of the river before them. Could a man but join to these enjoyments," he continued, "just a neighbor or two, — an old friend or so that he really liked, — one not alone agreeable from his tastes, but to whom the link of early companionship also attached us, with this addition I could call this a paradise."

"Well, I have the village doctor," croaked out M'Cor-mick, "and there's Barrington — old Peter — up at the 'Fisherman's Home.' I have *them* by way of society. I might have better, and I might have worse."

"They told me at Cobham that there was no getting you to 'go out;' that, like a regular old soldier, you liked your own chimney-corner, and could not be tempted away from it."

"They didn't try very hard, anyhow," said he, harshly. "I'll be nineteen years here if I live till November, and I think I got two invitations, and one of them to a 'dancing tea,' whatever that is; so that you may observe they did n't push the temptation as far as St. Anthony's!"

Stapylton joined in the laugh with which M'Cormick welcomed his own drollery.

"Your doctor," resumed he, "is, I presume, the father of the pretty girl who rides so cleverly?"

"So they tell me. I never saw her mounted but once, and she smashed a melon-frame for me, and not so much as 'I ask your pardon!' afterwards."

"And Barrington," resumed Stapylton, "is the ruined gentleman I have heard of, who has turned innkeeper. An extravagant son, I believe, finished him?"

"His own taste for law cost him just as much," muttered M'Cormick. "He had a trunk full of old title-deeds and bonds and settlements, and he was always poring over them, discovering, by the way, flaws in this and omissions in that, and then he 'd draw up a case for counsel, and get consultations on it, and before you could turn round, there he was, trying to break a will or get out of a covenant, with a special jury and the strongest Bar in Ireland. That's what ruined him."

"I gather from what you tell me that he is a bold, determined, and perhaps a vindictive man. Am I right?"

"You are not; he's an easy-tempered fellow, and careless, like every one of his name and race. If you said he hadn't a wise head on his shoulders, you 'd be nearer the mark. Look what he 's going to do now!" cried he, warming with his theme: "he 's going to give up the inn—"

"Give it up! And why?"

"Ay, that's the question would puzzle him to answer; but it's the haughty old sister persuades him that he ought to take this black girl—George Barrington's daughter—home to live with him, and that a shebeen is n't the place to bring her to, and she a negress. That's more of the family wisdom!"

"There may be affection in it."

"Affection! For what,—for a black! Ay, and a black that they never set eyes on! If it was old Withering had the affection for her, I wouldn't be surprised."

"What do you mean? Who is he?"

"The Attorney-General, who has been fighting the East India Company for her these sixteen years, and making more money out of the case than she 'll ever get back again. Did you ever hear of Barrington and Lot Rammadahn Mohr against the India Company? That's the case. Twelve millions of rupees and the interest on them! And I believe in my heart and soul old Peter would be well out of it for a thousand pounds."

"That is, you suspect he must be beaten in the end?"

"I mean that I am sure of it! We have a saying in Ireland, 'It's not fair for one man to fall on twenty,' and it's just the same thing to go to law with a great rich Company. You 're sure to have the worst of it."

"Did it never occur to them to make some sort of compromise?"

"Not a bit of it. Old Peter always thinks he has the game in his hand, and nothing would make him throw up the cards. No; I believe if you offered to pay the stakes, he 'd say, 'Play the game out, and let the winner take the money!'"

"His lawyer may, possibly, have something to say to this spirit."

"Of course he has; they are always bolstering each other up. It is, 'Barrington, my boy, you 'll turn the corner yet. You 'll drive up that old avenue to the house you were born in, Barrington, of Barrington Hall;' or, 'Withering, I never heard you greater than on that point before the twelve Judges;' or, 'Your last speech at Bar was finer than Curran.' They'd pass the evening that way, and call me a cantankerous old hound when my back was turned, just because I did n't hark in to the cry. Maybe I have the laugh at them, after all." And he broke out into one of his most discordant cackles to corroborate his boast.

"The sound sense and experience of an old Walcheren man might have its weight with them. I know it would with me."

"Ay," muttered the Major, half aloud, for he was thinking to himself whether this piece of flattery was a bait for a little whiskey-and-water.

"I 'd rather have the unbought judgment of a shrewd man of the world than a score of opinions based upon the quips and cranks of an attorney's instructions."

"Ay!" responded the other, as he mumbled to himself, "he's mighty thirsty."

"And what's more," said Stapylton, starting to his legs, "I 'd follow the one as implicitly as I'd reject the other. I 'd say, 'M'Cormick is an old friend; we have known each other since boyhood.'"

"No, we haven't I never saw Peter Barrington till I came to live here."

"Well, after a close friendship of years with his son—"

"Nor that, either," broke in the implacable Major. "He was always cutting his jokes on me, and I never could abide him, so that the close friendship you speak of is a mistake."

"At all events," said Stapylton, sharply, "it could be no interest of yours to see an old—an old acquaintance lavishing his money on lawyers and in the pursuit of the most improbable of all results. *You* have no design upon him. *You* don't want to marry his sister!"

"No, by Gemini! "—a favorite expletive of the Major's in urgent moments.

"Nor the Meer's daughter, either, I suppose?"

"The black! I think not. Not if she won the lawsuit, and was as rich as—she never will be."

"I agree with you there, Major, though I know nothing of the case or its merits; but it is enough to hear that a beggared squire is on one side, and Leadenhall Street on the other, to predict the upshot, and, for my own part, I wonder they go on with it."

"I'll tell you how it is," said M'Cormick, closing one eye so as to impart a look of intense cunning to his face. "It's the same with law as at a fox-hunt: when you 're tired out beating a cover, and ready to go off home, one dog—very often the worst in the whole pack—will yelp out. You know well enough he's a bad hound, and never found in his life. What does that signify? When you 're wishing a thing, whatever flatters your hopes is all right,—is n't that true?—and away you dash after the yelper as if he was a good hound."

"You have put the matter most convincingly before me."

"How thirsty he is now!" thought the Major; and grinned maliciously at his reflection.

"And the upshot of all," said Stapylton, like one summing up a case,—"the upshot of all is, that this old man is not satisfied with his ruin if it be not complete; he must see the last timbers of the wreck carried away ere he leaves the scene of his disaster. Strange, sad infatuation!"

"Ay," muttered the Major, who really had but few sympathies with merely moral abstractions.

"Not what I should have done in a like case; nor *you* either, Major, eh?"

"Very likely not"

"But so it is. There are men who cannot be practical, do what they will. This is above them."

A sort of grunt gave assent to this proposition; and Stapylton, who began to feel it was a drawn game, arose to take his leave.

"I owe you a very delightful morning, Major," said he. "I wish I could think it was not to be the last time I was to have this pleasure. Do you ever come up to Kilkenny? Does it ever occur to you to refresh your old mess recollections?"

Had M'Cormick been asked whether he did not occasionally drop in at Holland House, and brush up his faculties by intercourse with the bright spirits who resorted there, he could scarcely have been more astounded. That he, old Dan M'Cormick, should figure at a mess-table,—he, whose wardrobe, a mere skeleton battalion thirty years ago, had never since been recruited,—he should mingle with the gay and splendid young fellows of a "crack" regiment!

"I'd just as soon think of—of—" he hesitated how to measure an unlikelihood— "of marrying a young wife, and taking her off to Paris!"

"And I don't see any absurdity in the project There is certainly a great deal of brilliancy about it!"

"And something bitter too!" croaked out M'Cormick, with a fearful grin.

"Well, if you'll not come to see me, the chances are I'll come over and make *you* another visit before I leave the neighborhood." He waited a second or two, not more, for some recognition of this offer; but none came, and he con-tinned: "I'll get you to stroll down with me, and show me this 'Fisherman's Home,' and its strange proprietor."

"Oh, I 'll do *that!*" said the Major, who had no objection to a plan which by no possibility could involve himself in any cost.

"As it is an inn, perhaps they'd let us have a bit of dinner. What would you say to being my guest there to-morrow? Would that suit you?"

"It would suit *me* well enough!" was the strongly marked reply.

"Well, we'll do it this wise. You'll send one of your people over to order dinner for two at—shall we say five o'clock?—yes, five—to-morrow. That will give us a longer evening, and I'll call here for you about four. Is that agreed?"

"Yes, that might do," was M'Cormick's half-reluctant assent, for, in reality, there were details in the matter that he scarcely fancied. First of all, he had never hitherto crossed that threshold except as an invited guest, and he had his misgivings about the prudence of appearing in any other character, and secondly, there was a responsibility in ordering the dinner, which he liked just as little, and, as he muttered to himself, "Maybe I'll have to order the bill too!"

Some unlucky experiences of casualties of this sort had, perhaps, shadowed his early life; for so it was, that long after Stapylton had taken his leave and gone off, the Major stood there ruminating over this unpleasant contingency, and ingeniously imagining all the pleas he could put in, should his apprehension prove correct, against his own indebtedness.

"Tell Miss Dinah," said he to his messenger,—"tell her 't is an officer by the name of Captain Staples, or something like that, that's up at Cobham, that wants a dinner for two to-morrow at five o'clock; and mind that you don't say who the other is, for it's nothing to her. And if she asks you what sort of a dinner, say the best in the house, for the Captain—mind you say the Captain—is to pay for it, and the other man only dines with him. There, now, you have your orders, and take care that you follow them!"

There was a shrewd twinkle in the messenger's eye as he listened, which, if not exactly complimentary, guaranteed how thoroughly he comprehended the instructions that were given to him; and the Major saw him set forth on his mission, well assured that he could trust his envoy.

In that nothing-for-nothing world Major M'Cormick had so long lived in, and to whose practice and ways he had adapted all his thoughts, there was something puzzling in the fact of a dashing Captain of Hussars of "the Prince's Own," seeking him out, to form his acquaintance and invite him to dinner. Now, though the selfishness of an unimaginative man is the most complete of all, it yet exposes him to fewer delusions than the same quality when found allied with a hopeful or fanciful temperament. M'Cormick had no "distractions" from such sources. He thought very ill of the world at large; he expected extremely little from its generosity, and he resolved to be "quits" with it. To his often put question, "What brought him here?—what did he come for?" he could find no satisfactory reply. He scouted the notion of "love of scenery, solitude, and so forth," and as fully he ridiculed to himself the idea of a stranger caring to hear the gossip and small-talk of a mere country neighborhood. "I have it!" cried he at last, as a bright thought darted through his brain,—"I have it at last! He wants to pump me about the 'expedition.' It's for that he's come. He affected surprise, to be sure, when I said I was a Walcheren man, and pretended to be amazed, besides; but that was all make-believe. He knew well enough who and what I was before he came. And he was so cunning, leading the conversation away in another direction, getting me to talk of old Peter and his son George. Wasn't it deep?—was n't it sly? Well, maybe we are not so innocent as we look, ourselves; maybe we have a trick in our sleeves too! 'With a good dinner and a bottle of port wine,' says he, 'I 'll have the whole story, and be able to write it with the signature "One who was there."' But you 're mistaken this time, Captain; the sorrow bit of Walcheren you 'll hear out of my mouth to-morrow, be as pleasant and congenial as you like. I 'll give you the Barringtons, father and son,—ay, and old Dinah, too, if you fancy her,—but not a syllable about the expedition. It's the Scheldt you want, but you 'll have to 'take it out' in the Ganges." And his uncouth joke so tickled him that he laughed till his eyes ran over; and in the thought that he was going to obtain a dinner under false pretences, he felt something as nearly like happiness as he had tasted for many a long day before.

CHAPTER XVI.

COMING HOME

Miss Barrtngton waited with impatience for Conyers's appearance at the breakfast-table,—she had received such a pleasant note from her brother, and she was so eager to read it. That notion of imparting some conception of a dear friend by reading his own words to a stranger is a very natural one. It serves so readily to corroborate all we have already said, to fill up that picture of which wo have but given the mere outline, not to speak of the inexplicable charm there is in being able to say, "Here is the man without reserve or disguise; here he is in all the freshness and warmth of genuine feeling; no tricks of style, no turning of phrases to mar the honest expression of his nature. You see him as we see him."

"My brother is coming home, Mr. Conyers; he will be here to-day. Here is his note," said Miss Dinah, as she shook hands with her guest "I must read it for you:—

"'At last, my dear Dinah—at last I am free, and, with all my love of law and lawyers, right glad to turn my steps homeward. Not but I have had a most brilliant week of it; dined with my old schoolfellow Longmore, now Chief Baron, and was the honored guest of the "Home Circuit," not to speak of one glorious evening with a club called the "Unbriefed," the pleasantest dogs that ever made good speeches for nothing!—an amount of dissipation upon which I can well retire and live for the next twelve months. How strange it seems to me to be once more in the "world," and listening to scores of things in which I have no personal interest; how small it makes my own daily life appear, but how secure and how homelike, Dinah! You have often heard me grumbling over the decline of social agreeability, and the dearth of those pleasant speeches that could set the table in a roar. You shall never hear the same complaint from me again. These fellows are just as good as their fathers. If I missed anything, it was that glitter of scholarship, that classical turn which in the olden day elevated table-talk, and made it racy with the smart aphorisms and happy conceits of those who, even over their wine, were poets and orators. But perhaps I am not quite fair even in this. At all events, I am not going to disparage those who have brought back to my old age some of the pleasant memories of my youth, and satisfied me that even yet I have a heart for those social joys I once loved so dearly!

"'And we have won our suit, Dinah,—at least, a juror was withdrawn by consent,—and Brazier agrees to an arbitration as to the Moyalty lands, the whole of Clanebrach and Barrymaquilty property being released from the sequestration.'

"This is all personal matter, and technical besides," said Miss Barrington; "so I skip it."

"'Withering was finer than ever I heard him in the speech to evidence. We have been taunted with our defensive attitude so suddenly converted into an attack, and he compared our position to Wellington's at Torres Vedras. The Chief Justice said Curran, at his best, never excelled it, and they have called me nothing but Lord Wellington ever since. And now, Dinah, to answer the question your impatience has been putting these ten minutes: "What of the money part of all this triumph?" I fear much, my dear sister, we are to take little by our motion. The costs of the campaign cut up all but the glory! Hogan's bill extends to thirty-eight folio pages, and there's a codicil to it of eleven more, headed "Confidential between Client and Attorney," and though I have not in a rapid survey seen anything above five pounds, the gross total is two thousand seven hundred and forty-three pounds three and fourpence. I must and will say, however, it was a great suit, and admirably prepared. There was not an instruction Withering did not find substantiated, and Hogan is equally delighted with *him*, With all my taste for field sports and manly games, Dinah, I am firmly convinced that a good trial at bar is a far finer spectacle than the grandest tournament that ever was tilted. There was a skirmish yesterday that I 'd rather have witnessed than I 'd have seen Brian de Bois himself at Ashby-de-la-Zouch. And, considering that my own share for this passage at arms will come to a trifle above two thousand pounds, the confession may be taken as an honest one.

"'And who is your young guest whom I shall be so delighted to see? This gives no clew to him, Dinah, for you know well how I would welcome any one who has impressed you so favorably. Entreat of him to prolong his stay for a week at least, and if I can persuade Withering to come down with me, we 'll try and make his sojourn more agreeable. Look out for me—at least, about five o'clock—and have the green-room ready for W., and let Darby be at Holt's stile to take the trunks, for Withering likes that walk through the woods, and says that he leaves his wig and gown on the holly-bushes there till he goes back.'"

The next paragraph she skimmed over to herself. It was one about an advance that Hogan had let him have of two hundred pounds. "Quite ample," W. says, "for our excursion to fetch over Josephine." Some details as to the route followed, and some wise hints about travelling on the Continent, and a hearty concurrence on the old lawyer's part with the whole scheme.

"These are little home details," said she, hurriedly, "but you have heard enough to guess what my brother is like. Here is the conclusion:—

> "'I hope your young friend is a fisherman, which will give me more chance of his company than walking up the partridges, for which I am getting too old. Let him however understand that we mean him to enjoy himself in his own way, to have the most perfect liberty, and that the only despotism we insist upon is, not to be late for dinner.

> "'Your loving brother,

"'Peter Barrington.

"'There is no fatted calf to feast our return, Dinah, but Withering has an old weakness for a roast sucking-pig. Don't you think we could satisfy it?'"

Conyers readily caught the contagion of the joy Miss Barrington felt at the thought of her brother's return. Short as the distance was that separated him from home, his absences were so rare, it seemed as though he had gone miles and miles away, for few people ever lived more dependent on each other, with interests more concentrated, and all of whose hopes and fears took exactly the same direction, than this brother and sister, and this, too, with some strong differences on the score of temperament, of which the reader already has an inkling.

What a pleasant bustle that is of a household that prepares for the return of a well-loved master! What feeling pervades twenty little offices of every-day routine! And how dignified by affection are the smallest cares and the very humblest attentions! "He likes this!" "He is so fond of that!" are heard at every moment It is then that one marks how the observant eye of love has followed the most ordinary tricks of habit, and treasured them as things to be remembered. It is not the key of the street door in your pocket, nor the lease of the premises in your drawer, that make a home. Let us be grateful when we remember that, in this attribute, the humblest shealing on the hillside is not inferior to the palace of the king!

Conyers, I have said, partook heartily of Miss Barring-ton's delight, and gave a willing help to the preparations that went forward. All were soon busy within doors and without. Some were raking the gravel before the door; while others were disposing the flower-pots in little pyramids through the grass plats; and then there were trees to be nailed up, and windows cleaned, and furniture changed in various ways. What superhuman efforts did not Conyers make to get an old jet d'eau to play which had not spouted for nigh twenty years; and how reluctantly he resigned himself to failure and assisted Betty to shake a carpet!

And when all was completed, and the soft and balmy air sent the odor of the rose and the jessamine through the open windows, within which every appearance of ease and comfort prevailed, Miss Barrington sat down at the piano and began to refresh her memory of some Irish airs, old favorites of Withering's, which he was sure to ask for. There was that in their plaintive wildness which strongly interested Conyers; while, at the same time, he was astonished at the skill of one at whose touch, once on a time, tears had trembled in the eyes of those who listened, and whose fingers had not yet forgot their cunning.

"Who is that standing without there?" said Miss Barrington, suddenly, as she saw a very poor-looking countryman who had drawn close to the window to listen. "Who are you? and what do you want here?" asked she, approaching him.

"I 'm Terry, ma'am,—Terry Delany, the Major's man," said he, taking off his hat.

"Never heard of you; and what 's your business?"

"'T is how I was sent, your honor's reverence," began he, faltering at every word, and evidently terrified by her imperious style of address. "'Tis how I came here with the master's compliments, — not indeed his own but the other man's, — to say, that if it was plazing to you, or, indeed, anyhow at all, they 'd be here at five o'clock to dinner; and though it was yesterday I got it, I stopped with my sister's husband at Foynes Gap, and misremembered it all till this morning, and I hope your honor's reverence won't tell it on me, but have the best in the house all the same, for he's rich enough and can well afford it."

"What can the creature mean?" cried Miss Barrington. "Who sent you here?"

"The Major himself; but not for him, but for the other that's up at Cobham."

"And who is this other? What is he called?"

"'Twas something like Hooks, or Nails; but I can't remember," said he, scratching his head in sign of utter and complete bewilderment.

"Did any one ever hear the like! Is the fellow an idiot?" exclaimed she, angrily.

"No, my lady; but many a one might be that lived with ould M'Cormick!" burst out the man, in a rush of unguardedness.

"Try and collect yourself, my good fellow," said Miss Barrington, smiling, in spite of herself, at his confession, "and say, if you can, what brought you here?"

"It's just, then, what I said before," said he, gaining a little more courage. "It's dinner for two ye're to have; and it's to be ready at five o'clock; but ye 're not to look to ould Dan for the money, for he as good as said he would never pay sixpence of it, but 't is all to come out of the other chap's pocket, and well affordin' it. There it is now, and I defy the Pope o' Rome to say that I did n't give the message right!"

"Mr. Conyers," began Miss Barrington, in a voice shaking with agitation, "it is nigh twenty years since a series of misfortunes brought us so low in the world that—" She stopped, partly overcome by indignation, partly by shame; and then, suddenly turning towards the man, she continued, in a firm and resolute tone, "Go back to your master and say, 'Miss Barrington hopes he has sent a fool on his errand, otherwise his message is so insolent it will be far safer he should never present himself here again!' Do you hear me? Do you understand me?"

"If you mane you'd make them throw him in the river, the divil a straw I 'd care, and I would n't wet my feet to pick him out of it!"

"Take the message as I have given it you, and do not dare to mix up anything of your own with it."

"Faix, I won't. It's trouble enough I have without that! I 'll tell him there's no dinner for him here to-day, and that, if he 's wise, he won't come over to look for it."

"There, go—be off," cried Conyers, impatiently, for he saw that Miss Barrington's temper was being too sorely tried.

She conquered, however, the indignation that at one moment had threatened to master her, and in a voice of tolerable calm said, —

"May I ask you to see if Darby or any other of the workmen are in the garden?

It is high time to take down these insignia of our traffic, and tell our friends how we would be regarded in future."

"Will you let me do it? I ask as a favor that I may be permitted to do it," cried Conyers, eagerly; and without waiting for her answer, hurried away to fetch a ladder. He was soon back again and at work.

"Take care how you remove that board, Mr. Conyers," said she. "If there be the tiniest sprig of jessamine broken, my brother will miss it. He has been watching anxiously for the time when the white bells would shut out every letter of his name, and I like him not to notice the change immediately. There, you are doing it very handily indeed. There is another holdfast at this corner. Ah, be careful; that is a branch of the passion-tree, and though it looks dead, you will see it covered with flowers in spring. Nothing could be better. Now for the last emblem of our craft,—can you reach it?"

"Oh, easily," said Conyers, as he raised his eyes to where the little tin fish hung glittering above him. The ladder, however, was too short, and, standing on one of the highest rungs, still he could not reach the little iron stanchion. "I must have it, though," cried he; "I mean to claim that as my prize. It will be the only fish I ever took with my own hands." He now cautiously crept up another step of the ladder, supporting himself by the frail creepers which covered the walls. "Help me now with a crooked stick, and I shall catch it."

"I'll fetch you one," said she, disappearing within the porch.

Still wistfully looking at the object of his pursuit, Conyers never turned his eyes downwards as the sound of steps apprised him some one was near, and, concluding it to be Miss Barrington, he said, "I'm half afraid that I have torn some of this jessamine-tree from the wall; but see here's the prize!" A slight air of wind had wafted it towards him, and he snatched the fish from its slender chain and held it up in triumph.

"A poacher caught in the fact, Barrington!" said a deep voice from below; and Conyers, looking down, saw two men, both advanced in life, very gravely watching his proceedings.

Not a little ashamed of a situation to which he never expected an audience, he hastily descended the ladder; but before he reached the ground Miss Barrington was in her brother's arms, and welcoming him home with all the warmth of true affection. This over, she next shook hands cordially with his companion, whom she called Mr. Withering.

"And now, Peter," said she, "to present one I have been longing to make known to you. You, who never forget a well-known face, will recognize him."

"My eyes are not what they used to be," said Barrington, holding out his hand to Conyers, "but they are good enough to see the young gentleman I left here when I went away."

"Yes, Peter," said she, hastily; "but does the sight of him bring back to you no memory of poor George?"

POACHING

"George was dark as a Spaniard, and this gentleman—But pray, sir, forgive this rudeness of ours, and let us make ourselves better acquainted within doors. You mean to stay some time here, I hope."

"I only wish I could; but I have already overstayed my leave, and waited here only to shake your hand before I left."

"Peter, Peter," said Miss Dinah, impatiently, "must I then tell whom you are speaking to?"

Barrington seemed pazzled. He looked from the stranger to his sister, and back again.

She drew near and whispered in his ear: "The son of poor George's dearest friend on earth,—the son of Ormsby Conyers."

"Of whom?" said Barrington, in a startled and half-angry voice.

"Of Ormsby Conyers."

Barrington trembled from head to foot; his face, for an instant crimson, became suddenly of an ashy paleness, and his voice shook as he said,—

"I was not—I am not—prepared for this honor. I mean, I could not have expected that Mr. Conyers would have desired—Say this—do this for me, Withering, for I am not equal to it," said the old man, as, with his hands pressed over his face, he hurried within the house, followed by his sister.

"I cannot make a guess at the explanation my friend has left me to make," cried Withering, courteously; "but it is plain to see that your name has revived some sorrow connected with the great calamity of his life. You have heard of his son, Colonel Barrington?"

"Yes, and it was because my father had been his dearest friend that Miss Barrington insisted on my remaining here. She told me, over and over again, of the joy her brother would feel on meeting me—"

"Where are you going,—what's the matter?" asked Withering, as a man hurriedly passed out of the house and made for the river.

"The master is taken bad, sir, and I'm going to Inistioge for the doctor."

"Let me go with you," said Conyers; and, only returning by a nod the good-bye of Withering, he moved past and stepped into the boat.

"What an afternoon to such a morning!" muttered he to himself, as the tears started from his eyes and stole heavily along his cheeks.

CHAPTER XVII.

A SHOCK

If Conyers had been in the frame of mind to notice it, the contrast between the neat propriety of the "Fisherman's Home," and the disorder and slovenliness of the little inn at Inistioge could not have failed to impress itself upon him. The "Spotted Duck" was certainly, in all its details, the very reverse of that quiet and picturesque cottage he had just quitted. But what did he care at that moment for the roof that sheltered him, or the table that was spread before him? For days back he had been indulging in thoughts of that welcome which Miss Barrington had promised him. He fancied how, on the mere mention of his father's name, the old man's affection would have poured forth in a flood of kindest words; he had even prepared himself for a scene of such emotion as a father might have felt on seeing one who brought back to mind his own son's earlier years; and instead of all this, he found himself shunned, avoided, repulsed. If there was a thing on earth in which his pride was greatest, it was his name; and yet it was on the utterance of that word, "Conyers," old Barrington turned away and left him.

Over and over again had he found the spell of his father's name and title opening to him society, securing him attentions, and obtaining for him that recognition and acceptance which go so far to make life pleasurable; and now that word, which would have had its magic at a palace, fell powerless and cold at the porch of a humble cottage.

To say that it was part of his creed to believe his father could do no wrong is weak. It was his whole belief,—his entire and complete conviction. To his mind his father embodied all that was noble, high-hearted, and chivalrous. It was not alone the testimony of those who served under him could be appealed to. All India, the Government at home, his own sovereign knew it. From his earliest infancy he had listened to this theme, and to doubt it seemed like to dispute the fact of his existence. How was it, then, that this old man refused to accept what the whole world had stamped with its value? Was it that he impugned the services which had made his father's name famous throughout the entire East?

He endeavored to recall the exact words Barrington had used towards him, but he could not succeed. There was something, he thought, about intruding, unwarrantably intruding; or it might be a mistaken impression of the welcome that awaited him. Which was it? or was it either of them? At all events, he saw himself rejected and repulsed, and the indignity was too great to be borne.

While he thus chafed and fretted, hours went by; and Mr. M'Cabe, the landlord, had made more than one excursion into the room, under pretence of looking after the fire, or seeing that the windows were duly closed, but, in reality, very impatient to learn his guest's intentions regarding dinner.

"Was it your honor said that you'd rather have the chickens roast than biled?" said he at last, in a very submissive tone.

"I said nothing of the kind."

"Ah, it was No. 5 then, and I mistook; I crave your honor's pardon." Hoping that the chord he had thus touched might vibrate, he stooped down to arrange the turf, and give time for the response, but none came. Mr. M'Cabe gave a faint sigh, but returned to the charge. "When there's the laste taste of south in the wind, there 's no making this chimney draw."

Not a word of notice acknowledged this remark.

"But it will do finely yet; it's just the outside of the turf is a little wet, and no wonder; seven weeks of rain—glory be to Him that sent it—has nearly desthroyed us."

Still Conyers vouchsafed no reply.

"And when it begins to rain here, it never laves off. It isn't like in your honor's country. Your honor is English?"

A grunt,—it might be assent, it sounded like malediction.

"'T is azy seen. When your honor came out of the boat, I said, 'Shusy,' says I, 'he's English; and there's a coat they could n't make in Ireland for a king's ransom.'"

"What conveyances leave this for Kilkenny?" asked Conyers, sternly.

"Just none at all, not to mislead you," said M'Cabe, in a voice quite devoid of its late whining intonation.

"Is there not a chaise or a car to be had?"

"Sorrow one. Dr. Dill has a car, to be sure, but not for hire."

"Oh, Dr. Dill lives here. I forgot that. Go and tell him I wish to see him."

The landlord withdrew in dogged silence, but returned in about ten minutes, to say that the doctor had been sent for to the "Fisherman's Home," and Mr. Barrington was so ill it was not likely he would be back that night.

"So ill, did you say?" cried Conyers. "What was the attack,—what did they call it?"

"'T is some kind of a 'plexy, they said. He's a full man, and advanced in years, besides."

"Go and tell young Mr. Dill to come over here."

"He's just gone off with the cuppin' instruments. I saw him steppin' into the boat."

"Let me have a messenger; I want a man to take a note up to Miss Barrington, and fetch my writing-desk here."

In his eager anxiety to learn how Mr. Barrington was, Conyers hastily scratched off a few lines; but on reading them over, he tore them up: they implied a degree of interest on his part which, considering the late treatment extended to him, was scarcely dignified. He tried again; the error was as marked on the other side. It was a cold and formal inquiry. "And yet," said he, as he tore this in fragments, "one thing is quite clear,—this illness is owing to *me!* But for *my* presence there, that old man had now been hale and hearty; the impressions, rightfully or wrongfully, which the sight of *me* and the announcement of *my* name produced are the cause of this malady. I cannot deny it." With this revulsion of feeling he wrote a short but kindly worded note to Miss Barrington, in which, with the very faintest allusion to himself, he begged for a few lines to say how her brother was. He would have added something about the sorrow he experienced in requiting all her kindness by this calamitous return, but he felt that if the case should be a serious one, all reference to himself would be misplaced and impertinent.

The messenger despatched, he sat down beside his fire, the only light now in the room, which the shade of coming night had darkened. He was sad and dispirited, and ill at ease with his own heart. Mr. M'Cabe, indeed, appeared with a suggestion about candles, and a shadowy hint that if his guest speculated of dining at all, it was full time to intimate it; but Conyers dismissed him with a peremptory command not to dare to enter the room again until he was summoned to it. So odious to him was the place, the landlord, and all about him, that he would have set out on foot had his ankle been only strong enough to bear him. "What if he were to write to Stapylton to come and fetch him away? He never liked the man; he liked him less since the remark Miss Barrrington had made upon him from mere reading of his letter, but what was he to do?" While he was yet doubting what course to take, he heard the voices of some new arrivals outside, and, strange enough, one seemed to be Stapylton's. A minute or two after, the travellers had entered the room adjoining his own, and from which a very frail partition of lath and plaster alone separated him.

"Well, Barney," said a harsh, grating voice, addressing the landlord, "what have you got in the larder? We mean to dine with you."

"To dine here, Major!" exclaimed M'Cabe. "Well, well, wondhers will never cease." And then hurriedly seeking to cover a speech not very flattering to the Major's habits of hospitality, "Sure, I 've a loin of pork, and there 's two chickens and a trout fresh out of the water, and there's a cheese; it isn't mine, to be sure, but Father Cody's, but he 'll not miss a slice out of it; and barrin' you dined at the 'Fisherman's Home,' you 'd not get betther."

"That 's where we were to have dined by right," said the Major, crankily,—"myself and my friend here,—but we're disappointed, and so we stepped in here, to do the best we can."

"Well, by all accounts, there won't be many dinners up there for some time."

"Why so?"

"Ould Barrington was took with a fit this afternoon, and they say he won't get over it."

"How was it?—what brought it on?"

"Here's the way I had it. Ould Peter was just come home from Kilkenny, and had brought the Attorney-General with him to stay a few days at the cottage, and what was the first thing he seen but a man that come all the way from India with a writ out against him for some of mad George Barrington's debts; and he was so overcome by the shock, that he fainted away, and never came rightly to himself since."

"This is simply impossible," said a voice Conyers well knew to be Stapylton's.

"Be that as it may, I had it from the man that came for the doctor, and what's more, he was just outside the window, and could hear ould Barrington cursin' and swearin' about the man that ruined his son, and brought his poor boy to the grave; but I'll go and look after your honor's dinner, for I know more about that."

"I have a strange half-curiosity to know the correct version of this story," said Stapylton, as the host left the room. "The doctor is a friend of yours, I think. Would he step over here, and let us hear the matter accurately?"

"He's up at the cottage now, but I'll get him to come in here when he returns."

If Conyers was shocked to hear how even this loose version of what had occurred served to heighten the anxiety his own fears created, he was also angry with himself at having learned the matter as he did. It was not in his nature to play the eavesdropper, and he had, in reality, heard what fell between his neighbors, almost ere he was aware of it. To apprise them, therefore, of the vicinity of a stranger, he coughed and sneezed, poked the fire noisily, and moved the chairs about; but though the disturbance served to prevent him from hearing, it did not tend to impress any greater caution upon them, for they talked away as before, and more than once above the din of his own tumult, he heard the name of Barrington, and even his own, uttered.

Unable any longer to suffer the irritation of a position so painful, he took his hat, and left the house. It was now night, and so dark that he had to stand some minutes on the door-sill ere he could accustom his sight to the obscurity. By degrees, however, he was enabled to guide his steps, and, passing through the little square, he gained the bridge; and here he resolved to walk backwards and forwards till such time as he hoped his neighbors might have concluded their convivialities, and turned homeward.

A thin cold rain was falling, and the night was cheerless, and without a star; but his heart was heavy, and the dreariness without best suited that within him. For more than an hour he continued his lonely walk, tormented by all the miseries his active ingenuity could muster. To have brought sorrow and mourning beneath the roof where you have been sheltered with kindness is sad enough, but far sadder is it to connect the calamity you have caused with one dearer to you than yourself, and whose innocence, while assured of, you cannot vindicate. "My father never wronged this man, for the simple reason that he has never been unjust to any one. It is a gross injustice to accuse him! If Colonel Barrington forfeited my father's friendship, who could doubt where the fault lay? But I will not leave the matter questionable. I will write to my father and ask him to send me such a reply as may set the issue at rest forever; and then I will come down here, and, with my father's letter in my hand, say, 'The mention of my name was enough, once on a time, to make you turn away from me on the very threshold of your own door—'" When he had got thus far in his intended appeal, his ear was suddenly struck by the word "Conyers," uttered by one of two men who had passed him the moment before, and now stood still in one of the projections of the bridge to talk. He as hastily recognized Dr. Dill as the speaker. He went on thus: "Of course it was mere raving, but one must bear in mind that memory very often is the prompter of these wanderings; and it was strange how persistently he held to the one theme, and continued to call out, 'It was not fair, sir! It was not manly! You know it yourself, Conyers; you cannot deny it!'"

"But you attach no importance to such wanderings, doctor?" asked one whose deep-toned voice betrayed him to be Stapylton.

"I do; that is, to the extent I have mentioned. They are incoherencies, but they are not without some foundation. This Conyers may have had his share in that famous accusation against Colonel Barrington,—that well-known charge I told you of; and if so, it is easy to connect the name with these ravings."

"And the old man will die of this attack," said Stapylton, half musingly.

"I hope not. He has great vigor of constitution; and old as he is, I think he will rub through it."

"Young Conyers left for Kilkenny, then, immediately?" asked he.

"No; he came down here, to the village. He is now at the inn."

"At the inn, here? I never knew that. I am sorry I was not aware of it, doctor; but since it is so, I will ask of you not to speak of having seen me here. He would naturally take it ill, as his brother officer, that I did not make him out, while, as you see, I was totally ignorant of his vicinity."

"I will say nothing on the subject, Captain," said the doctor. "And now one word of advice from you on a personal matter. This young gentleman has offered to be of service to my son—"

Conyers, hitherto spellbound while the interest attached to his father, now turned hastily from the spot and walked away, his mind not alone charged with a heavy care, but full of an eager anxiety as to wherefore Stapylton should have felt so deeply interested in Barrington's illness, and the causes that led to it,—Stapylton, the most selfish of men, and the very last in the world to busy himself in the sorrows or misfortunes of a stranger. Again, too, why had he desired the doctor to preserve his presence there as a secret? Conyers was exactly in the frame of mind to exaggerate a suspicion, or make a mere doubt a grave question. While be thus mused, Stapylton and the doctor passed him on their way towards the village, deep in converse, and, to all seeming, in closest confidence.

"Shall I follow him to the inn, and declare that I overheard a few words on the bridge which give me a claim to explanation? Shall I say, 'Captain Stapylton, you spoke of my father, just now, sufficiently aloud to be overheard by me as I passed, and in your tone there was that which entitles me to question you? Then if he should say, 'Go on; what is it you ask for?' shall I not be sorely puzzled to continue? Perhaps, too, he might remind me that the mode in which I obtained my information precludes even a reference to it. He is one of those fellows not to throw away such an advantage, and I must prepare myself for a quarrel. Oh, if I only had Hunter by me! What would I not give for the brave Colonel's counsel at such a moment as this?"

Of this sort were his thoughts as he strolled up and down for hours, wearing away the long "night watches," till a faint grayish tinge above the horizon showed that morning was not very distant. The whole landscape was wrapped in that cold mysterious tint in which tower and hill-top and spire are scarcely distinguishable from each other, while out of the low-lying meadows already arose the bluish vapor that proclaims the coming day. The village itself, overshadowed by the mountain behind it, lay a black, unbroken mass.

Not a light twinkled from a window, save close to the river's bank, where a faint gleam stole forth and flickered on the water.

Who has not felt the strange interest that attaches to a solitary light seen thus in the tranquil depth of a silent night? How readily do we associate it with some incident of sorrow! The watcher beside the sick-bed rises to the mind, or the patient sufferer himself trying to cheat the dull hours by a book, or perhaps some poor son of toil arising to his daily round of labor, and seated at that solitary meal which no kind word enlivens, no companionship beguiles. And as I write, in what corner of earth are not such scenes passing, — such dark shadows moving over the battlefield of life?

In such a feeling did Conyers watch this light as, leaving the high-road, he took a path that led along the river towards it. As he drew nigher, he saw that the light came from the open window of a room which gave upon a little garden, — a mere strip of ground fenced off from the path by a low paling. With a curiosity he could not master, he stopped and looked in. At a large table, covered with books and papers, and on which a skull also stood, a young man was seated, his head leaning on his hand, apparently in deep thought, while a girl was slowly pacing the little chamber as she talked to him.

"It does not require," said she, in a firm voice, "any great effort of memory to bear in mind that a nerve, an artery, and a vein always go in company."

"Not for you, perhaps, — not for you, Polly."

"Not for any one, I 'm sure. Your fine dragoon friend with the sprained ankle might be brought to that amount of instruction by one telling of it."

"Oh, he 's no fool, I promise you, Polly. Don't despise him because he has plenty of money and can lead a life of idleness."

"I neither despise nor esteem him, nor do I mean that he should divert our minds from what we are at. Now for the popliteal space. Can you describe it? Do you know where it is, or anything about it?"

"I do," said he, doggedly, as he pushed his long hair back from his eyes, and tried to think,—"I do, but I must have time. You must n't hurry me."

She made no reply, but continued her walk in silence.

"I know all about it, Polly, but I can't describe it. I can't describe anything; but ask me a question about it."

"Where is it,—where does it lie?"

"Isn't it at the lower third of the humerus, where the flexors divide?"

"You are too bad,—too stupid!" cried she, angrily. "I cannot believe that anything short of a purpose, a determination to be ignorant, could make a person so unteach-able. If we have gone over this once, we have done so fifty times. It haunts me in my sleep, from very iteration."

"I wish it would haunt me a little when I 'm awake," said he, sulkily.

"And when may that be, I'd like to know? Do you fancy, sir, that your present state of intelligence is a very vigilant one?"

"I know one thing. I hope there won't be the like of you on the Court of Examiners, for I would n't bear the half of what *you've* said to me from another."

TOM DILL AT HIS STUDIES

"Rejection will be harder to bear, Tom. To be sent back as ignorant and incapable will be far heavier as a punishment than any words of mine. What are you laughing at, sir? Is it a matter of mirth to you?"

"Look at the skull, Polly,—look at the skull." And he pointed to where he had stuck his short, black pipe, between the grinning teeth of the skeleton.

She snatched it angrily away, and threw it out of the window, saying, "You may be ignorant, and not be able to help it. I will take care you shall not be irreverent, sir."

"There's my short clay gone, anyhow," said Tom, submissively, "and I think I 'll go to bed." And he yawned drearily as he spoke.

"Not till you have done this, if we sit here till breakfast-time," said she, resolutely. "There's the plate, and there's the reference. Read it till you know it!"

"What a slave-driver you 'd make, Polly!" said he, with a half-bitter smile.

"What a slave I am!" said she, turning away her head.

"That's true," cried he, in a voice thick with emotion; "and when I 'm thousands of miles away, I 'll be longing to hear the bitterest words you ever said to me, rather than never see you any more."

"My poor brother," said she, laying her hand softly on his rough head, "I never doubted your heart, and I ought to be better tempered with you, and I will. Come, now, Tom,"—and she seated herself at the table next him,—"see, now, if I cannot make this easy to you." And then the two heads were bent together over the table, and the soft brown hair of the girl half mingled with the rough wool of the graceless numskull beside her.

"I will stand by him, if it were only for her sake," said Conyers to himself. And he stole slowly away, and gained the inn.

So intent upon his purpose was he that he at once set about its fulfilment. He began a long letter to his father, and, touching slightly on the accident by which he made Dr. Dill's acquaintance, professed to be deeply his debtor for kindness and attention. With this prelude he introduced Tom. Hitherto his pen had glided along flippantly enough. In that easy mixture of fact and fancy by which he opened his case, no grave difficulty presented itself; but Tom was now to be presented, and the task was about as puzzling as it would have been to have conducted him bodily into society.

"I was ungenerous enough to be prejudiced against this poor fellow when I first met him," wrote he. "Neither his figure nor his manners are in his favor, and in his very diffidence there is an apparent rudeness and forwardness which are not really in his nature. These, however, are not mistakes you, my dear father, will fall into. With your own quickness you will see what sterling qualities exist beneath this rugged outside, and you will befriend him at first for my sake. Later on, I trust he will open his own account in your heart. Bear in mind, too, that it was all my scheme,—the whole plan mine. It was I persuaded him to try his luck in India; it was through me he made the venture; and if the poor fellow fail, all the fault will fall back upon *me*." From this he went into little details of Tom's circumstances, and the narrow means by which he was surrounded, adding how humble he was, and how ready to be satisfied with the most moderate livelihood. "In that great wide world of the East, what scores of things there must be for such a fellow to do; and even should he not turn out to be a Sydenham or a Harvey, he might administer justice, or collect revenue, or assist in some other way the process of that system which we call the British rule in India. In a word, get him something he may live by, and be able, in due time, to help those he has left behind here, in a land whose 'Paddy-fields' are to the full as pauperized as those of Bengal."

He had intended, having disposed of Tom Dill's case, to have addressed some lines to his father about the Barring-tons, sufficiently vague to be easily answered if the subject were one distasteful or unpleasing to him; but just as he reached the place to open this, he was startled by the arrival of a jaunting-car at the inn-door, whose driver stopped to take a drink. It was a chance conveyance, returning to Kilkenny, and Conyers at once engaged it; and, leaving an order to send on the reply when it arrived from the cottage, he wrote a hasty note to Tom Dill and departed. This note was simply to say that he had already fulfilled his promise of interesting his father in his behalf, and that whenever Tom had passed his examination, and was in readiness for his voyage, he should come or write to him, and he would find him fully disposed to serve and befriend him. "Meanwhile," wrote he, "let me hear of you. I am really anxious to learn how you acquit yourself at the ordeal, for which you have the cordial good wishes of your friend, F. Conyers."

Oh, if the great men of our acquaintance—and we all of us, no matter how hermit-like we may live, have our "great men"—could only know and feel what ineffable pleasure will sometimes be derived from the chance expressions they employ towards us,—words which, little significant in themselves, perhaps have some touch of good fellowship or good feeling, now reviving a "bygone," now far-seeing a future, tenderly thrilling through us by some little allusion to a trick of our temperament, noted and observed by one in whose interest we never till then knew we had a share,—if, I say, they were but aware of this, how delightful they might make themselves!—what charming friends!—and, it is but fair to own, what dangerous patrons!

I leave my reader to apply the reflection to the case before him, and then follow me to the pleasant quarters of a well-maintained country-house, full of guests and abounding in gayety.

CHAPTER XVIII.

COBHAM

My reader is already aware that I am telling of some forty years ago, and therefore I have no apologies to make for habits and ways which our more polished age has pronounced barbarous. Now, at Cobham, the men sat after dinner over their wine when the ladies had withdrawn, and, I grieve to say, fulfilled this usage with a zest and enjoyment that unequivocally declared it to be the best hour of the whole twenty-four.

Friends could now get together, conversation could range over personalities, egotisms have their day, and bygones be disinterred without need of an explanation. Few, indeed, who did not unbend at such a moment, and relax in that genial atmosphere begotten of closed curtains, and comfort, and good claret. I am not so certain that we are wise in our utter abandonment of what must have often conciliated a difference or reconciled a grudge. How many a lurking discontent, too subtle for intervention, must have been dissipated in the general burst of a common laugh, or the racy enjoyment of a good story! Decidedly the decanter has often played peacemaker, though popular prejudice inclines to give it a different mission.

On the occasion to which I would now invite my reader, the party were seated—by means of that genial discovery, a horseshoe-table—around the fire at Cobham. It was a true country-house society of neighbors who knew each other well, sprinkled with guests,—strangers to every one. There were all ages and all temperaments, from the hardy old squire, whose mellow cheer was known at the fox-cover, to the young heir fresh from Oxford and loud about Leicestershire; gentlemen-farmers and sportsmen, and parsons and soldiers, blended together with just enough disparity of pursuit to season talk and freshen experiences.

The conversation, which for a while was partly on sporting matters, varied with little episodes of personal achievement, and those little boastings which end in a bet, was suddenly interrupted by a hasty call for Dr. Dill, who was wanted at the "Fisherman's Home."

"Can't you stay to finish this bottle, Dill?" said the Admiral, who had not heard for whom he had been sent.

"I fear not, sir. It is a long row down to the cottage."

"So it 's poor Barrington again! I 'm sincerely sorry for it! And now I 'll not ask you to delay. By the way, take my boat. Elwes," said he to the servant, "tell the men to get the boat ready at once for Dr. Dill, and come and say when it is so."

The doctor's gratitude was profuse, though probably a dim vista of the "tip" that might be expected from him detracted from the fulness of the enjoyment.

"Find out if I could be of any use, Dill," whispered the Admiral, as the doctor arose. "Your own tact will show if there be anything I could do. You understand me; I have the deepest regard for old Barrington, and his sister too."

Dill promised to give his most delicate attention to the point, and departed.

While this little incident was occurring, Stapylton, who sat at an angle of the fireplace, was amusing two or three listeners by an account of his intended dinner at the "Home," and the haughty refusal of Miss Barrington to receive him.

"You must tell Sir Charles the story!" cried out Mr. Bushe. "He'll soon recognize the old Major from your imitation of him."

"Hang the old villain! he shot a dog-fox the other morning, and he knows well how scarce they are getting in the country," said another.

"I 'll never forgive myself for letting him have a lease of that place," said a third; "he's a disgrace to the neighborhood."

"You're not talking of Barrington, surely," called out Sir Charles.

"Of course not. I was speaking of M'Cormick. Harrington is another stamp of man, and here's his good health!"

"He'll need all your best wishes, Jack," said the host, "for Dr. Dill has just been called away to see him."

"To see old Peter! Why, I never knew him to have a day's illness!"

"He's dangerously ill now," said the Admiral, gravely. "Dill tells me that he came home from the Assizes hale and hearty, in high spirits at some verdict in his favor, and brought back the Attorney-General to spend a day or two with him; but that, on arriving, he found a young fellow whose father or grandfather—for I have n't it correctly—had been concerned in some way against George Barrington, and that high words passed between old Peter and this youth, who was turned out on the spot, while poor Barrington, overcome by emotion, was struck down with a sort of paralysis. As I have said, I don't know the story accurately, for even Dill himself only picked it up from the servants at the cottage, neither Miss Barrington nor Withering having told him one word on the subject."

"That is the very same story I heard at the village where we dined," broke in Stapylton, "and M'Cormick added that he remembered the name. Conyers—the young man is called Conyers—did occur in a certain famous accusation against Colonel Barrington."

"Well, but," interposed Bushe, "isn't all that an old story now? Is n't the whole thing a matter of twenty years ago?"

"Not so much as that," said Sir Charles. "I remember reading it all when I was in command of the 'Madagascar,'—I forget the exact year, but I was at Corfu."

"At all events," said Bushe, "it's long enough past to be forgotten or forgiven; and old Peter was the very last man I could ever have supposed likely to carry on an ancient grudge against any one."

"Not where his son was concerned. Wherever George's name entered, forgiveness of the man that wronged him was impossible," said another.

"You are scarcely just to my old friend," interposed the Admiral. "First of all, we have not the facts before us. Many of us here have never seen, some have never heard of the great Barrington Inquiry, and of such as have, if their memories be not better than mine, they can't discuss the matter with much profit."

"I followed the case when it occurred," chimed in the former speaker, "but I own, with Sir Charles, that it has gone clean out of my head since that time."

"You talk of injustice, Cobham, injustice to old Peter Barrington," said an old man from the end of the table; "but I would ask, are we quite just to poor George? I knew him well. My son served in the same regiment with him before he went out to India, and no finer nor nobler-hearted fellow than George Barrington ever lived. Talk of him ruining his father by his extravagance! Why, he'd have cut off his right hand rather than caused him one pang, one moment of displeasure. Barrington ruined himself; that insane passion for law has cost him far more than half what he was worth in the world. Ask Withering; he'll tell you something about it. Why, Withering's own fees in that case before 'the Lords' amount to upwards of two thousand guineas."

"I won't dispute the question with you, Fowndes," said the Admiral. "Scandal says you have a taste for a trial at bar yourself."

The hit told, and called for a hearty laugh, in which Fowndes himself joined freely.

"*I*'m a burned child, however, and keep away from the fire," said he, good-humoredly; "but old Peter seems rather to like being singed. There he is again with his Privy Council case for next term, and with, I suppose, as much chance of success as I should have in a suit to recover a Greek estate of some of my Phoenician ancestors."

It was not a company to sympathize deeply with such a litigious spirit. The hearty and vigorous tone of squiredom, young and old, could not understand it as a passion or a pursuit, and they mainly agreed that nothing but some strange perversion could have made the generous nature of old Barrington so fond of law. Gradually the younger members of the party slipped away to the drawing-room, till, in the changes that ensued, Stapylton found himself next to Mr. Fowndes.

"I'm glad to see, Captain," said the old squire, "that modern fashion of deserting the claret-jug has not invaded your mess. I own I like a man who lingers over his wine."

"We have no pretext for leaving it, remember that," said Stapylton, smiling.

"Very true. The *placeus uxor* is sadly out of place in a soldier's life. Your married officer is but a sorry comrade; besides, how is a fellow to be a hero to the enemy who is daily bullied by his wife?"

"I think you said that you had served?" interposed Stapylton.

"No. My son was in the army; he is so still, but holds a Governorship in the West Indies. He it was who knew this Barrington we were speaking of."

"Just so," said Stapylton, drawing his chair closer, so as to converse more confidentially.

"You may imagine what very uneventful lives we country gentlemen live," said the old squire, "when we can continue to talk over one memorable case for something like twenty years, just because one of the parties to it was our neighbor."

"You appear to have taken a lively interest in it," said Stapylton, who rightly conjectured it was a favorite theme with the old squire.

"Yes. Barrington and my son were friends; they came down to my house together to shoot; and with all his eccentricities—and they were many—I liked Mad George, as they called him."

"He was a good fellow, then?"

"A thoroughly good fellow, but the shyest that ever lived; to all outward seeming rough and careless, but sensitive as a woman all the while. He would have walked up to a cannon's mouth with a calm step, but an affecting story would bring tears to his eyes; and then, to cover this weakness, which he was well ashamed of, he 'd rush into fifty follies and extravagances. As he said himself to me one day, alluding to some feat of rash absurdity, 'I have been taking another inch off the dog's tail,'—he referred to the story of Alcibiades, who docked his dog to take off public attention from his heavier transgressions."

"There was no truth in these accusations against him?"

"Who knows? George was a passionate fellow, and he 'd have made short work of the man that angered him. I myself never so entirely acquitted him as many who loved him less. At all events, he was hardly treated; he was regularly hunted down. I imagine he must have made many enemies, for witnesses sprung up against him on all sides, and he was too proud a fellow to ask for one single testimony in his favor! If ever a man met death broken-hearted, he did!"

A pause of several minutes occurred, after which the old squire resumed,—

"My son told me that after Barrington's death there was a strong revulsion in his favor, and a great feeling that he had been hardly dealt by. Some of the Supreme Council, it is said, too, were disposed to behave generously towards his child, but old Peter, in an evil hour, would hear of nothing short of restitution of all the territory, and a regular rehabilitation of George's memory, besides; in fact, he made the most extravagant demands, and disgusted the two or three who were kindly and well disposed towards his cause. Had they, indeed,—as he said,—driven his son to desperation, he could scarcely ask them to declare it to the world; and yet nothing short of this would satisfy him! 'Come forth,' wrote he,—I read the letter myself,—'come forth and confess that your evidence was forged and your witnesses suborned; that you wanted to annex the territory, and the only road to your object was to impute treason to the most loyal heart that ever served the King!' Imagine what chance of favorable consideration remained to the man who penned such words as these."

"And he prosecutes the case still?"

"Ay, and will do to the day of his death. Withering—who was an old schoolfellow of mine—has got me to try what I could do to persuade him to come to some terms; and, indeed, to do old Peter justice, it is not the money part of the matter he is so obstinate about; it is the question of what he calls George's fair fame and honor; and one cannot exactly say to him, 'Who on earth cares a brass button whether George Barrington was a rebel or a true man? Whether he deserved to die an independent Rajah of some place with a hard name, or the loyal subject of his Majesty George the Third?' I own I, one day, did go so close to the wind, on that subject, that the old man started up and said, 'I hope I misapprehend you, Harry Fowndes. I hope sincerely that I do so, for if not, I'll have a shot at you, as sure as my name is Peter Barrington.' Of course I 'tried back' at once, and assured him it was a pure misconception of my meaning, and that until the East India folk fairly acknowledged that they had wronged his son, *he* could not, with honor, approach the question of a compromise in the money matter."

"That day, it may be presumed, is very far off," said Stapylton, half languidly.

"Well, Withering opines not. He says that they are weary of the whole case. They have had, perhaps, some misgivings as to the entire justice of what they did. Perhaps they have learned something during the course of the proceedings which may have influenced their judgment; and not impossible is it that they pity the old man fighting out his life; and perhaps, too, Barrington himself may have softened a little, since he has begun to feel that his granddaughter—for George left a child—had interests which his own indignation could not rightfully sacrifice; so that amongst all these perhapses, who knows but some happy issue may come at last?"

"That Barrington race is not a very pliant one," said Stapylton, half dreamily; and then, in some haste, added, "at least, such is the character they give them here."

"Some truth there may be in that. Men of a strong temperament and with a large share of self-dependence generally get credit from the world for obstinacy, just because the road *they* see out of difficulties is not the popular one. But even with all this, I'd not call old Peter self-willed; at least, Withering tells me that from time to time, as he has conveyed to him the opinions and experiences of old Indian officers, some of whom had either met with or heard of George, he has listened with much and even respectful attention. And as all their counsels have gone against his own convictions, it is something to give them a patient hearing."

"He has thus permitted strangers to come and speak with him on these topics?" asked Stapylton, eagerly.

"No, no,—not he. These men had called on Withering,—met him, perhaps, in society,—heard of his interest in George Barrington's case, and came good-naturedly to volunteer a word of counsel in favor of an old comrade. Nothing more natural, I think."

"Nothing. I quite agree with you; so much so, indeed, that having served some years in India, and in close proximity, too, to one of the native courts, I was going to ask you to present me to your friend Mr. Withering, as one not altogether incapable of affording him some information."

"With a heart and a half. I 'll do it."

"I say, Harry," cried out the host, "if you and Captain Stapylton will neither fill your glasses nor pass the wine, I think we had better join the ladies."

And now there was a general move to the drawing-room, where several evening guests had already assembled, making a somewhat numerous company. Polly Dill was there, too,—not the wearied-looking, careworn figure we last saw her, when her talk was of "dead anatomies," but the lively, sparkling, bright-eyed Polly, who sang the Melodies to the accompaniment of him who could make every note thrill with the sentiment his own genius had linked to it. I half wish I had not a story to tell,—that is, that I had not a certain road to take,—that I might wander at will through by-path and lane, and linger on the memories thus by a chance awakened! Ah, it was no small triumph to lift out of obscure companionship and vulgar associations the music of our land, and wed it to words immortal, to show us that the pebble at our feet was a gem to be worn on the neck of beauty, and to prove to us, besides, that our language could be as lyrical as Anacreon's own!

"I am enchanted with your singing," whispered Stapylton, in Polly's ear; "but I 'd forego all the enjoyment not to see you so pleased with your companion. I begin to detest the little Poet."

"I 'll tell him so," said she, half gravely; "and he 'll know well that it is the coarse hate of the Saxon."

"I'm no Saxon!" said he, flushing and darkening at the same time. And then, recovering his calm, he added, "There are no Saxons left amongst us, nor any Celts for us to honor with our contempt; but come away from the piano, and don't let him fancy he has bound you by a spell."

"But he has," said she, eagerly,—"he has, and I don't care to break it."

But the little Poet, running his fingers lightly over the keys, warbled out, in a half-plaintive whisper,—

"Oh, tell me, dear Polly, why is it thine eyes
Through their brightness have something of sorrow?
I cannot suppose that the glow of such skies
Should ever mean gloom for the morrow;

"Or must I believe that your heart is afar,
And you only make semblance to hear me,
While your thoughts are away to that splendid hussar,
And 't is only your image is near me?"

"An unpublished melody, I fancy," said Stapylton, with a malicious twinkle of his eye.

"Not even corrected as yet," said the Poet, with a glance at Polly.

What a triumph it was for a mere village beauty to be thus tilted for by such gallant knights; but Polly was practical as well as vain, and a certain unmistakable something in Lady Cobham's eye told her that two of the most valued guests of the house were not to be thus withdrawn from circulation; and with this wise impression on her mind, she slipped hastily away, on the pretext of something to say to her father. And although it was a mere pretence on her part, there was that in her look as they talked together that betokened their conversation to be serious.

"I tell you again," said he, in a sharp but low whisper, "she will not suffer it. You used not to make mistakes of this kind formerly, and I cannot conceive why you should do so now."

"But, dear papa," said she, with a strange half-smile, "don't you remember your own story of the gentleman who got tipsy because he foresaw he would never be invited again?"

But the doctor was in no jesting mood, and would not accept of the illustration. He spoke now even more angrily than before.

"You have only to see how much they make of him to know well that he is out of our reach," said he, bitterly.

"A long shot, Sir Lucius; there is such honor in a long shot," said she, with infinite drollery; and then with a sudden gravity, added, "I have never forgotten the man you cured, just because your hand shook and you gave him a double dose of laudanum."

This was too much for his patience, and he turned away in disgust at her frivolity. In doing so, however, he came in front of Lady Cobham, who had come up to request Miss Dill to play a certain Spanish dance for two young ladies of the company.

"Of course, your Ladyship, — too much honor for her, — she will be charmed; my little girl is overjoyed when she can contribute even thus humbly to the pleasure of your delightful house."

Never did a misdemeanist take his "six weeks" with a more complete consciousness of penalty than did Polly sit down to that piano. She well understood it as a sentence, and, let me own, submitted well and gracefully to her fate. Nor was it, after all, such a slight trial, for the fandango was her own speciality; she had herself brought the dance and the music to Cobham. They who were about to dance it were her own pupils, and not very proficient ones, either. And with all this she did her part well and loyally. Never had she played with more spirit; never marked the time with a firmer precision; never threw more tenderness into the graceful parts, nor more of triumphant daring into the proud ones. Amid the shower of "Bravos!" that closed the performance, — for none thought of the dancers, — the little Poet drew nigh and whispered, "How naughty!"

"Why so?" asked she, innocently.

"What a blaze of light to throw over a sorry picture!" said he, dangling his eyeglass, and playing that part of middle-aged Cupid he was so fond of assuming.

"Do you know, sir," said Lady Cobham, coming hastily towards him, "that I will not permit you to turn the heads of my young ladies? Dr. Dill is already so afraid of your fascinations that he has ordered his carriage,—is it not so?" she went on appealing to the doctor, with increased rapidity. "But you will certainly keep your promise to us. We shall expect you on Thursday at dinner."

Overwhelmed with confusion, Dill answered—he knew not what—about pleasure, punctuality, and so forth; and then turned away to ring for that carriage he had not ordered before.

"And so you tell me Barrington is better?" said the Admiral, taking him by the arm and leading him away. "The danger is over, then?"

"I believe so; his mind is calm, and he is only suffering now from debility. What with the Assizes, and a week's dissipation at Kilkenny, and this shock,—for it was a shock,—the whole thing was far more of a mental than a bodily ailment."

"You gave him my message? You said how anxious I felt to know if I could be of any use to him?"

"Yes; and he charged Mr. Withering to come and thank you, for he is passing by Cobham to-morrow on his way to Kilkenny."

"Indeed! Georgiana, don't forget that. Withering will call here to-morrow; try and keep him to dine, at least, if we cannot secure him for longer. He's one of those fellows I am always delighted to meet Where are you going, Dill? Not taking your daughter away at this hour, are you?"

The doctor sighed, and muttered something about dissipations that were only too fascinating, too engrossing. He did not exactly like to say that his passports had been sent him, and the authorities duly instructed to give him "every aid and assistance possible." For a moment, indeed, Polly looked as though she would make some explanation of the matter; but it was only for a moment, and the slight flush on her cheek gave way quickly, and she looked somewhat paler than her wont. Meanwhile, the little Poet had fetched her shawl, and led her away, humming, "Buona notte,—buona sera!" as he went, in that half-caressing, half-quizzing way he could assume so jauntily. Stapylton walked behind with the doctor, and whispered as he went, "If not inconvenient, might I ask the favor of a few minutes with you to-morrow?"

Dill assured him he was devotedly his servant; and having fixed the interview for two o'clock, away they drove. The night was calm and starlight, and they had long passed beyond the grounds of Cobham, and were full two miles on their road before a word was uttered by either.

"What was it her Ladyship said about Thursday next, at dinner?" asked the doctor, half pettishly.

"Nothing to me, papa."

"If I remember, it was that we had accepted the invitation already, and begging me not to forget it."

"Perhaps so," said she, dryly.

"You are usually more mindful about these matters," said he, tartly, "and not so likely to forget promised festivities."

"They certainly were not promised to me," said she, "nor, if they had been, should I accept of them."

"What do you mean?" said he, angrily.

"Simply, papa, that it is a house I will not re-enter, that's all."

"Why, your head is turned, your brains are destroyed by flattery, girl. You seem totally to forget that we go to these places merely by courtesy,—we are received only on sufferance; we are not *their* equals."

"The more reason to treat us with deference, and not render our position more painful than it need be."

"Folly and nonsense! Deference, indeed! How much deference is due from eight thousand a year to a dispensary doctor, or his daughter? I 'll have none of these absurd notions. If they made any mistake towards you, it was by over-attention,—too much notice."

"That is very possible, papa; and it was not always very flattering for that reason."

"Why, what is your head full of? Do you fancy you are one of Lord Carricklough's daughters, eh?"

"No, papa; for they are shockingly freckled, and very plain."

"Do you know your real station?" cried he, more angrily, "and that if, by the courtesy of society, my position secures acceptance anywhere, it entails nothing—positively nothing—to those belonging to me?"

"Such being the case, is it not wise of us not to want anything,—not to look for it,—not to pine after it? You shall see, papa, whether I fret over my exclusion from Cobham."

The doctor was not in a mood to approve of such philosophy, and he drove on, only showing—by an extra cut of his whip—the tone and temper that beset him.

"You are to have a visit from Captain Stapylton tomorrow, papa?" said she, in the manner of a half question.

"Who told you so?" said he, with a touch of eagerness in his voice; for suddenly it occurred to him if Polly knew of this appointment, she herself might be interested in its object.

"He asked me what was the most likely time to find you at home, and also if he might venture to hope he should be presented to mamma."

That was, as the doctor thought, a very significant speech; it might mean a great deal,—a very great deal, indeed; and so he turned it over and over in his mind for some time before he spoke again. At last he said,—

"I haven't a notion what he's coming about, Polly,—have you?"

"No, sir; except, perhaps, it be to consult you. He told me he had sprained his arm, or his shoulder, the other day, when his horse swerved."

"Oh no, it can't be that, Polly; it can't be that."

"Why not the pleasure of a morning call, then? He is an idle man, and finds time heavy on his hands."

A short "humph" showed that this explanation was not more successful than the former, and the doctor, rather irritated with this game of fence, for so he deemed it, said bluntly,—

"Has he been showing you any marked attentions of late? Have you noticed anything peculiar in his manner towards you?"

"Nothing whatever, sir," said she, with a frank boldness. "He has chatted and flirted with me, just as every one else presumes he has a right to do with a girl in a station below their own; but he has never been more impertinent in this way than any other young man of fashion."

"But there have been"—he was sorely puzzled for the word he wanted, and it was only as a resource, not out of choice, he said—"attentions?"

"Of course, papa, what many would call in the cognate phrase, marked attentions; but girls who go into the world as I do no more mistake what these mean than would you yourself, papa, if passingly asked what was good for a sore-throat fancy that the inquirer intended to fee you."

"I see, Polly, I see," muttered he, as the illustration came home to him. Still, after ruminating for some time, a change seemed to come over his thoughts, for he said,—

"But you might be wrong this time, Polly: it is by no means impossible that you might be wrong."

"My dear papa," said she, gravely, "when a man of his rank is disposed to think seriously of a girl in mine, he does not begin by flattery; he rather takes the line of correction and warning, telling her fifty little platitudes about trifles in manner, and so forth, by her docile acceptance of which he conceives a high notion of *himself*, and a half liking for *her*. But I have no need to go into these things; enough if I assure you Captain Stapylton's visit has no concern for me; he either comes out of pure idleness, or he wants to make use of *you*."

The last words opened a new channel to Dill's thoughts, and he drove on in silent meditation over them.

CHAPTER XIX.

THE HOUR OF LUNCHEON

If there be a special agreeability about all the meal-times of a pleasant country-house, there is not one of them which, in the charm of an easy, unconstrained gayety, can rival the hour of luncheon. At breakfast, one is too fresh; at dinner, too formal; but luncheon, like an opening manhood, is full of its own bright projects. The plans of the day have already reached a certain maturity, and fixtures have been made for riding-parties, or phaeton drives, or flirtations in the garden. The very strangers who looked coldly at each other over their morning papers have shaken into a semi-intimacy, and little traits of character and temperament, which would have been studiously shrouded in the more solemn festivals of the day, are now displayed with a frank and fearless confidence. The half-toilette and the tweed coat, mutton broth and "Balmorals," seem infinitely more congenial to acquaintanceship than the full-blown splendor of evening dress and the grander discipline of dinner.

Irish social life permits of a practice of which I do not, while recording, constitute myself the advocate or the apologist,—a sort of good-tempered banter called quizzing,—a habit I scarcely believe practicable in other lands; that is, I know of no country where it could be carried on as harmlessly and as gracefully, where as much wit could be expended innocuously, as little good feeling jeopardized in the display. The happiest hour of the day for such passages as these was that of luncheon, and it was in the very clash and clatter of the combat that a servant announced the Attorney-General!

What a damper did the name prove! Short of a bishop himself, no announcement could have spread more terror over the younger members of the company, embodying as it seemed to do all that could be inquisitorial, intolerant, and overbearing. Great, however, was the astonishment to see, instead of the stern incarnation of Crown prosecutions and arbitrary commitments, a tall, thin, slightly stooped man, dressed in a gray shooting-jacket, and with a hat plentifully garnished with fishing-flies. He came lightly into the room, and kissed the hand of his hostess with a mixture of cordiality and old-fashioned gallantry that became him well.

"My old luck, Cobham!" said he, as he seated himself at table. "I have fished the stream all the way from the Red House to this, and never so much as a rise to reward me.

"They knew you,—they knew you, Withering," chirped out the Poet, "and they took good care not to put in an appearance, with the certainty of a 'detainer.'"

"Ah! you here! That decanter of sherry screened you completely from my view," said Withering, whose sarcasm on his size touched the very sorest of the other's susceptibilities. "And talking of recognizances, how comes it you are here, and a large party at Lord Dunraney's all assembled to meet you?"

The Poet, as not infrequent with him, had forgotten everything of this prior engagement, and was now overwhelmed with his forgetfulness. The ladies, however, pressed eagerly around him with consolation so like caresses, that he was speedily himself again.

"How natural a mistake, after all!" said the lawyer. "The old song says,—

'Tell me where beauty and wit and wine
Are met, and I 'll say where I 'm asked to dine.'

Ah! Tommy, yours *is* the profession, after all; always sure of your retainer, and never but one brief to sustain—'T. M. *versus* the Heart of Woman.'"

"One is occasionally nonsuited, however," said the other, half pettishly. "By the way, how was it you got that verdict for old Barrington t'other day? Was it true that Plowden got hold of *your* bag by mistake?"

"Not only that, but he made a point for us none of us had discovered."

"How historical the blunder:—

'The case is classical, as I and you know;
He came from Venus, but made love to Juno.'"

"If Peter Barrington gained his cause by it I 'm heartily rejoiced, and I wish him health and years to enjoy it." The Admiral said this with a cordial good will as he drank off his glass.

"He's all right again," said Withering. "I left him working away with a hoe and a rake this morning, looking as hale and hearty as he did a dozen years ago."

"A man must have really high deserts in whose good fortune so many are well-wishers," said Stapylton; and by the courteous tone of the remark Withering's attention was attracted, and he speedily begged the Admiral to present him to his guest. They continued to converse together as they arose from table, and with such common pleasure that when Withering expressed a hope the acquaintance might not end there, Stapylton replied by a request that he would allow him to be his fellow-traveller to Kilkenny, whither he was about to go on a regimental affair. The arrangement was quickly made, to the satisfaction of each; and as they drove away, while many bewailed the departure of such pleasant members of the party, the little Poet simperingly said,—

"Shall I own that my heart is relieved of a care?—
Though you 'll think the confession is petty—
I cannot but feel, as I look on the pair,
It is 'Peebles' gone off with 'Dalgetty.'"

As for the fellow-travellers, they jogged along very pleasantly on their way, as two consummate men of the world are sure to do when they meet. For what Freemasonry equals that of two shrewd students of life? How flippantly do they discuss each theme! how easily read each character, and unravel each motive that presents itself! What the lawyer gained by the technical subtlety of his profession, the soldier made up for by his wider experience of mankind. There were, besides, a variety of experiences to exchange. Toga could tell of much that interested the "man of war," and he, in turn, made himself extremely agreeable by his Eastern information, not to say, that he was able to give a correct version of many Hindostanee phrases and words which the old lawyer eagerly desired to acquire.

"All you have been telling me has a strong interest for me, Captain Stapylton," said he, as they drove into Kilkenny. "I have a case which has engaged my attention for years, and is likely to occupy what remains to me of life,—a suit of which India is the scene, and Orientals figure as some of the chief actors,—so that I can scarcely say how fortunate I feel this chance meeting with you."

"I shall deem myself greatly honored if the acquaintance does not end here."

"It shall not, if it depend upon me," said Withering, cordially. "You said something of a visit you were about to make to Dublin. Will you do me a great—a very great—favor, and make my house your home while you stay? This is my address: '18 Merrion Square.' It is a bachelor's hall; and you can come and go without ceremony."

"The plan is too tempting to hesitate about. I accept your invitation with all the frankness you have given it. Meanwhile you will be my guest here." "'That is impossible. I must start for Cork this evening." And now they parted,—not like men who had been strangers a few hours back, but like old acquaintances, only needing the occasion to feel as old friends.

CHAPTER XX.

AN INTERIOR AT THE DOCTOR'S

When Captain Stapylton made his appointment to wait on Dr. Dill, he was not aware that the Attorney-General was expected at Cobham. No sooner, however, had he learned that fact than he changed his purpose, and intimated his intention of running up for a day to Kilkenny, to hear what was going on in the regiment. No regret for any disappointment he might be giving to the village doctor, no self-reproach for the breach of an engagement—all of his own making—crossed his mind. It is, indeed, a theme for a moralist to explore, the ease with which a certain superiority in station can divest its possessor of all care for the sensibilities of those below him; and yet in the little household of the doctor that promised visit was the source of no small discomfort and trouble. The doctor's study—the sanctum in which the interview should be held—had to be dusted and smartened up. Old boots, and overcoats, and smashed driving-whips, and odd stirrup-leathers, and stable-lanterns, and garden implements had all to be banished. The great table in front of the doctor's chair had also to be professionally littered with notes and cards and periodicals, not forgetting an ingenious admixture of strange instruments of torture, quaint screws, and inscrutable-looking scissors, destined, doubtless, to make many a faint heart the fainter in their dread presence. All these details had to be carried out in various ways through the rest of the establishment,—in the drawing-room, wherein the great man was to be ushered; in the dining-room, where he was to lunch. Upon Polly did the greater part of these cares devolve; not alone attending to the due disposal of chairs and sofas and tables, but to the preparation of certain culinary delicacies, which were to make the Captain forget the dainty luxuries of Cobham. And, in truth, there is a marvellous *esprit du corps* in the way a woman will fag and slave herself to make the humble household she belongs to look its best, even to the very guest she has least at heart; for Polly did not like Stapylton. Flattered at first by his notice, she was offended afterwards at the sort of conscious condescension of his manner,—a something which seemed to say, I can be charming, positively fascinating, but don't imagine for a moment that there is anything especial in it. I captivate—just as I fish, hunt, sketch, or shoot—to amuse myself. And with all this, how was it he was really not a coxcomb? Was it the grave dignity of his address, or the quiet state-liness of his person, or was it a certain uniformity, a keeping, that pervaded all he said or did? I am not quite sure whether all three did not contribute to this end, and make him what the world confessed,—a most well-bred gentleman.

Polly was, in her way, a shrewd observer, and she felt that Stapylton's manner towards her was that species of urbane condescension with which a great master of a game deigns to play with a very humble proficient. He moved about the board with an assumption that said, I can checkmate you when I will! Now this is hard enough to bear when the pieces at stake are stained ivory, but it is less endurable: still when they are our emotions and our wishes. And yet with all this before her, Polly ordered and arranged and superintended and directed with an energy that never tired, and an activity that never relaxed.

As for Mrs. Dill, no similar incident in the life of Clarissa had prepared her for the bustle and preparation she saw on every side, and she was fairly perplexed between the thought of a seizure for rent and a fire, — casualties which, grave as they were, she felt she could meet with Mr. Richardson beside her. The doctor himself was unusually fidgety and anxious. Perhaps he ascribed considerable importance to this visit; perhaps he thought Polly had not been candid with him, and that, in reality, she knew more of its object than she had avowed; and so he walked hurriedly from room to room, and out into the garden, and across the road to the river's side, and once as far as the bridge, consulting his watch, and calculating that as it now only wanted eight minutes of two o'clock, the arrival could scarcely be long delayed.

It was on his return he entered the drawing-room and found Polly, now plainly but becomingly dressed, seated at her work, with a seeming quietude and repose about her, strangely at variance with her late display of activity. "I 've had a look down the Graigue Road," said he, "but can see nothing. You are certain he said two o'clock?"

"Quite certain, sir."

"To be sure he might come by the river; there's water enough now for the Cobham barge."

She made no answer, though she half suspected some reply was expected.

"And of course," continued the doctor, "they'd have offered him the use of it. They seem to make a great deal of him up there."

"A great deal, indeed, sir," said she; but in a voice that was a mere echo of his own.

"And I suspect they know why. I 'm sure they know why. People in their condition make no mistakes about each other; and if he receives much attention, it is because it's his due."

No answer followed this speech, and he walked feverishly up and down the room, holding his watch in his closed hand. "I have a notion you must have mistaken him. It was not two he said."

"I 'm positive it was two, sir. But it can scarcely be much past that hour now."

"It is seventeen minutes past two," said he, solemnly. And then, as if some fresh thought had just occurred to him, asked, "Where 's Tom? I never saw him this morning."

"He 's gone out to take a walk, sir. The poor fellow is dead beat by work, and had such a headache that I told him to go as far as the Red House or Snow's Mill."

"And I 'll wager he did not want to be told twice. Anything for idleness with *him!*"

"Well, papa, he is really doing his very best now. He is not naturally quick, and he has a bad memory, so that labor is no common toil; but his heart is in it, and I never saw him really anxious for success before."

"To go out to India, I suppose," said Dill, sneeringly, "that notable project of the other good-for-nothing; for, except in the matter of fortune, there's not much to choose between them. There 's the half-hour striking now!"

"The project has done this for him, at least," said she, firmly, — "it has given him hope!"

"How I like to hear about hope!" said he, with a peculiarly sarcastic bitterness. "I never knew a fellow worth sixpence that had that cant of 'hope' in his mouth! How much hope had I when I began the world! How much have I now?"

"Don't you hope Captain Stapylton may not have forgotten his appointment, papa?" said she, with a quick drollery, which sparkled in her eye, but brought no smile to her lips.

"Well, here he is at last," said Dill, as he heard the sharp click made by the wicket of the little garden; and he started up, and rushed to the window. "May I never!" cried he, in horror, "if it isn't M'Cormick! Say we're out, — that I'm at Grai-gue, — that I won't be home till evening!"

But while he was multiplying these excuses, the old Major had caught sight of him, and was waving his hand in salutation from below. "It's too late, — it's too late!" sighed Dill, bitterly; "he sees me now, — there's no help for it!"

What benevolent and benedictory expressions were muttered below his breath, it is not for this history to record; but so vexed and irritated was he, that the Major had already entered the room ere he could compose his features into even a faint show of welcome.

"I was down at the Dispensary," croaked out M'Cormick, "and they told me you were not expected there to-day, and so I said, maybe he's ill, or maybe," — and here he looked shrewdly around him, — "maybe there 's something going on up at the house."

"What should there be going on, as you call it?" responded Dill, angrily, for he was now at home, in presence of the family, and could not compound for that tone of servile acquiescence he employed on foreign service.

"And, faix, I believe I was right; Miss Polly isn't so smart this morning for nothing, no more than the saving cover is off the sofa, and the piece of gauze taken down from before the looking-glass, and the 'Times' newspaper away from the rug!"

"Are there any other domestic changes you 'd like to remark upon, Major M'Cormick?" said Dill, pale with rage.

"Indeed, yes," rejoined the other; "there 's yourself, in the elegant black coat that I never saw since Lord Kilraney's funeral, and looking pretty much as lively and pleasant as you did at the ceremony."

"A gentleman has made an appointment with papa," broke in Polly, "and may be here at any moment."

"I know who it is," said M'Cormick, with a finger on the side of his nose to imply intense cunning. "I know all about it."

"What do you know?—what do you mean by all about it?" said Dill, with an eagerness he could not repress.

"Just as much as yourselves,—there now! Just as much as yourselves!" said he, sententiously.

"But apparently, Major, you know far more," said Polly.

"Maybe I do, maybe I don't; but I 'll tell you one thing, Dill, for your edification, and mind me if I 'm not right: you 're all mistaken about him, every one of ye!"

"Whom are you talking of?" asked the doctor, sternly.

"Just the very man you mean yourself, and no other! Oh, you need n't fuss and fume, I don't want to pry into your family secrets. Not that they 'll be such secrets tomorrow or next day,—the whole town will be talking of them,—but as an old friend that could, maybe, give a word of advice—"

"Advice about what? Will you just tell me about what?" cried Dill, now bursting with anger.

"I 've done now. Not another word passes my lips about it from this minute. Follow your own road, and see where it will lead ye?"

"Cannot you understand, Major M'Cormick, that we are totally unable to guess what you allude to? Neither papa nor I have the very faintest clew to your meaning, and if you really desire to serve us, you will speak out plainly."

"Not another syllable, if I sat here for two years!"

The possibility of such an infliction seemed so terrible to poor Polly that she actually shuddered as she heard it.

"Is n't that your mother I see sitting up there, with all the fine ribbons in her cap?" whispered M'Cormick, as he pointed to a small room which opened off an angle of the larger one. "That 's 'the boodoo,' is n't it?" said he, with a grin. This, I must inform my reader, was the M'Cormick for "boudoir." "Well, I'll go and pay my respects to her."

So little interest did Mrs. Dill take in the stir and movement around her that the Major utterly failed in his endeavors to torture her by all his covert allusions and ingeniously drawn inferences. No matter what hints he dropped or doubts he suggested, *she* knew "Clarissa" would come well out of her trials; and beyond a little unmeaning simper, and a muttered "To be sure," "No doubt of it," and, "Why not?" M'Cormick could obtain nothing from her.

Meanwhile, in the outer room the doctor continued to stride up and down with impatience, while Polly sat quietly working on, not the less anxious, perhaps, though her peaceful air betokened a mind at rest.

"That must be a boat, papa," said she, without lifting her head, "that has just come up to the landing-place. I heard the plash of the oars, and now all is still again."

"You 're right; so it is!" cried he, as he stopped before the window. "But how is this! That 's a lady I see yonder, and a gentleman along with her. That's not Stapylton, surely!"

"He is scarcely so tall," said she, rising to look out, "but not very unlike him. But the lady, papa,—the lady is Miss Barrington."

Bad as M'Cormick's visit was, it was nothing to the possibility of such an advent as this, and Dill's expressions of anger were now neither measured nor muttered.

"This is to be a day of disasters. I see it well, and no help for it," exclaimed he, passionately. "If there was one human being I 'd hate to come here this morning, it's that old woman! She's never civil. She's not commonly decent in her manner towards me in her own house, and what she 'll be in mine, is clean beyond me to guess. That's herself! There she goes! Look at her remarking,—I see, she's remarking on the weeds over the beds, and the smashed paling. She's laughing too! Oh, to be sure, it's fine laughing at people that's poor; and she might know something of that same herself. I know who the man is now. That 's the Colonel, who came to the 'Fisherman's Home' on the night of the accident."

"It would seem we are to hold a levee to-day," said Polly, giving a very fleeting glance at herself in the glass. And now a knock came to the door, and the man who acted gardener and car-driver and valet to the doctor announced that Miss Barrington and Colonel Hunter were below.

"Show them up," said Dill, with the peremptory voice of one ordering a very usual event, and intentionally loud enough to be heard below stairs.

If Polly's last parting with Miss Barrington gave little promise of pleasure to their next meeting, the first look she caught of the old lady on entering the room dispelled all uneasiness on that score. Miss Dinah entered with a pleasing smile, and presented her friend, Colonel Hunter, as one come to thank the doctor for much kindness to his young subaltern. "Whom, by the way," added he, "we thought to find here. It is only since we landed that we learned he had left the inn for Kilkenny."

While the Colonel continued to talk to the doctor, Miss Dinah had seated herself On the sofa, with Polly at her side.

"My visit this morning is to you," said she. "I have come to ask your forgiveness. Don't interrupt me, child; your forgiveness was the very word I used. I was very rude to you t' other morning, and being all in the wrong,—like most people in such circumstances,—I was very angry with the person who placed me so."

"But, my dear madam," said Polly, "you had such good reason to suppose you were in the right that this *amende* on your part is far too generous."

"It is not at all generous,—it is simply just. I was sorely vexed with you about that stupid wager, which you were very wrong to have had any share in; vexed with your father, vexed with your brother,—not that I believed his counsel would have been absolute wisdom,—and I was even vexed with my young friend Conyers, because he had not the bad taste to be as angry with you as I was. When I was a young lady," said she, bridling up, and looking at once haughty and defiant, "no man would have dared to approach me with such a proposal as complicity in a wager. But I am told that my ideas are antiquated, and the world has grown much wiser since that day."

"Nay, madam," said Polly, "but there is another difference that your politeness has prevented you from appreciating. I mean the difference in station between Miss Barrington and Polly Dill."

It was a well-directed shot, and told powerfully, for Miss Barrington's eyes became clouded, and she turned her head away, while she pressed Polly's hand within her own with a cordial warmth. "Ah!" said she, feelingly, "I hope there are many points of resemblance between us. I have always tried to be a good sister. I know well what you have been to your brother."

A very jolly burst of laughter from the inner room, where Hunter had already penetrated, broke in upon them, and the merry tones of his voice were heard saying, "Take my word for it, madam, nobody could spare time nowadays to make love in nine volumes. Life 's too short for it. Ask my old brother-officer here if he could endure such a thirty years' war; or rather let me turn here for an opinion. What does your daughter say on the subject?"

"Ay, ay," croaked out M'Cormick. "Marry in haste—"

"Or repent that you did n't. That 's the true reading of the adage."

"The Major would rather apply leisure to the marriage, and make the repentance come—"

"As soon as possible afterwards," said Miss Dinah, tartly.

"Faix, I 'll do better still; I won't provoke the repentance at all."

"Oh, Major, is it thus you treat me?" said Polly, affecting to wipe her eyes. "Are my hopes to be dashed thus cruelly?"

But the doctor, who knew how savagely M'Cormick could resent even the most harmless jesting, quickly interposed, with a question whether Polly had thought of ordering luncheon.

It is but fair to Dr. Dill to record the bland but careless way he ordered some entertainment for his visitors. He did it like the lord of a well-appointed household, who, when he said "serve," they served. It was in the easy confidence of one whose knowledge told him that the train was laid, and only waited for the match to explode it.

"May I have the honor, dear lady?" said he, offering his arm to Miss Barrington.

Now, Miss Dinah had just observed that she had various small matters to transact in the village, and was about to issue forth for their performance; but such is the force of a speciality, that she could not tear herself away without a peep into the dining-room, and a glance, at least, at arrangements that appeared so magically conjured up. Nor was Dill insensible to the astonishment expressed in her face as her eyes ranged over the table.

"If your daughter be your housekeeper, Dr. Dill," said she, in a whisper, "I must give her my very heartiest approbation. These are matters I can speak of with authority, and I pronounce her worthy of high commendation."

"What admirable salmon cutlets!" cried the Colonel. "Why, doctor, these tell of a French cook."

"There she is beside you, the French cook!" said the Major, with a malicious twinkle.

"Yes," said Polly, smiling, though with a slight flush on her face, "if Major M'Cormick will be indiscreet enough to tell tales, let us hope they will never be more damaging in their import."

"And do you say—do you mean to tell me that this curry is your handiwork? Why, this is high art."

"Oh, she's artful enough, if it's that ye're wanting," muttered the Major.

Miss Barrington, having apparently satisfied the curiosity she felt about the details of the doctor's housekeeping, now took her leave, not, however, without Dr. Dill offering his arm on one side, while Polly, with polite observance, walked on the other.

"Look at that now," whispered the Major. "They're as much afraid of that old woman as if she were the Queen of Sheba! And all because she was once a fine lady living at Barrington Hall."

"Here's their health for it," said the Colonel, filling his glass,—"and in a bumper too! By the way," added he, looking around, "does not Mrs. Dill lunch with us?"

"Oh, she seldom comes to her meals! She's a little touched here." And he laid his finger on the centre of his forehead. "And, indeed, no wonder if she is." The benevolent Major was about to give some details of secret family history, when the doctor and his daughter returned to the room.

The Colonel ate and talked untiringly. He was delighted with everything, and charmed with himself for his good luck in chancing upon such agreeable people. He liked the scenery, the village, the beetroot salad, the bridge, the pickled oysters, the evergreen oaks before the door. He was not astonished Conyers should linger on such a spot; and then it suddenly occurred to him to ask when he had left the village, and how.

The doctor could give no information on the point, and while he was surmising one thing and guessing another, M'Cormick whispered in the Colonel's ear, "Maybe it's a delicate point. How do you know what went on with—" And a significant nod towards Polly finished the remark.

"I wish I heard what Major M'Cormick has just said," said Polly.

"And it is exactly what I cannot repeat to you."

"I suspected as much. So that my only request will be that you never remember it."

"Isn't she sharp!—sharp as a needle!" chimed in the Major.

Checking, and not without some effort, a smart reprimand on the last speaker, the Colonel looked hastily at his watch, and arose from table.

"Past three o'clock, and to be in Kilkenny by six."

"Do you want a car? There's one of Rice's men now in the village; shall I get him for you?"

"Would you really do me the kindness?" While the Major bustled off on his errand, the Colonel withdrew the doctor inside the recess of a window. "I had a word I wished to say to you in private, Dr. Dill; but it must really be in private,—you understand me?"

"Strictly confidential, Colonel Hunter," said Dill, bowing.

"It is this: a young officer of mine, Lieutenant Conyers, has written to me a letter mentioning a plan he had conceived for the future advancement of your son, a young gentleman for whom, it would appear, he had formed a sudden but strong attachment. His project was, as I understand it, to accredit him to his father with such a letter as must secure the General's powerful influence in his behalf. Just the sort of thing a warm-hearted young fellow would think of doing for a friend he determined to serve, but exactly the kind of proceeding that might have a very unfortunate ending. I can very well imagine, from my own short experience here, that your son's claims to notice and distinction may be the very highest; I can believe readily what very little extraneous aid he would require to secure his success; but you and I are old men of the world, and are bound to look at things cautiously, and to ask, 'Is this scheme a very safe one?' 'Will General Conyers enter as heartily into it as his son?' 'Will the young surgeon be as sure to captivate the old soldier as the young one?' In a word, would it be quite wise to set a man's whole venture in life on such a cast, and is it the sort of risk that, with your experience of the world, you would sanction?"

It was evident, from the pause the Colonel left after these words, that he expected Dill to say something; but, with the sage reserve of his order, the doctor stood still, and never uttered a syllable. Let us be just to his acuteness, he never did take to the project from the first; he thought ill of it, in every way, but yet he did not relinquish the idea of making the surrender of it "conditional;" and so he slowly shook his head with an air of doubt, and smoothly rolled his hands one over the other, as though to imply a moment of hesitation and indecision.

"Yes, yes," muttered he, talking only to himself,—"disappointment, to be sure!—very great disappointment too! And his heart so set upon it, that's the hardship."

"Naturally enough," broke in Hunter, hastily. "Who would n't be disappointed under such circumstances? Better even that, however, than utter failure later on." The doctor sighed, but over what precise calamity was not so clear; and Hunter continued,—

"Now, as I have made this communication to you in strictest confidence, and not in any concert with Conyers, I only ask you to accept the view as a mere matter of opinion. I think you would be wrong to suffer your son to engage in such a venture. That's all I mean by my interference, and I have done."

Dill was, perhaps, scarcely prepared for the sudden summing up of the Colonel, and looked strangely puzzled and embarrassed.

"Might I talk the matter over with my daughter Polly? She has a good head for one so little versed in the world."

"By all means. It is exactly what I would have proposed. Or, better still, shall I repeat what I have just told you?"

"Do so," said the doctor, "for I just remember Miss Barrington will call here in a few moments for that medicine I have ordered for her brother, and which is not yet made up."

"Give me five minutes of your time and attention, Miss Dill," said Hunter, "on a point for which your father has referred me to your counsel."

"To mine?"

"Yes," said he, smiling at her astonishment. "We want your quick faculties to come to the aid of our slow ones. And here's the case." And in a few sentences he put the matter before her, as he had done to her father. While he thus talked, they had strolled out into the garden, and walked slowly side by side down one of the alleys.

"Poor Tom!—poor fellow!" was all that Polly said, as she listened; but once or twice her handkerchief was raised to her eyes, and her chest heaved heavily.

"I am heartily sorry for him—that is, if his heart be bent on it—if he really should have built upon the scheme already."

"Of course he has, sir. You don't suppose that in such lives as ours these are common incidents? If we chance upon a treasure, or fancy that we have, once in a whole existence, it is great fortune."

"It was a brief, a very brief acquaintance,—a few hours, I believe. The—What was that? Did you hear any one cough there?"

"No, sir; we are quite alone. There is no one in the garden but ourselves."

"So that, as I was saying, the project could scarcely have taken a very deep root, and—and—in fact, better the first annoyance than a mistake that should give its color to a whole lifetime. I'm certain I heard a step in that walk yonder."

"No, sir; we are all alone."

"I half wish I had never come on this same errand. I have done an ungracious thing, evidently very ill, and with the usual fate of those who say disagreeable things, I am involved in the disgrace I came to avert."

"But I accept your view."

"There! I knew there was some one there!" said Hunter, springing across a bed and coming suddenly to the side of M'Cormick, who was affecting to be making a nosegay.

"The car is ready at the door, Colonel," said he, in some confusion. "Maybe you 'd oblige me with a seat as far as Lyrath?"

"Yes, yes; of course. And how late it is!" cried he, looking at his watch. "Time does fly fast in these regions, no doubt of it."

"You see, Miss Polly, you have made the Colonel forget himself," said M'Cormick, maliciously.

"Don't be severe on an error so often your own, Major M'Cormick," said she, fiercely, and turned away into the house.

The Colonel, however, was speedily at her side, and in an earnest voice said: "I could hate myself for the impression I am leaving behind me here. I came with those excellent intentions which so often make a man odious, and I am going away with those regrets which follow all failures; but I mean to come back again one of these days, and erase, if I can, the ill impression."

"One who has come out of his way to befriend those who had no claim upon his kindness can have no fear for the estimation he will be held in; for my part, I thank you heartily, even though I do not exactly see the direct road out of this difficulty."

"Let me write to you. One letter—only one," said Hunter.

But M'Cormick had heard the request, and she flushed up with anger at the malicious glee his face exhibited.

"You 'll have to say my good-byes for me to your father, for I am sorely pressed for time; and, even as it is, shall be late for my appointment in Kilkenny." And before Polly could do more than exchange his cordial shake hands, he was gone.

CHAPTER XXI.

DARK TIDINGS

If I am not wholly without self-reproach when I bring my reader into uncongenial company, and make him pass time with Major M'Cormick he had far rather bestow upon a pleasanter companion, I am sustained by the fact—unpalatable fact though it be—that the highway of life is not always smooth, nor its banks flowery, and that, as an old Derry woman once remarked to me, "It takes a' kind o' folk to mak' a world."

Now, although Colonel Hunter did drive twelve weary miles of road with the Major for a fellow-traveller,—thanks to that unsocial conveniency called an Irish jaunting-car,—they rode back to back, and conversed but little. One might actually believe that unpopular men grow to feel a sort of liking for their unpopularity, and become at length delighted with the snubbings they meet with, as though an evidence of the amount of that discomfort they can scatter over the world at large; just, in fact, as a wasp or a scorpion might have a sort of triumphant joy in the consciousness of its power for mischief, and exult in the terror caused by its vicinity.

"Splendid road—one of the best I ever travelled on," said the Colonel, after about ten miles, during which he smoked on without a word.

"Why wouldn't it be, when they can assess the county for it? They're on the Grand Jury, and high up, all about here," croaked out the Major.

"It is a fine country, and abounds in handsome places." "And well mortgaged, too, the most of them." "You 'd not see better farming than that in Norfolk, cleaner wheat or neater drills; in fact, one might imagine himself in England."

"So he might, for the matter of taxes. I don't see much difference."

"Why don't you smoke? Things look pleasanter through the blue haze of a good Havannah," said Hunter, smiling.

"I don't want them to look pleasanter than they are," was the dry rejoinder.

Whether Hunter did or did not, he scarcely liked his counsellor, and, re-lighting a cigar, he turned his back once more on him.

"I'm one of those old-fashioned fellows," continued the Major, leaning over towards his companion, "who would rather see things as they are, not as they might be; and when I remarked you awhile ago so pleased with the elegant luncheon and Miss Polly's talents for housekeeping, I was laughing to myself over it all."

"How do you mean? What did you laugh at?" said Hunter, half fiercely.

"Just at the way you were taken in, that's all."

"Taken in?—taken in? A very strange expression for an hospitable reception and a most agreeable visit."

"Well, it's the very word for it, after all; for as to the hospitable reception, it was n't meant for us, but for that tall Captain,—the dark-complexioned fellow,—Staples, I think they call him."

"Captain Stapylton?"

"Yes, that's the man. He ordered Healey's car to take him over here; and I knew when the Dills sent over to Mrs. Brierley for a loan of the two cut decanters and the silver cruet-stand, something was up; and so I strolled down, by way of—to reconnoitre the premises, and see what old Dill was after."

"Well, and then?"

"Just that I saw it all,—the elegant luncheon, and the two bottles of wine, and the ginger cordials, all laid out for the man that never came; for it would seem he changed his mind about it, and went back to head-quarters."

"You puzzle me more and more at every word. What change of mind do you allude to? What purpose do you infer he had in coming over here to-day?"

The only answer M'Cormick vouchsafed to this was by closing one eye and putting his finger significantly to the tip of his nose, while he said, "Catch a weasel asleep!"

"I more than suspect," said Hunter, sternly, "that this half-pay life works badly for a man's habits, and throws him upon very petty and contemptible modes of getting through his time. What possible business could it be of yours to inquire why Stapylton came, or did not come here to-day, no more than for the reason of *my* visit?"

"Maybe I could guess that, too, if I was hard pushed," said M'Cormick, whose tone showed no unusual irritation from the late rebuke. "I was in the garden all the time, and heard everything."

"Listened to what I was saying to Miss Dill!" cried Hunter, whose voice of indignation could not now be mistaken.

"Every word of it," replied the unabashed Major. "I heard all you said about a short acquaintance—a few hours you called it—but that your heart was bent upon it, all the same. And then you went on about India; what an elegant place it was, and the fine pay and the great allowances. And ready enough she was to believe it all, for I suppose she was sworn at Highgate, and would n't take the Captain if she could get the Colonel."

By this time, and not an instant earlier, it flashed upon Hunter's mind that M'Cormick imagined he had overheard a proposal of marriage; and so amused was he by the blunder, that he totally drowned his anger in a hearty burst of laughter.

"I hope that, as an old brother-officer, you 'll be discreet, at all events," said he, at last. "You have not come by the secret quite legitimately, and I trust you will preserve it."

"My hearing is good, and my eyesight too, and I mean to use them both as long as they 're spared to me."

"It was your tongue that I referred to," said Hunter, more gravely.

"Ay, I know it was," said the Major, crankily. "My tongue will take care of itself also."

"In order to make its task the easier, then," said Hunter, speaking in a slow and serious voice, "let me tell you that your eaves-dropping has, for once at least, misled you. I made no proposal, such as you suspected, to Miss Dill. Nor did she give me the slightest encouragement to do so. The conversation you so unwarrantably and imperfectly overheard had a totally different object, and I am not at all sorry you should not have guessed it. So much for the past. Now one word for the future. Omit my name, and all that concerns me, from the narrative with which you amuse your friends, or, take my word for it, you 'll have to record more than you have any fancy for. This is strictly between ourselves; but if you have a desire to impart it, bear in mind that I shall be at my quarters in Kilkenny till Tuesday next."

"You may spend your life there, for anything I care," said the Major. "Stop, Billy; pull up. I'll get down here." And shuffling off the car, he muttered a "Good-day" without turning his head, and bent his steps towards a narrow lane that led from the high-road.

"Is this the place they call Lyrath?" asked the Colonel of the driver.

"No, your honor. We're a good four miles from it yet."

The answer showed Hunter that his fellow-traveller had departed in anger; and such was the generosity of his nature, he found it hard not to overtake him and make his peace with him.

"After all," thought he, "he 's a crusty old fellow, and has hugged his ill-temper so long, it may be more congenial to him now than a pleasanter humor." And he turned his mind to other interests that more closely touched him. Nor was he without cares, — heavier ones, too, than his happy nature had ever yet been called to deal with. There are few more painful situations in life than to find our advancement — the long-wished and strived-for promotion — achieved at the cost of some dearly loved friend; to know that our road to fortune had led us across the fallen figure of an old comrade, and that he who would have been the first to hail our success is already bewailing his own defeat. This was Hunter's lot at the present moment. He had been sent for to hear of a marvellous piece of good-fortune. His name and character, well known in India, had recommended him for an office of high trust, — the Political Resident of a great native court; a position not alone of power and influence, but as certain to secure, and within a very few years, a considerable fortune. It was the Governor-General who had made choice of him; and the Prince of Wales, in the brief interview he accorded him, was delighted with his frank and soldierlike manner, his natural cheerfulness, and high spirit. "We 're not going to unfrock you, Hunter," said he, gayly, in dismissing him. "You shall have your military rank, and all the steps of your promotion. We only make you a civilian till you have saved some lacs of rupees, which is what I hear your predecessor has forgotten to do."

THE MAJOR "DEPARTS," BUT NOT IN "PEACE"

It was some time before Hunter, overjoyed as he was, even bethought him of asking who that predecessor was. What was his misery when he heard the name of Ormsby Conyers, his oldest, best friend; the man at whose table he had sat for years, whose confidence he had shared, whose heart was open to him to its last secret! "No," said he, "this is impossible. Advancement at such a price has no temptation for me. I will not accept it" He wrote his refusal at once, not assigning any definite reasons, but declaring that, after much thought and consideration, he had decided the post was one he could not accept of. The Secretary, in whose province the affairs of India lay, sent for him, and, after much pressing and some ingenious cross-questioning, got at his reasons. "These may be all reasonable scruples on your part," said he, "but they will avail your friend nothing. Conyers must go; for his own interest and character's sake, he must come home and meet the charges made against him, and which, from their very contradictions, we all hope to see him treat triumphantly: some alleging that he has amassed untold wealth; others that it is, as a ruined man, he has involved himself in the intrigues of the native rulers. All who know him say that at the first whisper of a charge against him he will throw up his post and come to England to meet his accusers. And now let me own to you that it is the friendship in which he held you lay one of the suggestions for your choice. We all felt that if a man ill-disposed or ungenerously minded to Conyers should go out to Agra, numerous petty and vexatious accusations might be forthcoming; the little local injuries and pressure, so sure to beget grudges, would all rise up as charges, and enemies to the fallen man spring up in every quarter. It is as a successor, then, you can best serve your friend." I need not dwell on the force and ingenuity with which this view was presented; enough that I say it was successful, and Hunter returned to Ireland to take leave of his regiment, and prepare for a speedy departure to India.

Having heard, in a brief note from young Conyers, his intentions respecting Tom Dill, Hunter had hastened off to prevent the possibility of such a scheme being carried out. Not wishing, however, to divulge the circumstances of his friend's fortune, he had in his interview with the doctor confined himself to arguments on the score of prudence. His next charge was to break to Fred the tidings of his father's troubles, and it was an office he shrunk from with a coward's fear. With every mile he went his heart grew heavier. The more he thought over the matter the more difficult it appeared. To treat the case lightly, might savor of heartlessness and levity; to approach it more seriously, might seem a needless severity. Perhaps, too, Conyers might have written to his son; he almost hoped he had, and that the first news of disaster should not come from him.

That combination of high-heartedness and bashfulness, a blended temerity and timidity,—by no means an uncommon temperament,—renders a man's position in the embarrassments of life one of downright suffering. There are operators who feel the knife more sensitively than the patients. Few know what torments such men conceal under a manner of seeming slap-dash and carelessness. Hunter was of this order, and would, any day of his life, far rather have confronted a real peril than met a contingency that demanded such an address. It was, then, with a sense of relief he learned, on arrival at the barracks, that Conyers had gone out for a walk, so that there was a reprieve at least of a few hours of the penalty that overhung him.

The trumpet-call for the mess had just sounded as Conyers gained the door of the Colonel's quarters, and Hunter taking Fred's arm, they crossed the barrack-square together.

"I have a great deal to say to you, Conyers," said he, hurriedly; "part of it unpleasant,—none of it, indeed, very gratifying—"

"I know you are going to leave us, sir," said Fred, who perceived the more than common emotion in the other's manner. "And for myself, I own I have no longer any desire to remain in the regiment. I might go further, and say no more zest for the service. It was through your friendship for me I learned to curb many and many promptings to resistance, and when *you* go—"

"I am very sorry,—very, very sorry to leave you all," said Hunter, with a broken voice. "It is not every man that proudly can point to seven-and-twenty-years' service in a regiment without one incident to break the hearty cordiality that bound us. We had no bickerings, no petty jealousies amongst us. If a man joined us who wanted partisanship and a set, he soon found it better to exchange. I never expect again to lead the happy life I have here, and I 'd rather have led our bold squadrons in the field than have been a General of Division." Who could have believed that he, whose eyes ran over, as he spoke these broken words, was, five minutes after, the gay and rattling Colonel his officers always saw him, full of life, spirit, and animation, jocularly alluding to his speedy departure, and gayly speculating on the comparisons that would be formed between himself and his successor? "I'm leaving him the horses in good condition," said he; "and when Hargrave learns to give the word of command above a whisper, and Eyreton can ride without a backboard, he 'll scarcely report you for inefficiency." It is fair to add, that the first-mentioned officer had a voice like a bassoon, and the second was the beau-ideal of dragoon horsemanship.

It would not have consisted with military etiquette to have asked the Colonel the nature of his promotion, nor as to what new sphere of service he was called. Even the old Major, his contemporary, dared not have come directly to the question; and while all were eager to hear it, the utmost approach was by an insinuation or an innuendo. Hunter was known for no quality more remarkably than for his outspoken frankness, and some surprise was felt that in his returning thanks for his health being drank, not a word should escape him on this point; but the anxiety was not lessened by the last words he spoke. "It may be, it is more than likely, I shall never see the regiment again; but the sight of a hussar jacket or a scarlet busby will bring you all back to my memory, and you may rely on it, that whether around the mess-table or the bivouac fire my heart will be with you."

Scarcely had the cheer that greeted the words subsided, when a deep voice from the extreme end of the table said,—

"If only a new-comer in the regiment, Colonel Hunter, I am too proud of my good fortune not to associate myself with the feelings of my comrades, and, while partaking of their deep regrets, I feel it a duty to contribute, if in my power, by whatever may lighten the grief of our loss. Am I at liberty to do so? Have I your free permission, I mean?"

"I am fairly puzzled by your question, Captain Stapylton. I have not the very vaguest clew to your meaning, but, of course, you have my permission to mention whatever you deem proper."

"It is a toast I would propose, sir."

"By all means. The thing is not very regular, perhaps, but we are not exactly remarkable for regularity this evening. Fill, gentlemen, for Captain Stapylton's toast!"

"Few words will propose it," said Stapylton. "We have just drank Colonel Hunter's health with all the enthusiasm that befits the toast, but in doing so our tribute has been paid to the past; of the present and the future we have taken no note whatever, and it is to these I would now recall you. I say, therefore, bumpers to the health, happiness, and success of Major-General Hunter, Political Resident and Minister at the Court of Agra!"

"No, no!" cried young Conyers, loudly, "this is a mistake. It is my father—it is Lieutenant-General Conyers—who resides at Agra. Am I not right, sir?" cried he, turning to the Colonel.

But Hunter's face, pale as death even to the lips, and the agitation with which he grasped Fred's hand, so overcame the youth that with a sudden cry he sprang from his seat, and rushed out of the room. Hunter as quickly followed him; and now all were grouped around Stapylton, eagerly questioning and inquiring what his tidings might mean.

"The old story, gentlemen,—the old story, with which we are all more or less familiar in this best of all possible worlds: General Hunter goes out in honor, and General Conyers comes home in—well, under a cloud,—of course one that he is sure and certain to dispel. I conclude the Colonel would rather have had his advancement under other circumstances; but in this game of leap-frog that we call life, we must occasionally jump over our friends as well as our enemies."

"How and where did you get the news?"

"It came to me from town. I heard it this morning, and of course I imagined that the Colonel had told it to Conyers, whom it so intimately concerned. I hope I may not have been indiscreet in what I meant as a compliment."

None cared to offer their consolings to one so fully capable of supplying the commodity to himself, and the party broke up in twos or threes, moodily seeking their own quarters, and brooding gloomily over what they had just witnessed.

CHAPTER XXII.

LEAVING HOME

I will ask my reader now to turn for a brief space to the "Fisherman's Home," which is a scene of somewhat unusual bustle. The Barringtons are preparing for a journey, and old Peter's wardrobe has been displayed for inspection along a hedge of sweet-brier in the garden,—an arrangement devised by the genius of Darby, who passes up and down, with an expression of admiration on his face, the sincerity of which could not be questioned. A more reflective mind than his might have been carried away, at the sight to thoughts of the strange passages in the late history of Ireland, so curiously typified in that motley display. There, was the bright green dress-coat of Daly's club, recalling days of political excitement, and all the plottings and cabals of a once famous opposition. There was, in somewhat faded splendor it must be owned, a court suit of the Duke of Portland's day, when Irish gentlemen were as gorgeous as the courtiers of Versailles. Here came a grand colonel's uniform, when Barrington commanded a regiment of Volunteers; and yonder lay a friar's frock and cowl, relics of those "attic nights" with the Monks of the Screw, and recalling memories of Avonmore and Curran, and Day and Parsons; and with them were mixed hunting-coats, and shooting-jackets, and masonic robes, and "friendly brother" emblems, and long-waisted garments, and swallow-tailed affectations of all shades and tints,—reminders of a time when Buck Whalley was the eccentric, and Lord Llandaff the beau of Irish society. I am not certain that Monmouth Street would have endorsed Darby's sentiment as he said, "There was clothes there for a king on his throne!" but it was an honestly uttered speech, and came out of the fulness of an admiring heart, and although in truth he was nothing less than an historian, he was forcibly struck by the thought that Ireland must have been a grand country to live in, in those old days when men went about their ordinary avocations in such splendor as he saw there.

Nor was Peter Barrington himself an unmoved spectator of these old remnants of the past Old garments, like old letters, bring oftentimes very forcible memories of a long ago; and as he turned over the purple-stained flap of a waistcoat, he bethought him of a night at Daly's, when, in returning thanks for his health, his shaking hand had spilled that identical glass of Burgundy; and in the dun-colored tinge of a hunting-coat he remembered the day he had plunged into the Nore at Corrig O'Neal, himself and the huntsman, alone of all the field, to follow the dogs!

"Take them away, Darby, take them away; they only set me a-thinking about the pleasant companions of my early life. It was in that suit there I moved the amendment in '82, when Henry Grattan crossed over and said, 'Barrington will lead us here, as he does in the hunting-field.' Do you see that peach-colored waist-coat? It was Lady Caher embroidered every stitch of it with her own hands, for me."

MASTER AND MAN'S REFLECTIONS OVER OLD HABITS

"Them 's elegant black satin breeches," said Darby, whose eyes of covetous-ness were actually rooted on the object of his desire.

"I never wore them," said Barrington, with a sigh. "I got them for a duel with Mat Fortescue, but Sir Toby Blake shot him that morning. Poor Mat!"

"And I suppose you'll never wear them now. You couldn't bear the sight then," said Darby, insinuatingly.

"Most likely not," said Barrington, as he turned away with a heavy sigh. Darby sighed also, but not precisely in the same spirit.

Let me passingly remark that the total unsuitability to his condition of any object seems rather to enhance its virtue in the eyes of a lower Irishman, and a hat or a coat which he could not, by any possibility, wear in public, might still be to him things to covet and desire.

"What is the meaning of all this rag fair?" cried Miss Barrington, as she suddenly came in front of the exposed wardrobe. "You are not surely making any selections from these tawdry absurdities, brother, for your journey?"

"Well, indeed," said Barrington, with a droll twinkle of his eye, "it was a point that Darby and I were discussing as you came up. Darby opines that to make a suitable impression upon the Continent, I must not despise the assistance of dress, and he inclines much to that Corbeau coat with the cherry-colored lining."

"If Darby 's an ass, brother, I don't imagine it is a good reason to consult him," said she, angrily. "Put all that trash where you found it. Lay out your master's black clothes and the gray shooting-coat, see that his strong boots are in good repair, and get a serviceable lock on that valise."

It was little short of magic the spell these few and distinctly uttered words seemed to work on Darby, who at once descended from a realm of speculation and scheming to the commonplace world of duty and obedience. "I really wonder how you let yourself be imposed on, brother, by the assumed simplicity of that shrewd fellow."

"I like it, Dinah, I positively like it," said he, with a smile. "I watch him playing the game with a pleasure almost as great as his own; and as I know that the stakes are small, I 'm never vexed at his winning."

"But you seem to forget the encouragement this impunity suggests."

"Perhaps it does, Dinah; and very likely his little rogueries are as much triumphs to him as are all the great political intrigues the glories of some grand statesman."

"Which means that you rather like to be cheated," said she, scoffingly.

"When the loss is a mere trifle, I don't always think it ill laid out."

"And I," said she, resolutely, "so far from participating in your sentiment, feel it to be an insult and an outrage. There is a sense of inferiority attached to the position of a dupe that would drive me to any reprisals."

"I always said it; I always said it," cried he, laughing. "The women of our family monopolized all the com-bativeness."

Miss Barrington's eyes sparkled, and her cheek glowed, and she looked like one stung to the point of a very angry rejoinder, when by an effort she controlled her passion, and, taking a letter from her pocket, she opened it, and said, "This is from Withering. He has managed to obtain all the information we need for our journey. We are to sail for Ostend by the regular packet, two of which go every week from Dover. From thence there are stages or canal-boats to Bruges and Brussels, cheap and commodious, he says. He gives us the names of two hotels, one of which—the 'Lamb,' at Brussels—he recommends highly; and the Pension of a certain Madame Ochteroogen, at Namur, will, he opines, suit us better than an inn. In fact, this letter is a little road book, with the expenses marked down, and we can quietly count the cost of our venture before we make it."

"I 'd rather not, Dinah. The very thought of a limit is torture to me. Give me bread and water every day, if you like, but don't rob me of the notion that some fine day I am to be regaled with beef and pudding."

"I don't wonder that we have come to beggary," said she, passionately. "I don't know what fortune and what wealth could compensate for a temperament like yours."

"You may be right, Dinah. It may go far to make a man squander his substance, but take my word for it, it will help him to bear up under the loss."

If Barrington could have seen the gleam of affection that filled his sister's eyes, he would have felt what love her heart bore him; but he had stooped down to take a caterpillar off a flower, and did not mark it.

"Withering has seen young Conyers," she continued, as her eyes ran over the letter "He called upon him." Barrington made no rejoinder, though she waited for one. "The poor lad was in great affliction; some distressing news from India—of what kind Withering could not guess—had just reached him, and he appeared overwhelmed by it."

"He is very young for sorrow," said Barrington, feelingly.

"Just what Withering said;" and she read out, "'When I told him that I had come to make an *amende* for the reception he had met with at the cottage, he stopped me at once, and said, "Great grief s are the cure of small ones, and you find me under a very heavy affliction. Tell Miss Barrington that I have no other memories of the 'Fisherman's Home' than of all her kindness towards me.'"

"Poor boy!" said Barrington, with emotion. "And how did Withering leave him?"

"Still sad and suffering. Struggling too, Withering thought, between a proud attempt to conceal his grief and an ardent impulse to tell all about it 'Had *you* been there,' he writes, 'you'd have had the whole story; but I saw that he could n't stoop to open his heart to a man.'"

"Write to him, Dinah. Write and ask him down here for a couple of days."

"You forget that we are to leave this the day after tomorrow, brother."

"So I did. I forgot it completely. Well, what if he were to come for one day? What if you were to say come over and wish us good-bye?"

"It is so like a man and a man's selfishness never to consider a domestic difficulty," said she, tartly. "So long as a house has a roof over it, you fancy it may be available for hospitalities. You never take into account the carpets to be taken up, and the beds that are taken down, the plate-chest that is packed, and the cellar that is walled up. You forget, in a word, that to make that life you find so very easy, some one else must pass an existence full of cares and duties."

"There 's not a doubt of it, Dinah. There 's truth and reason in every word you 've said."

"I will write to him if you like, and say that we mean to be at home by an early day in October, and that if he is disposed to see how our woods look in autumn, we will be well pleased to have him for our guest."

"Nothing could be better. Do so, Dinah. I owe the young fellow a reparation, and I shall not have an easy conscience till I make it."

"Ah, brother Peter, if your moneyed debts had only given you one-half the torment of your moral ones, what a rich man you might have been to-day!"

Long after his sister had gone away and left him, Peter Barrington continued to muse over this speech. He felt it, felt it keenly too, but in no bitterness of spirit.

Like most men of a lax and easy temper, he could mete out to himself the same merciful measure he accorded to others, and be as forgiving to his own faults as to theirs. "I suppose Dinah is right, though," said he to himself. "I never did know that sensitive irritability under debt which insures solvency. And whenever a man can laugh at a dun, he is pretty sure to be on the high-road to bankruptcy! Well, well, it is somewhat late to try and reform, but I'll do my best!" And thus comforted, he set about tying up fallen rose-trees and removing noxious insects with all his usual zeal.

"I half wish the place did not look in such beauty, just as I must leave it for a while. I don't think that japonica ever had as many flowers before; and what a season for tulips! Not to speak of the fruit There are peaches enough to stock a market. I wonder what Dinah means to do with them? She 'll be sorely grieved to make them over as perquisites to Darby, and I know she 'll never consent to have them sold. No, that is the one concession she cannot stoop to. Oh, here she comes! What a grand year for the wall fruit, Dinah!" cried he, aloud.

"The apricots have all failed, and fully one-half of the peaches are worm-eaten," said she, dryly.

Peter sighed as he thought, how she does dispel an illusion, what a terrible realist is this same sister! "Still, my dear Dinah, one-half of such a crop is a goodly yield."

"Out with it, Peter Barrington. Out with the question that is burning for utterance. What's to be done with them? I have thought of that already. I have told Polly Dill to preserve a quantity for us, and to take as much more as she pleases for her own use, and make presents to her friends of the remainder. She is to be mistress here while we are away, and has promised to come up two or three times a week, and see after everything, for I neither desire to have the flower-roots sold, nor the pigeons eaten before our return."

"That is an admirable arrangement, sister. I don't know a better girl than Polly!"

"She is better than I gave her credit for," said Miss Barrington, who was not fully pleased at any praise not bestowed by herself. A man's estimate of a young woman's goodness is not so certain of finding acceptance from her own sex! "And as for that girl, the wonder is that with a fool for a mother, and a crafty old knave for a father, she really should possess one good trait or one amiable quality." Barrington muttered what sounded like concurrence, and she went on: "And it is for this reason I have taken an interest in her, and hope, by occupying her mind with useful cares and filling her hours with commendable duties, she will estrange herself from that going about to fine houses, and frequenting society where she is exposed to innumerable humiliations, and worse."

"Worse, Dinah!—what could be worse?"

"Temptations are worse, Peter Barrington, even when not yielded to; for like a noxious climate, which, though it fails to kill, it is certain to injure the constitution during a lifetime. Take my word for it, she 'll not be the better wife to the Curate for the memory of all the fine speeches she once heard from the Captain. Very old and ascetic notions I am quite aware, Peter; but please to bear in mind all the trouble we take that the roots of a favorite tree should not strike into a sour soil, and bethink you how very indifferent we are as to the daily associates of our children!"

"There you are right, Dinah, there you are right,—at least, as regards girls."

"And the rule applies fully as much to boys. All those manly accomplishments and out-of-door habits you lay such store by, could be acquired without the intimacy of the groom or the friendship of the gamekeeper. What are you muttering there about old-maids' children? Say it out, sir, and defend it, if you have the courage!"

But either that he had not said it, or failed in the requisite boldness to maintain it, he blundered out a very confused assurance of agreement on every point.

A woman is seldom merciful in argument; the consciousness that she owes victory to her violence far more than to her logic, prompts persistence in the course she has followed so successfully, and so was it that Miss Dinah contrived to gallop over the battlefield long after the enemy was routed! But Barrington was not in a mood to be vexed; the thought of the journey filled him with so many pleasant anticipations, the brightest of all being the sight of poor George's child! Not that this thought had not its dark side, in contrition for the long, long years he had left her unnoticed and neglected. Of course he had his own excuses and apologies for all this: he could refer to his overwhelming embarrassments, and the heavy cares that surrounded him; but then she—that poor friendless girl, that orphan—could have known nothing of these things; and what opinion might she not have formed of those relatives who had so coldly and heartlessly abandoned her! Barrington took down her miniature, painted when she was a mere infant, and scanned it well, as though to divine what nature might possess her! There was little for speculation there,—perhaps even less for hope! The eyes were large and lustrous, it is true, but the brow was heavy, and the mouth, even in infancy, had something that seemed like firmness and decision,—strangely at variance with the lips of childhood.

Now, old Barrington's heart was deeply set on that lawsuit—that great cause against the Indian Government—that had formed the grand campaign of his life. It was his first waking thought of a morning, his last at night. All his faculties were engaged in revolving the various points of evidence, and imagining how this and that missing link might be supplied; and yet, with all these objects of desire before him, he would have given them up, each and all, to be sure of one thing,—that his granddaughter might be handsome! It was not that he did not value far above the graces of person a number of other gifts; he would not, for an instant, have hesitated, had he to choose between mere beauty and a good disposition. If he knew anything of himself, it was his thorough appreciation of a kindly nature, a temper to bear well, and a spirit to soar nobly; but somehow he imagined these were gifts she was likely enough to possess. George's child would resemble him; she would have his light-heartedness and his happy nature, but would she be handsome? It is, trust me, no superficial view of life that attaches a great price to personal atractions, and Barrington was one to give these their full value. Had she been brought up from childhood under his roof, he had probably long since ceased to think of such a point; he would have attached himself to her by the ties of that daily domesticity which grow into a nature. The hundred little cares and offices that would have fallen to her lot to meet, would have served as links to bind their hearts; but she was coming to them a perfect stranger, and he wished ardently that his first impression should be all in her favor.

Now, while such were Barrington's reveries, his sister took a different turn. She had already pictured to herself the dark-orbed, heavy-browed child, expanded into a sallow-complexioned, heavy-featured girl, ungainly and ungraceful, her figure neglected, her very feet spoiled by the uncouth shoes of the convent, her great red hands untrained to all occupation save the coarse cares of that half-menial existence. "As my brother would say," muttered she, "a most unpromising filly, if it were not for the breeding."

Both brother and sister, however, kept their impressions to themselves, and of all the subjects discussed between them not one word betrayed what each forecast about Josephine. I am half sorry it is no part of my task to follow them on the road, and yet I feel I could not impart to my reader the almost boylike enjoyment old Peter felt at every stage of the journey. He had made the grand tour of Europe more than half a century before, and he was in ecstasy to find so much that was unchanged around him. There were the long-eared caps, and the monstrous earrings, and the sabots, and the heavily tasselled team horses, and the chiming church-bells, and the old-world equipages, and the strangely undersized soldiers,—all just as he saw them last! And every one was so polite and ceremonious, and so idle and so unoccupied, and the theatres were so large and the newspapers so small, and the current coin so defaced, and the order of the meats at dinner so inscrutable, and every one seemed contented just because he had nothing to do.

"Isn't it all I have told you, Dinah dear? Don't you perceive how accurate my picture has been? And is it not very charming and enjoyable?"

"They are the greatest cheats I ever met in my life, brother Peter; and when I think that every grin that greets us is a matter of five francs, it mars considerably the pleasure I derive from the hilarity."

It was in this spirit they journeyed till they arrived at Brussels.

CHAPTER XXIII.

THE COLONEL'S COUNSELS

When Conyers had learned from Colonel Hunter all that he knew of his father's involvement, it went no further than this, that the Lieutenant-General had either resigned or been deprived of his civil appointments, and Hunter was called upon to replace him. With all his habit of hasty and impetuous action, there was no injustice in Fred's nature, and he frankly recognized that, however painful to him personally, Hunter could not refuse to accede to what the Prince had distinctly pressed him to accept.

Young Conyers had heard over and over again the astonishment expressed by old Indian officials how his father's treatment of the Company's orders had been so long endured. Some prescriptive immunity seemed to attach to him, or some great patronage to protect him, for he appeared to do exactly as he pleased, and the despotic sway of his rule was known far and near. With the changes in the constitution of the Board, some members might have succeeded less disposed to recognize the General's former services, or endure so tolerantly his present encroachments, and Fred well could estimate the resistance his father would oppose to the very mildest remonstrance, and how indignantly he would reject whatever came in the shape of a command. Great as was the blow to the young man, it was not heavier in anything than the doubt and uncertainty about it, and he waited with a restless impatience for his father's letter, which should explain it all. Nor was his position less painful from the estrangement in which he lived, and the little intercourse he maintained with his brother-officers. When Hunter left, he knew that he had not one he could call friend amongst them, and Hunter was to go in a very few days, and even of these he could scarcely spare him more than a few chance moments!

It was in one of these flitting visits that Hunter bethought him of young Dill, of whom, it is only truth to confess, young Conyers had forgotten everything. "I took time by the forelock, Fred, about that affair," said he, "and I trust I have freed you from all embarrassment about it."

"As how, sir?" asked Conyers, half in pique.

"When I missed you at the 'Fisherman's Home,' I set off to pay the doctor a visit, and a very charming visit it turned out; a better pigeon-pie I never ate, nor a prettier girl than the maker of it would I ask to meet with. We became great friends, talked of everything, from love at first sight to bone spavins, and found that we agreed to a miracle. I don't think I ever saw a girl before who suited me so perfectly in all her notions. She gave me a hint about what they call 'mouth lameness' our Vet would give his eye for. Well, to come back to her brother,—a dull dog, I take it, though I have not seen him,—I said, 'Don't let him go to India, they 've lots of clever fellows out there; pack him off to Australia; send him to New Zealand.' And when she interrupted me, 'But young Mr. Conyers insisted,—he would have it so; his father is to make Tom's fortune, and to send him back as rich as a Begum,' I said, 'He has fallen in love with you, Miss Polly, that's the fact, and lost his head altogether; and I don't wonder at it, for here am I, close upon forty-eight,—I might have said forty-nine, but no matter,—close upon forty-eight, and I 'm in the same book!' Yes, if it was the sister, *vice* the brother, who wanted to make a fortune in India, I almost think I could say, 'Come and share mine!'"

"But I don't exactly understand. Am I to believe that they wish Tom to be off—to refuse my offer—and that the rejection comes from them?"

"No, not exactly. I said it was a bad spec, that you had taken a far too sanguine view of the whole thing, and that as I was an old soldier, and knew more of the world,—that is to say, had met a great many more hard rubs and disappointments,—my advice was, not to risk it. 'Young Conyers,' said I, 'will do all that he has promised to the letter. You may rely upon every word that he has ever uttered. But bear in mind that he's only a mortal man; he's not one of those heathen gods who used to make fellows invincible in a battle, or smuggle them off in a cloud, out of the way of demons, or duns, or whatever difficulties beset them. He might die, his father might die, any of us might die.' Yes, by Jove! there's nothing so uncertain as life, except the Horse Guards.' And putting one thing with another, Miss Polly,' said I, 'tell him to stay where he is,'—open a shop at home, or go to one of the colonies,—Heligoland, for instance, a charming spot for the bathing-season."

"And she, what did she say?"

"May I be cashiered if I remember! I never do remember very clearly what any one says. Where I am much interested on my own side, I have no time for the other fellow's arguments. But I know if she was n't convinced she ought to have been. I put the thing beyond a question, and I made her cry."

"Made her cry!"

"Not cry,—that is, she did not blubber; but she looked glassy about the lids, and turned away her head. But to be sure we were parting,—a rather soft bit of parting, too,—and I said something about my coming back with a wooden leg, and she said, 'No! have it of cork, they make them so cleverly now.' And I was going to say something more, when a confounded old half-pay Major came up and interrupted us, and—and, in fact, there it rests."

"I 'm not at all easy in mind as to this affair. I mean, I don't like how I stand in it."

"But you stand out of it,—out of it altogether! Can't you imagine that your father may have quite enough cares of his own to occupy him without needing the embarrassment of looking after this bumpkin, who, for aught you know, might repay very badly all the interest taken in him? If it had been the girl,—if it had been

Polly—" "I own frankly," said Conyers, tartly, "it did not occur to me to make such an offer to *her!*"

"Faith! then, Master Fred, I was deuced near doing it,—so near, that when I came away I scarcely knew whether I had or had not done so."

"Well, sir, there is only an hour's drive on a good road required to repair the omission."

"That's true, Fred,—that's true; but have you never, by an accident, chanced to come up with a stunning fence,—a regular rasper that you took in a fly a few days before with the dogs, and as you looked at the place, have you not said, 'What on earth persuaded me to ride at *that?*'"

"Which means, sir, that your cold-blooded reflections are against the project?"

"Not exactly that, either," said he, in a sort of confusion; "but when a man speculates on doing something for which the first step must be an explanation to this fellow, a half apology to that,—with a whimpering kind of entreaty not to be judged hastily, not to be condemned unheard, not to be set down as an old fool who couldn't stand the fire of a pair of bright eyes,—I say when it comes to this, he ought to feel that his best safeguard is his own misgiving!"

"If I do not agree with you, sir, it is because I incline to follow my own lead, and care very little for what the world says of it."

"Don't believe a word of that, Fred; it's all brag,—all nonsense! The very effrontery with which you fancy you are braving public opinion is only Dutch courage. What each of us in his heart thinks of himself is only the reflex of the world's estimate of him; at least, what he imagines it to be. Now, for my own part, I'd rather ride up to a battery in full fire than I'd sit down and write to my old aunt Dorothy Hunter a formal letter announcing my approaching marriage, telling her that the lady of my choice was twenty or thereabouts, not to add that her family name was Dill. Believe me, Fred, that if you want the concentrated essence of public opinion, you have only to do something which shall irritate and astonish the half-dozen people with whom you live in intimacy. Won't they remind you about the mortgages on your lands and the gray in your whiskers, that last loan you raised from Solomon Hymans, and that front tooth you got replaced by Cartwright, though it was the week before they told you you were a miracle of order and good management, and actually looking younger than you did five years ago! You're not minding me, Fred,—not following me; you're thinking of your *protégé*, Tom Dill, and what he'll think and say of your desertion of him."

"You have hit it, sir. It was exactly what I was asking myself."

"Well, if nothing better offers, tell him to get himself in readiness, and come out with me. I cannot make him a Rajah, nor even a Zemindar; but I'll stick him into a regimental surgeoncy, and leave him to fashion out his own future. He must look sharp, however, and lose no time. The 'Ganges' is getting ready in all haste, and will be round at Portsmouth by the 8th, and we expect to sail on the 12th or 13th at furthest."

"I'll write to him to-day. I'll write this moment."

"Add a word of remembrance on my part to the sister, and tell bumpkin to supply himself with no end of letters, recommendatory and laudatory, to muzzle our Medical Board at Calcutta, and lots of light clothing, and all the torturing instruments he 'll need, and a large stock of good humor, for he'll be chaffed unmercifully all the voyage." And, with these comprehensive directions, the Colonel concluded his counsels, and bustled away to look after his own personal interests.

Fred Conyers was not over-pleased with the task assigned him. The part he liked to fill in life, and, indeed, that which he had usually performed, was the Benefactor and the Patron, and it was but an ungracious office for him to have to cut the wings and disfigure the plumage of his generosity. He made two, three, four attempts at conveying his intentions, but with none was he satisfied; so he ended by simply saying, "I have something of importance to tell you, and which, not being altogether pleasant, it will be better to say than to write; so I have to beg you will come up here at once, and see me." Scarcely was this letter sealed and addressed than he bethought him of the awkwardness of presenting Tom to his brother-officers, or the still greater indecorum of not presenting him. "How shall I ask him to the mess, with the certainty of all the impertinences he will be exposed to? — and what pretext have I for not offering him the ordinary attention shown to every stranger?" He was, in fact, wincing under that public opinion he had only a few moments before declared he could afford to despise. "No," said he, "I have no right to expose poor Tom to this. I 'll drive over myself to the village, and if any advice or counsel be needed, he will be amongst those who can aid him."

He ordered his servant to harness his handsome roan, a thoroughbred of surpassing style and action, to the dog-cart, — not over-sorry to astonish his friend Tom by the splendor of a turn-out that had won the suffrages of Tattersall's, — and prepared for his mission to Inistioge.

Was it with the same intention of "astonishing" Tom Dill that Conyers bestowed such unusual attention upon his dress? At his first visit to the "Fisherman's Home" he had worn the homely shooting-jacket and felt hat which, however comfortable and conventional, do not always redound to the advantage of the wearer, or, if they do, it is by something, perhaps, in the contrast presented to his ordinary appearance, and the impression ingeniously insinuated that he is one so unmistakably a gentleman, no travesty of costume can efface the stamp.

It was in this garb Polly had seen him, and if Polly Dill had been a duchess it was in some such garb she would have been accustomed to see her brother or her cousin some six out of every seven mornings of the week; but Polly was not a duchess: she was the daughter of a village doctor, and might, not impossibly, have acquired a very erroneous estimate of his real pretensions from having beheld him thus attired. It was, therefore, entirely by a consideration for her ignorance of the world and its ways that he determined to enlighten her.

At the time of which I am writing, the dress of the British army was a favorite study with that Prince whose taste, however questionable, never exposed him to censure on grounds of over-simplicity and plainness. As the Colonel of the regiment Conyers belonged to, he had bestowed upon his own especial corps an unusual degree of splendor in equipment, and amongst other extravagances had given them an almost boundless liberty of combining different details of dress. Availing himself of this privilege, our young Lieutenant invented a costume which, however unmilitary and irregular, was not deficient in becomingness. Under a plain blue jacket very sparingly braided he wore the rich scarlet waistcoat, all slashed with gold, they had introduced at their mess. A simple foraging-cap and overalls, seamed with a thin gold line, made up a dress that might have passed for the easy costume of the barrack-yard, while, in reality, it was eminently suited to set off the wearer.

Am I to confess that he looked at himself in the glass with very considerable satisfaction, and muttered, as he turned away, "Yes, Miss Polly, this is in better style than that Quakerish drab livery you saw me last in, and I have little doubt that you 'll think so!"

"Is this our best harness, Holt?"

"Yes, sir."

"All right!"

CHAPTER XXIV.

CONYERS MAKES A MORNING CALL

When Conyers, to the astonishment and wonder of an admiring village public, drove his seventeen-hand-high roan into the market square of Inistioge, he learned that all of the doctor's family were from home except Mrs. Dill. Indeed, he saw the respectable lady at the window with a book in her hand, from which not all the noise and clatter of his arrival for one moment diverted her. Though not especially anxious to attract her attention, he was half piqued at her show of indifference. A dog-cart by Adams and a thoroughbred like Boanerges were, after all, worth a glance at. Little did he know what a competitor be had in that much-thumbed old volume, whose quaintly told miseries were to her as her own sorrows. Could he have assembled underneath that window all the glories of a Derby Day, Mr. Richardson's "Clarissa" would have beaten the field. While he occupied himself in dexterously tapping the flies from his horse with the fine extremity of his whip, and thus necessitating that amount of impatience which made the spirited animal stamp and champ his bit, the old lady read on undisturbed.

"Ask at what hour the doctor will be at home, Holt," cried he, peevishly.

"Not till to-morrow, sir; he has gone to Castle Durrow."

"And Miss Dill, is she not in the house?"

"No, sir; she has gone down to the 'Fisherman's Home' to look after the garden,—the family having left that place this morning."

After a few minutes' reflection, Conyers ordered his servant to put up the horse at the inn, and wait for him there; and then engaging a "cot," he set out for the "Fisherman's Home." "After having come so far, it would be absurd to go back without doing something in this business," thought he. "Polly, besides, is the brains carrier of these people. The matter would be referred to her; and why should I not go at once, and directly address her myself? With her womanly tact, too, she will see that for any reserve in my manner there must be a corresponding reason, and she'll not press me with awkward questions or painful inquiries, as the underbred brother might do. It will be enough when I intimate to her that my plan is not so practicable as when I first projected it." He reassured himself with a variety of reasonings of this stamp, which had the double effect of convincing his own mind and elevating Miss Polly in his estimation. There is a very subtle self-flattery in believing that the true order of person to deal with us—to understand and appreciate us—is one possessed of considerable ability united with the very finest sensibility. Thus dreaming and "mooning," he reached the "Fisherman's Home."

The air of desertion struck him even as he landed; and is there not some secret magic in the vicinity of life, of living people, which gives the soul to the dwelling-place? Have we to more than cross the threshold of the forsaken house to feel its desertion,—to know that our echoing step will track us along stair and corridor, and that through the thin streaks of light between the shutters phantoms of the absent will flit or hover, while the dimly descried objects of the room will bring memories of bright mornings and of happy eves? It is strange to measure the sadness of this effect upon us when caused even by the aspect of houses which we frequented not as friends but mere visitors; just as the sight of death thrills us, even though we had not loved the departed in his lifetime. But so it is: there is unutterable bitterness attached to the past, and there is no such sorrow as over the bygone!

All about the little cottage was silent and desolate; even the shrill peacock, so wont to announce the coming stranger with his cry, sat voiceless and brooding on a branch; and except the dull flow of the river, not a sound was heard. After tapping lightly at the door and peering through the partially closed shutters, Conyers turned towards the garden at the back, passing as he went his favorite seat under the great sycamore-tree. It was not a widely separated "long ago" since he had sat there, and yet how different had life become to him in the interval! With what a protective air he had talked to poor Tom on that spot,—how princely were the promises of his patronage, yet not exaggerated beyond his conscious power of performance! He hurried on, and came to the little wicket of the garden; it was open, and he passed in. A spade in some fresh-turned earth showed where some one had recently been at work, but still, as he went, he could find none. Alley after alley did he traverse, but to no purpose; and at last, in his ramblings, he came to a little copse which separated the main garden from a small flower-plat, known as Miss Dinah's, and on which the windows of her own little sitting-room opened. He had but seen this spot from the windows, and never entered it; indeed, it was a sort of sacred enclosure, within which the profane step of man was not often permitted to intrude. Nor was Conyers without a sting of self-reproach as he now passed in. He had not gone many steps when the reason of the seclusion seemed revealed to him. It was a small obelisk of white marble under a large willow-tree, bearing for inscription on its side, "To the Memory of George Barrington, the Truehearted, the Truthful, and the Brave, killed on the 19th February, 18—, at Agra, in the East Indies."

How strange that he should be standing there beside the tomb of his father's dearest friend, his more than brother! That George who shared his joys and perils, the comrade of his heart! No two men had ever lived in closer bonds of affection, and yet somehow of all that love he had never heard his father speak, nor of the terrible fate that befell his friend had one syllable escaped him. "Who knows if friendships ever survive early manhood?" said Fred, bitterly, as he sat himself down at the base of the monument: "and yet might not this same George Barrington, had he lived, been of priceless value to my father now? Is it not some such manly affection, such generous devotion as his, that he may stand in need of?" Thus thinking, his imagination led him over the wide sea to that far-distant land of his childhood, and scenes of vast arid plains and far-away mountains, and wild ghauts, and barren-looking nullahs, intersected with yellow, sluggish streams, on whose muddy shore the alligator basked, rose before him, contrasted with the gorgeous splendors of retinue and the glittering host of gold-adorned followers. It was in a vision of grand but dreary despotism, power almost limitless, but without one ray of enjoyment, that he lost himself and let the hours glide by. At length, as though dreamily, he thought he was listening to some faint but delicious music; sounds seemed to come floating towards him through the leaves, as if meant to steep him in a continued languor, and imparted a strange half-fear that he was under a spell. With an effort he aroused himself and sprang to his legs; and now he could plainly perceive that the sounds came through an open window, where a low but exquisitely sweet voice was singing to the accompaniment of a piano. The melody was sad and plaintive; the very words came dropping slowly, like the drops of a distilled grief; and they sank into his heart with a feeling of actual poignancy, for they were as though steeped in sorrow. When of a sudden the singer ceased, the hands ran boldly, almost wildly, over the keys; one, two, three great massive chords were struck, and then, in a strain joyous as the skylark, the clear voice carolled forth with,—

"But why should we mourn for the grief of the morrow?
Who knows in what frame it may find us?
Meeker, perhaps, to bend under our sorrow,
Or more boldly to fling it behind us."

And then, with a loud bang, the piano was closed, and Polly Dill, swinging her garden hat by its ribbon, bounded forth into the walk, calling for her terrier, Scratch, to follow.

"Mr. Conyers here!" cried she, in astonishment. "What miracle could have led you to this spot?"

"To meet you."

"To meet me!"

"With no other object. I came from Kilkenny this morning expressly to see you, and learning at your house that you had come on here, I followed. You still look astonished,—incredulous—"

"Oh, no; not incredulous, but very much astonished. I am, it is true, sufficiently accustomed to find myself in request in my own narrow home circle, but that any one out of it should come three yards—not to say three miles—to speak to me, is, I own, very new and very strange."

"Is not this profession of humility a little—a very little—bit of exaggeration, Miss Dill?"

"Is not the remark you have made on it a little—a very little—bit of a liberty, Mr. Conyers?"

So little was he prepared for this retort that he flushed up to his forehead, and for an instant was unable to recover himself: meanwhile, she was busy in rescuing Scratch from a long bramble that had most uncomfortably associated itself with his tail, in gratitude for which service the beast jumped up on her with all the uncouth activity of his race.

"He at least, Miss Dill, can take liberties unrebuked," said Conyers, with irritation.

"We are very old friends, sir, and understand each other's humors, not to say that Scratch knows well he'd be tied up if he were to transgress."

Conyers smiled; an almost irresistible desire to utter a smartness crossed his mind, and he found it all but impossible to resist saying something about accepting the bonds if he could but accomplish the transgression; but he bethought in time how unequal the war of banter would be between them, and it was with a quiet gravity he began: "I came to speak to you about Tom—"

"Why, is that not all off? Colonel Hunter represented the matter so forcibly to my father, put all the difficulties so clearly before him, that I actually wrote to my brother, who had started for Dublin, begging him on no account to hasten the day of his examination, but to come home and devote himself carefully to the task of preparation."

"It is true, the Colonel never regarded the project as I did, and saw obstacles to its success which never occurred to me; with all that, however, he never convinced me I was wrong."

"Perhaps not always an easy thing to do," said she, dryly.

"Indeed! You seem to have formed a strong opinion on the score of my firmness."

"I was expecting you to say obstinacy," said she, laughing, "and was half prepared with a most abject retractation. At all events, I was aware that you did not give way."

"And is the quality such a bad one?"

"Just as a wind may be said to be a good or a bad one; due west, for instance, would be very unfavorable if you were bound to New York."

It was the second time he had angled for a compliment, and failed; and he walked along at her side, fretful and discontented. "I begin to suspect," said he, at last, "that the Colonel was far more eager to make himself agreeable here than to give fair play to my reasons."

"He was delightful, if you mean that; he possesses the inestimable boon of good spirits, which is the next thing to a good heart."

"You don't like depressed people, then?"

"I won't say I dislike, but I dread them. The dear friends who go about with such histories of misfortune and gloomy reflections on every one's conduct always give me the idea of a person who should carry with him a watering-pot to sprinkle his friends in this Irish climate, where it rains ten months out of the twelve. There is a deal to like in life,—a deal to enjoy, as well as a deal to see and to do; and the spirit which we bring to it is even of more moment than the incidents that befall us."

"That was the burden of your song awhile ago," said he, smiling; "could I persuade you to sing it again?"

"What are you dreaming of, Mr. Conyers? Is not this meeting here—this strolling about a garden with a young gentleman, a Hussar!—compromising enough, not to ask me to sit down at a piano and sing for him? Indeed, the only relief my conscience gives me for the imprudence of this interview is the seeing how miserable it makes *you*."

"Miserable!—makes *me* miserable!"

"Well, embarrassed,—uncomfortable,—ill at ease; I don't care for the word. You came here to say a variety of things, and you don't like to say them. You are balked in certain very kind intentions towards us, and you don't know how very little of even intended good nature has befallen us in life to make us deeply your debtor for the mere project. Why, your very notice of poor Tom has done more to raise him in his own esteem and disgust him with low associates than all the wise arguments of all his family. There, now, if you have not done us all the good you meant, be satisfied with what you really have done."

"This is very far short of what I intended."

"Of course it is; but do not dwell upon that. I have a great stock of very fine intentions, too, but I shall not be in the least discouraged if I find them take wing and leave me."

"What would you do then?"

"Raise another brood. They tell us that if one seed of every million of acorns should grow to be a tree, all Europe would be a dense forest within a century. Take heart, therefore, about scattered projects; fully their share of them come to maturity. Oh dear! what a dreary sigh you gave! Don't you imagine yourself very unhappy?"

"If I did, I'd scarcely come to you for sympathy, certainly," said he, with a half-bitter smile.

"You are quite right there; not but that I could really condole with some of what I opine are your great afflictions: for instance, I could bestow very honest grief on that splint that your charger has just thrown out on his back tendon; I could even cry over the threatened blindness of that splendid steeple-chaser; but I 'd not fret about the way your pelisse was braided, nor because your new phaeton made so much noise with the axles."

"By the way," said Conyers, "I have such a horse to show you! He is in the village. Might I drive him up here? Would you allow me to take you back?"

"Not on any account, sir! I have grave misgivings about talking to you so long here, and I am mainly reconciled by remembering how disagreeable I have proved myself."

"How I wish I had your good spirits!"

"Why don't you rather wish for my fortunate lot in life,—so secure from casualties, so surrounded with life's comforts, so certain to attach to it consideration and respect? Take my word for it, Mr. Conyers, your own position is not utterly wretched; it is rather a nice thing to be a Lieutenant of Hussars, with good health, a good fortune, and a fair promise of mustachios. There, now, enough of impertinence for one day. I have a deal to do, and you 'll not help me to do it. I have a whole tulip-bed to transplant, and several trees to remove, and a new walk to plan through the beech shrubbery, not to speak of a change of domicile for the pigs,—if such creatures can be spoken of in your presence. Only think, three o'clock, and that weary Darby not got back from his dinner! has it ever occurred to you to wonder at the interminable time people can devote to a meal of potatoes?"

"I cannot say that I have thought upon the matter."

"Pray do so, then; divide the matter, as a German would, into all its 'Bearbeitungen,' and consider it ethnologically, esculently, and aesthetically, and you'll be surprised how puzzled you 'll be! Meanwhile, would you do me a favor?—I mean a great favor."

"Of course I will; only say what it is."

"Well; but I 'm about to ask more than you suspect."

"I do not retract. I am ready."

"What I want, then, is that you should wheel that barrow-ful of mould as far as the melon-bed. I 'd have done it myself if you had not been here."

With a seriousness which cost him no small effort to maintain, Conyers addressed himself at once to the task; and she walked along at his side, with a rake over her shoulder, talking with the same cool unconcern she would have bestowed on Darby.

"I have often told Miss Barrington," said she, "that our rock melons were finer than hers, because we used a peculiar composite earth, into which ash bark and soot entered,—what you are wheeling now, in fact, however hurtful it may be to your feelings. There! upset it exactly on that spot; and now let me see if you are equally handy with a spade."

"I should like to know what my wages are to be after all this," said he, as he spread the mould over the bed.

"We give boys about eightpence a day."

"Boys! what do you mean by boys?"

"Everything that is not married is boy in Ireland; so don't be angry, or I 'll send you off. Pick up those stones, and throw these dock-weeds to one side."

"You 'll send me a melon, at least, of my own raising, won't you?"

"I won't promise; Heaven knows where you'll be—where I 'll be, by that time! Would *you* like to pledge yourself to anything on the day the ripe fruit shall glow between those pale leaves?"

"Perhaps I might," said he, stealing a half-tender glance towards her.

A USEFUL HAND

"Well, I would not," said she, looking him full and steadfastly in the face.

"Then that means you never cared very much for any one?"

"If I remember aright, you were engaged as a gardener, not as father confessor. Now, you are really not very expert at the former; but you 'll make sad work of the latter."

"You have not a very exalted notion of my tact, Miss Dill."

"I don't know,—I'm not sure; I suspect you have at least what the French call 'good dispositions.' You took to your wheelbarrow very nicely, and you tried to dig—as little like a gentleman as need be."

"Well, if this does not bate Banagher, my name is n't Darby!" exclaimed a rough voice, and a hearty laugh followed his words. "By my conscience, Miss Polly, it's only yerself could do it; and it's truth they say of you, you 'd get fun out of an archdaycon!"

Conyers flung away his spade, and shook the mould from his boots in irritation.

"Come, don't be cross," said she, slipping her arm within his, and leading him away; "don't spoil a very pleasant little adventure by ill humor. If these melons come to good, they shall be called after you. You know that a Duke of Montmartre gave his name to a gooseberry; so be good, and, like him, you shall be immortal."

"I should like very much to know one thing," said he, thoughtfully.

"And what may that be?"

"I 'd like to know,—are you ever serious?"

"Not what you would call serious, perhaps; but I 'm very much in earnest, if that will do. That delightful Saxon habit of treating all trifles with solemnity I have no taste for. I'm aware it constitutes that great idol of English veneration, Respectability; but we have not got that sort of thing here. Perhaps the climate is too moist for it."

"I 'm not a bit surprised that the Colonel fell in love with you," blurted he out, with a frank abruptness.

"And did he,—oh, really did he?"

"Is the news so very agreeable, then?"

"Of course it is. I 'd give anything for such a conquest. There 's no glory in capturing one of those calf elephants who walk into the snare out of pure stupidity; but to catch an old experienced creature who has been hunted scores of times, and knows every scheme and artifice, every bait and every pitfall, there is a real triumph in that."

"Do I represent one of the calf elephants, then?"

"I cannot think so. I have seen no evidence of your capture—not to add, nor any presumption of my own—to engage in such a pursuit. My dear Mr. Conyers," said she, seriously, "you have shown so much real kindness to the brother, you would not, I am certain, detract from it by one word which could offend the sister. We have been the best of friends up to this; let us part so."

The sudden assumption of gravity in this speech seemed to disconcert him so much that he made no answer, but strolled along at her side, thoughtful and silent.

"What are you thinking of?" said she, at last.

"I was just thinking," said he, "that by the time I have reached my quarters, and begin to con over what I have accomplished by this same visit of mine, I 'll be not a little puzzled to say what it is."

"Perhaps I can help you. First of all, tell me what was your object in coming."

"Chiefly to talk about Tom."

"Well, we have done so. We have discussed the matter, and are fully agreed it is better he should not go to India, but stay at home here and follow his profession, like his father."

"But have I said nothing about Hunter's offer?"

"Not a word; what is it?"

"How stupid of me; what could I have been thinking of all this time?"

"Heaven knows; but what was the offer you allude to?"

"It was this: that if Tom would make haste and get his diploma or his license, or whatever it is, at once, and collect all sorts of testimonials as to his abilities and what not, that he'd take him out with him and get him an assistant-surgeoncy in a regiment, and in time, perhaps, a staff-appointment."

"I'm not very certain that Tom could obtain his diploma at once. I'm quite sure he could n't get any of those certificates you speak of. First of all, because he does not possess these same abilities you mention, nor, if he did, is there any to vouch for them. We are very humble people, Mr. Conyers, with a village for our world; and we contemplate a far-away country—India, for instance—pretty much as we should do Mars or the Pole-star."

"As to that, Bengal is more come-at-able than the Great Bear," said he, laughing.

"For you, perhaps, not for us. There is nothing more common in people's mouths than go to New Zealand or Swan River, or some far-away island in the Pacific, and make your fortune!—just as if every new and barbarous land was a sort of Aladdin's cave, where each might fill his pockets with gems and come out rich for life. But reflect a little. First, there is an outfit; next, there is a voyage; thirdly, there is need of a certain subsistence in the new country before plans can be matured to render it profitable. After all these come a host of requirements,—of courage, and energy, and patience, and ingenuity, and personal strength, and endurance, not to speak of the constitution of a horse, and some have said, the heartlessness of an ogre. *My* counsel to Tom would be, get the 'Arabian Nights' out of your head, forget the great Caliph Conyers and all his promises, stay where you are, and be a village apothecary."

These words were uttered in a very quiet and matter-of-fact way, but they wounded Conyers more than the accents of passion. He was angry at the cold realistic turn of a mind so devoid of all heroism; he was annoyed at the half-implied superiority a keener view of life than his own seemed to assert; and he was vexed at being treated as a well-meaning but very inconsiderate and inexperienced young gentleman.

"Am I to take this as a refusal," said he, stiffly; "am I to tell Colonel Hunter that your brother does not accept his offer?"

"If it depended on me,—yes; but it does not. I 'll write to-night and tell Tom the generous project that awaits him; he shall decide for himself."

"I know Hunter will be annoyed; he'll think it was through some bungling mismanagement of mine his plan has failed; he 'll be certain to say, If it was I myself bad spoken toner—"

"Well, there's no harm in letting him think so," said she, laughing. "Tell him I think him charming, that I hope he 'll have a delightful voyage and a most prosperous career after it, that I intend to read the Indian columns in the newspaper from this day out, and will always picture him to my mind as seated in the grandest of howdabs on the very tallest of elephants, humming 'Rule Britannia' up the slopes of the Himalaya, and as the penny-a-liners say, extending the blessings of the English rule in India." She gave her hand to him, made a little salutation,—half bow, half courtesy,—and, saying "Good-bye," turned back into the shrubbery and left him.

He hesitated,—almost turned to follow her; waited a second or two more, and then, with an impatient toss of his head, walked briskly to the river-side and jumped into his boat. It was a sulky face that he wore, and a sulky spirit was at work within him. There is no greater discontent than that of him who cannot define the chagrin that consumes him. In reality, he was angry with himself, but he turned the whole force of his displeasure upon her.

"I suppose she is clever. I 'm no judge of that sort of thing; but, for my own part, I'd rather see her more womanly, more delicate. She has not a bit of heart, that's quite clear; nor, with all her affectations, does she pretend it." These were his first meditations, and after them he lit a cigar and smoked it. The weed was a good one; the evening was beautifully calm and soft, and the river scenery looked its very best. He tried to think of a dozen things: he imagined, for instance, what a picturesque thing a boat-race would be in such a spot; he fancied he saw a swift gig sweep round the point and head up the stream; he caught sight of a little open in the trees with a background of dark rock, and he thought what a place for a cottage. But whether it was the "match" or the "chalet" that occupied him, Polly Dill was a figure in the picture; and he muttered unconsciously, "How pretty she is, what a deal of expression those gray-blue eyes possess! She's as active as a fawn, and to the full as graceful. Fancy her an Earl's daughter; give her station and all the advantages station will bring with it,—what a girl it would be! Not that she'd ever have a heart; I'm certain of that. She's as worldly—as worldly as—" The exact similitude did not occur; but he flung the end of his cigar into the river instead, and sat brooding mournfully for the rest of the way.

CHAPTER XXV.

DUBLIN REVISITED

The first stage of the Barringtons' journey was Dublin. They alighted at Reynolds's Hotel, in Old Dominick Street, the once favorite resort of country celebrities. The house, it is true, was there, but Reynolds had long left for a land where there is but one summons and one reckoning; even the old waiter, Foster, whom people believed immortal, was gone; and save some cumbrous old pieces of furniture,—barbarous relics of bad taste in mahogany,—nothing recalled the past. The bar, where once on a time the "Beaux" and "Bloods" had gathered to exchange the smart things of the House or the hunting-field, was now a dingy little receptacle for umbrellas and overcoats, with a rickety case crammed full of unacknowledged and unclaimed letters, announcements of cattle fairs, and bills of houses to let. Decay and neglect were on everything, and the grim little waiter who ushered them upstairs seemed as much astonished at their coming as were they themselves with all they saw. It was not for some time, nor without searching inquiry, that Miss Dinah discovered that the tide of popular favor had long since retired from this quarter, and left it a mere barren strand, wreck-strewn and deserted. The house where formerly the great squire held his revels had now fallen to be the resort of the traveller by canal-boat, the cattle salesman, or the priest. While she by an ingenious cross-examination was eliciting these details, Barrington had taken a walk through the city to revisit old scenes and revive old memories. One needs not to be as old as Peter Barrington to have gone through this process and experienced all its pain. Unquestionably, every city of Europe has made within such a period as five-and-thirty or forty years immense strides of improvement. Wider and finer streets, more commodious thoroughfares, better bridges, lighter areas, more brilliant shops, strike one on every hand; while the more permanent monuments of architecture are more cleanly, more orderly, and more cared for than of old. We see these things with astonishment and admiration at first, and then there comes a pang of painful regret,—not for the old dark alley and the crooked street, or the tumbling arch of long ago,—but for the time when they were there, for the time when they entered into our daily life, when with them were associated friends long lost sight of, and scenes dimly fading away from memory. It is for our youth, for the glorious spring and elasticity of our once high-hearted spirit, of our lives so free of care, of our days undarkened by a serious sorrow,—it is for these we mourn, and to our eyes at such moments the spacious street is but a desert, and the splendid monument but a whitened sepulchre!

"I don't think I ever had a sadder walk in my life, Dinah," said Peter Barrington, with a weary sigh. "'Till I got into the courts of the College, I never chanced upon a spot that looked as I had left it. There, indeed, was the quaint old square as of old, and the great bell—bless it for its kind voice!—was ringing out a solemn call to something, that shook the window-frames, and made the very air tremulous; and a pale-faced student or two hurried past, and those centurions in the helmets,—ancient porters or Senior Fellows,—I forget which,—stood in a little knot to stare at me. That, indeed, was like old times, Dinah, and my heart grew very full with the memory. After that I strolled down to the Four Courts. I knew you 'd laugh, Dinah. I knew well you 'd say, 'Was there nothing going on in the King's Bench or the Common Pleas?' Well, there was only a Revenue case, my dear, but it was interesting, very interesting; and there was my old friend Harry Bushe sitting as the Judge. He saw me, and sent round the tipstaff to have me come up and sit on the bench with him, and we had many a pleasant remembrance of old times—as the cross-examination went on—between us, and I promised to dine with him on Saturday."

"And on Saturday we will dine at Antwerp, brother, if I know anything of myself."

"Sure enough, sister, I forgot all about it Well, well, where could my head have been?"

"Pretty much where you have worn it of late years, Peter Barrington. And what of Withering? Did you see him?"

"No, Dinah, he was attending a Privy Council; but I got his address, and I mean to go over to see him after dinner."

"Please to bear in mind that you are not to form any engagements, Peter,—we leave this to-morrow evening by the packet,—if it was the Viceroy himself that wanted your company."

"Of course, dear, I never thought of such a thing. It was only when Harry said, 'You 'll be glad to meet Casey and Burrowes, and a few others of the old set,' I clean forgot everything of the present, and only lived in the long-past time, when life really was a very jolly thing."

"How did you find your friend looking?"

"Old, Dinah, very old! That vile wig has, perhaps, something to say to it; and being a judge, too, gives a sternness to the mouth and a haughty imperiousness to the brow. It spoils Harry; utterly spoils that laughing blue eye, and that fine rich humor that used to play about his lips."

"Which *did*, you ought to say,—which did some forty years ago. What are you laughing at, Peter? What is it amuses you so highly?"

"It was a charge of O'Grady's, that Harry told me,—a charge to one of those petty juries that, he says, never will go right, do what you may. The case was a young student of Trinity, tried for a theft, and whose defence was only by witnesses to character, and O'Grady said, 'Gentlemen of the jury, the issue before you is easy enough. This is a young gentleman of pleasing manners and the very best connections, who stole a pair of silk stockings, and you will find accordingly.' And what d'ye think, Dinah? They acquitted him, just out of compliment to the Bench."

"I declare, brother Peter, such a story inspires any other sentiment than mirth to me."

"I laughed at it till my sides ached," said he, wiping his eyes. "I took a peep into the Chancery Court and saw O'Connell, who has plenty of business, they tell me. He was in some altercation with the Court. Lord Manners was scowling at him, as if he hated him. I hear that no day passes without some angry passage between them."

"And is it of these jangling, quarrelsome, irritable, and insolent men your ideal of agreeable society is made up, brother Peter?"

"Not a doubt of it, Dinah. All these displays are briefed to them. They cannot help investing in their client's cause the fervor of their natures, simply because they are human; but they know how to leave all the acrimony of the contest in the wig-box, when they undress and come back to their homes,—the most genial, hearty, and frank fellows in all the world. If human nature were all bad, sister, he who saw it closest would be, I own, most like to catch its corruption, but it is not so, far from it. Every day and every hour reveals something to make a man right proud of his fellow-men."

Miss Barrington curtly recalled her brother from these speculations to the practical details of their journey, reminding him of much that he had to consult Withering upon, and many questions of importance to put to him. Thoroughly impressed with the perils of a journey abroad, she conjured up a vast array of imaginary difficulties, and demanded special instructions how each of them was to be met. Had poor Peter been—what he certainly was not—a most accomplished casuist, he might have been puzzled by the ingenious complexity of some of those embarrassments. As it was, like a man in the labyrinth, too much bewildered to attempt escape, he sat down in a dogged insensibility, and actually heard nothing.

"Are you minding me, Peter?" asked she, fretfully, at last; "are you paying attention to what I am saying?"

"Of course I am, Dinah dear; I'm listening with all ears."

"What was it, then, that I last remarked? What was the subject to which I asked your attention?"

Thus suddenly called on, poor Peter started and rubbed his forehead. Vague shadows of passport people, and custom-house folk, and waiters, and money-changers, and brigands; insolent postilions, importunate beggars, cheating innkeepers, and insinuating swindlers were passing through his head, with innumerable incidents of the road; and, trying to catch a clew at random, he said, "It was to ask the Envoy, her Majesty's Minister at Brussels, about a washerwoman who would not tear off my shirt buttons—eh, Dinah? wasn't that it?"

"You are insupportable, Peter Barrington," said she, rising in anger. "I believe that insensibility like this is not to be paralleled!" and she left the room in wrath.

Peter looked at his watch, and was glad to see it was past eight o'clock, and about the hour he meant for his visit to Withering. He set out accordingly, not, indeed, quite satisfied with the way he had lately acquitted himself, but consoled by thinking that Dinah rarely went back of a morning on the dereliction of the evening before, so that they should meet good friends as ever at the breakfast-table. Withering was at home, but a most discreet-looking butler intimated that he had dined that day *tête-à-tête* with a gentleman, and had left orders not to be disturbed on any pretext "Could you not at least, send in my name?" said Barrington; "I am a very old friend of your master's, whom he would regret not having seen." A little persuasion aided by an argument that butlers usually succumb to succeeded, and before Peter believed that his card could have reached its destination, his friend was warmly shaking him by both hands, as he hurried him into the dinner-room.

"You don't know what an opportune visit you have made me, Barrington," said he; "but first, to present you to my friend, Captain Stapylton—or Major— which is it?"

"Captain. This day week, the 'Gazette,' perhaps, may call me Major."

"Always a pleasure to me to meet a soldier, sir," said Barrington; "and I own to the weakness of saying, all the greater when a Dragoon. My own boy was a cavalryman."

"It was exactly of him we were talking," said Withering; "my friend here has had a long experience of India, and has frankly told me much I was totally ignorant of. From one thing to another we rambled on till we came to discuss our great suit with the Company, and Captain Stapylton assures me that we have never taken the right road in the case."

"Nay, I could hardly have had such presumption; I merely remarked, that without knowing India and its habits, you could scarcely be prepared to encounter the sort of testimony that would be opposed to you, or to benefit by what might tend greatly in your favor."

"Just so—continue," said Withering, who looked as though he had got an admirable witness on the table.

"I'm astonished to hear from the Attorney-General," resumed Stapylton, "that in a case of such magnitude as this you have never thought of sending out an efficient agent to India to collect evidence, sift testimony, and make personal inquiry as to the degree of credit to be accorded to many of the witnesses. This inquisitorial process is the very first step in every Oriental suit; you start at once, in fact, by sapping all the enemy's works,—countermining him everywhere."

"Listen, Barrington,—listen to this; it is all new to us."

"Everything being done by documentary evidence, there is a wide field for all the subtlety of the linguist; and Hindostanee has complexities enough to gratify the most inordinate appetite for quibble. A learned scholar—a Moonshee of erudition—is, therefore, the very first requisite, great care being taken to ascertain that he is not in the pay of the enemy."

"What rascals!" muttered Barrington.

"Very deep—very astute dogs, certainly, but perhaps not much more unprincipled than some fellows nearer home," continued the Captain, sipping his wine; "the great peculiarity of this class is, that while employing them in the most palpably knavish manner, and obtaining from them services bought at every sacrifice of honor, they expect all the deference due to the most umblemished integrity."

"I'd see them—I won't say where—first," broke out Barrington; "and I 'd see my lawsuit after them, if only to be won by their intervention."

"Remember, sir," said Stapylton, calmly, "that such are the weapons employed against you. That great Company does not, nor can it afford to, despise such auxiliaries. The East has its customs, and the natures of men are not light things to be smoothed down by conventionalities. Were you, for instance, to measure a testimony at Calcutta by the standard of Westminster Hall, you would probably do a great and grievous injustice."

"Just so," said Withering; "you are quite right there, and I have frequently found myself posed by evidence that I felt must be assailable. Go on, and tell my friend what you were mentioning to me before he came in."

"I am reluctant, sir," said Stapylton, modestly, "to obtrude upon you, in a matter of such grand importance as this, the mere gossip of a mess-table, but, as allusion has been made to it, I can scarcely refrain. It was when serving in another Presidency an officer of ours, who had been long in Bengal, one night entered upon the question of Colonel Barrington's claims. He quoted the words of an uncle—I think he said his uncle—who was a member of the Supreme Council, and said, 'Barrington ought to have known we never could have conceded this right of sovereignty, but he ought also to have known that we would rather have given ten lacs of rupees than have it litigated.'"

"Have you that gentleman's name?" asked Barrington, eagerly.

"I have; but the poor fellow is no more,—he was of that fatal expedition to Beloochistan eight years ago."

"You know our case, then, and what we claim?" asked Barrington.

"Just as every man who has served in India knows it,—popularly, vaguely. I know that Colonel Barrington was, as the adopted son of a Rajah, invested with supreme power, and only needed the ratification of Great Britain to establish a sovereignty; and I have heard"—he laid stress on the word "heard"—"that if it had not been for some allegation of plotting against the Company's government, he really might ultimately have obtained that sanction."

"Just what I have said over and over again?" burst in Barrington. "It was the worst of treachery that mined my poor boy."

"I have heard that also," said Stapylton, and with a degree of feeling and sympathy that made the old man's heart yearn towards him.

"How I wish you had known him!" said he, as he drew his hand over his eyes. "And do you know, sir," said he, warming, "that if I still follow up this suit, devoting to it the little that is left to me of life or fortune, that I do so less for any hope of gain than to place my poor boy before the world with his honor and fame unstained."

"My old friend does himself no more than justice there!" cried Withering.

"A noble object,—may you have all success in it!" said Stapylton. He paused, and then, in a tone of deeper feeling, added: "It will, perhaps, seem a great liberty, the favor I'm about to ask; but remember that, as a brother soldier with your son I have some slight claim to approach you. Will you allow me to offer you such knowledge as I possess of India, to aid your suit? Will you associate me, in fact, with your cause? No higher one could there be than the vindication of a brave man's honor."

"I thank you with all my heart and soul!" cried the old man, grasping his hand. "In my own name, and in that of my poor dear granddaughter, I thank you."

"Oh, then, Colonel Barrington has left a daughter? I was not aware of that," said Stapylton, with a certain coldness.

"And a daughter who knows no more of this suit than of our present discussion of it," said Withering.

In the frankness of a nature never happier than when indulging its own candor, Barrington told how it was to see and fetch back with him the same granddaughter he had left a spot he had not quitted for years. "She 's coming back to a very humble home, it is true; but if you, sir," said he, addressing Stapylton, "will not despise such lowly fare as a cottage can afford you, and would condescend to come and see us, you shall have the welcome that is due to one who wishes well to my boy's memory."

"And if you do," broke in Withering, "you'll see the prettiest cottage and the first hostess in Europe; and here 's to her health,—Miss Dinah Barrington!"

"I 'm not going to refuse that toast, though I have just passed the decanter," said Peter. "Here 's to the best of sisters!"

"Miss Barrington!" said Stapylton, with a courteous bow; and he drained his glass to the bottom.

"And that reminds me I promised to be back to tea with her," said Barrington; and renewing with all warmth his invitation to Stapylton, and cordially taking leave of his old friend, he left the house and hastened to his hotel.

"What a delightful evening I have passed, Dinah!" said he, cheerfully, as he entered.

"Which means that the Attorney-General gave you a grand review and sham fight of all the legal achievements of the term; but bear in mind, brother, there is no professional slang so odious to me as the lawyer's, and I positively hate a joke which cost six-and-eightpence, or even three-and-fourpence." <

"Nothing of this kind was there at all, Dinah! Withering had a friend with him, a very distinguished soldier, who had seen much Indian service, and entered with a most cordial warmth into poor George's case. He knew it,—as all India knows it, by report,—and frankly told us where our chief difficulties lay, and the important things we were neglecting."

"How generous! of a perfect stranger too!" said she, with a scarcely detectable tone of scorn.

"Not—so to say—an utter stranger, for George was known to him by reputation and character."

"And who is, I suppose I am to say, your friend, Peter?"

"Captain or Major Stapylton, of the Regent's Hussars?"

"Oh! I know him,—or, rather, I know of him."

"What and how, Dinah? I am very curious to hear this."

"Simply, that while young Conyers was at the cottage he showed me a letter from that gentleman, asking him in the Admiral's name, to Cobham, and containing, at the same time, a running criticism on the house and his guests far more flippant than creditable."

"Men do these things every day, Dinah, and there is no harm in it."

"That all depends upon whom the man is. The volatile gayety of a high-spirited nature, eager for effect and fond of a sensation, will lead to many an indiscretion; but very different from this is the well-weighed sarcasm of a more serious mind, who not only shots his gun home, but takes time to sight ere he fires it. I hear that Captain Stapylton is a grand, cold, thoughtful man, of five or six-and-thirty. Is that so?"

"Perhaps he may be. He 's a splendid fellow to look at, and all the soldier. But you shall see for yourself, and I 'll warrant you 'll not harbor a prejudice against him."

"Which means, you have asked him on a visit, brother Peter?"

"Scarcely fair to call it on a visit, Dinah," blundered he out, in confusion; "but I have said with what pleasure we should see him under our roof when we returned."

"I solemnly declare my belief, that if you went to a cattle-show you 'd invite every one you met there, from the squire to the pig-jobber, never thinking the while that nothing is so valueless as indiscriminate hospitality, even if it were not costly. Nobody thanks you,—no one is grateful for it."

"And who wants them to be grateful, Dinah? The pleasure is in the giving, not in receiving. You see your friends with their holiday faces on, when they sit round the table. The slowest and dreariest of them tries to look cheery; and the stupid dog who has never a jest in him has at least a ready laugh for the wit of his neighbor."

"Does it not spoil some of your zest for this pleasantry to think how it is paid for, brother?"

"It might, perhaps, if I were to think of it; but, thank Heaven! it's about one of the last things would come into my head. My dear sister, there's no use in always treating human nature as if it was sick, for if you do, it will end by being hypochondriac!"

"I protest, brother Peter, I don't know where you meet all the good and excellent people you rave about, and I feel it very churlish of you that you never present any of them to *me!*" And so saying, she gathered her knitting materials hastily together, and reminding him that it was past eleven o'clock, she uttered a hurried good-night, and departed.

CHAPTER XXVI.
A VERY SAD GOOD-BYE

Conyers sat alone in his barrack-room, very sad and dispirited. Hunter had left that same morning, and the young soldier felt utterly friendless. He had obtained some weeks' leave of absence, and already two days of the leave had gone over, and he had not energy to set out if he had even a thought as to the whither. A variety of plans passed vaguely through his head. He would go down to Portsmouth and see Hunter off; or he would nestle down in the little village of Inistioge and dream away the days in quiet forgetfulness; or he would go over to Paris, which he had never seen, and try whether the gay dissipations of that brilliant city might not distract and amuse him. The mail from India had arrived and brought no letter from his father, and this, too, rendered him irritable and unhappy. Not that his father was a good correspondent; he wrote but rarely, and always like one who snatched a hurried moment to catch a post. Still, if this were a case of emergency, any great or critical event in his life, he was sure his father would have informed him; and thus was it that he sat balancing doubt against doubt, and setting probability against probability, till his very head grew addled with the labor of speculation.

It was already late; all the usual sounds of barrack life had subsided, and although on the opposite side of the square the brilliant lights of the mess-room windows showed where the convivial spirits of the regiment were assembled, all around was silent and still. Suddenly there came a dull heavy knock to the door, quickly followed by two or three others.

Not caring to admit a visitor, whom, of course, he surmised would be some young brother-officer full of the plans and projects of the mess, he made no reply to the summons, nor gave any token of his presence. The sounds, however, were redoubled, and with an energy that seemed to vouch for perseverance; and Conyers, partly in anger, and partly in curiosity, went to the door and opened it. It was not till after a minute or two that he was able to recognize the figure before him. It was Tom Dill, but without a hat or neckcloth, his hair dishevelled, his face colorless, and his clothes torn, while from a recent wound in one hand the blood flowed fast, and dropped on the floor. The whole air and appearance of the young fellow so resembled drunkenness that Conyers turned a stern stare upon him as he stood in the centre of the room, and in a voice of severity said, "By what presumption, sir, do you dare to present yourself in this state before me?"

"You think I'm drunk, sir, but I am not," said he, with a faltering accent and a look of almost imploring misery.

"What is the meaning of this state, then? What disgraceful row have you been in?"

"None, sir. I have cut my hand with the glass on the barrack-wall, and torn my trousers too; but it's no matter, I 'll not want them long."

"What do you mean by all this? Explain yourself."

"May I sit down, sir, for I feel very weak?" but before the permission could be granted, his knees tottered, and he fell in a faint on the floor. Conyers knelt down beside him, bathed his temples with water, and as soon as signs of animation returned, took him up in his arms and laid him at full length on a sofa.

In the vacant, meaningless glance of the poor fellow as he looked first around him, Conyers could mark how he was struggling to find out where he was.

"You are with me, Tom,—with your friend Conyers," said he, holding the cold clammy hand between his own.

"Thank you, sir. It is very good of you. I do not deserve it," said he, in a faint whisper.

"My poor boy, you mustn't say that; I am your friend. I told you already I would be so."

"But you 'll not be my friend when I tell you—when I tell you—all;" and as the last word dropped, he covered his face with both his hands, and burst into a heavy passion of tears.

"Come, come, Tom, this is not manly; bear up bravely, bear up with courage, man. You used to say you had plenty of pluck if it were to be tried."

"So I thought I had, sir, but it has all left me;" and he sobbed as if his heart was breaking. "But I believe I could bear anything but this," said he, in a voice shaken by convulsive throes. "It is the disgrace,—that 's what unmans me."

"Take a glass of wine, collect yourself, and tell me all about it."

"No, sir. No wine, thank you; give me a glass of water. There, I am better now; my brain is not so hot. You are very good to me, Mr. Conyers, but it 's the last time I'll ever ask it,—the very last time, sir; but I 'll remember it all my life."

"If you give way in this fashion, Tom, I 'll not think you the stout-hearted fellow I once did."

"No, sir, nor am I. I 'll never be the same again. I feel it here. I feel as if something gave, something broke." And he laid his hand over his heart and sighed heavily.

"Well, take your own time about it, Tom, and let me hear if I cannot be of use to you."

"No, sir, not now. Neither you nor any one else can help me now. It's all over, Mr. Conyers,—it's all finished."

"What is over,—what is finished?"

"And so, as I thought it would n't do for one like me to be seen speaking to you before people, I stole away and climbed over the barrack-wall. I cut my hand on the glass, too, but it's nothing. And here I am, and here's the money you gave me; I've no need of it now." And as he laid some crumpled bank-notes on the table, his overcharged heart again betrayed him, and he burst into tears. "Yes, sir, that's what you gave me for the College, but I was rejected."

"Rejected, Tom! How was that? Be calm, my poor fellow, and tell me all about it quietly."

"I'll try, sir, I will, indeed; and I'll tell you nothing but the truth, that you may depend upon." He took a great drink of water, and went on. "If there was one man I was afraid of in the world, it was Surgeon Asken, of Mercer's Hospital. I used to be a dresser there, and he was always angry with me, exposing me before the other students, and ridiculing me, so that if anything was done badly in the wards, he 'd say, 'This is some of Master Dill's work, is n't it?' Well, sir, would you believe it, on the morning I went up for my examination, Dr. Coles takes ill, and Surgeon Asken is called on to replace him. I did n't know it till I was sent for to go in, and my head went round, and I could n't see, and a cold sweat came over me, and I was so confused that when I got into the room I went and sat down beside the examiners, and never knew what they were laughing at.

"'I have no doubt, Mr. Dill, you 'll occupy one of these places at some future day,' says Dr. Willes, 'but for the present your seat is yonder.' I don't remember much more after that, till Mr. Porter said, 'Don't be so nervous, Mr. Dill; collect yourself; I am persuaded you know what I am asking you, if you will not be flurried.' And all I could say was, 'God bless you for that speech, no matter how it goes with me' and they all laughed out.

"It was Asken's turn now, and he began. 'You are destined for the navy, I understand, sir?'

"'No, sir; for the army,' said I.

"'From what we have seen to-day, you 'll prove an ornament to either service. Meanwhile, sir, it will be satisfactory to the court to have your opinion on gunshot wounds. Describe to us the case of a man laboring under the worst form of concussion of the brain, and by what indications you would distinguish it from fracture of the base of the skull, and what circumstances might occur to render the distinction more difficult, and what impossible?' That was his question, and if I was to live a hundred years I 'll never forget a word in it,—it's written on my heart, I believe, for life.

"'Go on, sir,' said he, 'the court is waiting for you.'

"'Take the case of concussion first,' said Dr. Willes.

"'I hope I may be permitted to conduct my own examination in my own manner,' said Asken.

"That finished me, and I gave a groan that set them all laughing again.

"'Well, sir, I 'm waiting,' said Asken. 'You can have no difficulty to describe concussion, if you only give us your present sensations.'

"'That's as true as if you swore it,' said I. 'I 'm just as if I had a fall on the crown of my head. There's a haze over my eyes, and a ringing of bells in my ears, and a feeling as if my brain was too big.'

"'Take my word for it, Mr. Dill,' said he, sneeringly, 'the latter is a purely deceptive sensation; the fault lies in the opposite direction. Let us, however, take something more simple;' and with that he described a splinter wound of the scalp, with the whole integuments torn in fragments, and gunpowder and sticks and sand all mixed up with the flap that hung down over the patient's face. 'Now,' said he, after ten minutes' detail of this,—'now,' said he, 'when you found the man in this case, you 'd take out your scalpel, perhaps, and neatly cut away all these bruised and torn integuments?'

"'I would, sir,' cried I, eagerly.

"'I knew it,' said he, with a cry of triumph,—'I knew it. I 've no more to ask you. You may retire.'

"I got up to leave the room, but a sudden flash went through me, and I said out boldly,—

"'Am I passed? Tell me at once. Put me out of pain, for I can't bear any more!'

"'If you'll retire for a few minutes,' said the President—

"'My heart will break, sir,' said I, 'if I 'm to be in suspense any more. Tell me the worst at once.'

"And I suppose they did tell me, for I knew no more till I found myself in the housekeeper's room, with wet cloths on my head, and the money you see there in the palm of my hand. *That* told everything. Many were very kind to me, telling how it happened to this and to that man, the first time; and that Asken was thought very unfair, and so on; but I just washed my face with cold water, and put on my hat and went away home, that is, to where I lodged, and I wrote to Polly just this one line: 'Rejected; I 'm not coming back.' And then I shut the shutters and went to bed in my clothes as I was, and I slept sixteen hours without ever waking. When I awoke, I was all right. I could n't remember everything that happened for some time, but I knew it all at last, and so I went off straight to the Royal Barracks and 'listed."

"Enlisted?—enlisted?"

"Yes, sir, in the Forty-ninth Regiment of Foot, now in India, and sending off drafts from Cork to join them on Tuesday. It was out of the dépôt at the bridge I made my escape to-night to come and see you once more, and to give you this with my hearty blessing, for you were the only one ever stood to me in the world,—the only one that let me think for a moment I *could* be a gentleman!"

"Come, come, this is all wrong and hasty and passionate, Tom. You have no right to repay your family in this sort; this is not the way to treat that fine-hearted girl who has done so much for you; this is but an outbreak of angry selfishness."

"These are hard words, sir, very hard words, and I wish you had not said them."

"Hard or not, you deserve them; and it is their justice that wounds you."

"I won't say that it is *not*, sir. But it isn't justice I'm asking for, but forgiveness. Just one word out of your mouth to say, 'I'm sorry for you, Tom;' or, 'I wish you well.'"

"So I do, my poor fellow, with all my heart," cried Con-yers, grasping his hand and pressing it cordially, "and I'll get you out of this scrape, cost what it may."

"If you mean, sir, that I am to get my discharge, it's better to tell the truth at once. I wouldn't take it. No, sir, I'll stand by what I've done. I see I never could be a doctor, and I have my doubts, too, if I ever could be a gentleman; but there's something tells me I could be a soldier, and I'll try."

Conyers turned from him with an impatient gesture, and walked the room in moody silence.

"I know well enough, sir," continued Tom, "what every one will say; perhaps you yourself are thinking it this very minute: 'It's all out of his love of low com-pany he's gone and done this; he's more at home with those poor ignorant boys there than he would be with men of education and good manners.' Perhaps it's true, perhaps it is'n't! But there's one thing certain, which is, that I'll never try again to be anything that I feel is clean above me, and I'll not ask the world to give me credit for what I have not the least pretension to."

"Have you reflected," said Conyers, slowly, "that if you reject my assistance now, it will be too late to ask for it a few weeks, or even a few days hence?"

"I *have* thought of all that, sir. I'll never trouble you about myself again."

"My dear Tom," said Conyers, as he laid his arm on the other's shoulder, "just think for one moment of all the misery this step will cause your sister, — that kind, true-hearted sister, who has behaved so nobly by you."

"I have thought of that, too, sir; and in my heart I believe, though she'll fret herself at first greatly, it will all turn out best in the end. What could I ever be but a disgrace to her? Who'd ever think the same of Polly after seeing *me*? Don't I bring her down in spite of herself; and is n't it a hard trial for her to be a lady when I am in the same room with her? No, sir, I'll not go back; and though I haven't much hope in me, I feel I'm doing right."

"I know well," said Conyers, pettishly, "that your sister will throw the whole blame on me. She'll say, naturally enough, *You* could have obtained his dis-charge, — *you* should have insisted on his leaving."

"That's what you could not, sir," said Tom, sturdily. "It's a poor heart hasn't some pride in it; and I would not go back and meet my father, after my disgrace, if it was to cost me my right hand, — so don't say another word about it. Good-bye, sir, and my blessing go with you wherever you are. I'll never forget how you stood to me."

"That money there is yours, Dill," said Conyers, half haughtily. "You may re-fuse my advice and reject my counsel, but I scarcely suppose you 'll ask me to take back what I once have given."

Tom tried to speak, but he faltered and moved from one foot to the other, in an embarrassed and hesitating way. He wanted to say how the sum originally intended for one object could not honestly be claimed for another; he wanted to say, also, that he had no longer the need of so much money, and that the only ob-ligation he liked to submit to was gratitude for the past; but a consciousness that in attempting to say these things some unhappy word, some ill-advised or ungra-cious expression might escape him, stopped him, and he was silent.

"You do not wish that we should part coldly, Tom?"

"No, sir,—oh, no!" cried he, eagerly.

"Then let not that paltry gift stand in the way of our esteem. Now, another thing. Will you write to me? Will you tell me how the world fares with you, and honestly declare whether the step you have taken to-day brings with it regret or satisfaction?"

"I'm not over-much of a letter-writer," said he, falter-ingly, "but I'll try. I must be going, Mr. Conyers," said he, after a moment's silence; "I must get back before I'm missed."

"Not as you came, Tom, however. I'll pass you out of the barrack-gate."

As they walked along side by side, neither spoke till they came close to the gate; then Conyers halted and said, "Can you think of nothing I can do for you, or is there nothing you would leave to my charge after you have gone?"

"No, sir, nothing." He paused, and then, as if with a struggle, said, "Except you 'd write one line to my sister Polly, to tell her that I went away in good heart, that I did n't give in one bit, and that if it was n't for thinking that maybe I 'd never see her again—" He faltered, his voice grew thick, he tried to cough down the ris-ing emotion, but the feeling overcame him, and he burst out into tears. Ashamed at the weakness he was endeavoring to deny, he sprang through the gate and disappeared.

Conyers slowly returned to his quarters, very thoughtful and very sad.

CHAPTER XXVII.

THE CONVENT ON THE MEUSE

While poor Tom Dill, just entering upon life, went forth in gloom and disappointment to his first venture, old Peter Barrington, broken by years and many a sorrow, set out on his journey with a high heart and a spirit well disposed to see everything in its best light and be pleased with all around him. Much of this is, doubtless, matter of temperament; but I suspect, too, that all of us have more in our power in this way than we practise. Barrington had possibly less merit than his neighbors, for nature had given him one of those happy dispositions upon which the passing vexations of life produce scarcely any other effect than a stimulus to humor, or a tendency to make them the matter of amusing memory.

He had lived, besides, so long estranged from the world, that life had for him all the interests of a drama, and he could no more have felt angry with the obtrusive waiter or the roguish landlord than he would with their fictitious representatives on the stage. They were, in his eyes, parts admirably played, and no more; he watched them with a sense of humorous curiosity, and laughed heartily at successes of which he was himself the victim. Miss Barrington was no disciple of this school; rogues to her were simply rogues, and no histrionic sympathies dulled the vexation they gave her. The world, out of which she had lived so long, had, to her thinking, far from improved in the mean while. People were less deferential, less courteous than of old. There was an indecent haste and bustle about everything, and a selfish disregard of one's neighbor was the marked feature of all travel. While her brother repaid himself for many an inconvenience by thinking over some strange caprice, or some curious inconsistency in human nature, — texts for amusing afterthought, — she only winced under the infliction, and chafed at every instance of cheating or impertinence that befell them.

The wonderful things she saw, the splendid galleries rich in art, the gorgeous palaces, the grand old cathedrals, were all marred to her by the presence of the loquacious lackey whose glib tongue had to be retained at the salary of the "vicar of our parish," and who never descanted on a saint's tibia without costing the price of a dinner; so that old Peter at last said to himself, "I believe my sister Dinah would n't enjoy the garden of Eden if Adam had to go about and show her its beauties."

The first moment of real enjoyment of her tour was on that morning when they left Namur to drive to the Convent of Bramaigne, about three miles off, on the banks of the Meuse. A lovelier day never shone upon a lovelier scene. The river, one side guarded by lofty cliffs, was on the other bounded by a succession of rich meadows, dotted with picturesque homesteads half hidden in trees. Little patches of cultivation, labored to the perfection of a garden, varied the scene, and beautiful cattle lay lazily under the giant trees, solemn voluptuaries of the peaceful happiness of their lot.

Hitherto Miss Dinah had stoutly denied that anything they had seen could compare with their own "vale and winding river," but now she frankly owned that the stream was wider, the cliffs higher, the trees taller and better grown, while the variety of tint in the foliage far exceeded all she had any notion of; but above all these were the evidences of abundance, the irresistible charm that gives the poetry to peasant life; and the picturesque cottage, the costume, the well-stored granary, bespeak the condition with which we associate our ideas of rural happiness. The giant oxen as they marched proudly to their toil, the gay-caparisoned pony who jingled his bells as he trotted by, the peasant girls as they sat at their lace cushions before the door, the rosy urchins who gambolled in the deep grass, all told of plenty,—that blessing which to man is as the sunlight to a landscape, making the fertile spots more beautiful, and giving even to ruggedness an aspect of stern grandeur.

"Oh, brother Peter, that we could see something like this at home," cried she. "See that girl yonder watering the flowers in her little garden,—how prettily that old vine is trained over the balcony,—mark the scarlet tassels in the snow-white team,—are not these signs of an existence not linked to daily drudgery? I wish our people could be like these."

"Here we are, Dinah: there is the convent!" cried Barrington, as a tall massive roof appeared over the tree-tops, and the little carriage now turned from the high-road into a shady avenue of tall elms. "What a grand old place it is! some great seigniorial château once on a time."

As they drew nigh, nothing bespoke the cloister. The massive old building, broken by many a projection and varied by many a gable, stood, like the mansion of some rich proprietor, in a vast wooded lawn. The windows lay open, the terrace was covered with orange and lemon trees and flowering plants, amid which seats were scattered; and in the rooms within, the furniture indicated habits of comfort and even of luxury. With all this, no living thing was to be seen; and when Barrington got down and entered the hall, he neither found a servant nor any means to summon one.

"You'll have to move that little slide you see in the door there," said the driver of the carriage, "and some one will come to you."

He did so; and after waiting a few moments, a somewhat ruddy, cheerful face, surmounted by a sort of widow's cap, appeared, and asked his business.

"They are at dinner, but if you will enter the drawing-room she will come to you presently."

They waited for some time; to them it seemed very long, for they never spoke, but sat there in still thoughtfulness, their hearts very full, for there was much in that expectancy, and all the visions of many a wakeful night or dreary day might now receive their shock or their support. Their patience was to be further tested; for, when the door opened, there entered a grim-looking little woman in a nun's costume, who, without previous salutation, announced herself as Sister Lydia. Whether the opportunity for expansiveness was rare, or that her especial gift was fluency, never did a little old woman hold forth more volubly. As though anticipating all the worldly objections to a conventual existence, or rather seeming to suppose that every possible thing had been actually said on that ground, she assumed the defence the very moment she sat down. Nothing short of long practice with this argument could have stored her mind with all her instances, her quotations, and her references. Nor could anything short of a firm conviction have made her so courageously indifferent to the feelings she was outraging, for she never scrupled to arraign the two strangers before her for ignorance, apathy, worldliness, sordid and poor ambitions, and, last of all, a levity unbecoming their time of life.

A LECTURE

"I 'm not quite sure that I understand her aright," whispered Peter, whose familiarity with French was not what it had once been; "but if I do, Dinah, she 's giving us a rare lesson."

"She's the most insolent old woman I ever met in my life," said his sister, whose violent use of her fan seemed either likely to provoke or to prevent a fit of apoplexy.

"It is usual," resumed Sister Lydia, "to give persons who are about to exercise the awful responsibility now devolving upon you the opportunity of well weighing and reflecting over the arguments I have somewhat faintly shadowed forth."

"Oh, not faintly!" groaned Barrington.

But she minded nothing the interruption, and went on, —

"And for this purpose a little tract has been composed, entitled 'A Word to the Worldling.' This, with your permission, I will place in your hands. You will there find at more length than I could bestow — But I fear I impose upon this lady's patience?"

"It has left me long since, madam," said Miss Dinah, as she actually gasped for breath.

In the grim half-smile of the old nun might be seen the triumphant consciousness that placed her above the "mundane;" but she did not resent the speech, simply saying that, as it was the hour of recreation, perhaps she would like to see her young ward in the garden with her companions.

"By all means. We thank you heartily for the offer," cried Barrington, rising hastily.

With another smile, still more meaningly a reproof, Sister Lydia reminded him that the profane foot of a man had never transgressed the sacred precincts of the convent garden, and that he must remain where he was.

"For Heaven's sake! Dinah, don't keep me a prisoner here a moment longer than you can help it," cried he, "or I'll not answer for my good behavior."

As Barrington paced up and down the room with impatient steps, he could not escape the self-accusation that all his present anxiety was scarcely compatible with the long, long years of neglect and oblivion he had suffered to glide over.

The years in which he had never heard of Josephine — never asked for her — was a charge there was no rebutting. Of course he could fall back upon all that special pleading ingenuity and self-love will supply about his own misfortunes, the crushing embarrassments that befell him, and such like. But it was no use, it was desertion, call it how he would; and poor as he was he had never been without a roof to shelter her, and if it had not been for false pride he would have offered her that refuge long ago. He was actually startled as he thought over all this. Your generous people, who forgive injuries with little effort, who bear no malice nor cherish any resentment, would be angels — downright angels — if we did not find that they are just as indulgent, just as merciful to themselves as to the world at large. They become perfect adepts in apologies, and with one cast of the net draw in a whole shoal of attenuating circumstances. To be sure, there will now and then break in upon them a startling suspicion that all is not right, and that conscience has been "cooking" the account; and when such a moment does come, it is a very painful one.

"Egad!" muttered he to himself, "we have been very heartless all this time, there's no denying it; and if poor George's girl be a disciple of that grim old woman with the rosary and the wrinkles, it is nobody's fault but our own." He looked at his watch; Dinah had been gone more than half an hour. What a time to keep him in suspense! Of course there were formalities,—the Sister Lydia described innumerable ones,—jail delivery was nothing to it, but surely five-and-thirty minutes would suffice to sign a score of documents. The place was becoming hateful to him. The grand old park, with its aged oaks, seemed sad as a graveyard, and the great silent house, where not a footfall sounded, appeared a tomb. "Poor child! what a dreary spot you have spent your brightest years in,—what a shadow to throw over the whole of a lifetime!"

He had just arrived at that point wherein his granddaughter arose before his mind a pale, careworn, sorrow-struck girl, crushed beneath the dreary monotony of a joyless life, and seeming only to move in a sort of dreamy melancholy, when the door opened, and Miss Barrington entered with her arm around a young girl tall as herself, and from whose commanding figure even the ungainly dress she wore could not take away the dignity.

"This is Josephine, Peter," said Miss Dinah; and though Barrington rushed forward to clasp her in his arms, she merely crossed hers demurely on her breast and courtesied deeply.

"It is your grandpapa, Josephine," said Miss Dinah, half tartly.

The young girl opened her large, full, lustrous eyes, and stared steadfastly at him, and then, with infinite grace, she took his hand and kissed it.

"My own dear child," cried the old man, throwing his arms around her, "it is not homage, it is your love we want."

"Take care, Peter, take care," whispered his sister; "she is very timid and very strange."

"You speak English, I hope, dear?" said the old man.

"Yes, sir, I like it best," said she. And there was the very faintest possible foreign accent in the words.

"Is n't that George's own voice, Dinah? Don't you think you heard himself there?"

"The voice is certainly like him," said Miss Dinah, with a marked emphasis.

"And so are—no, not her eyes, but her brow, Dinah. Yes, darling, you have his own frank look, and I feel sure you have his own generous nature."

"They say I'm like my mother's picture," said she, unfastening a locket she wore from its chain and handing it. And both Peter and his sister gazed eagerly at the miniature. It was of a very dark but handsome woman in a rich turban, and who, though profusely ornamented with costly gems, did, in reality, present a resemblance to the cloistered figure before them.

"Am I like her?" asked the girl, with a shade more of earnestness in her voice.

"You are, darling; but like your father, too, and every word you utter brings back his memory; and see, Dinah, if that is n't George's old trick, — to lay one hand in the palm of the other."

As if corrected, the young girl dropped her arms to her sides and stood like a statue.

"Be like him in everything, dearest child," said the old man, "if you would have my heart all your own."

"I must be what I am," said she, solemnly.

"Just so, Josephine; well said, my good girl. Be natural," said Miss Dinah, kissing her, "and our love will never fail you."

There was the faintest little smile of acknowledgment to this speech; but faint as it was, it dimpled her cheek, and seemed to have left a pleasant expression on her face, for old Peter gazed on her with increased delight as he said, "That was George's own smile; just the way he used to look, half grave, half merry. Oh, how you bring him back to me!"

"You see, my dear child, that you are one of us; let us hope you will share in the happiness this gives us."

The girl listened attentively to Miss Dinah's words, and after a pause of apparent thought over them, said, "I will hope so."

"May we leave this, Dinah? Are we free to get away?" whispered Barrington to his sister, for an unaccountable oppression seemed to weigh on him, both from the place and its belongings.

"Yes; Josephine has only one good-bye to say; her trunks are already on the carriage, and there is nothing more to detain us."

"Go and say that farewell, dear child," said he, affectionately; "and be speedy, for there are longing hearts here to wish for your return."

With a grave and quiet mien she walked away, and as she gained the door turned round and made a deep, respectful courtesy, — a movement so ceremonious that the old man involuntarily replied to it by a bow as deep and reverential.

CHAPTER XXVIII.

GEORGE'S DAUGHTER

I suppose, nay, I am certain, that the memory of our happiest moments ought ever to be of the very faintest and weakest, since, could we recall them in all their fulness and freshness, the recollection would only serve to deepen the gloom of age, and imbitter all its daily trials. Nor is it, altogether, a question of memory! It is in the very essence of happiness to be indescribable. Who could impart in words the simple pleasure he has felt as he lay day-dreaming in the deep grass, lulled by the humming insect, or the splash of falling water, with teeming fancy peopling the space around, and blending the possible with the actual? The more exquisite the sense of enjoyment, the more will it defy delineation. And so, when we come to describe the happiness of others, do we find our words weak, and our attempt mere failure.

It is in this difficulty that I now find myself. I would tell, if I could, how enjoyably the Barringtons sauntered about through the old villages on the Rhine and up the Moselle, less travelling than strolling along in purposeless indolence, resting here, and halting there, always interested, always pleased. It was strange into what perfect harmony these three natures—unlike as they were—blended!

Old Peter's sympathies went with all things human, and he loved to watch the village life and catch what he could of its ways and instincts. His sister, to whom the love of scenery was a passion, never wearied of the picturesque land they travelled; and as for Josephine, she was no longer the demure pensionnaire of the convent,—thoughtful and reserved, even to secrecy,—but a happy child, revelling in a thousand senses of enjoyment, and actually exulting in the beauty of all she saw around her. What depression must come of captivity, when even its faintest image, the cloister, could have weighed down a heart like hers! Such was Barrington's thought as he beheld her at play with the peasant children, weaving garlands for a village *fête*, or joyously joining the chorus of a peasant song. There was, besides, something singularly touching in the half-consciousness of her freedom, when recalled for an instant to the past by the tinkling bell of a church. She would seem to stop in her play, and bethink her how and why she was there, and then, with a cry of joy, bound away after her companions in wild delight.

"Dearest aunt," said she, one day, as they sat on a rocky ledge over the little river that traverses the Lahnech, "shall I always find the same enjoyment in life that I feel now, for it seems to me this is a measure of happiness that could not endure?"

"Some share of this is owing to contrast, Fifine. Your convent life had not too many pleasures."

"It was, or rather it seems to me now, as I look back, a long and weary dream; but, at the same time, it appears more real than this; for do what I may I cannot imagine this to be the world of misery and sorrow I have heard so much of. Can any one fancy a scene more beautiful than this before us? Where is the perfume more exquisite than these violets I now crush in my hand? The peasants, as they salute us, look happy and contented. Is it, then, only in great cities that men make each other miserable?"

Dinah shook her head, but did not speak.

"I am so glad grandpapa does not live in a city. Aunt, I am never wearied of hearing you talk of that dear cottage beside the river; and through all my present delight I feel a sense of impatience to be there, to be at 'home.'"

"So that you will not hold us to our pledge to bring you back to Bramaigne, Fifine," said Miss Dinah, smiling.

"Oh no, no! Not if you will let me live with you. Never!"

"But you have been happy up to this, Fifine? You have said over and over again that your convent life was dear to you, and all its ways pleasant."

"It is just the same change to me to live as I now do, as in my heart I feel changed after reading out one of those delightful stories to grandpapa,—Rob Roy, for instance. It all tells of a world so much more bright and beautiful than I know of, that it seems as though new senses were given to me. It is so strange and so captivating, too, to hear of generous impulses, noble devotion,—of faith that never swerved, and love that never faltered."

"In novels, child; these were in novels."

"True, aunt; but they had found no place there had they been incredible; at least, it is clear that he who tells the tale would have us believe it to be true."

Miss Dinah had not been a convert to her brother's notions as to Fifine's readings; and she was now more disposed to doubt than ever. To overthrow of a sudden, as though by a great shock, all the stem realism of a cloister existence, and supply its place with fictitious incidents and people, seemed rash and perilous; but old Peter only thought of giving a full liberty to the imprisoned spirit,—striking off chain and fetter, and setting the captive free,—free in all the glorious liberty of a young imagination.

"Well, here comes grandpapa," said Miss Dinah, "and, if I don't mistake, with a book in his hand for one of your morning readings."

Josephine ran eagerly to meet him, and, fondly drawing her arm within his own, came back at his side.

"The third volume, Fifine, the third volume," said he, holding the book aloft. "Only think, child, what fates are enclosed within a third volume! What a deal of happiness or long-living misery are here included!"

THE THIRD VOLUME

She straggled to take the book from his hand, but he evaded her grasp, and placed it in his pocket, saying, —

"Not till evening, Fifine. I am bent on a long ramble up the Glen this morning, and you shall tell me all about the sisterhood, and sing me one of those little Latin canticles I'm so fond of."

"Meanwhile, I 'll go and finish my letter to Polly Dill. I told her, Peter, that by Thursday next, or Friday, she might expect us."

"I hope so, with all my heart; for, beautiful as all this is, it wants the greatest charm, — it's not home! Then I want, besides, to see Fifine full of household cares."

"Feeding the chickens instead of chasing the butterflies, Fifine. Totting up the house-bills, in lieu of sighing over 'Waverley.'"

"And, if I know Fifine, she will be able to do one without relinquishing the other," said Peter, gravely. "Our daily life is all the more beautiful when it has its landscape reliefs of light and shadow."

"I think I could, too," cried Fifine, eagerly. "I feel as though I could work in the fields and be happy, just in the conscious sense of doing what it was good to do, and what others would praise me for."

"There's a paymaster will never fail you in such hire," said Miss Dinah, pointing to her brother; and then, turning away, she walked back to the little inn. As she drew nigh, the landlord came to tell her that a young gentleman, on seeing her name in the list of strangers, had made many inquiries after her, and begged he might be informed of her return. On learning that he was in the garden, she went thither at once.

"I felt it was you. I knew who had been asking for me, Mr. Conyers," said she, advancing towards Fred with her hand out. "But what strange chance could have led you here?"

"You have just said it, Miss Barrington; a chance,—a mere chance. I had got a short leave fron l my regiment, and came abroad to wander about with no very definite object; but, growing impatient of the wearisome hordes of our countrymen on the Rhine, I turned aside yesterday from that great high-road and reached this spot, whose greatest charm—shall I own it?—was a fancied resemblance to a scene I loved far better."

"You are right. It was only this morning my brother said it was so like our own cottage."

"And he is here also?" said the young man, with a half-constraint.

"Yes, and very eager to see you, and ask your forgive ness for his ungracious manner to you; not that I saw it, or understand what it could mean, but he says that he has a pardon to crave at your hands."

So confused was Conyers for an instant that he made no answer, and when he did speak it was falteringly and with embarrassment, "I never could have anticipated meeting you here. It is more good fortune than I ever looked for."

"We came over to the Continent to fetch away my grand-niece, the daughter of that Colonel Barrington you have heard so much of."

"And is she—" He stopped, and grew scarlet with confusion; but she broke in, laughingly,—

"No, not black, only dark-complexioned; in fact, a brunette, and no more."

"Oh, I don't mean,—I surely could not have said—"

"No matter what you meant or said. Your unuttered question was one that kept occurring to my brother and myself every morning as we journeyed here, though neither of us had the courage to speak it. But our wonders are over; she is a dear good, girl, and we love her better every day we see her. But now a little about yourself. Why do I find you so low and depressed?"

"I have had much to fret me, Miss Barrington. Some were things that could give but passing unhappiness; others were of graver import."

"Tell me so much as you may of them, and I will try to help you to bear up against them."

"I will tell you all,—everything!" cried he. "It is the very moment I have been longing for, when I could pour out all my cares before you and ask, What shall I do?"

Miss Barrington silently drew her arm within his, and they strolled along the shady alley without a word.

"I must begin with my great grief,—it absorbs all the rest," said he, suddenly. "My father is coming home; he has lost, or thrown up, I can't tell which, his high employment. I have heard both versions of the story; and his own few words, in the only letter he has written me, do not confirm either. His tone is indignant; but far more it is sad and depressed,—he who never wrote a line but in the joyousness of his high-hearted nature; who met each accident of life with an undaunted spirit, and spurned the very thought of being cast down by fortune. See what he says here." And he took a much crumpled letter from his pocket, and folded down a part of it "Read that. 'The time for men of my stamp is gone by in India. We are as much bygones as the old flint musket or the matchlock. Soldiers of a different temperament are the fashion now; and the sooner we are pensioned or die off the better. For my own part, I am sick of it. I have lost my liver and have not made my fortune, and like men who have missed their opportunities, I come away too discontented with myself to think well of any one. They fancied that by coldness and neglect they might get rid of me, as they did once before of a far worthier and better fellow; but though I never had the courage that he had, they shall not break *my* heart.' Does it strike you to whom he alludes there?" asked Conyers, suddenly; "for each time that I read the words I am more disposed to believe that they refer to Colonel Barrington."

"I am sure of it!" cried she. "It is the testimony of a sorrow-stricken heart to an old friend's memory; but I hear my brother's voice; let me go and tell him you are here." But Barrington was already coming towards them.

"Ah, Mr. Conyers!" cried he. "If you knew how I have longed for this moment! I believe you are the only man in the world I ever ill treated on my own threshold; but the very thought of it gave me a fit of illness, and now the best thing I know on my recovery is, that I am here to ask your pardon."

"I have really nothing to forgive. I met under your roof with a kindness that never befell me before; nor do I know the spot on earth where I could look for the like to-morrow."

"Come back to it, then, and see if the charm should not be there still."

"Where 's Josephine, brother?" asked Miss Barrington, who, seeing the young man's agitation, wished to change the theme.

"She's gone to put some ferns in water; but here she comes now."

Bounding wildly along, like a child in joyous freedom, Josephine came towards them, and, suddenly halting at sight of a stranger, she stopped and courtesied deeply, while Conyers, half ashamed at his own unhappy blunder about her, blushed deeply as he saluted her. Indeed, their meeting was more like that of two awkward timid children than of two young persons of their age; and they eyed each other with the distrust school boys and girls exchange on a first acquaintance.

"Brother, I have something to tell you," said Miss Barrington, who was eager to communicate the news she had just heard of General Conyers; and while she drew him to one side, the young people still stood there, each seeming to expect the other would make some advance towards acquaintanceship. Conyers tried to say some commonplace,—some one of the fifty things that would have occurred so naturally in presence of a young lady to whom he had been just presented; but he could think of none, or else those that *he* thought of seemed inappropriate. How talk, for instance, of the world and its pleasures to one who had been estranged from it! While he thus struggled and contended with himself, she suddenly started as if with a flash of memory, and said, "How forgetful!"

"Forgetful!—and of what?" asked he.

"I have left the book I was reading to grandpapa on the rock where we were sitting. I must go and fetch it."

"May I go with you?" asked he, half timidly.

"Yes, if you like."

"And your book,—what was it?"

"Oh, a charming book,—such a delightful story! So many people one would have loved to know!—such scenes one would have loved to visit!—incidents, too, that keep the heart in intense anxiety, that you wonder how he who imagined them could have sustained the thrilling interest, and held his own heart so long in terrible suspense!"

"And the name of this wonderful book is—"

"'Waverley.'"

"I have read it," said he, coldly.

"And have you not longed to be a soldier? Has not your heart bounded with eagerness for a life of adventure and peril?"

"I am a soldier," said he, quietly.

"Indeed!" replied she, slowly, while her steadfast glance scanned him calmly and deliberately.

"You find it hard to recognize as a soldier one dressed as I am, and probably wonder how such a life as this consorts with enterprise and danger. Is not that what is passing in your mind?"

"Mayhap," said she, in a low voice.

"It is all because the world has changed a good deal since Waverley's time."

"How sorry I am to hear it!"

"Nay, for your sake it is all the better. Young ladies have a pleasanter existence now than they had sixty years since. They lived then lives of household drudgery or utter weariness."

"And what have they now?" asked she, eagerly.

"What have they not! All that can embellish life is around them; they are taught in a hundred ways to employ the faculties which give to existence its highest charm. They draw, sing, dance, ride, dress becomingly, read what may give to their conversation an added elegance and make their presence felt as an added lustre."

"How unlike all this was our convent life!" said she, slowly. "The beads in my rosary were not more alike than the days that followed each other, and but for the change of season I should have thought life a dreary sleep. Oh, if you but knew what a charm there is in the changeful year to one who lives in any bondage!"

"And yet I remember to have heard how you hoped you might not be taken away from that convent life, and be compelled to enter the world," said he, with a malicious twinkle of the eye.

"True; and had I lived there still I had not asked for other. But how came it that you should have heard of me? I never heard of *you!*"

"That is easily told. I was your aunt's guest at the time she resolved to come abroad to see you and fetch you home. I used to hear all her plans about you, so that at last—I blush to own—I talked of Josephine as though she were my sister."

"How strangely cold you were, then, when we met!" said she, quietly. "Was it that you found me so unlike what you expected?"

"Unlike, indeed!"

"Tell me how—tell me, I pray you, what you had pictured me."

"It was not mere fancy I drew from. There was a miniature of you as a child at the cottage, and I have looked at it till I could recall every line of it."

"Go on!" cried she, as he hesitated.

"The child's face was very serious,—actually grave for childhood,—and had something almost stern in its expression; and yet I see nothing of this in yours."

"So that, like grandpapa," said she, laughing, "you were disappointed in not finding me a young tiger from Bengal; but be patient, and remember how long it is since I left the jungle."

Sportively as the words were uttered, her eyes flashed and her cheek colored, and Conyers saw for the first time how she resembled her portrait in infancy.

"Yes," added she, as though answering what was passing in his mind, "you are thinking just like the sisters, 'What years and years it would take to discipline one of such a race!' I have heard that given as a reason for numberless inflictions. And now, all of a sudden, comes grandpapa to say, 'We love you so because you are one of us.' Can you understand this?"

"I think I can,—that is, I think I can understand why—" he was going to add, "why they should love you;" but he stopped, ashamed of his own eagerness.

She waited a moment for him to continue, and then, herself blushing, as though she had guessed his embarrassment, she turned away.

"And this book that we have been forgetting,—let us go and search for it," said she, walking on rapidly in front of him; but he was speedily at her side again.

"Look there, brother Peter,—look there!" said Miss Dinah, as she pointed after them, "and see how well fitted we are to be guardians to a young lady!"

"I see no harm in it, Dinah,—I protest, I see no harm in it."

"Possibly not, brother Peter, and it may only be a part of your system for making her—as you phrase it—feel a holy horror of the convent."

"Well," said he, meditatively, "he seems a fine, frank-hearted young fellow, and in this world she is about to enter, her first experiences might easily be worse."

"I vow and declare," cried she, warmly, "I believe it is your slipshod philosophy that makes me as severe as a holy inquisitor!"

"Every evil calls forth its own correction, Dinah," said he, laughing. "If there were no fools to skate on the Serpentine, there had been no Humane Society."

"One might grow tired of the task of resuscitating, Peter Barrington," said she, hardly.

"Not you, not you, Dinah,—at least, if I was the drowned man," said he, drawing her affectionately to his side; "and as for those young creatures yonder, it's like gathering dog-roses, and they 'll stop when they have pricked their fingers."

"I'll go and look after the nosegay myself," said she, turning hastily away, and following them.

A real liking for Conyers, and a sincere interest in him were the great correctives to the part of Dragon which Miss Dinah declared she foresaw to be her future lot in life. For years and years had she believed that the cares of a household and the rule of servants were the last trials of human patience. The larder, the dairy, and the garden were each of them departments with special opportunities for deception and embezzlement, and it seemed to her that new discoveries in roguery kept pace with the inventions of science; but she was energetic and active, and kept herself at what the French would call "the level of the situation;" and neither the cook nor the dairymaid nor Darby could be vainglorious over their battles with her. And now, all of a sudden, a new part was assigned her, with new duties, functions, and requirements; and she was called on to exercise qualities which had lain long dormant and in disuse, and renew a knowledge she had not employed for many a year. And what a strange blending of pleasure and pain must have come of that memory of long ago! Old conquests revived, old rivalries and jealousies and triumphs; glorious little glimpses of brilliant delight, and some dark hours, too, of disappointment,—almost despair!

"Once a bishop, always a bishop," says the canon; but might we not with almost as much truth say, "Once a beauty, always a beauty"?—not in lineament and feature, in downy cheek or silky tresses, but in the heartfelt consciousness of a once sovereign power, in that sense of having been able to exact a homage and enforce a tribute. And as we see in the deposed monarch how the dignity of kingcraft clings to him, how through all he does and says there runs a vein of royal graciousness as from one the fount of honor, so it is with beauty. There lives through all its wreck the splendid memory of a despotism the most absolute, the most fascinating of all!

"I am so glad that young Conyers has no plans, Dinah," said Barrington; "he says he will join us if we permit him."

"Humph!" said Miss Barrington, as she went on with her knitting.

"I see nothing against it, sister."

"Of course not, Peter," said she, snappishly; "it would surprise me much if you did."

"Do *you*, Dinah?" asked he, with a true simplicity of voice and look.

"I see great danger in it, if that be what you mean. And what answer did you make him, Peter?"

"The same answer that I make to every one,—I would consult my sister Dinah. 'Le Roi s'avisera' meant, I take it, that he 'd be led by a wiser head than his own."

"He was wise when he knew it," said she, sententiously, and continued her work.

And from that day forth they all journeyed together, and one of them was very happy, and some were far more than happy; and Aunt Dinah was anxious even beyond her wont.

CHAPTER XXIX.

THE RAMBLE

Day after day, week after week rolled on, and they still rambled about among the picturesque old villages on the Moselle, almost losing themselves in quaint unvisited spots, whose very names were new to them. To Barrington and his sister this picture of a primitive peasant life, with its own types of costume and custom, had an indescribable charm. Though debarred, from his ignorance of their dialect, of anything like intercourse with the people, he followed them in their ways with intense interest, and he would pass hours in the market-place, or stroll through the fields watching the strange culture, and wondering at the very implements of their labor. And the young people all this while? They were never separate. They read, and walked, and sat together from dawn to dark. They called each other Fifine and Freddy. Sometimes she sang, and he was there to listen; sometimes he drew, and she was as sure to be leaning over him in silent wonder at his skill; but with all this there was no love-making between them,—that is, no vows were uttered, no pledges asked for. Confidences, indeed, they interchanged, and without end. She told the story of her friendless infancy, and the long dreary years of convent life passed in a dull routine that had almost barred the heart against a wish for change; and he gave her the story of his more splendid existence, charming her imagination with a picture of that glorious Eastern life, which seemed to possess an instinctive captivation for her. And at last he told her, but as a great secret never to be revealed, how his father and her own had been the dearest, closest friends; that for years and years they had lived together like brothers, till separated by the accidents of life. *Her* father went away to a long distant station, and *his* remained to hold a high military charge, from which he was now relieved and on his way back to Europe. "What happiness for you, Freddy," cried she, as her eyes ran over, "to see him come home in honor! What had I given that such a fate were mine!"

For an instant he accepted her words in all their flattery, but the hypocrisy was brief; her over-full heart was bursting for sympathy, and he was eager to declare that his sorrows were scarcely less than her own. "No, Fifine," said he, "my father is coming back to demand satisfaction of a Government that has wronged him, and treated him with the worst ingratitude. In that Indian life men of station wield an almost boundless power; but if they are irresponsible as to the means, they are tested by the results, and whenever an adverse issue succeeds they fall irrevocably. What my father may have done, or have left undone, I know not. I have not the vaguest clew to his present difficulty, but, with his high spirit and his proud heart, that he would resent the very shadow of a reproof I can answer for, and so

I believe, what many tell me, that it is a mere question of personal feeling,—some small matter in which the Council have not shown him the deference he felt his due, but which his haughty nature would not forego."

Now these confidences were not love-making, nor anything approaching to it, and yet Josephine felt a strange half-pride in thinking that she had been told a secret which Conyers had never revealed to any other; that to her he had poured forth the darkest sorrow of his heart, and actually confided to her the terrors that beset him, for he owned that his father was rash and headstrong, and if he deemed himself wronged would be reckless in his attempt at justification.

"You do not come of a very patient stock, then," said she, smiling.

"Not very, Fifine."

"Nor I," said she, as her eyes flashed brightly. "My poor Ayah, who died when I was but five years old, used to tell me such tales of my father's proud spirit and the lofty way he bore himself, so that I often fancy I have seen him and heard him speak. You have heard he was a Rajah?" asked she, with a touch of pride.

The youth colored deeply as he muttered an assent, for he knew that she was ignorant of the details of her father's fate, and he dreaded any discussion of her story.

"And these Rajahs," resumed she, "are really great princes, with power of life and death, vast retinues, and splendid armies. To my mind, they present a more gorgeous picture than a small European sovereignty with some vast Protectorate looming over it. And now it is my uncle," said she, suddenly, "who rules there."

"I have heard that your own claims, Fifine, are in litigation," said he, with a faint smile.

"Not as to the sovereignty," said she, with a grave look, half rebukeful of his levity. "The suit grandpapa prosecutes in my behalf is for my mother's jewels and her fortune; a woman cannot reign in the Tannanoohr."

There was a haughty defiance in her voice as she spoke, that seemed to say, "This is a theme I will not suffer to be treated lightly,—beware how you transgress here."

"And yet it is a dignity would become you well," said he, seriously.

"It is one I would glory to possess," said she, as proudly.

"Would you give me a high post, Fifine, if you were on the throne?—would you make me Commander-in-Chief of your army?"

"More likely that I would banish you from the realm," said she, with a haughty laugh; "at least, until you learned to treat the head of the state more respectfully."

"Have I ever been wanting in a proper deference?" said he, bowing, with a mock humility.

"If you had been, sir, it is not now that you had first heard of it," said she, with a proud look, and for a few seconds it seemed as though their jesting was to have a serious ending. She was, however, the earliest to make terms, and in a tone of hearty kindliness said: "Don't be angry, Freddy, and I 'll tell you a secret. If that theme be touched on, I lose my head: whether it be in the blood that circles in my veins, or in some early teachings that imbued my childhood, or long dreaming over what can never be, I cannot tell, but it is enough to speak of these things, and at once my imagination becomes exalted and my reason is routed."

"I have no doubt your Ayah was to blame for this; she must have filled your head with ambitions, and hopes of a grand hereafter. Even I myself have some experiences of this sort; for as my father held a high post and was surrounded with great state and pomp, I grew at a very early age to believe myself a very mighty personage, and gave my orders with despotic insolence, and suffered none to gainsay me."

"How silly!" said she, with a supercilious toss of her head that made Conyers flush up; and once again was peace endangered between them.

"You mean that what was only a fair and reasonable assumption in *you* was an absurd pretension in me, Miss Barrington; is it not so?" asked he, in a voice tremulous with passion.

"I mean that we must both have been very naughty children, and the less we remember of that childhood the better for us. Are we friends, Freddy?" and she held out her hand.

"Yes, if you wish it," said he, taking her hand half coldly in his own.

"Not that way, sir. It is *I* who have condescended; not *you.*"

"As you please, Fifine, — will this do?" and kneeling with well-assumed reverence, he lifted her hand to his lips.

"If my opinion were to be asked, Mr. Conyers, I would say it would *not* do at all," said Miss Dinah, coming suddenly up, her cheeks crimson, and her eyes flashing.

"It was a little comedy we were acting, Aunt Dinah," said the girl, calmly.

"I beg, then, that the piece may not be repeated," said she, stiffly.

"Considering how ill Freddy played his part, aunt, he will scarcely regret its withdrawal."

Conyers, however, could not get over his confusion, and looked perfectly miserable for very shame.

"My brother has just had a letter which will call us homeward, Mr. Conyers," said Miss Dinah, turning to him, and now using a tone devoid of all irritation. "Mr. Withering has obtained some information which may turn out of great consequence in our suit, and he wishes to consult with my brother upon it."

"I hope—I sincerely hope—you do not think—" he began, in a low voice.

"I do not think anything to your disadvantage, and I hope I never may," replied she, in a whisper low as his own; "but bear in mind, Josephine is no finished coquette like Polly Dill, nor must she be the mark of little gallantries, however harmless. Josephine, grandpapa has some news for you; go to him."

"Poor Freddy," whispered the girl in the youth's ear as she passed, "what a lecture you are in for!" "You mustn't be angry with me if I play Duenna a little harshly, Mr. Conyers," said Miss Dinah; "and I am far more angry with myself than you can be. I never concurred with my brother that romance reading and a young dragoon for a companion were the most suitable educational means for a young lady fresh from a convent, and I have only myself to blame for permitting it."

Poor Conyers was so overwhelmed that he could say nothing; for though he might, and with a safe conscience, have answered a direct charge, yet against a general allegation he was powerless. He could not say that he was the best possible companion for a young lady, though he felt, honestly felt, that he was not a bad one. He had never trifled with her feelings, nor sought to influence her in his favor. Of all flirtation, such as he would have adventured with Polly Dill, for instance, he was guiltless. He respected her youth and ignorance of life too deeply to take advantage of either. He thought, perhaps, how ungenerous it would have been for a man of the world like himself to entrap the affections of a young, artless creature, almost a child in her innocence. He was rather fond of imagining himself "a man of the world," old soldier, and what not,—a delusion which somehow very rarely befalls any but very young men, and of which the experience of life from thirty to forty is the sovereign remedy. And so overwhelmed and confused and addled was he with a variety of sensations, he heard very little of what Miss Dinah said to him, though that worthy lady talked very fluently and very well, concluding at last with words which awoke Conyers from his half-trance with a sort of shock. "It is for these reasons, my dear Mr. Conyers,—reasons whose force and nature you will not dispute,—that I am forced to do what, were the occasion less important, would be a most ungenerous task. I mean, I am forced to relinquish all the pleasure that I had promised ourselves from seeing you our guest at the cottage. If you but knew the pain I feel to speak these words—"

"There is no occasion to say more, madam," said he; for, unfortunately, so unprepared was he for the announcement, its chief effect was to wound his pride. "It is the second time within a few months destiny has stopped my step on your threshold. It only remains for me to submit to my fate, and not adventure upon an enterprise above my means."

"You are offended with me, and yet you ought not," said she, sorrowfully; "you ought to feel that I am consulting *your* interests fully as much as ours."

"I own, madam," said he, coldly, "I am unable to take the view you have placed before me."

"Must I speak out, then?—must I declare my meaning in all its matter-of-fact harshness, and say that your family and your friends would have little scruple in estimating the discretion which encouraged your intimacy with my niece,—the son of the distinguished and highly favored General Conyers with the daughter of the ruined George Barring-ton? These are hard words to say, but I have said them."

"It is to my father you are unjust now, Miss Harrington."

"No, Mr. Conyers; there is no injustice in believing that a father loves his son with a love so large that it cannot exclude even worldliness. There is no injustice in believing that a proud and successful man would desire to see his son successful too; and we all know what we call success. I see you are very angry with me. You think me very worldly and very small-minded; perhaps, too, you would like to say that all the perils I talk of are of my own inventing; that Fifine and you could be the best of friends, and never think of more than friendship; and that I might spare my anxieties, and not fret for sorrows that have no existence;—and to all this I would answer, I 'll not risk the chance. No, Mr. Conyers, I 'll be no party to a game where the stakes are so unequal. What might give *you* a month's sorrow might cost *her* the misery of a life long."

"I have no choice left me. I will go,—I will go to-night, Miss Barrington."

"Perhaps it would be better," said she, gravely, and walked slowly away.

I will not tell the reader what harsh and cruel things Conyers said of every one and everything, nor how severely he railed at the world and its ways. Lord Byron had taught the youth of that age a very hearty and wholesome contempt for all manner of conventionalities, into which category a vast number of excellent customs were included, and Conyers could spout "Manfred" by heart, and imagine himself, on very small provocation, almost as great a man-hater; and so he set off on a long walk into the forest, determined not to appear at dinner, and equally determined to be the cause of much inquiry, and, if possible, of some uneasiness. "I wonder what that old-maid,"—alas for his gallantry, it was so he called her,— "what she would say if her harsh, ungenerous words had driven me to—" what he did not precisely define, though it was doubtless associated with snow peaks and avalanches, eternal solitudes and demoniac possessions. It might, indeed, have been some solace to him had he known how miserable and anxious old Peter became at his absence, and how incessantly he questioned every one about him.

"I hope that no mishap has befallen that boy, Dinah; he was always punctual. I never knew him stray away in this fashion before."

"It would be rather a severe durance, brother Peter, if a young gentleman could not prolong his evening walk without permission."

"What says Fifine? I suspect she agrees with me."

"If that means that he ought to be here, grandpapa, I do."

"I must read over Withering's letter again, brother," said Miss Dinah, by way of changing the subject "He writes, you say, from the Home?"

"Yes; he was obliged to go down there to search for some papers he wanted, and he took Stapylton with him; and he says they had two capital days at the partridges. They bagged,—egad! I think it was eight or ten brace before two o'clock, the Captain or Major, I forget which, being a first-rate shot."

"What does he say of the place,—how is it looking?"

"In perfect beauty. Your deputy, Polly, would seem to have fulfilled her part admirably. The garden in prime order; and that little spot next your own sitting-room, he says, is positively a better flower-show than one he paid a shilling to see in Dublin. Polly herself, too, comes in for a very warm share of his admiration."

"How did he see her, and where?"

"At the Home. She was there the evening they arrived, and Withering insisted on her presiding at the tea-table for them."

"It did not require very extraordinary entreaty, I will make bold to say, Peter."

"He does not mention that; he only speaks of her good looks, and what he calls her very pretty manners. In a situation not devoid of a certain awkwardness he says she displayed the most perfect tact; and although doing the honors of the house, she, with some very nice ingenuity, insinuated that she was herself but a visitor."

"She could scarce have forgotten herself so far as to think anything else, Peter," said Miss Dinah, bridling up. "I suspect her very pretty manners were successfully exercised. That old gentleman is exactly of the age to be fascinated by her."

"What! Withering, Dinah,—do you mean Withering?" cried he, laughing.

"I do, brother; and I say that he is quite capable of making her the offer of his hand. You may laugh, Peter Barrington, but my observation of young ladies has been closer and finer than yours." And the glance she gave at Josephine seemed to say that her gun had been double-shotted.

"But your remark, sister Dinah, rather addresses itself to old gentlemen than to young ladies."

"Who are much the more easily read of the two," said she, tartly. "But really, Peter, I will own that I am more deeply concerned to know what Mr. Withering has to say of our lawsuit than about Polly Dill's attractions."

"He speaks very hopefully,—very hopefully, indeed. In turning over George's papers some Hindoo documents have come to light, which Stapylton has translated, and it appears that there is a certain Moonshee, called Jokeeram, who was, or is, in the service of Meer Rustum, whose testimony would avail us much. Stapylton inclines to think he could trace this man for us. His own relations are principally in Madras, but he says he could manage to institute inquiries in Bengal."

"What is our claim to this gentleman's interest for us, Peter?"

"Mere kindness on his part; he never knew George, except from hearsay. Indeed, they could not have been contemporaries. Stapylton is not, I should say, above five-and-thirty."

"The search after this creature with the horrid name will be, of course, costly, brother Peter. It means, I take it, sending some one out to India; that is to say, sending one fool after another. Are you prepared for this expense?"

"Withering opines it would be money well spent. What he says is this: The Company will not willingly risk another inquiry before Parliament, and if we show fight and a firm resolve to give the case publicity, they will probably propose terms. This Moonshee had been in his service, but was dismissed, and his appearance as a witness on our side would occasion great uneasiness."

"You are going to play a game of brag, then, brother Peter, well aware that the stronger purse is with your antagonist?"

"Not exactly, Dinah; not exactly. We are strengthening our position so far that we may say, 'You see our order of battle; would it not be as well to make peace?' Listen to what Withering says." And Peter opened a letter of several sheets, and sought out the place he wanted.

"Here it is, Dinah. 'From one of these Hindoo papers we learn that Ram Sham-soolah Sing was not at the Meer's residence during the feast of the Rhamadan, and could not possibly have signed the document to which his name and seal are appended. Jokeeram, who was himself the Moon-shee interpreter in Luckerabad, writes to his friend Cossien Aga, and says—'"

"Brother Peter, this is like the Arabian Nights in all but the entertainment to me, and the jumble of these abominable names only drives me mad. If you flatter yourself that you can understand one particle of the matter, it must be that age has sharpened your faculties, that's all."

"I'm not quite sure of that, Dinah," said he, laughing. "I 'm half disposed to believe that years are not more merciful to our brains than to our ankles; but I'll go and take a stroll in the shady alleys under the linden-trees, and who knows how bright it will make me!"

"Am I to go with you, grandpapa?" said the young girl, rising.

"No, Fifine; I have something to say to you here," said Miss Dinah; and there was a significance in the tone that was anything but reassuring.

CHAPTER XXX.

UNDER THE LINDEN

That shady alley under the linden-trees was a very favorite walk with Peter Barrington. It was a nice cool lane, with a brawling little rivulet close beside it, with here and there a dark silent pool for the dragon-fly to skim over and see his bronzed wings reflected in the still water; and there was a rustic bench or two, where Peter used to sit and fancy he was meditating, while, in reality, he was only watching a speckled lizard in the grass, or listening to the mellow blackbird over his head. I have had occasion once before to remark on the resources of the man of imagination, but I really suspect that for the true luxury of idleness there is nothing like the temperament devoid of fancy. There is a grand breadth about those quiet, peaceful minds over which no shadows flit, and which can find sufficient occupation through the senses, and never have to go "within" for their resources. These men can sit the livelong day and watch the tide break over a rock, or see the sparrow teach her young to fly, or gaze on the bee as he dives into the deep cup of the foxglove, and actually need no more to fill the hours. For them there is no memory with its dark bygones, there is no looming future with its possible misfortunes; there is simply a half-sleepy present, with soft sounds and sweet odors through it,—a balmy kind of stupor, from which the awaking comes without a shock.

When Barrington reached his favorite seat, and lighted his cigar,—it is painting the lily for such men to smoke,—he intended to have thought over the details of Withering's letter, which were both curious and interesting; he intended to consider attentively certain points which, as Withering said, "he must master before he could adopt a final resolve;" but they were knotty points, made knottier, too, by hard Hindoo words for things unknown, and names totally unpronounceable. He used to think that he understood "George's claim" pretty well; he had fancied it was a clear and very intelligible case, that half a dozen honest men might have come to a decision on in an hour's time; but now he began to have a glimmering perception that George must have been egregiously duped and basely betrayed, and that the Company were not altogether unreasonable in assuming their distrust of him. Now, all these considerations coming down upon him at once were overwhelming, and they almost stunned him. Even his late attempt to enlighten his sister Dinah on a matter he so imperfectly understood now recoiled upon him, and added to his own mystification.

"Well, well," muttered he, at last, "I hope Tom sees his way through it,"—Tom was Withering,—"and if *he* does, there's no need of my bothering *my* head about it.

What use would there be in lawyers if they hadn't got faculties sharper than other folk? and as to 'making up my mind,' my mind is made up already, that I want to win the cause if he'll only show me how." From these musings he was drawn off by watching a large pike,—the largest pike, he thought, he had ever seen,—which would from time to time dart out from beneath a bank, and after lying motionless in the middle of the pool for a minute or so, would, with one whisk of its tail, skim back again to its hiding-place. "That fellow has instincts of its own to warn him," thought he; "he knows he was n't safe out there. *He* sees some peril that *I* cannot see; and that ought to be the way with Tom, for, after all, the lawyers are just pikes, neither more nor less." At this instant a man leaped across the stream, and hurriedly passed into the copse. "What! Mr. Conyers—Conyers, is that you?" cried Barrington; and the young man turned and came towards him. "I am glad to see you all safe and sound again," said Peter; "we waited dinner half an hour for you, and have passed all the time since in conjecturing what might have befallen you."

"Did n't Miss Barrington say—did not Miss Barrington know—" He stopped in deep confusion, and could not finish his speech.

"My sister knew nothing,—at least, she did not tell me any reason for your absence."

"No, not for my absence," began he once more, in the same embarrassment; "but as I had explained to her that I was obliged to leave this suddenly,—to start this evening—"

"To start this evening! and whither?"

"I cannot tell; I don't know,—that is, I have no plans."

"My dear boy," said the old man, affectionately, as he laid his hand on the other's arm, "if you don't know where you are going, take my word for it there is no such great necessity to go."

"Yes, but there is," replied he, quickly; "at least Miss Barrington thinks so, and at the time we spoke together she made me believe she was in the right."

"And are you of the same opinion *now?*" asked Peter, with a humorous drollery in his eye.

"I am,—that is, I was a few moments back. I mean, that whenever I recall the words she spoke to me, I feel their full conviction."

"Come, now, sit down here beside me! It can scarcely be anything I may not be a party to. Just let me hear the case like a judge in chamber"—and he smiled at an illustration that recalled his favorite passion, "I won't pretend to say my sister has not a wiser head—as I well know she has a far better heart—than myself, but now and then she lets a prejudice or a caprice or even a mere apprehension run away with her, and it's just possible it is some whim of this kind is now uppermost."

Conyers only shook his head dissentingly, and said nothing.

"Maybe I guess it,—I suspect that I guess it," said Peter, with a sly drollery about his mouth. "My sister has a notion that a young man and a young woman ought no more to be in propinquity than saltpetre and charcoal. She has been giving me a lecture on my blindness, and asking if I can't see this, that, and the other; but, besides being the least observant of mankind, I'm one of the most hopeful as regards whatever I wish to be. Now we have all of us gone on so pleasantly together, with such a thorough good understanding—such loyalty, as the French would call it—that I can't, for the life of me, detect any ground for mistrust or dread. Have n't I hit the blot, Conyers—eh?" cried he, as the young fellow grew redder and redder, till his face became crimson.

"I assured Miss Barrington," began he, in a faltering, broken voice, "that I set too much store on the generous confidence you extended to me to abuse it; that, received as I was, like one of your own blood and kindred, I never could forget the frank trustfulness with which you discussed everything before me, and made me, so to say, 'One of you.' The moment, however, that my intimacy suggested a sense of constraint, I felt the whole charm of my privilege would have departed, and it is for this reason I am going!" The last word was closed with a deep sigh, and he turned away his head as he concluded.

"And for this reason you shall not go one step," said Peter, slapping him cordially on the shoulder. "I verily believe that women think the world was made for nothing but love-making, just as the crack engineer believed rivers were intended by Providence to feed navigable canals; but you and I know a little better, not to say that a young fellow with the stamp gentleman indelibly marked on his forehead would not think of making a young girl fresh from a convent—a mere child in the ways of life—the mark of his attentions. Am I not right?"

"I hope and believe you are!"

"Stay where you are, then; be happy, and help us to feel so; and the only pledge I ask is, that whenever you suspect Dinah to be a shrewder observer and a truer prophet than her brother—you understand me—you'll just come and say, 'Peter Barrington, I'm off; good-bye!'"

"There's my hand on it," said he, grasping the old man's with warmth. "There's only one point—I have told Miss Barrington that I would start this evening."

"She'll scarcely hold you very closely to your pledge."

"But, as I understand her, you are going back to Ireland?"

"And you are coming along with us. Isn't that a very simple arrangement?"

"I know it would be a very pleasant one."

"It shall be, if it depend on me. I want to make you a fisherman too. When I was a young man, it was my passion to make every one a good horseman. If I liked a fellow, and found out that he couldn't ride to hounds, it gave me a shock little short of hearing that there was a blot on his character, so associated in my mind had become personal dash and prowess in the field with every bold and manly characteristic. As I grew older, and the rod usurped the place of the hunting-whip, I grew to fancy that your angler would be the truest type of a companion; and if you but knew," added he, as a glassy fulness dulled his eyes, "what a flattery it is to an old fellow when a young one will make a comrade of him,—what a smack of bygone days it brings up, and what sunshine it lets in on the heart,—take my word for it, you young fellows are never so vain of an old companion as we are of a young one! What are you so thoughtful about?"

"I was thinking how I was to make this explanation to Miss Barrington."

"You need not make it at all; leave the whole case in my hands. My sister knows that I owe you an *amende* and a heavy one. Let this go towards a part payment of it. But here she comes in search of me. Step away quietly, and when we meet at the tea-table all will have been settled."

Conyers had but time to make his escape, when Miss Barrington came up.

"I thought I should find you mooning down here, Peter," said she, sharply. "Whenever there is anything to be done or decided on, a Barrington is always watching a fly on a fish-pond."

"Not the women of the family, Dinah,—not the women. But what great emergency is before us now?"

"No great emergency, as you phrase it, at all, but what to men like yourself is frequently just as trying,—an occasion that requires a little tact. I have discovered—what I long anticipated has come to pass—Conyers and Fifine are on very close terms of intimacy, which might soon become attachment. I have charged him with it, and he has not altogether denied it. On the whole he has behaved well, and he goes away to-night."

"I have just seen him, Dinah. I got at his secret, not without a little dexterity on my part, and learned what had passed between you. We talked the thing over very calmly together, and the upshot is—he's not going."

"Not going! not going! after the solemn assurance he gave me!"

"But of which I absolved him, sister Dinah; or rather, which I made him retract."

"Peter Barrington, stop!" cried she, holding her hands to her temples. "I want a little time to recover myself. I must have time, or I'll not answer for my senses. Just reply to one question. I 'll ask you, have you taken an oath—are you under a vow to be the ruin of your family?"

"I don't think I have, Dinah. I 'm doing everything for the best."

"If there's a phrase in the language condemns the person that uses it, it's 'Doing everything for the best.' What does it mean but a blind, uninquiring, inconsiderate act, the work of a poor brain and sickly conscience? Don't talk to me, sir, of doing for the best, but do the best, the very best, according to the lights that guide you. You know well, perfectly well, that Fifine has no fortune, and that this young man belongs to a very rich and a very ambitious family, and that to encourage what might lead to attachment between them would be to store up a cruel wrong and a great disappointment."

"My dear Dinah, you speak like a book, but I don't agree with you."

"You don't. Will you please to state why?"

"In the first place, Dinah, forgive me for saying it, but we men do not take *your* view of these cases. We neither think that love is as catching or as dangerous as the smallpox. We imagine that two young people can associate together every day and yet never contract a lien that might break their hearts to dissolve."

"Talking politics together, perhaps; or the state of the Three per Cents?"

"Not exactly that, but talking of fifty other things that interest their time of life and tempers. Have they not songs, drawings, flowers, landscapes, and books, with all their thousand incidents, to discuss? Just remember what that writer who calls himself 'Author of Waverley'—what he alone has given us of people to talk over just as if we knew them."

"Brother Peter, I have no patience with you. You enumerate one by one all the ingredients, and you disparage the total. You tell of the flour, and the plums, and the suet, and the candied lemon, but you cry out against the pudding! Don't you see that the very themes you leave for them all conduce to what you ignore, and that your music and painting and romance-reading only lead to love-making? Don't you see this, or are you in reality—I didn't want to say it, but you have made me—are you an old fool?"

"I hope not, Dinah; but I'm not so sure you don't think me one."

"It's nothing to the purpose whether I do or not," said she; "the question is, have you asked this young man to come back with us to Ireland?"

"I have, and he is coming."

"I could have sworn to it," said she, with a sudden energy; "and if there was anything more stupid, you 'd have done it also." And with this speech, more remarkable for its vigor than its politeness, she turned away and left him.

Ere I close the chapter and the subject, let me glance, and only glance, at the room where Conyers is now standing beside Josephine. She is drawing, not very attentively or carefully, perhaps, and he is bending over her and relating, as it seems, something that has occurred to him, and has come to the end with the words, "And though I was to have gone this evening, it turns out that now I am to stay and accompany you to Ireland."

"Don't sigh so painfully over it, however," said she, gravely; "for when you come to mention how distressing it is, I 'm sure they 'll let you off."

"Fifine," said he, reproachfully, "is this fair, is this generous?"

"I don't know whether it be unfair, I don't want it to be generous," said she, boldly.

"In point of fact, then, you only wish for me here to quarrel with, is that the truth?"

"I think it better fun disagreeing with you than always saying how accurate you are, and how wise, and how well-judging. That atmosphere of eternal agreement chokes me; I feel as if I were suffocating."

"It's not a very happy temperament; it's not a disposition to boast of."

"You never did hear me boast of it; but I have heard *you* very vainglorious about your easy temper and your facile nature, which were simply indolence. Now, I have had more than enough of that in the convent, and I long for a little activity."

"Even if it were hazardous?"

"Even if it were hazardous," echoed she. "But here comes Aunt Dinah, with a face as stern as one of the sisters, and an eye that reminds me of penance and bread and water; so help me to put up my drawings, and say nothing of what we were talking."

"My brother has just told me, Mr. Conyers," said she, in a whisper, "a piece of news which it only depends upon you to make a most agreeable arrangement."

"I trust you may count upon me, madam," said he, in the same tone, and bowed low as he spoke.

"Then come with me and let us talk it over," said she, as she took his arm and led him away.

END OF VOL. I.

VOLUME II.

"WOULD I DO?"

CHAPTER I.

FIFINE AND POLLY

There are a few days in our autumnal season—very few and rare!—when we draw the curtain against the glare of the sun at breakfast, and yet in the evening are glad to gather around the cheerful glow of the fire. These are days of varied skies, with fleecy clouds lying low beneath a broad expanse of blue, with massive shadows on the mountains, and here and there over the landscape tips of sunlight that make the meanest objects pictures; and, with all these, a breezy wind that scatters the yellow leaves and shakes the tree-tops, while it curls the current of the bright river into mimic waves. The sportsman will tell you that on such days the birds are somewhat wild, and the angler will vow that no fish will rise to the fly, nor is it a scent-lying day for the harriers; and yet, with all this, there is a spring and elasticity in the air that impart themselves to the temperament, so that the active grow energetic, and even the indolent feel no touch of lassitude.

It was on the morning of such a day that Barrington, with his sister and grand-daughter, drew nigh the Home. Conyers had parted with them at Dublin, where his regiment was now stationed, but was to follow in a day or two. All the de-scriptions—descriptions which had taken the shape of warnings—which they had given Josephine of the cottage could not prevent her asking at each turn of the road if that large house yonder, if that sombre tower over the trees, if that massive gate-lodge were not theirs. "I know this is it, grandpapa," said she, clapping her hands with delight as they came opposite a low wall within which lay the spacious lawn of Cobham Park, a portion of the house itself being just visible through the trees; "don't tell me, aunt," cried she, "but let me guess it."

"It is the seat of Sir Charles Cobham, child, one of the richest baronets in the kingdom."

"There it is at last,—there it is!" cried she, straining oat of the carriage to see the handsome portico of a very large building, to which a straight avenue of oaks led up from the high-road. "My heart tells me, aunt, that this is ours!"

"It was once on a time, Fifiue," said the old man, with a quivering voice, and a glassy film over his eyes; "it was once, but it is so no longer."

"Barrington Hall has long ceased to belong to us," said Miss Dinah; "and after all the pains I have taken in description, I cannot see how you could possibly con-found it with our little cottage."

The young girl sat back without a word, and, whether from disappointment or the rebuke, looked forth no more.

"We are drawing very near now, Fifine," said the old man, after a long silence, which lasted fully two miles of the way. "Where you see the tall larches yonder—not there—lower down, at the bend of the stream; those are the trees. I declare, Dinah, I fancy they have grown since we saw them last."

"I have no doubt you do, Peter; not that you will find the cottage far more commodious and comfortable than you remembered it."

"Ah, they've repaired that stile, I see," cried he; "and very well they've done it, without cutting away the ivy. Here we are, darling; here we are!" and he grasped the young girl's hand in one of his, while he drew the other across his eyes.

"They're not very attentive, I must say, brother Peter, or they would not leave us standing, with our own gate locked against us."

"I see Darby running as fast as he can. Here he comes!"

"Oh, by the powers, ye're welcome home, your honor's reverence, and the mistresses!" cried Darby, as he fumbled at the lock, and then failing in all his efforts,—not very wonderful, seeing that he had taken a wrong key,—he seized a huge stone, and, smashing the padlock at a blow, threw wide the gate to admit them.

"You are initiated at once into our Irish ways, Fifine," said Miss Barrington. "All that you will see here is in the same style. Let that be repaired this evening, sir, and at your own cost," whispered she to Darby, into whose hand at the same moment Peter was pressing a crown piece.

"'T is the light of my eyes to see your honors home again! 'Tis like rain to the new potatoes what I feel in my heart, and looking so fresh and well too! And the young lady, she isn't—"

From what dread anticipation Darby's sudden halt saved him the expression is not for me to say, but that Peter Barrington guessed it is probable, for he lay back in the carriage and shook with laughter.

"Drive on, sir," said Miss Dinah to the postilion, "and pull up at the stone cross."

"You can drive to the door now, ma'am," said Darby, "the whole way; Miss Polly had the road made while you were away."

"What a clever girl! Who could have thought it?" said Barrington.

"I opine that we might have been consulted as to the change. On a matter as important as this, Peter, I think our voices might have been asked."

"And how well she has done it too!" muttered he, half aloud; "never touched one of those copper beeches, and given us a peep of the bright river through the meadows."

As the carriage rolled briskly along, Darby, who trotted alongside, kept up a current narrative of the changes effected during their absence.

"The ould pigeon-house is tuck down, and an iligant new one put up in the island; and the calves' paddock is thrown into the flower-garden, and there's a beautiful flight of steps down to the river, paved with white stones,—sorrow one is n't white as snow."

"It is a mercy we had not a sign over the door, brother Peter," whispered Miss Dinah, "or this young lady's zeal would have had it emblazoned like a shield in heraldry."

"Oh, how lovely, how beautiful, how exquisite!" cried Josephine, as they came suddenly round the angle of a copse and directly in front of the cottage.

Nor was the praise exaggerated. It was all that she had said. Over a light trellis-work, carried along under the thatch, the roses and jessamine blended with the clematis and the passion-flower, forming a deep eave of flowers, drooping in heavy festoons across the spaces between the windows, and meeting the geraniums which grew below. Through the open sashes the rooms might be seen, looking more like beautifnl bowers than the chambers of a dwelling-house. And over all, in sombre grandeur, bent the great ilex-trees, throwing their grand and tranquil shade over the cottage and the little grass-plot and even the river itself, as it swept smoothly by. There was in the stillness of that perfumed air, loaded with the sweet-brier and the rose, a something of calm and tranquillity; while in the isolation of the spot there was a sense of security that seemed to fill op the measure of the young girl's hopes, and made her exclaim with rapture, "Oh, this, indeed, is beautiful!"

"Yes, my darling Fifine!" said the old man, as he pressed her to his heart; "your home, your own home! I told you, my dear child, it was not a great castle, no fine château, like those on the Meuse and the Sambre, but a lowly cottage with a thatched roof and a rustic porch."

"In all this ardor for decoration and smartness," broke in Miss Dinah, "it would not surprise me to find that the peacock's tail had been picked out in fresh colors and varnished."

"Faix! your honor is not far wrong," interposed Darby, who had an Irish tendency to side with the majority. "She made us curry and wash ould Sheela, the ass, as if she was a race-horse."

"I hope poor Wowsky escaped," said Barrington, laughing.

"That's what he didn't! He has to be scrubbed with soap and water every morning, and his hair divided all the way down his back, like a Christian's, and his tail looks like a bunch of switch grass."

"That 's the reason he has n't come out to meet me; the poor fellow is like his betters,—he's not quite sure that his altered condition improves him."

"You have at least one satisfaction, brother Peter," said Miss Dinah, sharply; "you find Darby just as dirty and uncared for as you left him."

"By my conscience, there 's another of us is n't much changed since we met last," muttered Darby, but in a voice only audible to himself.

"Oh, what a sweet cottage! What a pretty summer-house!" cried Josephine, as the carriage swept round the copse, and drew short up at the door.

"This summer-house is your home, Fifine," said Miss Barrington, tartly.

"Home! home! Do you mean that we live here,—live here always, aunt?"

"Most distinctly I do," said she, descending and addressing herself to other cares. "Where's Jane? Take these trunks round by the back door. Carry this box to the green-room,—to Miss Josephine's room," said she, with a stronger stress on the words.

"Well, darling, it is a very humble, it is a very lowly," said Barrington, "but let us see if we cannot make it a very happy home;" but as he turned to embrace her, she was gone.

"I told you so, brother Peter,—I told you so, more than once; but, of course, you have your usual answer, 'We must do the best we can!' which simply means, doing worse than we need do."

Barrington was in no mood for a discussion; he was too happy to be once more at home to be ruffled by any provocation his sister could give him. Wherever he turned, some old familiar object met his eye and seemed to greet him, and he bustled in and out from his little study to the garden, and then to the stable, where he patted old Roger; and across to the cow-house, where Maggie knew him, and bent her great lazy eyes softly on him; and then down to the liver-side, where, in gilt letters, "Josephine" shone on the trim row-boat he had last seen half rotten on the bank; for Polly had been there too, and her thoughtful good-nature, forgetting nothing which might glad them on their coming.

Meanwhile, Josephine had reached her chamber, and, locking the door, sat down and leaned her head on the table. Though no tears fell from her eyes, her bosom heaved and fell heavily, and more than one deep sigh escaped her. Was it disappointment that had so overcome her? Had she fancied something grander and more pretentious than this lonely cottage? Was it that Aunt Dinah's welcome was wanting in affection? What revulsion could it be that so suddenly overwhelmed her? Who can tell these things, who can explain how it is that, without any definite picture of an unexpected joy, imagination will so work upon us that reality will bring nothing but a blank? It is not that the object is less attractive than is hoped for, it is simply that a dark shadow has passed over our own hearts; the sense of enjoyment has been dulled, and we are sad without a reason. If we underrate sorrows of our youth,—and this is essentially one of them,—it is because our mature age leaves us nothing of that temperament on which such afflictions preyed.

Josephine, without knowing why, without even a reason, wished herself back in the convent. There, if there was a life of sombre monotony and quietude, there was at least companionship; she had associates of her own age. They had pursuits in common, shared the same hopes and wishes and fears; but here—but here—Just as her thoughts had carried her so far, a tap—a very gentle tap—came to the door. Josephine heard it, but made no answer. It was repeated a little louder, and then a low pleasing voice she had never heard before said, "May I come in?"

"No," said Josephine,—"yes—that is—who are you?"

"Polly Dill," was the answer; and Josephine arose and unlocked the door.

"Miss Barrington told me I might take this liberty," said Polly, with a faint smile. "She said, 'Go and make acquaintance for yourself; I never play master of the ceremonies.'"

"And you are Polly,—the Polly Dill I have heard so much of?" said Josephine, regarding her steadily and fixedly.

"How stranded your friends must have been for a topic when they talked of *me!*" said Polly, laughing.

"It is quite true you have beautiful teeth,—I never saw such beautiful teeth," said Josephine to herself, while she still gazed earnestly at her.

"And you," said Polly, "are so like what I had pictured you,—what I hoped you would be. I find it hard to believe I see you for the first time."

"So, then, *you* did not think the Rajah's daughter should be a Moor?" said Josephine, half haughtily. "It is very sad to see what disappointments I had caused." Neither the saucy toss of the head, nor the tone that accompanied these words, were lost upon Polly, who began to feel at once that she understood the speaker.

"And your brother," continued Josephine, "is the famous Tom Dill I have heard such stories about?"

"Poor Tom! he is anything rather than famous."

"Well, he is remarkable; he is odd, original, or whatever you would call it. Fred told me he never met any one like him."

"Tom might say as much of Mr. Conyers, for, in truth, no one ever showed him such kindness."

"Fred told me nothing of that; but perhaps," added she, with a flashing eye, "you were more in his confidence than I was."

"I knew very little of Mr. Conyers; I believe I could count on the fingers of one hand every time I met him."

"How strange that you should have made so deep an impression, Miss Dill!"

"I am flattered to hear it, but more surprised than flattered."

"But I don't wonder at it in the least," said Josephine, boldly. "You are very handsome, you are very graceful, and then—" She hesitated and grew confused, and stammered, and at last said, "and then there is that about you which seems to say, 'I have only to wish, and I can do it.'"

"I have no such gift, I assure you," said Polly, with a half-sad smile.

"Oh, I know you are very clever; I have heard how accomplished you were, how beautifully you rode, how charmingly you sang. I wish he had not told me of it all—for if—for if—"

"If what? Say on!"

"If you were not so superior to me, I feel that I could love you;" and then with a bound she threw her arms around Polly's neck, and clasped her affectionately to her bosom.

Sympathy, like a fashionable physician, is wonderfully successful where there is little the matter. In the great ills of life, when the real afflictions come down to crush, to wound, or to stun us, we are comparatively removed from even the kindest of our comforters. Great sorrows are very selfish things. In the lighter maladies, however, in the smaller casualties of fortune, sympathy is a great remedy, and we are certain to find that, however various our temperaments, it has a sort of specific for each. Now Josephine Barrington had not any great cares upon her heart; if the balance were to be struck between them, Polly Dill could have numbered ten, ay, twenty, for her one, but she thought hers was a case for much commiseration, and she liked commiseration, for there are moral hypochondrias as well as physical ones. And so she told Polly how she had neither father nor mother, nor any other belongings than "dear old grandpapa and austere Aunt Dinah;" that she had been brought up in a convent, never knowing one of the pleasures of youth, or her mind being permitted to stray beyond the dreary routine of prayer and penance. Of music she knew nothing but the solemn chants of the organ, and even flowers were to her eyes but the festal decorations of the high altar; and, lastly, she vaguely balanced between going back to the dismal existence of the cloister, or entering upon the troubled sea of life, so full of perils to one unpractised and unskilled as she was. Now Polly was a very pretty comforter through these afflictions; her own home experiences were not all rose-colored, but the physician who whispers honeyed consolations to the patient has often the painful consciousness of a deeper malady within than that for which he ministers. Polly knew something of a life of struggle and small fortune, with its daily incident of debt and dun. She knew what it was to see money mix itself with every phase of existence, throwing its damper over joy, arresting the hand of benevolence, even denying to the sick-bed the little comforts that help to cheat misery. She knew how penury can eat its canker into the heart till all things take the color of thrift, and life becomes at last the terrible struggle of a swimmer storm-tossed and weary; and yet, with all this experience in her heart, she could whisper cheerful counsels to Josephine, and tell her that the world had a great many pleasant paths through it, though one was occasionally footsore before reaching them; and in this way they talked till they grew very fond of each other, and Josephine was ready to confess that the sorrow nearest to her heart was parting with her. "But must you go, dearest Polly,—must you really go?"

"I must, indeed," said she, laughing; "for if I did not, two little sisters of mine would go supperless to bed, not to speak of a small boy who is waiting for me with a Latin grammar before him; and the cook must get her orders for to-morrow; and papa must have his tea; and this short, stumpy little key that you see here unlocks the oat-bin, without which an honest old pony would share in the family fast: so that, all things considered, my absence would be far from advisable."

"And when shall we meet again, Polly?"

"Not to-morrow, dear; for to-morrow is our fair at Inistioge, and I have yarn to buy, and some lambs to sell."

"And could you sell lambs, Polly?" said Josephine, with an expression of blank disappointment in her face.

Polly smiled, but not without a certain sadness, as she said, "There are some sentimentalities which, to one in my condition, would just be as unsuitable as Brussels lace or diamonds. They are born of luxury and indolence, and pertain to those whose existence is assured to them; and my own opinion is, they are a poor privilege. At all events," added she, rapidly, "they are not for me, and I do not wish for them."

"The day after to-morrow, then, you will come here,—promise me that."

"It will be late, then, towards evening, for I have made an engagement to put a young horse in harness,—a three-year-old, and a sprightly one, they tell me,—so that I may look on the morning as filled. I see, my dear child, how shocked you are with all these unladylike cares and duties; but poor Tom and I used to weld our lives together, and while I took my share of boat-building one day, he helped me in the dairy the day after; but now that he is gone, our double functions devolve upon me."

"How happy you must be!"

"I think I am; at least, I have no time to spare for unhappiness."

"If I could but change with you, Polly!"

"Change what, my dear child?"

"Condition, fortune, belongings,—everything."

"Take my word for it, you are just as well as you are; but I suppose it's very natural for one to fancy he could carry another's burden easier than his own, for it was only a few moments back I thought how I should like to be you."

"To be me,—to be me!"

"Of course I was wrong, dearest. It was only a passing, fleeting thought, and I now see how absurd I was to wish to be very beautiful, dearly loved, and affection-ately cared for, with a beautiful home to live in, and every hour free to be happy. Oh, what a sigh, dearest, what a sigh! but I assure you I have my calamities too; the mice have got at the seeds in my onion-bed, and I don't expect to see one come up."

If Josephine's first impulse was to feel angry, her next was to laugh out, which she did heartily; and passing her arm fondly round Polly's waist, she said, "I'll get used to your raillery, Polly, and not feel sore at it; but remember, too, it's a spirit I never knew before."

"How good and generous, then, to bear it so well!" said Polly, affectionately; "your friend Mr. Conyers did not show the same patience."

"You tried him, then?" said Josephine, with a half-eager glance.

"Of course; I talked to him as I do to every one. But there goes your dinner-bell." Checking herself on a reflection over the pretension of this summons of three people to a family meal in a cottage, Polly tied on her bonnet and said "Good-bye."

CHAPTER II.

AT HOME AGAIN

The Barringtons had not been quite a fortnight settled in their home, when a note came from Conyers, lamenting, in most feeling terms, that he could not pay them his promised visit. If the epistle was not very long, it was a grumble from beginning to end. "Nobody would know," wrote he, "it was the same regiment poor Colonel Hunter commanded. Our Major is now in command,—the same Stapylton you have heard me speak of; and if we never looked on him too favorably, we now especially detest him. His first step was to tell us we were disorderly, ill-dressed, and ill-disciplined; but we were even less prepared to hear that we could not ride. The result of all this is, we have gone to school again,—even old captains, who have served with distinction in the field, have been consigned to the riding-house; and we poor subs are treated as if we were the last refuse of all the regiments of the army, sent here to be reformed and corrected. We have incessant drills, parades, and inspections, and, worse again, all leave is stopped. If I was not in the best of temper with the service before, you may judge how I feel towards it now. In fact, if it were not that I expect my father back in England by the middle of May, I'd send in my papers and leave at once. How I fall back now in memory to the happy days of my ramble with you, and wonder if I shall ever see the like again. And how I hate myself for not having felt at the time how immeasurably delightful they were! Trust me never to repeat the mistake if I have the opportunity given me. I asked this morning for three days—only three—to run down and see you once more before we leave,—for we are ordered to Honnslow,—and I was refused. But this was not all: not content with rejecting my request, he added what he called an expression of astonishment that an officer so deficient in his duties should care to absent himself from regimental discipline."

"Poor boy!—this is, indeed, too bad," said Miss Dinah, as she had read thus far; "only think, Peter, how this young fellow, spoiled and petted as he was as a child,—denied nothing, pampered as though he were a prince,—should find himself the mark of so insulting a tyranny. Are you listening to me, Peter Barrington?"

"Eh,—what? No, thank you, Dinah; I have made an excellent breakfast," said Barrington, hurriedly, and again addressed himself to the letter he was reading. "That's what I call a Trump, Dinah,—a regular Trump."

"Who is the especial favorite that has called for the very choice eulogy?" said she, bridling up.

"Gone into the thing, too, with heart and soul,—a noble fellow!" continued

Barrington.

"Pray enlighten us as to the name that calls forth such enthusiasm."

"Stapylton, my dear Dinah,—Major Stapylton. In all my life I do not remember one instance to parallel with this generous and disinterested conduct. Listen to what Withering says,—not a man given to take up rash impressions in favor of a stranger. Listen to this: 'Stapylton has been very active,—written to friends, both at Calcutta and Agra, and shown, besides, an amount of acuteness in pursuit of what is really important, that satisfies me a right good common lawyer has been lost by his being a soldier.' And here, again he recurs to him: it is with reference to certain documents: 'S. persists in believing that with proper diligence these may be recovered; he says that it is a common practice with the Moonshees to retain papers, in the hope of their being one day deemed of value; and he is fully persuaded that they have not been destroyed. There is that about the man's manner of examining a question,—his patience, his instinctive seizure of what is of moment, and his invariable rejection of whatever is immaterial; and, lastly, his thorough appreciation of the character of that evidence which would have most weight with the Indian Board, which dispose me to regard him as an invaluable ally to our cause.'"

"Do me the favor to regard this picture of your friend now," said Miss Barrington, as she handed the letter from Conyers across the table.

Barrington read it over attentively. "And what does this prove, my dear sister?" said he. "This is the sort of stereotyped complaint of every young fellow who has been refused a leave. I have no doubt Hunter was too easy-tempered to have been strict in discipline, and the chances are these young dogs had everything their own way till Stapylton came amongst them. I find it hard to believe that any man likes unpopularity."

"Perhaps not, Peter Barrington; but he may like tyranny more than he hates unpopularity; and, for my own part, this man is odious to me."

"Don't say so, Dinah,—don't say so, I entreat of you, for he will be our guest here this very day."

"Our guest!—why, is not the regiment under orders to leave?"

"So it is; but Withering says it would be a great matter if we could have a sort of consultation together before the Major leaves Ireland. There are innumerable little details which he sees ought to be discussed between us; and so he has persuaded him to give us a day,—perhaps two days,—no small boon, Dinah, from one so fully occupied as he is."

"I wish he would not make the sacrifice, Peter."

"My dear sister, are we so befriended by Fortune that we can afford to reject the kindness of our fellows?"

"I'm no believer in chance friendships, Peter Barrington; neither you nor I are such interesting orphans as to inspire sympathy at first sight."

Josephine could not help a laugh at Miss Dinah's illustration, and old Barriqgton himself heartily joined in the merriment, not sorry the while to draw the discussion into a less stern field. "Come, come, Dinah," said he, gayly, "let us put out a few bottles of that old Madeira in the sun; and if Darby can find us a salmon-trout, we 'll do our best to entertain our visitors."

"It never occurred to me to doubt the probability of their enjoying themselves, Peter; my anxieties were quite on another score."

"Now, Fifine," continued Barrington, "we shall see if Polly Dill has really made you the perfect housekeeper she boasted. The next day or two will put your talents to the test."

"Oh, if we could only have Polly herself here!"

"What for?—on what pretext, Miss Barrington?" said Dinah, haughtily. "I have not, so far as I am aware, been accounted very ignorant of household cares."

"Withering declares that your equal is not in Europe, Dinah."

"Mr. Withering's suffrage can always be bought by a mock-turtle soup, and a glass of Roman punch after it."

"How he likes it,—how he relishes it! He says that he comes back to the rest of the dinner with the freshness of a man at an assize case."

"So like him!" said Dinah, scornfully; "he has never an illustration that is not taken from the Four Courts. I remember one day, when asking for the bill of fare, he said, 'Will you kindly let me look at the cause list.' Prepare yourself, Josephine, for an avalanche of law anecdotes and Old Bailey stories, for I assure you you will hear nothing for the next three days but drolleries that have been engrossed on parchment and paid stamp duty to the Crown."

Barrington gave a smile, as though in protest against the speech, and left the room. In truth, he was very anxious to be alone, and to think over, at his leisure, a short passage in his letter which he had not summoned courage to read aloud. It was Withering's opinion that to institute the inquiries in India a considerable sum of money would be required, and he had left it for Barrington's consideration whether it were wiser to risk the great peril of this further involvement, or once more to try what chance there might be of a compromise. Who knows what success might have attended the suggestion if the old lawyer had but employed any other word! Compromise, however, sounded to his ears like an unworthy concession,—a surrender of George's honor. Compromise might mean money for his granddaughter, and shame to her father's memory. Not, indeed, that Withering was, as a man, one to counsel such a course, but Withering was a lawyer, and in the same spirit that he would have taken a verdict for half his claim if he saw an adverse feeling in the jury-box, so he would bow to circumstances that were stronger than him, and accept the best he could, if he might not have all that he ought But could Barrington take this view? He thought not. His conviction was that the main question to establish was the fair fame and honor of his son; his guide was, how George himself would have acted—would have felt—in the same contingency; and he muttered, "He'd have been a hardy fellow who would have hinted at compromise to *him*."

The next point was how the means for the coming campaign were to be provided. He had already raised a small sum by way of mortgage on the "Home," and nothing remained but to see what further advance could be made on the same security. When Barrington was a great estated gentleman with a vast fortune at his command, it cost him wonderfully little thought to contract a loan, or even to sell a farm. A costly election, a few weeks of unusual splendor, an unfortunate night at play, had made such sacrifices nothing very unusual, and he would give his orders on this score as unconcernedly as he would bid his servant replenish his glass at table. Indeed, he had no more fear of exhausting his fortune than he felt as to out-drinking his cellar. There was enough there, as he often said, for those who should come after him. And now, what a change! He stood actually appalled at the thought of a mortgage for less than a thousand pounds. But so it is; the cockboat may be more to a man than was once the three-decker. The cottage was his all now; that lost, and they were houseless. Was it not a bold thing to risk everything on one more throw? There was the point over which he now pondered as he walked slowly along in the little shady alley between the laurel hedges. He had no friend nearer his heart than Withering, no one to whom he could unbosom himself so frankly and so freely, and yet this was a case on which he could not ask his counsel. All his life long he had strenuously avoided suffering a question of the kind to intervene between them. Of his means, his resources, his straits, or his demands, Withering knew positively nothing. It was with Barrington a point of delicacy to maintain this reserve towards one who was always his lawyer, and often his guest. The very circumstance of his turning innkeeper was regarded by Withering as savoring far more of caprice than necessity, and Barrington took care to strengthen this impression.

If, then, Withering's good sense and worldly knowledge would have been invaluable aids to him in this conjunction, he saw he could not have them. The same delicacy which debarred him heretofore, would still interpose against his appeal to that authority. And then he thought how he had once troops of friends to whom he could address himself for counsel. There is nothing more true, indeed, than the oft-uttered scoff on the hollowness of those friendships which attach to the days of prosperous fortune, and the world is very prone to point to the utter loneliness of him who has been shipwrecked by Fate; but let us be just in our severity, and let us own that a man's belongings, his associates, his—what common parlance calls—friends, are the mere accidents of his station, and they no more accompany him in his fall than do the luxuries he has forfeited. From the level from which he has lapsed they have not descended. They are there, living to-day as they lived yesterday. If their sympathy is not with him, it is because neither are they themselves; they cross each other no more. Such friendships are like the contracts made with a crew for a particular voyage,—they end with the cruise. No man ever understood this better than Barrington; no man ever bore the world less of ill will for its part towards himself. If now and then a sense of sadness would cloud him at some mark of passing forgetfulness, he would not own to the gloomy feeling; while to any show of recognition, to any sign of a grateful remembrance of the past, he would grow boastful to very vanity. "Look there, Dinah," he would say, "what a noble-hearted fellow that is! I scarcely was more than commonly civil to him formerly, and you saw how courteous he was in making a place for us, how heartily he hoped I was in good health."

"I'll send over to Dill and have a talk with him," was Barrington's last resolve, as he turned the subject over and over in his mind. "Dill 's a shrewd fellow, and I 'm not sure that he has not laid by a little money; he might feel no objection to a good investment for it, with such security." And he looked around as he spoke on the trees, some of which he planted, every one of which he knew, and sighed heavily. "He 'll scarce love the spot more than I did," muttered he, and walked along with his head down. After a while he took out Withering's letter from his pocket and re-read it. Somehow, it was hard to say why, it did not read so promisingly as at first. The difficulties to be encountered were very stubborn ones, so much so that he very palpably hinted how much better some amicable settlement would be than an open contest wherein legal subtlety and craft should be evoked. There was so much of that matter always taken for granted, to be proved, to be demonstrated true on evidence, that it actually looked appalling. "Of the searches and inquiries instituted in India," wrote Withering, "I can speak but vaguely; but I own the very distance magnifies them immensely to my eyes." "Tom is growing old, not a doubt of it," muttered Barrington; "these were not the sort of obstacles that could have terrified him once on a time. He 'd have said, 'If there 's evidence, we 'll have it; if there's a document, we 'll find it.' It's India, that far-away land, that has frightened him. These lawyers, like certain sportsmen, lose their nerve if you take them out of their own country. It 's the new style of fences they can't face. Well, thanks to him who gave it, I have my stout heart still, and I 'll go on."

"Going on" was, however, not the easy task it first seemed, nor was the pleasantest part of it the necessity of keeping the secret from his sister. Miss Dinah had from the first discouraged the whole suit. The adversary was too powerful, the odds against them were too great; the India Board had only to protract and prolong the case and *they* must be beaten from sheer exhaustion. How, then, should he reconcile her to mortgaging the last remnant of all their fortune for "one more throw on the table"? "No chance of persuading a woman that this would be wise," said he. And he thought, when he had laid the prejudice of sex as the ground of error, he had completed his argument.

"Going on" had its fine generous side about it, also, that cheered and elevated him. It was for George he was doing it, and that dear girl, whose every trait recalled her father; for let those explain it who can, she, who had never seen nor even heard of her father since her infancy, inherited all his peculiar ways and habits, and every trick of his manner. Let me own that these, even more than any qualities of sterling worth, endeared her to her grandfather; and just as he had often declared no rank or position that could befall George would have been above his deserts, so he averred that if Josephine were to be the greatest heiress in England to-morrow, she would be a grace and an ornament to the station. If Aunt Dinah would occasionally attempt to curb this spirit, or even limit its extravagance, his invariable answer was, "It may be all as you say, sister, but for the life of me I cannot think my swans to be geese."

As he thus mused and meditated, he heard the wicket of the garden open and shut, and shortly afterwards a half-shambling shuffling step on the gravel. Before he had time to speculate on whose it should be, he saw Major M'Cormick limping laboriously towards him.

"How is this, Major?" cried he; "has the change of weather disagreed with your rheumatism?"

"It's the wound; it's always worse in the fall of the year," croaked the other. "I'd have been up to see you before but for the pains, and that old fool Dill—a greater fool myself for trusting him—made me put on a blister down what he calls the course of the nerve, and I never knew torture till I tried it."

"My sister Dinah has, I verily believe, the most sovereign remedy for these pains."

"Is it the green draught? Oh, don't I know it," burst out the Major. "You might hear my shouts the day I took it down at Inistioge. There was n't a bit of skin left on my lips, and when I wiped the perspiration off my head my hair came off too. Aquafortis is like egg-flip compared to that blessed draught; and I remember well how I crawled to my writing-desk and wrote, 'Have me opened,' for I knew I was poisoned."

"Did you tell my sister of your sufferings?"

"To be sure I did, and she only smiled and said that I took it when I was fasting, or when I was full, I forget which; and that I ought to have taken a brisk walk, and I only able to creep; and only one spoonful at a time, and it was the whole bottle I swallowed. In fact, she owned afterwards that nothing but the strength of a horse could have saved me."

Peter found it very hard to maintain a decent gravity at the play of the Major's features, which during the narrative recalled every dire experience of his medicine.

"Well, come into the house and we'll give you something better," said Barrington, at last.

"I think I saw your granddaughter at the window as I came by,—a good-looking young woman, and not so dark as I suspected she 'd be."

"There's not a handsomer girl in Ireland; and as to skin, she 's not as brown as her father."

"It wouldn't be easy to be that; he was about three shades deeper than a Portuguese."

"George Barrington was confessedly the finest-looking fellow in the King's army, and as English-looking a gentleman as any man in it."

The tone of this speech was so palpably that of one who would not stand the very shadow of a rejoinder, that the Major held his peace, and shuffled along without a word. The thought, however, of administering a rebuke to any one within the precincts of his home was so repugnant to Barrington's nature, that he had scarcely uttered the words than he was eager to repair them, and with a most embarrassed humility he stammered out something about their recent tour abroad and all the enjoyment it had given them.

"Maybe so," rejoined the other, dryly; "but I never saw any pleasure in spending money you could keep."

"My dear Major, that is precisely the very money that does procure pleasure."

"Wasn't that a post-chaise I saw through the trees? There it is again; it's making straight for the 'Home,'" said M'Cormick, pointing with his stick.

"Yes," said Peter; "I was expecting a couple of friends to pass a day or so with me here. Will you excuse me if I hurry forward to welcome them?"

"Don't make a stranger of me; I'll saunter along at my leisure," said the Major, as Barrington walked briskly on towards the cottage.

CHAPTER III.

A SMALL DINNER-PARTY

Withering and Stapylton had arrived fully two hoars earlier than they were expected, and Miss Dinah was too deeply engaged in the household cares that were to do them honor to receive them. Josephine, too, was not less busily occupied, for her conventual education had made her wonderfully skilful in all sorts of confectionery, and she was mistress of devices in spun sugar and preserved fruits, which rose in Aunt Dinah's eyes to the dignity of high art. Barrington, however, was there to meet them, and with a cordial welcome which no man could express more gracefully. The luncheon hour passed pleasantly over, for all were in good humor and good spirits. Withering's holiday always found him ready to enjoy it, and when could old Peter feel so happy as when he had a guest beneath his roof who thoroughly appreciated the cottage, and entered into the full charm of its lovely scenery! Such was Stapylton; he blended a fair liking for the picturesque with a natural instinct for comfort and homeliness, and he saw in this spot what precisely embraced both elements. It was very beautiful; but, better still, it was very lovable. "It was so rare"—so, at least, he told Barrington—"to find a cottage wherein internal comfort had not been sacrificed to some requirement of outward show. There was only one way of doing this," said he, as Barrington led him through the little flower-garden, giving glimpses of the rooms within as they passed,—"only one way, Mr. Barrington; a man must have consummate taste, and strong credit at his banker's." Barrington's cheek grew a thought redder, and he smiled that faint sad smile which now and then will break from one who feels that he could rebut what he has just heard, if it were but right or fitting he should do so. Of course, amongst really distressing sensations this has no place; but yet there is a peculiar pain in being complimented by your friend on the well-to-do condition of your fortune when your conscience is full of the long watching hours of the night, or, worse still, the first awaking thought of difficulties to which you open your eyes of a morning. It is not often, nor are there many to whom you can say, "I cannot tell the day or the hour when all this shall pass away from me; my head is racked with care, and my heart heavy with anxiety." How jarring to be told of all the things you ought to do! You who could so well afford it! And how trying to have to take shelter from your necessity under the shadow of a seeming stinginess, and to bear every reflection on your supposed thrift rather than own to your poverty!

If Withering had been with them as they strolled, this, perhaps, might have been avoided; he had all a lawyer's technical skill to change a topic; but Withering had gone to take his accustomed midday nap, the greatest of all the luxuries his time of idleness bestowed upon him.

Now, although Stapylton's alludings—and they were no more—to Barrington's gifts of fortune were such as perfectly consisted with good taste and good breeding, Barring-ton felt them all painfully, and probably nothing restrained him from an open disclaimer of their fitness save the thought that from a host such an avowal would sound ungracefully. "It is my duty now," reasoned he, "to make my guest feel that all the attentions he receives exact no sacrifice, and that the pleasure his presence affords is unalloyed by a single embarrassment. If he must hear of my difficulties, let it be when he is not beneath my roof." And so he let Stapylton talk away about the blessings of tranquil affluence, and the happiness of him whose only care was to find time for the enjoyments that were secured to him. He let him quote Pope and Wharton and Edmund Burke, and smiled the blandest concurrence with what was irritating him almost to fever.

"This is Withering's favorite spot," said Peter, as they gained the shade of a huge ilex-tree, from which two distinct reaches of the river were visible.

"And it shall be mine, too," said Stapylton, throwing himself down in the deep grass; "and as I know you have scores of things which claim your attention, let me release you, while I add a cigar—the only possible enhancement—to the delight of this glorious nook."

"Well, it shall be as you wish. We dine at six. I'll go and look after a fish for our entertainment;" and Barrington turned away into the copse, not sorry to release his heart by a heavy sigh, and to feel he was alone with his cares.

Let us turn for a moment to M'Cormick, who continued to saunter slowly about the garden, in the expectation of Barrington's return. Wearied at length with waiting, and resolved that his patience should not go entirely unrequited, he turned into a little shady walk on which the windows of the kitchen opened. Stationing himself there, in a position to see without being seen, he took what he called an observation of all within. The sight was interesting, even if he did not bring to it the appreciation of a painter. There, upon a spacious kitchen table, lay a lordly sirloin, richly and variously colored, flanked by a pair of plump guinea-hens and a fresh salmon of fully twenty pounds' weight. Luscious fruit and vegetables were heaped and mingled in a wild profusion, and the speckled plumage of game was half hidden under the massive bunches of great hot-house grapes. It is doubtful if Sneyders himself could have looked upon the display with a higher sense of enjoyment It is, indeed, a question between the relative merits of two senses, and the issue lies between the eye and the palate.

Wisely reasoning that such preparations were not made for common guests, M'Cormick ran over in his mind all the possible and impossible names he could think of, ending at last with the conviction it was some "Nob" he must have met abroad, and whom in a moment of his expansive hospitality he had invited to visit him. "Isn't it like them!" muttered he. "It would be long before they'd think of such an entertainment to an old neighbor like myself; but here they are spending—who knows how much?—for somebody that to-morrow or next day won't remember their names, or maybe, perhaps, laugh when they think of the funny old woman they saw, — the 'Fright' with the yellow shawl and the orange bonnet. Oh, the world, the world!"

It is not for me to speculate on what sort of thing the world had been, if the Major himself had been intrusted with the control and fashion of it; but I have my doubts that we are just as well off as we are. "Well, though they haven't the manners to say 'M'Cormick; will you stop and dine?' they haven't done with me yet; not a bit!" And with this resolve he entered the cottage, and found his way to the drawing-room. It was unoccupied; so he sat himself down in a comfortable armchair, to await events and their issue. There were books and journals and newspapers about; but the Major was not a reader, and so he sat musing and meditating, while the time went by. Just as the clock struck five, Miss Dinah, whose various cares of housewifery had given her a very busy day, was about to have a look at the drawing-room before she went to dress, and being fully aware that one of her guests was asleep, and the other full stretched beside the river, she felt she could go her "rounds" without fear of being observed. Now, whatever had been the peculiar functions she was lately engaged in, they had exacted from her certain changes in costume more picturesque than flattering. In the first place, the sleeves of her dress were rolled up above the elbows, displaying arms more remarkable for bone than beauty. A similar curtailment of her petticoats exhibited feet and ankles which — not to be ungallant — might be called massive rather than elegant; and lastly, her two long curls of auburn hair — curls which, in the splendor of her full toilette, were supposed to be no mean aids to her captivating powers — were now tastefully festooned and fastened to the back of her head, pretty much as a pair of hawsers are occasionally disposed on the bow of a merchantman! Thus costumed, she had advanced into the middle of the room before she saw the Major.

"A pleasure quite unexpected, sir, is this," said she, with a vigorous effort to shake out what sailors would call her "lower courses." "I was not aware that you were here."

"Indeed, then, I came in myself, just like old times. I said this morning, if it 's fine to-day, I 'll just go over to the 'Fisherman's Home.'"

"'The Home,' sir, if you please. We retain so much of the former name." But just as she uttered the correction, a chance look at the glass conveyed the condition of her head-gear, — a startling fact which made her cheeks perfectly crimson. "I lay stress upon the change of name, sir," continued she, "as intimating that we are no longer innkeepers, and expect something, at least, of the deference rendered to those who call their house their own."

"To be sure, and why not?" croaked out the Major, with a malicious grin. "And I forgot all about it, little thinking, indeed, to surprise you in 'dishabille,' as they call it."

"*You* surprise me, sir, every time we meet," said she, with flashing eyes. "And you make me feel surprised with myself for my endurance!" And so saying, she retired towards the door, covering her retreat as she went by every object of furniture that presented itself, and, like a skilful general, defending her rear by every artifice of the ground. Thus did she exit, and with a bang of the door—as eloquent as any speech—close the colloquy.

"Faix! and the Swiss costume doesn't become you at all!" said the Major, as he sat back in his chair, and cackled over the scene.

As Miss Barrington, boiling with passion, passed her brother's door, she stopped to knock.

"Peter!" cried she. "Peter Barrington, I say!" The words were, however, not well out, when she heard a step ascending the stair. She could not risk another discovery like the last; so, opening the door, she said, "That hateful M'Cormick is below. Peter, take care that on no account—"

There was no time to finish, and she had barely an instant to gain her own room, when Stapylton reached the corridor.

Peter Barrington had, however, heard enough to inform him of his sister's high behest. Indeed, he was as quick at interpreting brief messages as people have grown in these latter days of telegraphic communication. Oracular utterings had been more than once in his life his only instructors, and he now knew that he had been peremptorily ordered not to ask the Major to dinner.

There are, doubtless, people in this world—I almost fancy I have met one or two such myself—who would not have felt peculiar difficulty in obeying this command; who would have gone down to the drawing-room and talked coolly to the visitor, discussing commonplaces, easily and carelessly, noting the while how at every pause of the conversation each was dwelling on the self-same point, and yet, with a quiet abstinence, never touching it, till with a sigh, that was half a malediction, the uninvited would rise to take leave. Barrington was not of this number. The man who sat under his roof was sacred. He could have no faults; and to such a pitch had this punctilio carried him, that had an actual enemy gained the inside of his threshold, he would have spared nothing to treat him with honor and respect.

"Well, well," muttered he, as he slowly descended the stairs, "it will be the first time in my life I ever did it, and I don't know how to go about it now."

When a frank and generous man is about to do something he is ashamed of, how readily will a crafty and less scrupulous observer detect it! M'Cormick read Barrington's secret before he was a minute in the room. It was in vain Peter affected an off-hand easy manner, incidentally dropping a hint that the Attorney-General and another friend had just arrived,—a visit, a mere business visit it was, to be passed with law papers and parchments. "Poor fun when the partridges were in the stubble, but there was no help for it. Who knew, however, if he could not induce them to give him an extra day, and if I can, Major, you must promise to come over and meet them. You 'll be charmed with Withering, he has such a fund of agreeability. One of the old school, but not the less delightful to you and me. Come, now, give me your word—for—shall we say Saturday?—Yes, Saturday!"

"I 've nothing to say against it," grumbled out M'Cormick, whose assent was given, as attorneys say, without prejudice to any other claim.

MISS DINAH IN DISHABILLE

"You shall hear from me in the morning, then," said Peter. "I 'll send you a line to say what success I have had with my friends."

"Any time in the day will do," said the Major, unconcernedly; for, in truth, the future never had in his estimation the same interest as the present. As for the birds in the bush, he simply did not believe in them at all.

"No, no," said Barrington, hurriedly. "You shall hear from me early, for I am anxious you should meet Withering and his companion, too,—a brother-soldier."

"Who may he be?" asked M'Cormick.

"That's my secret, Major,—that's my secret," said Peter, with a forced laugh, for it now wanted but ten minutes to six; "but you shall know all on Saturday."

Had he said on the day of judgment, the assurance would have been as palatable to M'Cormick. Talking to him of Saturday on a Monday was asking him to speculate on the infinite. Meanwhile he sat on, as only they sit who understand the deep and high mystery of that process. Oh, if you who have your fortunes to make in life, without any assignable mode for so doing, without a craft, a calling, or a trade, knew what success there was to be achieved merely by sitting—by simply being "there," eternally "there"—a warning, an example, an illustration, a what you will, of boredom or infliction; but still "there." The butt of this man, the terror of that,—hated, feared, trembled at,—but yet recognized as a thing that must be, an institution that was, and is, and shall be, when we are all dead and buried.

Long and dreary may be the days of the sitter, but the hour of his reward will come at last. There will come the time when some one—any one—will be wanted to pair off with some other bore, to listen to his stories and make up his whist-table; and then he will be "there." I knew a man who, merely by sitting on patiently for years, was at last chosen to be sent as a Minister and special Envoy to a foreign Court just to get rid of him. And for the women sitters,—the well-dressed and prettily got-up simperers, who have sat their husbands into Commissionerships, Colonial Secretaryships, and such like,—are they not written of in the Book of Beauty?

"Here 's M'Cormick, Dinah," said Barrington, with a voice shaking with agitation and anxiety, "whom I want to pledge himself to us for Saturday next. Will you add your persuasions to mine, and see what can be done?"

"Don't you think you can depend upon me?" cackled out the Major.

"I am certain of it, sir; I feel your word like your bond on such a matter," said Miss Dinah. "My grandniece, Miss Josephine Barrington," said she, presenting that young lady, who courtesied formally to the unprepossessing stranger.

"I'm proud of the honor, ma'am," said M'Cormick, with a deep bow, and resumed his seat; to rise again, however, as Withering entered the room and was introduced to him.

"This is intolerable, Peter," whispered Miss Barrington, while the lawyer and the Major were talking together. "You are certain you have not asked him?"

"On my honor, Dinah! on my honor!"

"I hope I am not late?" cried Stapylton, entering; then turning hastily to Barrington, said, "Pray present me to your niece."

"This is my sister, Major Stapylton; this is my granddaughter;" and the ladies courtesied, each with a degree of satisfaction which the reader shall be left to assign them.

After a few words of commonplace civility, uttered, however, with a courtesy and tact which won their way for the speaker, Stapylton recognized and shook hands with M'Cormick.

"You know my neighbor, then?" said Barrington, in some surprise.

"I am charmed to say I do; he owes me the *denouement* of a most amusing story, which was suddenly broken off when we last parted, but which I shall certainly claim after dinner."

"He has been kind enough to engage himself to us for Saturday," began Dinah. But M'Cormick, who saw the moment critical, stepped in, —

"You shall hear every word of it before you sleep. It's all about Walcheren, though they think Waterloo more the fashion now."

"Just as this young lady might fancy Major Stapylton a more interesting event than one of us," said Withering, laughing. "But what 's become of your boasted punctuality, Barrington? A quarter past, — are you waiting for any one?"

"Are we, Dinah?" asked Barrington, with a look of sheepishness.

"Not that I am aware of, Peter. There is no one to *come*;" and she laid such an emphasis on the word as made the significance palpable.

To Barrington it was painful as well as palpable; so painful, indeed, that he hurriedly rang the bell, saying, in a sharp voice, "Of course, we are all here, — there are six of us. Dinner, Darby!"

The Major had won, but he was too crafty to show any triumph at his victory, and he did not dare even to look towards where Miss Barrington stood, lest he should chance to catch her eye. Dinner was at length announced. Withering gave his arm to Miss Barrington, Stapylton took charge of Josephine, and old Peter, pleasantly drawing his arm within M'Cormick's, said, "I hope you 've got a good appetite, Major, for I have a rare fish for you to-day, and your favorite sauce, too, — smelt, not lobster."

Poor Barrington! it was a trying moment for him, that short walk into the dinner-room, and he felt very grateful to M'Cormick that he said nothing peevish or sarcastic to him on the way. Many a dinner begins in awkwardness, but warms as it proceeds into a pleasant geniality. Such was the case here. Amongst those, besides, who have not the ties of old friendship between them, or have not as yet warmed into that genial good-fellowship which is, so to say, its foster-brother, a character of the M'Cormick class is not so damaging an element as might be imagined, and at times there is a positive advantage in having one of whose merits, by a tacit understanding, all are quite agreed. Withering and Stapylton both read the man at once, and drew out his salient points — his parsimony, his malice, and his prying curiosity — in various ways, but so neatly and so advisedly as to make him fancy he was the attacking party, and very successful, too, in his assaults upon the enemy. Even Barrington, in the honest simplicity of his nature, was taken in, and more than once thought that the old Major was too severe upon the others, and sat in wondering admiration of their self-command and good temper. No deception of this sort prevailed with Miss Barrington, who enjoyed to the fullest extent the subtle raillery with which they induced him to betray every meanness of his nature, and yet never suffered the disclosure to soar above the region of the ludicrous.

"You have been rather hard upon them, Major," said Barrington, as they strolled about on the greensward after dinner to enjoy their coffee and a cigar.

"Don't you think you have been a shade too severe?"

"It will do them good. They wanted to turn me out like a bagged fox, and show the ladies some sport; but I taught them a thing or two."

"No, no, M'Cormick, you wrong them there; they had no such intentions, believe me."

"I know that *you* did n't see it," said he, with emphasis, "but your sister did, and liked it well, besides; ay, and the young one joined in the fun. And, after all, I don't see that they got much by the victory, for Withering was not pleased at my little hit about the days when he used to be a Whig and spout liberal politics; and the other liked just as little my remark about the fellows in the Company's service, and how nobody knew who they were or where they came from. He was in the Madras army himself, but I pretended not to know it; but I found his name written on the leaf of an old book he gave me, and the regiment he was in: and did you see how he looked when I touched on it? But here he comes now."

"Make your peace with him, M'Cormick, make your peace!" said Barrington, as he moved away, not sorry, as he went, to mark the easy familiarity with which Stapylton drew his arm within the other's, and walked along at his side.

"Wasn't that a wonderful dinner we had to-day, from a man that hasn't a cross in his pocket?" croaked out M'Cormick to Stapylton.

"Is it possible?"

"Sherry and Madeira after your soup, then Sauterne,—a thing I don't care for any more than the oyster patties it came with; champagne next, and in tumblers too! Do you ever see it better done at your mess? Or where did you ever taste a finer glass of claret?"

"It was all admirable."

"There was only one thing forgotten,—not that it signifies to me."

"And what might that be?"

"It was n't paid for! No, nor will it ever be!"

"You amaze me, Major. My impression was that our friend here was, without being rich, in very comfortable circumstances; able to live handsomely, while he carried on a somewhat costly suit."

"That 's the greatest folly of all," broke out M'Cormick; "and it's to get money for that now that he's going to mortgage this place here,—ay, the very ground under our feet!" And this he said with a sort of tremulous indignation, as though the atrocity bore especially hard upon *them*. "Kinshela, the attorney from Kilkenny, was up with me about it yesterday. 'It's an elegant investment, Major,' says he, 'and you 're very likely to get the place into your hands for all the chance old Peter has of paying off the charge. His heart is in that suit, and he 'll not stop as long as he has a guinea to go on with it.'

"I said, 'I 'd think of it: I 'd turn it over in my mind;' for there's various ways of looking at it."

"I fancy I apprehend one of them," said Stapylton, with a half-jocular glance at his companion. "You have been reflecting over another investment, eh? Am I not right? I remarked you at dinner. I saw how the young brunette had struck you, and I said to myself, 'She has made a conquest already!'"

"Not a bit of it; nothing of the kind," said M'Cormick, awkwardly. "I 'm too 'cute to be caught that way."

"Yes, but remember it might be a very good catch. I don't speak of the suit, because I agree with you, the chances in that direction are very small, indeed, and I cannot understand the hopeful feeling with which he prosecutes it; but she is a fine, handsome girl, very attractive in manner, and equal to any station."

"And what's the good of all that to me? Wouldn't it be better if she could make a pease-pudding, like Polly Dill, or know how to fatten a turkey, or salt down a side of bacon?"

"I don't think so; I declare, I don't think so," said Stapylton, as he lighted a fresh cigar. "These are household cares, and to be bought with money, and not expensively, either. What a man like you or I wants is one who should give a sort of tone, — impart a degree of elegance to his daily life. We old bachelors grow into self-indulgence, which is only another name for barbarism. With a mistaken idea of comfort we neglect scores of little observances which constitute the small currency of civilization, and without which all intercourse is unpleasing and ungraceful."

"I'm not quite sure that I understand you aright, but there's one thing I know, I 'd think twice of it before I 'd ask that young woman to be Mrs. M'Cormick. And, besides," added he, with a sly side-look, "if it's so good a thing, why don't you think of it for yourself?"

"I need not tell an old soldier like *you* that full pay and a wife are incompatible. Every wise man's experience shows it; and when a fellow goes to the bishop for a license, he should send in his papers to the Horse Guards. Now, I 'm too poor to give up my career. I have not, like you, a charming cottage on a river's bank, and a swelling lawn dotted over with my own sheep before my door. I cannot put off the harness."

"Who talks of putting off the harness?" cried Withering, gayly, as he joined them. "Who ever dreamed of doing anything so ill-judging and so mistaken? Why, if it were only to hide the spots where the collar has galled you, you ought to wear the trappings to the last. No man ever knew how to idle, who had n't passed all his life at it! Some go so far as to say that for real success a man's father and grandfather should have been idlers before him. But have you seen Barrington? He has been looking for you all over the grounds."

"No," said Stapylton; "my old brother-officer and myself got into pipeclay and barrack talk, and strolled away down here unconsciously."

"Well, we 'd better not be late for tea," broke in the Major, "or we 'll hear of it from Miss Dinah!" And there was something so comic in the seriousness of his tone, that they laughed heartily as they turned towards the house.

CHAPTER IV.

A MOVE IN ADVANCE

How pleasantly did the next day break on the "Home"! Polly Dill arrived in the best of possible spirits. A few lines from Tom had just reached them. They were written at sea; but the poor fellow's notions of latitude and longitude were so confused that it was not easy to say from whence. They were cheery, however, he was in good health, his comrades were kind-hearted creatures, and evidently recognized in him one of a station above their own. He said that he could have been appointed hospital sergeant-if he liked, but that whatever reminded him of his old calling was so distasteful that he preferred remaining as he was, the rather as he was given to believe he should soon be a corporal.

"Not that I mean to stop there, Polly; and now that I have n't got to study for it, I feel a courage as to the future I never knew before. Give my love to Mr. Conyers, and say that I 'm never tired of thinking over the last night I saw him, and of all his good nature to me, and that I hope I 'll see his father some day or other to thank him. I suppose father does n't miss me? I 'm sure mother does n't; and it 's only yourself, Polly, will ever feel a heavy heart for the poor castaway! But cheer up! for as sure as my name is Tom, I 'll not bring discredit on you, and you 'll not be ashamed to take my arm down the main street when we meet. I must close now, for the boat is going.

"P. S. I dreamed last night you rode Sid Davis's brown mare over the Millrace at Graigue. Would n't it be strange if it came true? I wish I could know it."

"May I show this to my friend here, Polly?" said Barrington, pointing to Withering. "It's a letter he 'd like to read; and as she nodded assent, he handed it across the breakfast-table.

"What is your brother's regiment, Miss Dill?" said Stapylton, who had just caught a stray word or two of what passed.

"The Forty-ninth."

"The Forty-ninth," said he, repeating the words once or twice. "Let me see, — don't I know some Forty-ninth men? To be sure I do. There's Rep ton and Hare. Your brother will be delighted with Hare."

"My brother is in the ranks, Major Stapylton," said she, flushing a deep scarlet; and Barrington quickly interposed, —

"It was the wild frolic of a young man to escape a profession he had no mind for."

"But in foreign armies every one does it," broke in Stapylton, hurriedly. "No matter what a man's rank may be, he must carry the musket; and I own I like the practice,—if for nothing else for that fine spirit of *camaraderie* which it engenders."

Fifine's eyes sparkled with pleasure at what she deemed the well-bred readiness of this speech, while Polly became deadly pale, and seemed with difficulty to repress the repartee that rose to her mind. Not so Miss Dinah, who promptly said, "No foreign customs can palliate a breach of our habits. We are English, and we don't desire to be Frenchmen or Germans."

"Might we not occasionally borrow from our neighbors with advantage?" asked Stapylton, blandly.

"I agree with Miss Barrington," said Withering,—"I agree with Miss Barrington, whose very prejudices are always right. An army formed by a conscription which exempts no man is on a totally different footing from one derived from voluntary enlistment."

"A practice that some say should be reserved for marriage," said Barrington, whose happy tact it was to relieve a discussion by a ready joke.

They arose from table soon after,—Polly to accompany Miss Barrington over the garden and the shrubberies, and show all that had been done in their absence, and all that she yet intended to do, if approved of; Withering adjourned to Barrington's study to pore over parchments; and Stapylton, after vainly seeking to find Josephine in the drawing-room, the flower-garden, or the lawn, betook himself with a book, the first he could find on the table, to the river's side, and lay down, less to read than to meditate and reflect.

A breezy morning of a fine day in early autumn, with slow sailing clouds above and a flickering sunlight on the grass below, besides a rippling river, whose banks are glowing with blue and purple heath-bells,—all these and a Waverley novel were not enough to distract Stapylton from the cares that pressed upon his mind; for so it is, look where we may on those whom Fortune would seem to have made her especial favorites, and we shall find some unsatisfied ambition, some craving wish doomed to disappointment, some hope deferred till the heart that held it has ceased to care for its accomplishment. To the world's eyes, here was a man eminently fortunate: already high up in the service, with health, vigor, and good looks, a reputation established for personal gallantry in the field, and an amount of capacity that had already won for him more than one distinction, and yet all these, great and solid advantages as they are, were not sufficient to give the ease of mind we call happiness.

He had debts, some of them heavy debts, but these sat lightly on him. He was one of those men creditors never crush, some secret consciousness seeming to whisper that, however ill the world may go with them for a while, in the long run they must triumph; and thus Mr. Hirman Davis, to whom he owed thousands, would have cashed him another bill to-morrow, all on the faith of that future which Stapylton talked about with the careless confidence of a mind assured.

He had enemies, too,—powerful and determined enemies,—who opposed his advancement for many a year, and were still adverse to him; but, like the creditors, they felt he was not a man to be crushed, and so he and his ill-wishers smiled blandly when they met, exchanged the most cordial greetings, and even imparted little confidences of their several fortunes with all that well-bred duplicity which so simulates friendship.

He had been crossed,—no, not in love, but in his ambition to marry one greatly above him in station; but her subsequent marriage had been so unfortunate that he felt in part recompensed for the slight she passed upon him; so that, taking it all and all, fate had never been cruel to him without a compensation.

There are men who feel their whole existence to be a hand-to-hand struggle with the world, who regard the world as an adversary to be worsted, and all whose efforts are devoted to reach that point upon which they can turn round and say, "You see that I have won the game. I was unknown, and I am famous; I was poor, and I am rich; I was passed over and ignored, and now the very highest are proud to recognize me!" Stapylton was one of these. All the egotism of his nature took this form, and it was far more in a spirit against his fellows than in any indulgence of himself he fought and struggled with Fortune. Intrusted by Withering with much of the secret history of Barring-ton's claim against the India Company, he had learned considerably more through inquiries instituted by himself, and at length arrived at the conclusion that if old Barring-ton could be persuaded to limit his demands within moderate bounds, and not insist upon the details of that personal reparation which he assumed so essential to his son's honor, a very ample recompense would not be refused him. It was to induce Barrington to take this course Stapylton had consented to come down with Withering,—so, at least, he said, and so Withering believed. Old lawyer that he was, with a hundred instincts of distrust about him, he had conceived a real liking for Stapylton, and a great confidence in his judgment. "We shall have to divide our labors here, Major," said he, as they travelled along together; "I will leave the ladies to your care. Barrington shall be mine." A very brief acquaintance with Miss Dinah satisfied Stapylton that she was one to require nice treatment, and what he called "a very light hand." The two or three little baits he had thrown out took nothing; the stray bits of sentimentality, or chance scraps of high-toned principle he had addressed to her, had failed. It was only when he had with some sharpness hit off some small meanness in M'Cormick's nature that she had even vouchsafed him so much as a half-smile of approval, and he saw that even then she watched him closely.

"No," said he, half aloud to himself, "that old woman is not one easily to be dealt with; and the younger one, too, would have a will of her own if she had but the way to use it. If Polly had been in her place,—the clever, quickwitted Polly,— she would have gone with me in my plans, associated herself in all my projects, and assured their success. Oh for a good colleague just to keep the boat's head straight when one is weary of rowing!"

"Would I do?" said a low voice near. And, on looking up, he saw Josephine standing over him, with an arch smile on her face as though she had surprised him in a confession.

"How long have you been there?" asked he, hurriedly.

"A few seconds."

"And what have you heard me say?"

"That you wanted a colleague, or a companion of some sort; and as I was the only useless person here, I offered myself."

"In good faith?"

"In good faith!—why not? I am more likely to gain by the association than you are; at least, if you can only be as pleasant of a morning as you were yesterday at dinner."

"I 'll try," said he, springing to his feet; "and as a success in these efforts is mainly owing to the amount of zeal that animates them, I am hopeful."

"Which means a flattery at the outset," said she, smiling.

"Only as much as your friend Mr. Withering would throw out to dispose the court in his favor; and now, which way shall we walk? Are you to be the guide, or I?"

"You, by all means, since you know nothing of the locality."

"Agreed. Well, here is my plan. We cross the river in this boat, and take that path yonder that leads up by the waterfall. I know, from the dark shadow of the mountain, that there is a deep glen, very wild, very romantic, and very solemn, through which I mean to conduct you."

"All this means a very long excursion, does it not?"

"You have just told me that you were free from all engagement."

"Yes; but not from all control. I must ask Aunt Dinah's leave before I set out on this notable expedition."

"Do nothing of the kind. It would be to make a caprice seem a plan. Let us go where you will,—here, along the river's side; anywhere, so that we may affect to think that we are free agents, and not merely good children sent out for a walk."

"What a rebel against authority you are for one so despotic yourself!"

"I despotic! Who ever called me so?"

"Your officers say as much."

"I know from what quarter that came," said he; and his bronzed face grew a shade deeper. "That dilettante soldier, young Conyers, has given me this character; but I 'd rather talk of you than myself. Tell me all about your life. Is it as delightful as everything around would bespeak it? Are these trees and flowers, this sunny bank, this perfumed sward, true emblems of the existence they embellish, or is Paradise only a cheat?"

"I don't think so. I think Paradise is very like what it looks, not but I own that the garden is pleasanter with guests in it than when only Adam and Eve were there. Mr. Withering is charming, and you can be very agreeable."

"I would I knew how to be so," said he, seriously, "just at this moment; for I am going away from Ireland, and I am very desirous of leaving a good impression behind me."

"What could it signify to you how you were thought of in this lonely spot?"

"More than you suspect,—more than you would, perhaps, credit," said he, feelingly.

There was a little pause, during which they walked along side by side.

"What are you thinking of?" said she, at last

"I was thinking of a strange thing,—it was this: About a week ago there was no effort I was not making to obtain the command of my regiment. I wanted to be Lieutenant-Colonel; and so bent was I on gaining my object, that if giving away three or four years of that life that I may hope for would have done it, I'd have closed the bargain; and now the ambition is gone, and I am speculating whether I 'll not take the cottage of your friend Major M'Cormick,—he offered it to me last night,—and become your neighbor. What say you to the project?"

"For us the exchange will be all a gain."

"I want your opinion,—your own," said he, with a voice reduced to a mere whisper.

"I'd like it of all things; although, if I were your sister or your daughter, I'd not counsel it."

"And why not, if you were my sister?" said he, with a certain constraint in his manner.

"I'd say it was inglorious to change from the noble activity of a soldier's life to come and dream away existence here."

"But what if I have done enough for this same thing men call fame? I have had my share of campaigning, and as the world looks there is wondrous little prospect of any renewal of it. These peace achievements suit your friend Conyers better than me."

"I think you are not just to him. If I read him aright, he is burning for an occasion to distinguish himself."

A cold shrug of the shoulders was his only acknowledgment of this speech, and again a silence fell between them.

"I would rather talk of you, if you would let me," said he, with much significance of voice and manner. "Say would you like to have me for your neighbor?"

"It would be a pleasant exchange for Major M'Cormick," said she, laughing.

"I want you to be serious now. What I am asking you interests me too deeply to jest over."

"First of all, is the project a serious one?"

"It is."

"Next, why ask advice from one as inexperienced as I am?"

"Because it is not counsel I ask,—it is something more. Don't look surprised, and, above all, don't look angry, but listen to me. What I have said now, and what more I would say, might more properly have been uttered when we had known each other longer; but there are emergencies in life which give no time for slow approaches, and there are men, too, that they suit not. Imagine such now before you,—I mean, both the moment and the man. Imagine one who has gone through a great deal in life, seen, heard, and felt much, and yet never till now, never till this very morning, understood what it was to know one whose least word or passing look was more to him than ambition, higher than all the rewards of glory."

"We never met till yesterday," said she, calmly.

"True; and if we part to-morrow, it will be forever. I feel too painfully," added he, with more eagerness, "how I compromise all that I value by an avowal abrupt and rash as this is; but I have had no choice. I have been offered the command of a native force in India, and must give my answer at once. With hope—the very faintest, so that it be hope—I will refuse. Remember I want no pledge, no promise; all I entreat is that you will regard me as one who seeks to win your favor. Let time do the rest."

"I do not think I ought to do this—I do not know if you should ask it."

"May I speak to your grandfather—may I tell him what I have told you—may I say, 'It is with Josephine's permission—'"

"I am called Miss Barrington, sir, by all but those of my own family."

"Forgive me, I entreat you," said he, with a deep humility in his tone. "I had never so far forgotten myself if calm reason had not deserted me. I will not transgress again."

"This is the shortest way back to the cottage," said she, turning into a narrow path in the wood.

"It does not lead to my hope," said he, despondingly; and no more was uttered between them for some paces.

"Do not walk so very fast, Miss Barrington," said he, in a tone which trembled slightly. "In the few minutes—the seconds you could accord me—I might build the whole fortune of my life. I have already endangered my hopes by rashness; let me own that it is the fault I have struggled against in vain. This scar"—and he showed the deep mark of a sabre-wound on the temple—"was the price of one of my offendings; but it was light in suffering to what I am now enduring."

"Can we not talk of what will exact no such sacrifice?" said she, calmly.

"Not now, not now!" said he, with emotion; "if you pass that porch without giving me an answer, life has no longer a tie for me. You know that I ask for no pledge, no promise, merely time,—no more than time,—a few more of those moments of which you now would seem eager to deny me. Linger an instant here, I beseech you, and remember that what to *you* may be a caprice may to *me* be a destiny."

"I will not hear more of this," said she, half angrily. "If it were not for my own foolish trustfulness, you never would have dared to address such words to one whom you met yesterday for the first time."

"It is true your generous frankness, the nature they told me you inherited, gives me boldness, but it might teach you to have some pity for a disposition akin to it. One word,—only one word more."

"Not one, sir! The lesson my frankness has taught me is, never to incur this peril again."

"Do you part from me in anger?"

"Not with *you*; but I will not answer for myself if you press me further."

"Even this much is better than despair," said he, mournfully; and she passed into the cottage, while he stood in the porch and bowed respectfully as she went by. "Better than I looked for, better than I could have hoped," muttered he to himself, as he strolled away and disappeared in the wood.

CHAPTER V.

A CABINET COUNCIL

"What do you think of it, Dinah?" said Barrington, as they sat in conclave the next morning in her own sitting-room.

She laid down a letter she had just finished reading on the table, carefully folding it, like one trying to gain time before she spoke: "He's a clever man, and writes well, Peter; there can be no second opinion upon that."

"But his proposal, Dinah,—his proposal?"

"Pleases me less the more I think of it. There is great disparity of age,—a wide discrepancy in character. A certain gravity of demeanor would not be undesirable, perhaps, in a husband for Josephine, who has her moments of capricious fancy; but if I mistake not, this man's nature is stern and unbending."

"There will be time enough to consider all that, Dinah. It is, in fact, to weigh well the chances of his fitness to secure her happiness that he pleads; he asks permission to make himself known to her, rather than to make his court."

"I used to fancy that they meant the same thing,—I know that they did in my day, Peter," said she, bridling; "but come to the plain question before us. So far as I understand him, his position is this: 'If I satisfy you that my rank and fortune are satisfactory to you, have I your permission to come back here as your granddaughter's suitor?'"

"Not precisely, Dinah,—not exactly this. Here are his words: 'I am well aware that I am much older than Miss Barrington, and it is simply to ascertain from herself if, in that disparity of years, there exists that disparity of tastes and temper which would indispose her to regard me as one to whom she would intrust her happiness. I hope to do this without any offence to her delicacy, though not without peril to my own self-love. Have I your leave for this experiment?'"

"Who is he? Who are his friends, connections, belongings? What is his station independently of his military rank, and what are his means? Can you answer these questions?"

"Not one of them. I never found myself till to-day in a position to inquire after them."

"Let us begin, then, by that investigation, Peter. There is no such test of a man as to make him talk of himself. With you alone the matter, perhaps, would not present much difficulty to him, but I intend that Mr. Withering's name and my own shall be on the committee; and, take *my* word for it, we shall sift the evidence carefully."

"Bear in mind, sister Dinah, that this gentleman is, first of all, our guest."

"The first of all that I mean to bear in mind is, that he desires to be your grandson."

"Of course,—of course. I would only observe on the reserve that should be maintained towards one who honors us with his presence."

"Peter Barrington, the Arabs, from whom you seem to borrow your notions on hospitality, seldom scruple about cutting a guest's head off when he passes the threshold; therefore I would advise you to adopt habits that may be more suited to the land we live in."

"All I know is," said Barrington, rising and pacing the room, "that I could no more put a gentleman under my roof to the question as to his father and mother and his fortune, than I could rifle his writing-desk and read his letters."

"Brother Peter, the weakness of your disposition has cost you one of the finest estates in your country, and if it could be restored to you to-morrow, the same imbecility would forfeit it again. I will, however, take the matter into my own hands."

"With Withering, I suppose, to assist you?"

"Certainly not. I am perfectly competent to make any inquiry I deem requisite without a legal adviser. Perhaps, were I to be so accompanied, Major Stapylton would suppose that he, too, should appear with his lawyer."

Barrington smiled faintly at the dry jest, but said nothing.

"I see," resumed she, "that you are very much afraid about my want of tact and delicacy in this investigation. It is a somewhat common belief amongst men that in all matters of business women err on the score of hardness and persistence. I have listened to some edifying homilies from your friend Withering on female incredulity and so forth,—reproaches which will cease to apply when men shall condescend to treat us as creatures accessible to reason, and not as mere dupes. See who is knocking at the door, Peter," added she, sharply. "I declare it recalls the old days of our innkeeping, and Darby asking for the bill of the lame gentleman in No. 4."

"Upon my life, they were pleasant days, too," said Barrington, but in a tone so low as to be unheard by his sister.

"May I come in?" said Withering, as he opened the door a few inches, and peeped inside. "I want to show you a note I have just had from Kinshela, in Kilkenny."

"Yes, yes; come in," said Miss Barrington. "I only wish you had arrived a little earlier. What is your note about?"

"It's very short and very purpose-like. The first of it is all about Brazier's costs, which it seems the taxing-officer thinks fair and reasonable,—all excepting that charge for the additional affidavits. But here is what I want to show you. 'Major M'Cormick, of M'Cormick's Grove, has just been here; and although I am not entitled to say as much officially on his part, I entertain no doubt whatever but that he is ready to advance the money we require. I spoke of fifteen hundred, but said twelve might possibly be taken, and twelve would be, I imagine, his limit, since he held to this amount in all our conversation afterwards. He appears to be a man of strange and eccentric habits, and these will probably be deemed a sufficient excuse for the singular turn our interview took towards its conclusion. I was speaking of Mr. Barrington's wish for the insertion in the deed of a definite period for redemption, and he stopped me hastily with, "What if we could strike out another arrangement? What if he was to make a settlement of the place on his granddaughter? I am not too old to marry, and I'd give him the money at five per cent." I have been careful to give you the very expressions he employed, and of which I made a note when he left the office; for although fully aware how improper it would be in me to submit this proposal to Mr. Barrington, I have felt it my duty to put you in possession of all that has passed between us.'"

"How can you laugh, Peter Barrington?—how is it possible you can laugh at such an insult,—such an outrage as this? Go on, sir," said she, turning to Withering; "let us hear it to the end, for nothing worse can remain behind."

"There is no more; at least, there is not anything worth hearing. Kinshela winds up with many apologies, and hopes that I will only use his communication for my own guidance, and not permit it in any case to prejudice him in your estimation." As he spoke, he crumpled up the note in his hand in some confusion.

"Who thinks of Mr. Kinshela, or wants to think of him, in the matter?" said she, angrily. "I wish, however, I were a man for a couple of hours, to show Major M'Cormick the estimate I take of the honor he intends us."

"After all, Dinah, it is not that he holds us more cheaply, but rates himself higher."

"Just so," broke in Withering; "and I know, for my own part, I have never been able to shake off the flattery of being chosen by the most nefarious rascal to defend him on his trial. Every man is a great creature in his own eyes."

"Well, sir, be proud of your client," said she, trembling with anger.

"No, no,—he's no client of mine, nor is this a case I would plead for him. I read you Kinshela's note because I thought you were building too confidently on M'Cormick's readiness to advance this money."

"I understood what that readiness meant, though my brother did not. M'Cormick looked forward to the day—and not a very distant day did he deem it—when he should step into possession of this place, and settle down here as its owner."

Barrington's face grew pale, and a glassy film spread over his eyes, as his sister's words sunk into his heart. "I declare, Dinah," said he, falteringly, "that never did strike me before."

"'It never rains but it pours,' says the Irish adage," resumed she. "My brother and I were just discussing another proposal of the same kind when you knocked.

Read that letter. It is from a more adroit courtier than the other, and, at least, he does n't preface his intentions with a bargain." And she handed Stapylton's letter to Withering.

"Ah!" said the lawyer, "this is another guess sort of man, and a very different sort of proposal."

"I suspected that he was a favorite of yours," said Miss Dinah, significantly.

"Well, I own to it. He is one of those men who have a great attraction for me, — men who come out of the conflict of life and its interests without any exaggerated notions of human perfectibility or the opposite, who recognize plenty of good and no small share of bad in the world, but, on the whole, are satisfied that, saving ill health, very few of our calamities are not of our own providing."

"All of which is perfectly compatible with an odious egotism, sir," said she, warmly; "but I feel proud to say such characters find few admirers amongst women."

"From which I opine that he is not fortunate enough to number Miss Dinah Barrington amongst his supporters?"

"You are right there, sir. The prejudice I had against him before we met has been strengthened since I have seen him."

"It is candid of you, however, to call it a prejudice," said he, with a smile.

"Be it so, Mr. Withering; but prejudice is only another word for an instinct."

"I 'm afraid if we get into ethics we 'll forget all about the proposal," said Barrington.

"What a sarcasm!" cried Withering, "that if we talk of morals we shall ignore matrimony."

"I like the man, and I like his letter," said Barrington.

"I distrust both one and the other," said Miss Dinah.

"I almost fancy I could hold a brief on either side," interposed Withering.

"Of course you could, sir; and if the choice were open to you, it would be the defence of the guilty."

"My dear Miss Barrington," said Withering, calmly, "when a great legal authority once said that he only needed three lines of any man's writing 'to hang him,' it ought to make us very lenient in our construction of a letter. Now, so far as I can see in this one before us, he neither asks nor protests too much. He begs simply for time, he entreats leave to draw a bill on your affections, and he promises to meet it."

"No, sir, he wishes to draw at sight, though he has never shown us the letter of credit."

"I vow to Heaven it is hopeless to expect anything practical when you two stand up together for a sparring-match," cried Barrington.

"Be practical, then, brother Peter, and ask this gentleman to give you a quarter of an hour in your study. Find out who he is; I don't expect you to learn what he is, but what he has. With his fortune we shall get the clew to himself."

"Yes," chimed in Withering, "all that is very businesslike and reasonable."

"And it pledges us to nothing," added she. "We take soundings, but we don't promise to anchor."

"If you go off again with your figures of speech, Dinah, there is an end of me, for I have one of those unhappy memories that retain the illustration and forget what it typified. Besides this, here is a man who, out of pure good nature and respect for poor George's memory, has been doing us most important services, written letters innumerable, and taken the most active measures for our benefit. What sort of a figure shall I present if I bring him to book about his rental and the state of his bank account?"

"With the exercise of a little tact, Barrington,—a little management—"

"Ask a man with a club-foot to walk gingerly! I have no more notion of getting at anything by address than I have of tying the femoral artery."

"The more blunt the better, Peter Barrington. You may tumble into the truth, though you'd never pick your way into it. Meanwhile, leave me to deal with Major M'Cor-mick."

"You'll do it courteously, Dinah; you'll bear in mind that he is a neighbor of some twenty years' standing?" said Barrington, in a voice of anxiety.

"I 'll do it in a manner that shall satisfy *my* conscience and *his* presumption."

She seated herself at the table as she said this, and dashed off a few hasty lines. Indeed, so hurried was the action, that it looked far more like one of those instances of correspondence we see on the stage than an event of real life.

"Will that do?" said she, showing the lines to Withering.

The old lawyer read them over to himself, a faint twitching of the mouth being the only sign his face presented of any emotion. "I should say admirably,—nothing better."

"May I see it, Dinah?" asked Peter.

"You shall hear it, brother," said she, taking the paper and reading,—

"'Miss Barrington informs Mr. Kinshela that if he does not at once retract his epistle of this morning's date, she will place it in the hands of her legal adviser, and proceed against it as a threatening letter.'"

"Oh, sister, you will not send this?"

"As sure as my name is Dinah Barrington."

CHAPTER VI.

AN EXPRESS

In the times before telegraphs,—and it is of such I am writing,—a hurried express was a far more stirring event than in these our days of incessant oracles. While, therefore, Barrington and his sister and Withering sat in deep consultation on Josephine's fate and future, a hasty summons arrived from Dublin, requiring the instantaneous departure of Stapylton, whose regiment was urgently needed in the north of England, at that time agitated by those disturbances called the Bread Riots. They were very formidable troubles, and when we look back upon them now, with the light which the great events of later years on the Continent afford us, seem more terrible still. It was the fashion, however, then, to treat them lightly, and talk of them contemptuously; and as Stapylton was eating a hasty luncheon before departure, he sneered at the rabble, and scoffed at the insolent pretension of their demands. Neither Barrington nor Withering sympathized with the spirit of the revolt, and yet each felt shocked at the tone of haughty contempt Stapylton assumed towards the people. "You'll see," cried he, rising, "how a couple of brisk charges from our fellows will do more to bring these rascals to reason than all the fine pledges of your Parliament folk; and I promise you, for my own part, if I chance upon one of their leaders, I mean to lay my mark on him."

"I fear, sir, it is your instinctive dislike to the plebeian that moves you here," said Miss Dinah. "You will not entertain the question whether these people may not have some wrongs to complain of."

"Perhaps so, madam," said he; and his swarthy face grew darker as he spoke. "I suppose this is the case where the blood of a gentleman boils indignantly at the challenge of the *canaille*."

"I will not have a French word applied to our own people, sir," said she, angrily.

"Well said," chimed in Withering. "It is wonderful how a phrase can seem to carry an argument along with it."

And old Peter smiled, and nodded his concurrence with this speech.

"What a sad minority do I stand in!" said Stapylton, with an effort to smile very far from successful. "Will not Miss Josephine Barrington have generosity enough to aid the weaker side?"

"Not if it be the worst cause," interposed Dinah. "My niece needs not to be told she must be just before she is generous."

"Then it is to your own generosity I will appeal," said Stapylton, turning to her; "and I will ask you to ascribe some, at least, of my bitterness to the sorrow I feel at being thus summoned away. Believe me it is no light matter to leave this place and its company."

"But only for a season, and a very brief season too, I trust," said Barrington. "You are going away in our debt, remember."

"It is a loser's privilege, all the world over, to withdraw when he has lost enough," said Stapylton, with a sad smile towards Miss Dinah; and though the speech was made in the hope it might elicit a contradiction, none came, and a very awkward silence ensued.

"You will reach Dublin to-night, I suppose?" said Withering, to relieve the painful pause in the conversation.

"It will be late,—after midnight, perhaps."

"And embark the next morning?"

"Two of our squadrons have sailed already; the others will, of course, follow to-morrow."

"And young Conyers," broke in Miss Dinah,—"he will, I suppose, accompany this—what shall I call it?—this raid?"

"Yes, madam. Am I to convey to him your compliments upon the first opportunity to flesh his maiden sword?"

"You are to do nothing of the kind, sir; but tell him from me not to forget that the angry passions of a starving multitude are not to be confounded with the vindictive hate of our natural enemies."

"Natural enemies, my dear Miss Barrington! I hope you cannot mean that there exists anything so monstrous in humanity as a natural enemy?"

"I do, sir; and I mean all those whose jealousy of us ripens into hatred, and who would spill their heart's blood to see us humbled. When there exists a people like this, and who at every fresh outbreak of a war with us have carried into the new contest all the bitter animosities of long past struggles as debts to be liquidated, I call these natural enemies; and, if you prefer a shorter word for it, I call them Frenchmen."

"Dinah, Dinah!"

"Peter, Peter! don't interrupt me. Major Stapylton has thought to tax me with a blunder, but I accept it as a boast!"

"Madam, I am proud to be vanquished by you," said Stapylton, bowing low.

"And I trust, sir," said she, continuing her speech, and as if heedless of his interruption, "that no similarity of name will make you behave at Peterloo—if that be the name—as though you were at Waterloo."

"Upon my life!" cried he, with a saucy laugh, "I don't know how I am to win your good opinion, except it be by tearing off my epaulettes, and putting myself at the head of the mob."

"You know very little of my sister, Major Stapylton," said Barrington, "or you would scarcely have selected that mode of cultivating her favor."

"There is a popular belief that ladies always side with the winning cause," said Stapylton, affecting a light and easy manner; "so I must do my best to be successful. May I hope I carry your *good* wishes away with me?" said he, in a lower tone to Josephine.

"I hope that nobody will hurt you, and you hurt nobody," said she, laughingly.

"And this, I take it, is about as much sympathy as ever attends a man on such a campaign. Mr. Barrington, will you grant me two minutes of conversation in your own room?" And, with a bow of acquiescence, Barrington led the way to his study.

"I ought to have anticipated your request, Major Stapyl-ton," said Barrington, when they found themselves alone. "I owe you a reply to your letter, but the simple fact is, I do not know what answer to give it; for while most sensible of the honor you intend us, I feel still there is much to be explained on both sides. We know scarcely anything of each other, and though I am conscious of the generosity which prompts a man with *your* prospects and in *your* position to ally himself with persons in *ours*, yet I owe it to myself to say, it hangs upon a contingency to restore us to wealth and station. Even a portion of what I claim from the East India Company would make my granddaughter one of the richest heiresses in England."

Stapylton gave a cold, a very cold smile, in reply to this speech. It might mean that he was incredulous or indifferent, or it might imply that the issue was one which need not have been introduced into the case at all. Whatever its signification, Barrington felt hurt by it, and hastily said, —

"Not that I have any need to trouble you with these details: it is rather my province to ask for information regarding *your* circumstances than to enter upon a discussion of *ours*."

"I am quite ready to give you the very fullest and clearest, — I mean to yourself personally, or to your sister; for, except where the lawyer intervenes of necessity and *de droit*, I own that I resent his presence as an insult. I suppose few of us are devoid of certain family circumstances which it would be more agreeable to deal with in confidence; and though, perhaps, I am as fortunate as most men in this respect, there are one or two small matters on which I would ask your attention. These, however, are neither important nor pressing. My first care is to know, — and I hope I am not peremptory in asking it, — have I your consent to the proposition contained in my letter; am I at liberty to address Miss Barrington?"

Barrington flushed deeply and fidgeted; he arose and sat down again, — all his excitement only aggravated by the well-bred composure of the other, who seemed utterly unconscious of the uneasiness he was causing.

"Don't you think, Major, that this is a case for a little time to reflect, — that in a matter so momentous as this, a few days at least are requisite for consideration? We ought to ascertain something at least of my granddaughter's own sentiments,—I mean, of course, in a general way. It might be, too, that a day or two might give us some better insight into her future prospects."

"Pardon my interrupting you; but, on the last point, I am perfectly indifferent. Miss Barrington with half a province for her dower, would be no more in my eyes than Miss Barrington as she sat at breakfast this morning. Nor is there anything of high-flown sentiment in this declaration, as my means are sufficiently ample for all that I want or care."

"There, at least, is one difficulty disposed of. You are an eldest son?" said he; and he blushed at his own boldness in making the inquiry.

"I am an only son."

"Easier again," said Barrington, trying to laugh off the awkward moment. "No cutting down one's old timber to pay off the provisions for younger brothers."

"In my case there is no need of this."

"And your father. Is he still living, Major Stapylton?"

"My father has been dead some years."

Barrington fidgeted again, fumbled with his watch-chain and his eye-glass, and would have given more than he could afford for any casualty that should cut short the interview. He wanted to say, "What is the amount of your fortune? What is it? Where is it? Are you Wiltshire or Staffordshire? Who are your uncles and aunts, and your good friends that you pray for, and where do you pray for them?" A thousand questions of this sort arose in his mind, one only more prying and impertinent than another. He knew he ought to ask them; he knew Dinah would have asked them. Ay, and would have the answers to them as plain and palpable as the replies to a life assurance circular; but he could n't do it. No; not if his life depended on it.

He had already gone further in his transgression of good manners than it ever occurred to him before to do, and he felt something between a holy inquisitor and a spy of the police.

Stapylton looked at his watch, and gave a slight start.

"Later than you thought, eh?" cried Peter, overjoyed at the diversion.

Stapylton smiled a cold assent, and put up his watch without a word. He saw all the confusion and embarrassment of the other, and made no effort to relieve him. At last, but not until after a considerable pause, he said,—"I believe, Mr. Barrington,—I hope, at least,—I have satisfactorily answered the questions which, with every right on your part, you have deemed proper to put to me. I cannot but feel how painful the task has been to you, and I regret it the more, since probably it has set a limit to inquiries which you are perfectly justified in making, but which closer relations between us may make a matter far less formidable one of these days."

"Yes, yes,—just so; of course," said Barrington, hurriedly assenting to he knew not what.

"And I trust I take my leave of you with the understanding that when we meet again, it shall be as in the commencement of these pleasanter relations. I own to you I am the more eager on this point, that I perceive your sister, Miss Barrington, scarcely regards me very favorably, and I stand the more in need of your alliance."

"I don't think it possible, Major Stapylton," said Barrington, boldly, "that my sister and I could have two opinions upon anything or anybody."

"Then I only ask that she may partake of yours on this occasion," said Stapylton, bowing. "But I must start; as it is, I shall be very late in Dublin. Will you present my most respectful adieux to the ladies, and say also a goodbye for me to Mr. Withering?"

"You'll come in for a moment to the drawing-room, won't you?" cried Barrington.

"I think not. I opine it would be better not. There would be a certain awkwardness about it,—that is, until you have informed Miss Dinah Barrington of the extent to which you have accorded me your confidence, and how completely I have opened every detail of my circumstances. I believe it would be in better taste not to present myself. Tell Withering that if he writes, Manchester will find me. I don't suspect he need give himself any more trouble about establishing the proofs of marriage. They will scarcely contest that point. The great question will and must be, to ascertain if the Company will cease to oppose the claim on being fully convinced that the letter to the Meer Busherat was a forgery, and that no menace ever came from Colonel Barrington's hand as to the consequences of opposing his rule. Get them to admit this,—let the issue rest upon this,—and it will narrow the whole suit within manageable limits."

"Would you not say this much to him before you go? It would come with so much more force and clearness from yourself."

"I have done so till I was wearied. Like a true lawyer, he insists upon proving each step as he goes, and will not condescend to a hypothetical conclusion, though I have told him over and over again we want a settlement, not a victory. Good-bye, good-bye! If I once launch out into the cause, I cannot tear myself away again."

"Has your guest gone, Peter?" said Miss Dinah, as her brother re-entered the drawing-room.

"Yes; it was a hurried departure, and he had no great heart for it, either. By the way, Withering, while it is fresh in my head, let me tell you the message he has sent you."

"Was there none for *me*, Peter?" said she, scoffingly.

"Ay, but there was, Dinah! He left with me I know not how many polite and charming things to say for him."

"And am I alone forgotten in this wide dispensation of favors?" asked Josephine, smiling.

"Of course not, dear," chimed in Miss Dinah. "Your grandpapa has been charged with them all. You could not expect a gentleman so naturally timid and bashful as our late guest to utter them by his own lips."

"I see," said Withering, laughing, "that you have not forgiven the haughty aristocrat for his insolent estimate of the people!"

"He an aristocrat! Such bitter words as his never fell from any man who had a grandfather!"

"Wrong for once, Dinah," broke in Barrington. "I can answer for it that you are unjust to him."

"We shall see," said she. "Come, Josephine, I have a whole morning's work before me in the flower-garden, and I want your help. Don't forget, Peter, that Major M'Cormick's butler, or boatman, or bailiff, whichever he be, has been up here with a present of seakale this morning. Give him something as you pass the kitchen; and you, Mr. Withering, whose trade it is to read and unravel mysteries, explain if you can the meaning of this unwonted generosity."

"I suppose we can all guess it," said he, laughing. "It's a custom that begins in the East and goes round the whole world till it reaches the vast prairie in the Far West."

"And what can that custom be, Aunt Dinah?" asked Josephine, innocently.

"It's an ancient rite Mr. Withering speaks, of, child, pertaining to the days when men offered sacrifices. Come along; I 'm going!"

CHAPTER VII.

CROSS-EXAMININGS.

While Barrington and his lawyer sat in conclave over the details of the great suit, Stapylton hurried along his road with all the speed he could summon. The way, which for some miles led along the river-side, brought into view M'Cormick's cottage, and the Major himself, as he stood listlessly at his door.'

Halting his carriage for a moment, Stapylton jumped out and drew nigh the little quickset hedge which flanked the road.

"What can I do for you in the neighborhood of Manchester, Major? We are just ordered off there to ride down the Radicals."

"I wish it was nearer home you were going to do it," said he, crankily. "Look here,"—and he pointed to some fresh-turned earth,—"they were stealing my turnips last night."

"It would appear that these fellows in the North are growing dangerous," said Stapylton.

"'T is little matter to us," said M'Cormick, sulkily. "I'd care more about a blight in the potatoes than for all the politics in Europe."

"A genuine philosopher! How snug you are here, to be sure! A man in a pleasant nook like this can well afford to smile at the busy ambitions of the outer world. I take it you are about the very happiest fellow I know?"

"Maybe I am, maybe I'm not," said he, peevishly.

"This spot only wants what I hinted to you t'other evening, to be perfection."

"Ay!" said the other, dryly.

"And you agree with me heartily, if you had the candor to say it. Come, out with it, man, at once. I saw your gardener this morning with a great basketful of greenery, and a large bouquet on the top of it,—are not these significant signs of a projected campaign? You are wrong, Major, upon my life you are wrong, not to be frank with me. I could, by a strange hazard, as the newspapers say, 'tell you something to your advantage.'"

"About what?"

"About the very matter you were thinking of as I drove up. Come, I will be more generous than you deserve." And, laying his arm on M'Cormick's shoulder, he halt whispered in his ear; "It is a good thing,—a deuced good thing! and I promise you, if I were a marrying man, you 'd have a competitor. I won't say she 'll have one of the great fortunes people rave about, but it will be considerable,—very considerable."

"How do you know, or what do you know?"

"I 'll tell you in three words. How I know is, because I have been the channel for certain inquiries they made in India. What I know is, the Directors are sick of the case, they are sorely ashamed of it, and not a little uneasy lest it should come before the public, perhaps before the Parliament. Old Barrington has made all ne-gotiation difficult by the extravagant pretensions he puts forward about his son's honor, and so forth. If, however, the girl were married, her husband would be the person to treat with, and I am assured with him they would deal handsomely, even generously."

"And why would n't all this make a marrying man of you, though you were n't before?"

"There's a slight canonical objection, if you must know," said Stapylton, with a smile.

"Oh, I perceive,—a wife already! In India, perhaps?"

"I have no time just now for a long story, M'Cormick," said he, familiarly, "nor am I quite certain I 'd tell it if I had. However, you know enough for all practical purposes, and I repeat to you this is a stake I can't enter for,—you understand me?"

"There's another thing, now," said M'Cormick; "and as we are talking so free-ly together, there's no harm in mentioning it. It 's only the other day, as I may call it, that we met for the first time?"

"Very true: when I was down here at Cobham."

"And never heard of each other before?"

"Not to my knowledge, certainly."

"That being the case, I 'm curious to hear how you took this wonderful interest in me. It wasn't anything in my appearance, I 'm sure, nor my manner; and as to what you 'd hear about me among those blackguards down here, there's nothing too bad to say of me."

"I'll be as frank as yourself," said Stapylton, boldly; "you ask for candor, and you shall have it. I had n't talked ten minutes with you till I saw that you were a thorough man of the world; the true old soldier, who had seen enough of life to know that whatever one gets for nothing in this world is just worth nothing, and so I said to myself, 'If it ever occurs to me to chance upon a good opportunity of which I cannot from circumstances avail myself, there's my man. I'll go to him and say, "M'Cormick, that's open to you, there's a safe thing!" And when in return he 'd say, "Stapylton, what can I do for you?" my answer would be, "Wait till you are satisfied that I have done you a good turn; be perfectly assured that I have really served you." And then, if I wanted a loan of a thousand or fifteen hundred to lodge for the Lieutenant-Colonelcy, I 'd not be ashamed to say, "M'Cormick, let me have so much."""

"That's *it*, is it?" said M'Cormick, with a leer of intense cunning. "Not a bad bargain for *you*, anyhow. It is not every day that a man can sell what is n't his own."

"I might say, it's not every day that a man regards a possible loan as a gift, but I 'm quite ready to reassure all your fears on that score; I'll even pledge myself never to borrow a shilling from you."

"Oh, I don't mean that; you took me up so quick," said the old fellow, reddening with a sense of shame he had not felt for many a year. "I may be as stingy as they call me, but for all that I 'd stand to a man who stands to *me*."

"Between gentlemen and men of the world these things are better left to a sense of an honorable understanding than made matters of compact. There is no need of another word on the matter. I shall be curious, however, to know how your project speeds. Write to me,—you have plenty of time,—and write often. I 'm not unlikely to learn something about the Indian claim, and if I do, you shall hear of it."

"I'm not over good at pen and ink work; indeed, I haven't much practice, but I'll do my best."

"Do, by all means. Tell me how you get on with Aunt Dinah, who, I suspect, has no strong affection for either of us. Don't be precipitate; hazard nothing by a rash step; secure your way by intimacy, mere intimacy: avoid particular attentions strictly; be always there, and on some pretext or other—But why do I say all this to an old soldier, who has made such sieges scores of times?"

"Well, I think I see my way clear enough," said the old fellow, with a grin. "I wish I was as sure I knew why you take such an interest in me."

"I believe I have told you already; I hope there is nothing so strange in the assurance as to require corroboration. Come, I must say good-bye; I meant to have said five words to you, and I have stayed here five-and-twenty minutes."

"Would n't you take something?—could n't I offer you anything?" said M'Cormick, hesitatingly.

"Nothing, thanks. I lunched before I started; and although old Dinah made several assaults upon me while I ate, I managed to secure two cutlets and part of a grouse-pie, and a rare glass of Madeira to wash them down."

"That old woman is dreadful, and I'll take her down a peg yet, as sure as my name is Dan."

"No, don't, Major; don't do anything of the kind. The people who tame tigers are sure to get scratched at last, and nobody thanks them for their pains. Regard her as the sailors do a fire-ship; give her a wide berth, and steer away from her."

"Ay, but she sometimes gives chase."

"Strike your flag, then, if it must be; for, trust me, you 'll not conquer *her*."

"We 'll see, we 'll see," muttered the old fellow, as he waved his adieux, and then turned back into the house again.

As Stapylton lay back in his carriage, he could not help muttering a malediction on the "dear friend" he had just parted with. When the *bourgeois gentilhomme* objected to his adversary pushing him *en tierce* while he attacked him *en quarte*, he was expressing a great social want, applicable to those people who in conversation will persist in saying many things which ought not to be uttered, and expressing doubts and distrusts which, however it be reasonable to feel, are an outrage to avow.

"The old fox," said Stapylton, aloud, "taunted me with selling what did not belong to me; but he never suspects that I have bought something without paying for it, and that something himself! Yes, the mock siege he will lay to the fortress will occupy the garrison till it suits me to open the real attack, and I will make use of him, besides, to learn whatever goes on in my absence. How the old fellow swallowed the bait! What self-esteem there must be in such a rugged nature, to make him imagine he could be successful in a cause like this! He is, after all, a clumsy agent to trust one's interest to. If the choice had been given me, I'd far rather have had a woman to watch over them. Polly Dill, for instance, the very girl to understand such a mission well. How adroitly would she have played the game, and how clearly would her letters have shown me the exact state of events!"

Such were the texts of his musings as he drove along, and deep as were his thoughts, they never withdrew him, when the emergency called, from attention to every detail of the journey, and he scrutinized the post-horses as they were led out, and apportioned the rewards to the postilions as though no heavier care lay on his heart than the road and its belongings. While he rolled thus smoothly along, Peter Barrington had been summoned to his sister's presence, to narrate in full all that he had asked, and all that he had learned of Stapylton and his fortunes.

Miss Dinah was seated in a deep armchair, behind a formidable embroidery-frame,—a thing so complex and mysterious in form as to suggest an implement of torture. At a short distance off sat Withering, with pen, ink, and paper before him, as if to set down any details of unusual importance; and into this imposing presence poor Barrington entered with a woful sense of misgiving and humiliation.

"We have got a quiet moment at last, Peter," said Miss Barrington. "I have sent the girls over to Brown's Barn for the tulip-roots, and I have told Darby that if any visitors came they were to be informed we were particularly occupied by business, and could see no one."

"Just so," added Withering; "it is a case before the Judge in Chamber."

"But what have we got to hear?" asked Barrington, with an air of innocence.

"We have got to hear your report, brother Peter; the narrative of your late conversation with Major Stapylton; given, as nearly as your memory will serve, in the exact words and in the precise order everything occurred."

"October the twenty-third," said Withering, writing as he spoke; "minute of interview between P. B. and Major S. Taken on the same morning it occurred, with remarks and observations explanatory."

"Begin," said Dinah, imperiously, while she worked away without lifting her head. "And avoid, so far as possible, anything beyond the precise expression employed."

"But you don't suppose I took notes in shorthand of what we said to each other, do you?"

"I certainly suppose you can have retained in your memory a conversation that took place two hours ago," said Miss Dinah, sternly.

"And can relate it circumstantially and clearly," added Withering.

"Then I 'm very sorry to disappoint you, but I can do nothing of the kind."

"Do you mean to say that you had no interview with Major Stapylton, Peter?"

"Or that you have forgotten all about it?" said Withering.

"Or is it that you have taken a pledge of secrecy, brother Peter?"

"No, no, no! It is simply this, that though I retain a pretty fair general impression of what I said myself, and what he said afterwards, I could no more pretend to recount it accurately than I could say off by heart a scene in 'Romeo and Juliet.'"

"Why don't you take the 'Comedy of Errors' for your illustration, Peter Barrington? I ask you, Mr. Withering, have you in all your experience met anything like this?"

"It would go hard with a man in the witness-box to make such a declaration, I must say."

"What would a jury think of, what would a judge say to him?" said she, using the most formidable of all penalties to her brother's imagination. "Wouldn't the court tell him that he would be compelled to speak out?"

"They'd have it out on the cross-examination, at all events, if not on the direct."

"In the name of confusion, what do you want with me?" exclaimed Peter, in despair.

"We want everything,—everything that you heard about this man. Who he is, what he is; what by the father's side, what by the mother's; what are his means, and where; who knows him, who are his associates. Bear in mind that to us, here, he has dropped out of the clouds."

"And gone back there too," added Withering.

"I wish to Heaven he had taken me with him!" sighed Peter, drearily.

"I think in this case, Miss Barrington," said Withering, with a well-affected gravity, "we had better withdraw a juror, and accept a nonsuit."

"I have done with it altogether," said she, gathering up her worsted and her needles, and preparing to leave the room.

"My dear Dinah," said Barrington, entreatingly, "imagine a man as wanting in tact as I am,—and as timid, too, about giving casual offence,—conducting such an inquiry as you committed to my hands. Fancy how, at every attempt to obtain information, his own boldness, I might call it rudeness, stared him in the face, till at last, rather than push his investigations, he grew puzzled how to apologize for his prying curiosity."

"Brother, brother, this is too bad! It had been better to have thought more of your granddaughter's fate and less of your own feelings." And with this she flounced out of the room, upsetting a spider-table, and a case of stuffed birds that stood on it, as she passed.

MISS DINAH'S INDIGNATION

"I don't doubt but she 's right, Tom," said Peter, when the door closed.

"Did he not tell you who he was, and what his fortune? Did you really learn nothing from him?"

"He told me everything; and if I had not been so cruelly badgered, I could have repeated every word of it; but you never made a hound true to the scent by flogging him, Tom,—is n't that a fact, eh?" And consoled by an illustration that seemed so pat to his case, he took his hat and strolled out into the garden.

CHAPTER VIII.

GENERAL CONYERS

In a snug little room of the Old Ship Hotel, at Dover, a large, heavy man, with snow-white hair, and moustaches,—the latter less common in those days than the present,—sat at table with a younger one, so like him that no doubt could have existed as to their being father and son. They had dined, and were sitting over their wine, talking occasionally, but oftener looking fondly and affectionately at each other; and once, by an instinct of sudden love, grasping each other's hand, and sitting thus several minutes without a word on either side.

"You did not expect me before to-morrow, Fred," said the old man, at last.

"No, father," replied young Conyers. "I saw by the newspapers that you were to dine at the Tuileries on Tuesday, and I thought you would not quit Paris the same evening."

"Yes; I started the moment I took off my uniform. I wanted to be with you, my boy; and the royal politeness that detained me was anything but a favor. How you have grown, Fred,—almost my own height, I believe."

"The more like you the better," said the youth, as his eyes ran over, and the old man turned away to hide his emotion.

After a moment he said: "How strange you should not have got my letters, Fred; but, after all, it is just as well as it is. I wrote in a very angry spirit, and was less just than a little cool reflection might have made me. They made no charges against me, though I thought they had. There were grumblings and discontents, and such-like. They called me a Rajah, and raked up all the old stories they used to circulate once on a time about a far better fellow—"

"You mean Colonel Barrington, don't you?" said Fred.

"Where or how did you hear of that name?" said the old man, almost sternly.

"An accident made me the guest of his family, at a little cottage they live in on an hish river. I passed weeks there, and, through the favor of the name I bore, I received more kindness than I ever before met in life."

"And they knew you to be a Conyers, and to be my son?"

"It was Colonel Barrington's aunt was my hostess, and she it was who, on hearing my name, admitted me at once to all the privileges of old friendship. She told me of the close companionship which once subsisted between you and her nephew, and gave me rolls of his letters to read wherein every line spoke of you."

"And Mr. Barrington, the father of George, how did he receive you?"

"At first with such coolness that I could n't bring myself to recross his threshold. He had been away from home when I arrived, and the day of his return I was unexpectedly presented to him by his sister, who evidently was as unprepared as myself for the reception I met with."

"And what was that reception,—how was it? Tell me all as it happened."

"It was the affair of a moment. Miss Barrington introduced me, saying, 'This is the son of poor George's dearest friend,—this is a Conyers;' and the old man faltered, and seemed like to faint, and after a moment stammered out something about an honor he had never counted upon,—a visit he scarcely could have hoped for; and, indeed, so overcome was he that he staggered into the house only to take to his bed, where he lay seriously ill for several days after."

"Poor fellow! It was hard to forgive,—very hard."

"Ay, but he has forgiven it—whatever it was—heartily, and wholly forgiven it. We met afterwards by a chance in Germany, and while I was hesitating how to avoid a repetition of the painful scene which marked our first meeting, he came manfully towards me with his hand out, and said, 'I have a forgiveness to beg of you; and if you only know how I long to obtain it, you would scarce say me no.'"

"The worthy father of poor George! I think I hear him speak the very words himself. Go on, Fred,—go on, and tell me further."

"There is no more to tell, sir, unless I speak of all the affectionate kindness he has shown,—the trustfulness and honor with which he has treated me. I have been in his house like his own son."

"Ah! if you had known that son! If you had seen what a type of a soldier he was! The most intrepid, the boldest fellow that ever breathed; but with a heart of childlike simplicity and gentleness. I could tell you traits of him, of his forbearance, his forgiveness, his generous devotion to friendship, that would seem to bespeak a nature that had no room for other than soft and tender emotion; and yet, if ever there was a lion's heart within a man's bosom it was his." For a moment or two the old man seemed overcome by his recollections, and then, as if by an effort, rallying himself, he went on: "You have often heard the adage, Fred, that enjoins watching one's pennies and leaving the pounds to take care of themselves; and yet, trust me, the maxim is truer as applied to our morals than our money. It is by the smaller, finer, and least important traits of a man that his fate in life is fashioned. The caprices we take no pains to curb, the tempers we leave unchecked, the petty indulgences we extend to our vanity and self-love,—these are the great sands that wreck us far oftener than the more stern and formidable features of our character. I ought to know this truth; I myself lost the best and truest and the noblest friend that ever man had, just from the exercise of a spirit of bantering and ridicule which amused those about me, and gave me that pre-eminence which a sarcastic and witty spirit is sure to assert. You know already how George Barrington and I lived together like brothers. I do not believe two men ever existed more thoroughly and sincerely attached to each other. All the contrarieties of our dispositions served but to heighten the interest that linked us together. As for myself, I was never wearied in exploring the strange recesses of that great nature that seemed to unite all that could be daring and dashing in man with the tenderness of a woman. I believe I knew him far better than he knew himself. But to come to what I wanted to tell you, and which is an agony to me to dwell on. Though for a long while our close friendship was known in the regiment, and spoken of as a thing incapable of change, a sort of rumor—no, not even a rumor, but an impression—seemed to gain, that the ties between us were looser on my side than his; that George looked up to *me*, and that I, with the pride of a certain superiority, rather lorded it over *him*. This feeling became painfully strengthened when it got about that Barrington had lent me the greater part of the purchase-money for my troop,—a promotion, by the way, which barred his own advancement,—and it was whispered, so at least I heard, that Barrington was a mere child in my hands, whom I rebuked or rewarded at pleasure. If I could have traced these rumors to any direct source, I could have known how to deal with them. As it was, they were vague, shadowy, and unreal; and their very unsubstantiality maddened me the more. To have told George of them would have been rasher still. The thought of a wrong done to *me* would have driven him beyond all reason, and he would infallibly have compromised himself beyond recall. It was the very first time in my life I had a secret from him, and it eat into my heart like a virulent disease. The consciousness that I was watched, the feeling that eyes were upon me marking all I did, and tongues were commenting on all I said, exasperated me, and at one moment I would parade my friendship for Barrington in a sort of spirit of defiance, and at another, as though to give the lie to my slanderers, treat him with indifference and carelessness, as it were, to show that I was not bound to him by the weight of a direct obligation, and that our relations involved nothing of dependence. It was when, by some cruel mischance, I had been pursuing this spirit to its extreme, that the conversation one night at mess turned upon sport and tiger-hunting. Many stories were told, of course, and we had the usual narratives of hairbreadth escapes and perils of the most appalling kind; till, at length, some one—I forget exactly who it was—narrated a single-handed encounter with a jaguar, which in horror exceeded anything we had heard before. The details were alone not so terrible, but the circumstances so marvellous, that one and all who listened cried out, 'Who did it?'

"'The man who told me the tale,' replied the narrator, 'and who will probably be back to relate it here to you in a few days,—Colonel Barrington.'

"I have told you the devilish spirit which had me in possession. I have already said that I was in one of those moods of insolent mockery in which nothing was sacred to me. No sooner, then, did I hear Barrington's name than I burst into a hearty laugh, and said, 'Oh! if it was one of George Barrington's tigers, you ought to have mentioned that fact at the outset. You have been exciting our feelings unfairly.'

"'I assume that his statement was true,' said the other, gravely.

"'Doubtless; just as battle-pieces are true, that is, pic-torially true. The tiger did nothing that a tiger ought not to do, nor did George transgress any of those "unities" which such combats require. At the same time, Barring-ton's stories have always a something about them that stamps the authorship, and you recognize this trait just as you do a white horse in a picture by Wouvermans.'

"In this strain I went on, heated by my own warmed imagination, and the approving laughter of those around me. I recounted more than one feat of Barrington's,—things which I knew he had done, some of them almost incredible in boldness. These I told with many a humorous addition and many an absurd commentary, convulsing the listeners with laughter, and rendering my friend ridiculous.

"He came back from the hills within the week, and before he was two hours in his quarters he had heard the whole story. We were at luncheon in the mess-room when he entered, flushed and excited, but far more moved by emotion than resentment.

"'Ormsby,' said he, 'you may laugh at me to your heart's content and I'll never grumble at it; but there are some young officers here who, not knowing the ties that attach us, may fancy that these quizzings pass the limits of mere drollery, and even jeopardize something of my truthfulness. *You*, I know, never meant this any more than I have felt it, but others might, and might, besides, on leaving this and sitting at other tables, repeat what they had heard here. Tell them that you spoke of me as you have a free right to do, in jest, and that your ridicule was the good-humored banter of a friend,—of a friend who never did, never could, impugn my honor.'

"His eyes were swimming over, and his lips trembling, as he uttered the last words. I see him now, as he stood there, his very cheek shaking in agitation. That brave, bold fellow, who would have marched up to a battery without quailing, shook like a sickly girl.

"'Am I to say that you never draw the long-bow, George?' asked I, half insolently.

"'You are to say, sir, that I never told a lie,' cried he, dark with passion.

"'Oh, this discussion will be better carried on elsewhere,' said I, as I arose and left the room.

"As I was in the wrong, totally in the wrong, I was passionate and headstrong. I sat down and wrote a most insolent letter to Barrington. I turned all the self-hate that was consuming *me* against my friend, and said I know not what of outrage and insult. I did worse; I took a copy of my letter, and declared that I would read it to the officers in the mess-room. He sent a friend to me to beg I would not take this course of open insult. My answer was, 'Colonel Barrington knows his remedy.' When I sent this message, I prepared for what I felt certain would follow. I knew Barrington so well that I thought even the delay of an hour, then two hours, strange. At length evening drew nigh, and, though I sat waiting in my quarters, no one came from him,—not a letter nor a line apprised me what course he meant to take.

"Not caring to meet the mess at such a moment, I ordered my horses and drove up to a small station about twenty miles off, leaving word where I was to be found. I passed three days there in a state of fevered expectancy. Barrington made no sign, and, at length, racked and distressed by the conflict with myself,—now summoning up an insolent spirit of defiance to the whole world, now humbling myself in a consciousness of the evil line I had adopted,—I returned one night to my quarters. The first news that greeted me was that Barrington had left us. He had accepted the offer of a Native command which had been made to him some months before, and of which we had often canvassed together all the advantages and disadvantages. I heard that he had written two letters to me before he started, and torn them up after they were sealed. I never heard from him, never saw him more, till I saw his dead body carried into camp the morning he fell.

"I must get to the end of this quickly, Fred, and I will tell you all at once, for it is a theme I will never go back on. I came to England with despatches about two years after Barrington's death. It was a hurried visit, for I was ordered to hold myself in readiness to return almost as soon as I arrived. I was greatly occupied, going about from place to place, and person to person, so many great people desired to have a verbal account of what was doing in India, and to hear confidentially what I thought of matters there. In the midst of the mass of letters which the post brought me every morning, and through which, without the aid of an officer on the staff, I could never have got through, there came one whose singular address struck me. It was to 'Captain Ormsby Conyers, 22d Light Dragoons,' a rank I had held fourteen years before that time in that same regiment. I opined at once that my correspondent must have been one who had known me at that time and not followed me in the interval. I was right. It was from old Mr. Barrington,—George Barrington's father. What version of my quarrel with his son could have reached him, I cannot even guess, nor by what light he read my conduct in the affair; but such a letter I never read in my life. It was a challenge to meet him anywhere, and with any weapon, but couched in language so insulting as to impugn my courage, and hint that I would probably shelter myself behind the pretext of his advanced age. 'But remember,' said he, 'if God has permitted me to be an old man, it is *you* who have made me a childless one!'"

For a few seconds he paused, overcome by emotion, and then went on: "I sat down and wrote him a letter of contrition, almost abject in its terms. I entreated him to believe that for every wrong I had done his noble-hearted son, my own conscience had repaid me in misery ten times told; that if he deemed my self-condemnation insufficient, it was open to him to add to it whatever he wished of obloquy or shame; that if he proclaimed me a coward before the world, and degraded me in the eyes of men, I would not offer one word in my defence. I cannot repeat all that I said in my deep humiliation. His answer came at last, one single line, re-enclosing my own letter to me: 'Lest I should be tempted to make use of this letter, I send it back to you; there is no need of more between us.'

"With this our intercourse ceased. When a correspondence was published in the 'Barrington Inquiry,' as it was called, I half hoped he would have noticed some letters of mine about George; but he never did, and in his silence I thought I read his continued unforgiveness."

"I hope, father, that you never believed the charges that were made against Captain Barrington?"

"Not one of them; disloyalty was no more his than cowardice. I never knew the Englishman with such a pride of country as he had, nor could you have held out a greater bribe to him, for any achievement of peril, than to say, 'What a gain it would be for England!'"

"How was it that such a man should have had a host of enemies?"

"Nothing so natural. Barrington was the most diffident of men; his bashfulness amounted to actual pain. With strangers, this made him cold to very sternness, or, as is often seen in the effort to conquer a natural defect, gave him a manner of over-easy confidence that looked like impertinence. And thus the man who would not have wounded the self-love of the meanest beggar, got the reputation of being haughty, insolent, and oppressive. Besides this, when he was in the right, and felt himself so, he took no pains to convince others of the fact. His maxim was,—have I not heard it from his lips scores of times,—'The end will show.'"

"And yet the end will not show, father; his fame has not been vindicated, nor his character cleared."

"In some measure the fault of those who took up his cause. They seemed less to insist on reparation than punishment. They did not say, 'Do justice to this man's memory;' but, 'Come forward and own you wronged him, and broke his heart.' Now, the accusation brought against George Barrington of assuming sovereign power was not settled by his death; his relatives forgot this, or merged it in their own charge against the Company. They mismanaged everything."

"Is it too late to put them on the right track, father; or could you do it?" asked the youth, eagerly.

"It is not too late, boy! There is time for it yet. There is, however, one condition necessary, and I do not see how that is to be secured."

"And what is that?"

"I should see Mr. Barrington and confer with him alone; he must admit me to his confidence, and I own to you, I scarcely deem that possible."

"May I try—may I attempt this?"

"I do not like to refuse you, Fred: but if I say Yes, it will be to include you in my own defeated hopes. For many a year Mr. Barrington has refused to give one sign of his forgiveness; for in his treatment of you I only recognize the honorable feeling of exempting the son from the penalty due to the father. But perhaps defeat is better than self-reproach, and as I have a strong conviction I could serve him, I am ready to risk a failure."

"I may make the attempt, then?" said Fred, eagerly. "I will write to Miss Barrington to-day."

"And now of yourself. What of your career? How do you like soldiering, boy?"

"Less than ever, sir; it is only within the last week or two that we have seen anything beyond barrack or parade duty. Now, however, we have been called to repress what are called risings in the northern shires; and our task has been to ride at large unarmed mobs and charge down masses, whose grape-shot are brickbats. Not a very glorious campaign!"

The old man smiled, but said nothing for a moment.

"Your colonel is on leave, is he not?" asked he.

"Yes. We are commanded by that Major Stapylton I told you of."

"A smart officer, but no friend of yours, Fred," said the General, smiling.

"No, sir; certainly no friend of mine," said the young man, resolutely. "To refuse me a week's leave to go and meet my father, whom I have not seen for years, and, when pressed, to accord me four days, is to disgust me with himself and the service together."

"Well, as you cannot be my guest, Fred, I will be yours. I 'll go back with you to headquarters. Stapylton is a name I used to be familiar with long ago. It may turn out that I know his family; but let us talk of Barrington. I have been thinking it would be better not to link any question of his own interests with my desire to meet him, but simply to say I 'm in England, and wish to know if he would receive me."

"It shall be as you wish, sir. I will write to his sister by this post."

"And after one day in town, Fred, I am ready to accompany you anywhere."

CHAPTER IX.

MAJOR M'CORMICK'S LETTER

As it was not often that Major M'Cormick performed the part of a letter-writer, perhaps my reader will pardon me if I place him before him on one of these rare occasions. If success would always respond to labor, his would have been a real triumph; for the effort cost him many days, two sleepless nights, a headache, and half a quire of paper.

Had not Stapylton retained him by an admirably selected hamper of good things from a celebrated Italian warehouse in the Strand, I am afraid that M'Cormick's zeal might have cooled down to the zero of forgetfulness; but the reindeer hams and the Yarmouth bloaters, the potted shrimps and the preserved guavas, were an appeal that addressed themselves to that organ which with him paid the double debt of digestion and emotion. He felt that such a correspondent was worth a sacrifice, and he made it That my reader may appreciate the cost of the achievement, I would have him imagine how a mason about to build a wall should be obliged to examine each stone before he laid it, test its constituent qualities, its shape and its size,—for it was thus that almost every word occasioned the Major a reference to the dictionary, spelling not having been cultivated in his youth, nor much practised in his riper years. Graces of style, however, troubled him little; and, to recur to my figure of the stone-mason, if he was embarrassed in his search for the materials, he cared wonderfully little for the architecture. His letter ran thus, and the reader will perceive that it must have been written some weeks after the events recorded in the last chapter:—

"Mac's Nest, October, Thursday.

"Dear S.,—A touch of my old Walcheren complaint has laid me up since Tuesday, and if the shakes make me illegible now, that's the reason why. Besides this the weather is dreadful; cold east winds and rains, sometimes sleet, every day; and the turf so wet, it 's only smoke, not fire. I believe it is the worst climate in Europe, and it gets wetter every year.

"The hamper came to hand, but though it was marked 'Carriage paid, this side up,' they upset it and broke two bottles, and charged seven and fourpence-half-penny for the bringing it, which is, I think, enormous; at least, Tim Hacket got over a thrashing-machine from Scotland last spring for twelve and four, and there 's no comparison between the two. Thanks to you, however, all the same; but if you can get any of this charge reduced, so much the better, not to speak of the bottles,—both mixed pickles—which they ought to make good.

"I am glad to see you are touching up the Radicals in the North; powder and ball will do more to bring them to reason than spouting in Parliament. The papers say there was nine killed and twenty-three wounded; and one fellow, the 'Stockport Bee,' says, that 'if the Butcher that led the dragoons is n't turned out of the service with disgrace no gentleman will degrade himself by entering the army.' Isn't the Butcher yourself? Miss Barrington, always your friend, says it is; and that if the account of another paper, called the 'Ægis,' be true, you 'll have to go to a court-martial. I stood stoutly to you through it all, and declared that when the niggers was up at Jamaica, we had n't time to take the names of the prisoners, and we always cut one of their ears off to know them again. Old Peter laughed till the tears ran down his face, but Dinah said, 'If I did not suppose, sir, that you were inventing a very graceless joke, I'd insist on your leaving this room and this house on the instant.' It was ten o'clock at night, and raining hard; so you may guess I gave in. Bad as she is, the young one is her equal, and I gave up all thoughts of what you call 'prosecuting my suit' in that quarter. She isn't even commonly civil to me, and when I ask her for, maybe, the mustard at dinner, she turns away her head, and says, 'Darby, give Major M'Cormick the salt.' That's French politeness, perhaps; but I'll pay them all off yet, for they can't get sixpence on the mortgage, and I 'm only drinking out that bin of old Madeira before I tell them that I won't advance the money. Why should I? The women treat me worse than a dog, and old B. is neither more nor less than a fool. Dill, the doctor, however he got it, says it's all up about the suit with the India Company; that there's no proof of the Colonel's marriage at all, that the charges against him were never cleared up, and that nothing can come out of it but more disgrace and more exposure.

"I wish you 'd send me the correct account of what took place between you and one of your subalterns, for old Dinah keeps harping on it in a sort of mysterious and mischievous way of her own, that provokes me. Was it that he refused to obey orders, or that *you*, as *she* says, used such language towards him that he wrote to report you? Give it to me in black and white, and maybe I won't try her temper with it. At all events, make out some sort of a case, for the old woman is now intolerable. She said yesterday, 'Major Stapylton, to whom I write by this post, will see that his visit here must be preceded by an explanation.' There's her words for you, and I hope you like them!

"I think you are right to be in no hurry about purchasing, for many say the whole system will be changed soon, and the money would be clean thrown away. Besides this, I have been looking over my bauk-book, and I find I could n't help you just now. Two bad harvests, and the smut in the wheat last year, are running me mighty close. I won't finish this till to-morrow, for I 'm going to dine at 'The Home' to-day. It is the granddaughter's birthday, and there was a regular shindy about who was going to be asked. Old Peter was for a grand celebration, and inviting the Admiral, and the Gores, and God knows who besides; and Dinah was for what she called a family party, consisting, I suppose, of herself and Darby. I 'll be able, before I close this, to tell you how it was ended; for I only know now that Dill and his daughter are to be there.

"Wednesday.—I sit down with a murdering headache to finish this letter.

Maybe it was the pickled lobster, or the ice punch, or the other drink they called champagne-cup that did it. But I never passed such a night since I was in the trenches, and I am shaking still, so that I can scarce hold the pen. It was a grand dinner, to be sure, for ruined people to give. Venison from Carrick Woods, and game of every kind, with all kinds of wine; and my Lord Car-rickmore talking to Miss Dinah, and the Admiral following up with the niece, and Tom Brabazon, and Dean of Deanspark, and the devil knows who besides, bringing up the rear, with Dill and your obedient servant. Every dish that came in, and every bottle that was uncorked, I said to myself, 'There goes another strap on the property;' and I felt as if we were eating the trees and the timber and the meadows all the time at table.

"It's little of the same sympathy troubled the others. My Lord was as jolly as if he was dining with the King; and old Cobham called for more of the Madeira, as if it was an inn; and Peter himself—the heartless old fool—when he got up to thank the company for drinking his granddaughter's health, said, 'May I trust that even at my advanced age this may not be the last time I may have to speak my gratitude to you all for the generous warmth with which you have pledged this toast; but even should it be so, I shall carry away with me from this evening's happiness a glow of pleasure that will animate me to the last. It was only this morning I learned what I know you will all hear with satisfaction, that there is every probability of a speedy arrangement of my long-pending suit with the Company, and that my child here will soon have her own again.' Grand applause and huzzas, with a noise that drowned 'Bother!' from myself, and in the middle of the row up jumps the Admiral, and cries out, 'Three cheers more for the Rajah's daughter!' I thought the old roof would come down; and the blackguards in the kitchen took up the cry and shouted like mad, and then we yelled again, and this went on for maybe five minutes. 'What does it all mean,' says I, 'but a cheer for the Court of Bankruptcy, and Hip, hip, hurray! for the Marshalsea Prison!' After that, he had half an hour or more of flatteries and compliments. My Lord was so happy, and Peter Barrington so proud, and the Admiral so delighted, and the rest of us so much honored, that I could n't stand it any longer, but stole away, and got into the garden, to taste a little fresh air and quietness. I had n't gone ten paces, when I came plump upon Miss Dinah, taking her coffee under a tree. 'You are a deserter, I fear, sir,' said she, in her own snappish way; so I thought I 'd pay her off, and I said, 'To tell you the truth, Miss Barrington, at our time of life these sort of things are more full of sadness than pleasure. We know how hollow they are, and how little heart there is in the cheers of the people that are so jolly over your wine, but would n't stop to talk to you when you came down to water!'

"'The worse we think of the world, Major M'Cormick,' says she, 'the more risk we run of making ourselves mean enough to suit it.'

"'I don't suspect, ma'am,' says I, 'that when people have known it so long as you and I, that they are greatly in love with it.'

"'They may, however, be mannerly in their dealings with it, sir,' said she, fiercely; and so we drew the game, and settled the men for another battle.

"'Is there anything new, ma'am?' says I, after a while.

"'I believe not, sir. The bread riots still continue in the North, where what would seem the needless severity of some of the military commanders has only exasperated the people. You have heard, I suppose, of Major Stapylton's business?'

"'Not a word, ma'am,' says I; 'for I never see a paper.'

"'I know very little of the matter myself,' says she. 'It was, it would appear, at some night assemblage at a place called Lund's Common. A young officer sent forward by Major Stapylton to disperse the people, was so struck by the destitution and misery he witnessed, and the respectful attitude they exhibited, that he hesitated about employing force, and restricted himself to counsels of quietness and submission. He did more,—not perhaps very prudently, as some would say,—he actually emptied his pockets of all the money he had, giving even his watch to aid the starving horde before him. What precise version of his conduct reached his superior, I cannot say; but certainly Major Stapylton commented on it in terms of the harshest severity, and he even hinted at a reason for the forbearance too offensive for any soldier to endure.'

"She did not seem exactly to know what followed after this, but some sort of inquiry appeared to take place, and witnesses were examined as to what really occurred at Lund's Common; and amongst others, a Lascar, who was one of the factory hands,—having come to England a great many years before with an officer from India. This fellow's evidence was greatly in favor of young Conyers, and was subjected to a very severe cross-examination from yourself, in the middle of which he said something in Hindostanee that nobody in the court understood but you; and after this he was soon dismissed and the case closed for that day.

"'What do you think, Major M'Cormick,' said she, 'but when the court of inquiry opened the next morning, Lal-Adeen, the Lascar, was not to be found high or low. The court have suspended their sittings to search for him; but only one opinion prevails,—that Major Stapylton knows more of this man's escape than he is likely to tell.' I have taken great pains to give you her own very words in all this business, and I wrote them down the moment I got home, for I thought to myself you 'd maybe write about the matter to old Peter, and you ought to be prepared for the way they look at it; the more because Miss Dinah has a liking for young Conyers,—what she calls a motherly affection; but I don't believe in the motherly part of it! But of course you care very little what the people here say about you at all. At least, I know it would n't trouble *me* much, if I was in your place. At all events, whatever you do, do with a high hand, and the Horse Guards is sure to stand to you. Moderation may be an elegant thing in civil life, but I never knew it succeed in the army. There's the rain coming on again, and I just sent out six cars to the bog for turf; so I must conclude, and remain, yours sincerely,

"Daniel T. M'Cormick.

"I 'm thinking of foreclosing the small mortgage I hold on 'The Home,' but as they pay the interest regularly, five per cent, I would n't do it if I knew things were going on reasonably well with them; send me a line about what is doing regarding the 'claim,' and it will guide me."

While Major M'Cormick awaited the answer to his postscript, which to him—

as to a lady—was the important part of his letter, a short note arrived at 'The Home' from Mr. Withering, enclosing a letter he had just received from Major Stapylton. Withering's communication was in answer to one from Barrington, and ran thus:—

"Dear B.,—All things considered, I believe you are right in not receiving General Conyers at this moment. It would probably, as you suspect, enable calumnious people to say that you could make your resentments play second when they came in the way of your interests. If matters go on well, as I have every hope they will, you can make the *amende* to him more satisfactorily and more gracefully hereafter. Buxton has at length consented to bring the case before the House; of course it will not go to a division, nor, if it did, could it be carried; but the discussion will excite interest, the Press will take it up, and after a few regretful and half-civil expressions from the Ministry, the India Board will see the necessity of an arrangement.

"It is somewhat unfortunate and *mal à propos* that Stapylton should at this moment have got into an angry collision with young Conyers. I have not followed the case closely, but, as usual in such things, they seem each of them in the wrong,—the young sub wanting to make his generous sympathy supply the place of military obedience, and the old officer enforcing discipline at the cost of very harsh language. I learn this morning that Conyers has sold out, intending to demand a personal satisfaction. You will see by S.'s letter that he scarcely alludes to this part of the transaction at all. S. feels very painfully the attacks of the Press, and sees, perhaps, more forcibly than I should in his place, the necessity of an exchange. Read attentively the portion I have underlined."

It is to this alone I have to direct my readers' attention, the first two sides of the letter being entirely filled with details about the "claim":—

"'The newspapers have kept me before you for some days back, much more, I doubt not, to their readers' amusement than to my own gratification. I could, if I pleased, have told these slanderers that I did not charge a crowd of women and children,—that I did not cut down an elderly man at his own door-sill,—that I did not use language "offensive and unbecoming" to one of my officers, for his having remonstrated in the name of humanity against the cruelty of my orders. In a word, I might have shown the contemptible scribblers that I knew how to temper duty with discretion, as I shall know how, when the occasion offers, to make the punishment of a calumniator a terror to his colleagues. However, there is a very absurd story going about of a fellow whose insolence I certainly *did* reply to with the flat of my sabre, and whom I should be but too happy to punish legally, if he could be apprehended. That he made his escape after being captured, and that I connived at or assisted in it,—I forget which,—you have probably heard. In fact, there is nothing too incredible to say of me for the moment; and what is worse, I begin to suspect that the Home Secretary, having rather burned his fingers in the business, will not be very sorry to make an Admiral Byng of a Major of Hussars. For each and all these reasons I mean to exchange, and, if possible, into a regiment in India. This will, of course, take some time; meanwhile, I have asked for and obtained some months' leave. You will be surprised at my troubling you with so much of purely personal matters, but they are the necessary preface to what I now come. You are aware of the letter I wrote some time back to Mr. Barrington, and the request it preferred. If the reply I received was not discouraging, neither was it conclusive. The ordinary commonplaces as to the shortness of our acquaintance, the want of sufficient knowledge of each other's tastes, characters, &c, were duly dwelt upon; but I could not at the end say, was I an accepted or a rejected suitor. Now that the critical moment of my life draws nigh,—for such I feel the present emergency,—an act of confidence in me would have more than double value. Can you tell me that this is the sentiment felt towards me, or am I to learn that the yells of a rabble have drowned the voices of my friends? In plain words, will Miss Josephine Barrington accept my offer? Will she intrust her happiness to my keeping, and change the darkest shadow that ever lowered over my life into a gleam of unspeakable brightness? You have given me too many proofs of a friendly disposition towards me, not to make me feel that you are the best fitted to bring this negotiation to a good issue. If I do not mistake you much, you look with favor on my suit and wish it success. I am ashamed to say how deeply my hopes have jeopardized my future happiness, but I tell you frankly life has no such prize to my ambition, nor, in fact, any such alternative of despair before me.'

"Now, my dear Barrington," continued Withering's letter, "there is a great deal in this that I like, and something with which I am not so much pleased. If, however, I am not the Major's advocate to the extent he asks, or expects me, it is because I feel that to be unjustly dealt with is a stronger claim on *your* heart than that of any other man I ever met with, and the real danger here would be that you should suffer that feeling to predominate over all others. Consult your granddaughter's interests, if you can, independently of this; reflect well if the plan be one likely to promise her happiness. Take your sensible, clear-headed sister into your counsels; but, above all, ascertain Josephine's own sentiments, and do nothing in direct opposition to them."

"There, Dinah," said Barrington, placing the letter in her hands, "this is as much to your address as to mine. Read it over carefully, and you'll find me in the garden when you have done."

Miss Barrington laid down her great roll of worsted work, and began her task without a word. She had not proceeded very far, however, when Josephine entered in search of a book. "I beg pardon, aunt, if I derange you."

"We say disturb, or inconvenience, in English, Miss Barrington. What is it you are looking for?"

"The 'Legend of Montrose,' aunt. I am so much amused by that Major Dalgetty that I can think of nothing but him."

"Umph!" muttered the old lady. "It was of a character not altogether dissimilar I was thinking myself at that moment. Sit down here, child, and let me talk to you. This letter that I hold here, Josephine, concerns you."

"Me, aunt—concerns *me?* And who on earth could have written a letter in which I am interested?"

"You shall hear it." She coughed only once or twice, and then went on: "It's a proposal of marriage,—no less. That gallant soldier who left us so lately has fallen in love with you,—so he says, and of course he knows best. He seems fully aware that, being older than you, and graver in temperament, his offer must come heralded with certain expressions almost apologetic; but he deals with the matter skillfully, and tells us that being well off as regards fortune, of good blood, and with fair prospects before him, he does not wish to regard his suit as hopeless. Your grandfather was minded to learn how you might feel disposed to accept his addresses by observing your demeanor, by watching what emotion mention of him might occasion, by seeing how far you felt interested in his good or ill repute. I did not agree with him. I am never for the long road when there is a short one, and therefore I mean to let you hear his letter. This is what he writes." While Miss Dinah read the extract which the reader has just seen, she never noticed, or, if noticed, never attended to, the agitation in her niece's manner, or seemed to remark that from a deep-crimson at first her cheeks grew pale as death, and her lips-tremulous. "There, child," said Miss Dinah, as she finished—"there are his own words; very ardent words, but withal respectful. What do you think of them,—of them and of him?"

Josephine hung down her head, and with her hands firmly clasped together, she sat for a few moments so motionless that she seemed scarcely to breathe.

"Would you like to think over this before you speak of it, Josephine? Would you like to take this letter to your room and ponder over it alone?" No answer came but a low, half-subdued sigh.

"If you do not wish to make a confidante of me, Josephine, I am sorry for it, but not offended."

"No, no, aunt, it is not that," burst she in; "it is to *you* and you alone, I wish to speak, and I will be as candid as yourself. I am not surprised at the contents of this letter. I mean, I was in a measure prepared for them."

"That is to say, child, that he paid you certain attentions?"

She nodded assent.

"And how did you receive them? Did you let him understand that you were not indifferent to him,—that his addresses were agreeable to you?"

Another, but shorter, nod replied to this question.

"I must confess," said the old lady, bridling up, "all this amazes me greatly. Why, child, it is but the other day you met each other for the first time. How, when, and where you found time for such relations as you speak of, I cannot imagine. Do you mean to tell me, Josephine, that you ever talked alone together?"

"Constantly, aunt!"

"Constantly!"

"Yes, aunt. We talked a great deal together."

"But how, child,—where?"

"Here, aunt, as we used to stroll together every morning through the wood or in the garden; then as we went on the river or to the waterfall."

"I can comprehend nothing of all this, Josephine. I know you mean to deal openly with me; so say at once, how did this intimacy begin?"

"I can scarcely say how, aunt, because I believe we drifted into it. We used to talk a great deal of ourselves, and at length we grew to talk of each other,—of our likings and dislikings, our tastes and our tempers. And these did not always agree!"

"Indeed!"

"No, aunt," said she, with a heavy sigh. "We quarrelled very often; and once,—I shall not easily forget it,—once seriously."

"What was it about?"

"It was about India, aunt; and he was in the wrong, and had to own it afterwards and ask pardon."

"He must know much more of that country than you, child. How came it that you presumed to set up your opinion against his?"

"The presumption was his," said she, haughtily. "He spoke of *his* father's position as something the same as *my* father's. He talked of him as a Rajah!"

"I did not know that he spoke of his father," said Miss Dinah, thoughtfully.

"Oh, he spoke much of him. He told me, amongst other things, how he had been a dear friend of papa's; that as young men they lived together like brothers, and never were separate till the fortune of life divided them."

"What is all this I am listening to? Of whom are you telling me, Josephine?"

"Of Fred, Aunt Dinah; of Fred, of course."

"Do you mean young Conyers, child?"

"Yes. How could I mean any other?"

"Ta, ta, ta!" said the old lady, drumming with her heel on the floor and her fingers on the table. "It has all turned out as I said it would! Peter, Peter, will you never be taught wisdom? Listen to me, child!" said she, turning almost sternly towards Josephine. "We have been at cross-purposes with each other all this time. This letter which I have just read for you—" She stopped suddenly as she reached thus far, and after a second's pause, said, "Wait for me here; I will be back presently. I have a word to say to your grandfather."

Leaving poor Josephine in a state of trepidation and bewilderment,—ashamed at the confession she had just made, and trembling with a vague sense of some danger that impended over her,—Miss Dinah hurried away to the garden.

"Here's a new sort of worm got into the celery, Dinah," said he, as she came up, "and a most destructive fellow he is. He looks like a mere ruffling of the leaf, and you 'd never suspect him."

"It is your peculiarity never to suspect anything, brother Peter, even after you have had warning of peril. Do you remember my telling you, when we were up the Rhine, what would come of that intimacy between Conyers and Josephine?"

THE LETTER

"I think I do," said he, making what seemed an effort of memory.

"And can you recall the indolent slipshod answer you made me about it? But of course you cannot. It was an old-maid's apprehensions, and you forgot the whole thing. Well, Peter, I was right and you were wrong."

"Not the first time that the double event has come off so!" said he, smiling.

"You are too fond of that cloak of humility, Peter Barrington. The plea of

Guilty never saved any one from transportation!" Waiting a moment to recover her breath after this burst of passion, she went on: "After I had read that letter you gave me, I spoke to Josephine; I told her in a few words how it referred to her, and frankly asked her what she thought of it. She was very candid and very open, and, I must say, also very collected and composed. Young ladies of the present day possess that inestimable advantage over their predecessors. Their emotions do not overpower them." This was the second time of "blowing off the steam," and she had to wait a moment to rally. "She told me, frankly, that she was not unprepared for such an offer; that tender passages had already been exchanged between them. The usual tomfoolery, I conclude,—that supreme effort of selfishness people call love,—in a word, Peter, she was in no wise disinclined to the proposal; the only misfortune was, she believed it came from young Conyers."

Barrington would have laughed, and laughed heartily, if he dared. As it was, the effort to restrain himself sent the blood to his head, and made his eyes run over.

"You may well blush, Peter Barrington," said she, shaking her finger at him. "It's all your own doing."

"And when you undeceived her, Dinah, what did she say?"

"I have not done so yet; but my impression is that so susceptible a young lady should find no great difficulty in transferring her affections. For the present I mean to limit myself to declaring that this offer is not from Conyers; if she has curiosity to know the writer, she shall learn it. I always had my doubts about these convents Bread and water diet makes more epicures than abstinents!"

CHAPTER X.

INTERCHANGED CONFESSIONS

Miss Barrington, with Josephine at one side and Polly Dill on the other, sat at work in her little room that opened on the garden. Each was engaged in some peculiar task, and each seemed bent upon her labor in that preoccupied way which would imply that the cares of needlework make no mean call upon human faculties. A close observer would, however, have remarked that though Miss Barrington stitched vigorously away at the background for a fierce tiger with measly spots over him, Polly seemed oftener to contemplate than continue her handiwork; while Josephine's looks strayed constantly from the delicate tracery she was following, to the garden, where the roses blended with the jasmine, and the drooping honeysuckles hung listlessly over the boughs of the apple-tree.

"If your work wearies you, Fifine," said Miss Dinah, "you had better read for us."

"Oh no, not at all, aunt; I like it immensely. I was only wondering why one should devise such impossible foliage, when we have the real thing before us, in all its grace and beauty."

"Humph!" said the old lady; "the sight of a real tiger would not put me out of countenance with my own."

"It certainly ought not, ma'am," said Polly; while she added, in a faint whisper, "for there is assuredly no rivalry in the case."

"Perhaps Miss Dill is not too absorbed in her study of nature, as applied to needlework, to read out the newspaper."

"I will do it with pleasure, ma'am. Where shall I begin?"

"Deaths and marriages first, of course, child. Then fashion and varieties; take the accidents afterwards, and close with anything remarkable in politics, or any disastrous occurrence in high life."

Polly obeyed to the letter; once only straying into an animated account of a run with the Springfield fox-hounds, where three riders out of a large field came in at the death; when Miss Dinah stopped her abruptly, saying, "I don't care for the obituary of a fox, young lady. Go on with something else."

"Will you have the recent tragedy at Ring's End, ma'am?"

"I know it by heart Is there nothing new in the fashions,—how are bonnets worn? What's the latest sleeve? What's the color in vogue?"

"A delicate blue, ma'am; a little off the sky, and on the hyacinth."

"Very becoming to fair people," said Miss Dinah, with a shake of her blond ringlets.

"'The Prince's Hussars!' Would you like to hear about *them*, ma'am?"

"By all means."

"It's a very short paragraph. 'The internal troubles of this unhappy regiment would seem to be never ending. We last week informed our readers that a young subaltern of the corps, the son of one of our most distinguished generals, had thrown up his commission and repaired to the Continent, to enable him to de-mand a personal satisfaction from his commanding officer, and we now learn that the Major in question is precluded from accepting the gage of battle by something stronger than military etiquette.'"

"Read it again, child; that vile newspaper slang always puzzles me."

Polly recited the passage in a clear and distinct voice.

"What do you understand by it, Polly?"

"I take it to mean nothing, madam. One of those stirring pieces of intelligence which excites curiosity, and are no more expected to be explained than a bad rid-dle."

"It cannot surely be that he shelters himself under his position towards us? That I conclude is hardly possible!"

Though Miss Barrington said this as a reflection, she addressed herself almost directly to Josephine.

"As far as I am concerned, aunt," answered Josephine, promptly, "the Major may fight the monster of the Drachenfels to-morrow, if he wishes it."

"Oh, here is another mystery apparently on the same subject. 'The Lascar, Lal-Adeen, whom our readers will remember as having figured in a police-court a few days back, and was remanded till the condition of his wound—a severe sabre-cut on the scalp—should permit his further examination, and on the same night made his escape from the hospital, has once again, and very unexpectedly, turned up at Boulogne-sur-Mer. His arrival in this country—some say voluntarily, others un-der a warrant issued for his apprehension—will probably take place to-day or to-morrow, and, if report speak truly, be followed by some of the most singular confessions which the public has heard for a long time back.' 'The Post' contradicts the statement, and declares 'no such person has ever been examined before the magistrate, if he even have any existence at all.'"

"And what interest has all this for us?" asked Miss Dinah, sharply.

"You do not forget, ma'am, that this is the same man Major Stapylton was said to have wounded; and whose escape scandal hinted he had connived at, and who now 'does not exist.'"

"I declare Miss Dill, I remember no such thing; but it appears to me that Major Stapylton occupies a very considerable space in your own thoughts."

"I fancy Polly likes him, aunt," said Josephine, with a slight smile.

"Well, I will own he interests me; there is about him a mysterious something that says, 'I have more in my head and on my heart than you think of, and more, perhaps, than you could carry if the burden were yours.'"

"A galley-slave might say the same, Miss Dill."

"No doubt of it, ma'am; and if there be men who mix in the great world, and dine at grand houses, with something of the galley-slave on their conscience, they assuredly impress us with an amount of fear that is half a homage. One dreads them as he does a tiger, but the terror is mingled with admiration."

"This is nonsense, young lady, and baneful nonsense, too, begotten of French novels and a sickly sentimentality. I hope Fifine despises it as heartily as I do." The passionate wrath which she displayed extended to the materials of her work-basket, and while rolls of worsted were upset here, needles were thrown there; and at last, pushing her embroidery-frame rudely away, she arose and left the room.

"Dearest Polly, how could you be so indiscreet! You know, far better than I do, how little patience she has with a paradox."

"My sweet Fifine," said the other, in a low whisper, "I was dying to get rid of her, and I knew there was only one way of effecting it. You may remark that whenever she gets into a rage, she rushes out into the flower-garden, and walks round and round till she's ready to drop. There she is already; you may gauge her anger by the number of her revolutions in a minute."

"But why did you wish her away, Polly?"

"I'll tell you why; that is, there is a charming French word for what I mean, the verb 'agacer,' all untranslatable as it is. Now there are moments when a person working in the same room—reading, writing, looking out of the window—becomes an insupportable infliction. You reason, and say, 'How absurd, how childish, how ungenerous,' and so forth. It won't do; for as you look round he is there still, and by his mere presence keeps up the ferment in your thoughts. You fancy, at last, that he stands between you and your inner self, a witness that won't let your own conscience whisper to you, and you come in the end to hate him. Your dear aunt was on the high-road to this goal, when I bethought me of my expedient! And now we are all alone, dearest, make me a confession."

"What is it?"

"You do not like Major Stapylton?"

"No."

"And you do like somebody else?"

"Perhaps," said she, slowly, and dividing the syllables as she spoke them.

"That being the case, and seeing, as you do, that your aunt is entirely of your own mind, at least as to the man you do not care for, why don't you declare as much frankly to your grandfather, and break off the negotiation at once?"

"Just because that dear old grandpapa asked me not to be precipitate, not to be rash. He did not tell me that I must love Major Stapylton, or must marry him; but he said, 'If you only knew, Fifine, what a change in our fortune would come of a change in *your* feelings; if you could but imagine, child, how the whole journey of life might be rendered easier, all because you took the right-hand road instead of the left; if you could guess these things, and what might follow them —'" She stopped.

"Well, go on."

"No. I have said all that he said; he kissed my cheek as he got thus far, and hurried away from the room."

"And you, like a sweet, obedient child, hastened away to yours; wrote a farewell, a heart-broken farewell, to Fred Conyers; and solemnly swore to your own conscience you 'd marry a man you disliked. These are the sort of sacrifices the world has a high admiration for; but do you know, Fifine, the world limps a little in its morality sometimes, and is not one-half the fine creature it thinks itself. For instance, in the midst of all its enthusiasm for you, it has forgotten that in accepting for your husband a man you do not love, you are doing a dishonesty; and that, besides this, you really love another. It is what the French call the aggravating circumstance."

"I mean to do nothing of the kind!" broke in Fifine, boldly. "Your lecture does not address itself to *me*."

"Do not be angry, Fifine," said the other, calmly.

"It is rather too hard to be rebuked for the faults one might have, but has not committed. It's like saying how wet you 'd have been had you fallen into that pool!"

"Well, it also means, don't fall into the pool!"

"Do you know, Polly," said Josephine, archly, "I have a sort of suspicion that you don't dislike this Major yourself! Am I right?"

"I'm not say you were altogether wrong; that is, he interests me, or, rather, he puzzles me, and it piques my ingenuity to read him, just as it would to make out a cipher to which I had only one-half the key."

"Such a feeling as that would never inspire a tender interest, at least, with *me*."

"Nor did I say it was, Fifine. I have read in some book of my father's how certain physicians inoculated themselves with plague, the better to note the phenomena, and trace the course; and I own I can understand their zeal, and I 'd risk something to decipher this man."

"This may be very nice in medicine, Polly, but very bad in morals! At all events, don't catch the plague for the sake of saving *me*?"

"Oh! I assure you any step I take shall be done in the interests of science solely; not but that I have a small debt to acquit towards the gallant Major."

"You have! What can it possibly be?"

"Well, it was this wise," said she, with a half-sigh. "We met at a country-house here, and he paid me certain attentions, made me compliments on my riding, which I knew to be good, and my singing, which was just tolerable; said the usual things which mean nothing, and a few of those more serious ones which are supposed to be more significant; and then he asked my father's leave to come and visit him, and actually fixed a day and an hour. And we, poor people, all delighted with the flattery of such high notice, and thinking of the effect upon our neighbors so splendid a visitor would produce, made the most magnificent preparations to receive him,—papa in a black satin waistcoat, mamma in her lilac ribbons. I myself,—having put the roof on a pigeon-pie, and given the last finishing touch to a pagoda of ruby jelly,—I, in a charming figured muslin and a blush rose in my hair, awaited the hour of attack! And, after all, he never came. No, Fifine, never came! He forgot us, or he changed his mind, or something else turned up that he liked better; or—which is just as likely as any of the three—he thought it would be a charming piece of impertinence to pass off on such small folk, who presumed to fancy themselves company for him. At all events, Fifine, we saw him no more. He went his way somewhere, and we were left lamenting."

"And you really liked him, Polly?"

"No, of the two, I disliked him; but I wished very much that he might like *me!* I saw him very overbearing and very insolent to those who were certainly his equals, assuming a most offensive superiority everywhere and to any one, and I thought what an awful humiliation it would be if so great a personage were to be snubbed by the doctor's daughter. I wanted to give a lesson which could only be severe if it came from one humble as myself; but he defeated me, Fifine, and I am still his debtor! If I did not like him before, you may believe that I hate him now; and I came off here this morning, in hot haste, for no other purpose than to set you against him, and induce you to regard him as I do."

"There was little need," said Fifine, calmly; "but here comes my aunt back again. Make your submission quickly, Polly, or it will be too late to expect mercy."

"I 'll do better," said Polly, rising. "I 'll let my trial go on in my absence;" and with this she stepped out of the window as Miss Barrington entered by the door.

CHAPTER XI.

STAPYLTON'S VISIT AT "THE HOME"

So secretly had Barrington managed, that he negotiated the loan of five hundred pounds on a mortgage of the cottage without ever letting his sister hear of it; and when she heard on a particular day that her brother expected Mr. Kinshela, the attorney, from Kilkenny, on business, she made the occasion the pretext of a visit to Dr. Dill, taking Josephine with her, to pass the day there.

Barrington was therefore free to receive his lawyer at his ease, and confer with him alone. Not that he cared much for his company; he felt towards the attorney pretty much as an ardent soldier feels to a non-combatant, the commissary, or the paymaster. Had he been a barrister, indeed, old Peter would have welcomed him with the zest of true companionship; he would have ransacked his memory for anecdotes, and prepared for the meeting as for an encounter of sharp wits. Now it is no part of my task to present Mr. Kinshela more than passingly to my reader, and I will merely say that he was a shrewd, commonplace man, whose practice rarely introduced him to the higher classes of his county, and who recognized Barrington, even in his decline, as a person of some consideration.

They had dined well, and sat over their wine in the little dining-room over the river, a favorite spot of Barrington's when he wished to be confidential, for it was apart from the rest of the cottage, and removed from all intrusion.

"So, you won't tell me, Kinshela, who lent us this money?" said the old man, as he passed the decanter across the table.

"It is not that I won't, sir, but I can't. It was in answer to an advertisement I inserted in the 'Times,' that I got an application from Granger and Wood to supply particulars; and I must say there was no unnecessary security on their part. It was as speedily settled a transaction as I ever conducted, and I believe in my heart we might have had a thousand pounds on it just as easily as five hundred."

"As well as it is, Kinshela. When the day of repayment comes round, I'll perhaps find it heavy enough;" and he sighed deeply as he spoke.

"Who knows, sir? There never was a time that capital expended on land was more remunerative than the present."

Now, Mr. Kinshela well knew that the destination of the money they spoke of was not in this direction, and that it had as little to say to subsoil drainage or top dressing as to the conversion of the heathen; but he was angling for a confidence, and he did not see how to attain it.

Barrington smiled before he answered,—one of those sad, melancholy smiles which reveal a sorrow a man is not able to suppress,—and then he said, "I 'm afraid, Kinshela, I 'll not test the problem this time."

"It will be better employed, perhaps, sir. You mean, probably, to take your granddaughter up to the drawing-room at the Castle?"

"I never so much as thought of it, Joe Kinshela; the fact is, that money is going where I have sent many a hundred before it,—in law! I have had a long, wearisome, costly suit, that has well-nigh beggared me; and of that sum you raised for me I don't expect to have a shilling by this day week."

"I heard something about that, sir," said the other, cautiously.

"And what was it you heard?"

"Nothing, of course, worth repeating; nothing from any one that knew the matter himself; just the gossip that goes about, and no more."

"Well, let us hear the gossip that goes about, and I'll promise to tell you if it's true."

"Well, indeed," said Kinshela, drawing a long breath, "they say that your claim is against the India Board."

Barring ton nodded.

"And that it is a matter little short of a million is in dispute."

He nodded again twice.

"And they say, too,—of course, on very insufficient knowledge,—that if you would have abated your demands once on a time, you might readily have got a hundred thousand pounds, or even more."

"That's not impossible," muttered Barrington.

"But that, now—" he stammered for an instant, and then stopped.

"But now? Go on."

"Sure, sir, they can know nothing about it; it's just idle talk, and no more."

"Go on, and tell me what they say *now*," said Barrington, with a strong force on the last word.

"They say you 'll be beaten, sir," said he, with an effort.

"And do they say why, Kinshela?"

"Yes, sir; they say you won't take advice; and no matter what Mr. Withering counsels, or is settled in consultation, you go your own way and won't mind them; and that you have been heard to declare you 'll have all, or nothing."

"They give me more credit than I deserve, Kinshela. It is, perhaps, what I ought to have said, for I have often *thought it*. But in return for all the kind interest my neighbors take about me, let them know that matters look better for us than they once did. Perhaps," added he, with a laugh,—"perhaps I have overcome my obstinacy, or perhaps my opponents have yielded to it. At all events, Joe, I believe

I see land at last, and it was a long 'lookout' and many a fog-bank I mistook for it."

"And what makes you think now you'll win?" said the other, growing bolder by the confidence reposed in him.

Barrington half started at the presumption of the question; but he suddenly remembered how it was he himself who had invited the discussion, so he said calmly,—

"My hope is not without a foundation. I expect by the mail to-night a friend who may be able to tell me that I have won, or as good as won."

Kinshela was dying to ask who the friend was, but even his curiosity had its prudential limits; so he merely took out his watch, and, looking at it, remarked that the mail would pass in about twenty minutes or so.

"By the way, I must n't forget to send a servant to wait on the roadside;" and he rang the bell and said, "Let Darby go up to the road and take Major Stapylton's luggage when he arrives."

"Is that the Major Stapylton is going to be broke for the doings at Manchester, sir?" asked Kinshela.

"He is the same Major Stapylton that a rascally press is now libelling and calumniating," said Barrington, hotly. "As to being broke, I don't believe that we have come yet to that pass in England that the discipline of our army is administered by every scribbler in a newspaper."

"I humbly crave your pardon, sir, if I have said the slightest thing to offend; but I only meant to ask, was he the officer they were making such a fuss about?" "He is an officer of the highest distinction, and a wellborn gentleman to boot,— two admirable reasons for the assaults of a contemptible party. Look you, Kinshela; you and I are neither of us very young or inexperienced men, but I would ask you, have we learned any wiser lesson from our intercourse with life than to withhold our judgment on the case of one who rejects the sentence of a mob, and appeals to the verdict of his equals?"

"But if he cut the people down in cold blood,—if it be true that he laid open that poor black fellow's cheek from the temple to the chin—"

"If he did no such thing," broke in Barrington; "that is to say, if there is no evidence whatever that he did so, what will your legal mind say then, Joe Kinshela?"

"Just this, sir. I'd say—what all the newspapers are saying—that he got the man out of the way,—bribed and sent him off."

"Why not hint that he murdered him, and buried him within the precincts of the jail? I declare I wonder at your moderation."

"I am sure, sir, that if I suspected he was an old friend of yours—"

"Nothing of the kind,—a friend of very short standing; but what has that to say to it? Is he less entitled to fair play whether he knew me or not?"

"All I know of the case is from the newspapers; and as I scarcely see one word in his favor, I take it there is not much to be said in his defence."

"Well, if my ears don't deceive me, that was the guard's horn I heard then. The man himself will be here in five minutes or so. You shall conduct the prosecution, Kinshela, and I 'll be judge between you."

"Heaven forbid, sir; on no account whatever!" said Kinshela, trembling all over. "I'm sure, Mr. Barrington, you couldn't think of repeating what I said to you in confidence—"

"No, no, Kinshela. You shall do it yourself; and it's only fair to tell you that he is a right clever fellow, and fully equal to the task of defending himself." Peter arose as he spoke, and walked out upon the lawn, affectedly to meet his coming guest, but in reality to cover a laugh that was half smothering him, so comical was the misery expressed in the attorney's face, and so ludicrous was his look of terror.

Of course I need not say that it never occurred to Barrington to realize his threat, which he merely uttered in the spirit of that quizzing habit that was familiar to him. "Yes, Kinshela," cried he, "here he comes. I recognize his voice already;" and Barrington now walked forward to welcome his friend.

It was not till after some minutes of conversation, and when the light fell strongly on Stapylton's features, that Barrington saw how changed a few weeks of care had made him. He looked at the least ten years older than before. His eyes had lost their bold and daring expression, too, and were deep sunk, and almost furtive in their glance.

"You are tired, I fear," said Barrington, as the other moved his hand across his forehead, and, with a slight sigh, sank down upon a sofa.

"Less tired than worried,—harassed," said he, faintly. "Just as at a gaming-table a man may lose more in half an hour's high play than years of hard labor could acquire, there are times of life when we dissipate more strength and vigor than we ever regain. I have had rough usage since I saw you last," said he, with a very sickly smile. "How are the ladies,—well, I hope?"

"Perfectly well. They have gone to pass the day with a neighbor, and will be home presently. By the way, I left a friend here a few moments ago. What can have become of him?" and he rang the bell hastily. "Where's Mr. Kinshela, Darby?"

"Gone to bed, sir. He said he 'd a murthering headache, and hoped your honor would excuse him."

Though Barrington laughed heartily at this message, Stapylton never asked the reason, but sat immersed in thought and unmindful of all around him.

"I half suspect you ought to follow his good example, Major," said Peter. "A mug of mulled claret for a nightcap, and a good sleep, will set you all right."

"It will take more than that to do it," said the Major, sadly. Then suddenly rising, and pacing the room with quick, impatient steps, he said, "What could have induced you to let them bring your claim before the House? They are going to do so, ain't they?"

"Yes. Tom Withering says that nothing will be so effectual, and I thought you agreed with him."

"Never. Nothing of the kind. I said, threaten it; insist that if they continue the opposition, that you will,—that you must do so; but I never was the fool to imagine that it could really be a wise step. What 's the fate of all such motions? I ask you. There's a speech—sometimes an able one—setting forth a long catalogue of unmerited injuries and long suffering. There's a claim made out that none can find a flaw in, and a story that, if Parliament was given to softness, might move men almost to tears, and at the end of it up rises a Minister to say how deeply he sympathizes with the calamity of the case, but that this house is, after all, not the fitting locality for a discussion which is essentially a question of law, and that, even if it were, and if all the allegations were established,—a point to which he by no means gave adhesion,—there was really no available fund at the disposal of the Crown to make reparation for such losses. Have you not seen this, or something like this, scores of times? Can you tell me of one that succeeded?"

"A case of such wrong as this cannot go without reparation," said Peter, with emotion. "The whole country will demand it."

"The country will do no such thing. If it were a question of penalty or punishment,—yes! the country would demand it. Fine, imprison, transport, hang him! are easy words to utter, and cheap ones; but pay him, reinstate him, reward him! have a very different sound and significance. They figure in the budget, and are formidable on the hustings. Depend on it, Mr. Barrington, the step will be a false one."

"It has been my fate never to have got the same advice for two weeks together since the day I entered on this weary suit," said Barrington, with a peevishness not natural to him.

"I may as well tell you the whole truth at once," said Stapylton. "The Board have gone back of all their good intentions towards us; some recent arrivals from India, it is said, have kindled again the old fire of opposition, and we are to be met by a resistance bold and uncompromising. They are prepared to deny everything we assert; in fact, they have resolved to sweep all the pieces off the board and begin the whole game again, and all because you have taken this unfortunate course of appeal to Parliament."

"Have you told Withering this?"

"Yes; I have talked the matter over for nearly four hours with him. Like a lawyer, he was most eager to know from what source came the new evidence so damaging to us. I could only guess at this."

"And your guess was—"

"I scarcely like to own to you that I take a less favorable view of mankind than you do, who know it better; but in this case my suspicion attaches to a man who was once your son's dearest friend, but grew to be afterwards his deadliest enemy."

"I will not have this said, Major Stapylton. I know whom you mean, and I don't believe a word of it."

Stapylton simply shrugged his shoulders, and continued to pace the room without speaking, while Barrington went on muttering, half aloud: "No, no, impossible; quite impossible. These things are not in nature. I don't credit them."

"You like to think very well of the world, sir!" said the Major, with a faint scorn, so faint as scarcely to color his words.

"Think very badly of it, and you 'll soon come down to the level you assign it," said Peter, boldly.

"I 'm afraid I 'm not in the humor just now to give it my best suffrages. You 've seen, I doubt not, something of the treatment I have met with from the Press for the last few weeks; not very generous usage,—not very just. Well! what will you say when I tell you that I have been refused an inquiry into my conduct at Manchester; that the Government is of opinion that such an investigation might at the moment be prejudicial to the public peace, without any counterbalancing advantage on the score of a personal vindication; that they do not deem the time favorable for the calm and unbiassed judgment of the country; in one short word, sir, they 'd rather ruin a Major of Hussars than risk a Cabinet. I am to exchange into any corps or any service I can; and they are to tide over these troubles on the assumption of having degraded me."

"I hope you wrong them,—I do hope you wrong them!" cried Barrington, passionately.

"You shall see if I do," said he, taking several letters from his pocket, and searching for one in particular. "Yes, here it is. This is from Aldridge, the private secretary of the Commander-in-chief. It is very brief, and strictly secret:—

> "'Dear S.,—The "Chief" does not like your scrape at all. You did rather too much, or too little,—a fatal mistake dealing with a mob. You must consent—there's no help for it—to be badly used, and an injured man. If you don't like the half-pay list,—which would, in my mind, be the best step,—there 's the Seventeenth ordered to Baroda, and Maidstone refuses to go. This, or the Second West India, are the only things open. Above all, don't show fight; don't rally a party round you, for there is not a man in England whose influence is sufficiently great to stand between you and the public. A conple of years' patience and a hot climate will set all right, and reinstate you everywhere. Come over here at once and I 'll do my best for you.
>
> "'Yours ever,
"'St. George Aldridge.'

"This is a friend's letter," said Stapylton, with a sneer; "and he has no better counsel to give me than to plead guilty, and ask for a mitigated punishment."

Harrington was silenced; he would not by any expression of indignation add to the great anger of the other, and he said nothing. At last he said, "I wish from my heart—I wish I could be of any service to you."

"You are the only man living who can," was the prompt answer.

"How so—in what way? Let me hear."

"When I addressed a certain letter to you some time back, I was in a position both of fortune and prospect to take at least something from the presumption of my offer. Now, though my fortune remains, my future is more than clouded, and if I ask you to look favorably on my cause now, it is to your generosity I must appeal; I am, in fact, asking you to stand by a fallen man."

This speech, uttered in a voice slightly shaken by agitation, went to Barrington's heart. There was not a sentiment in his nature so certain to respond to a call upon it as this one of sympathy with the beaten man; the weaker side was always certain of his adherence. With a nice tact Stapylton said no more, but, pushing open the window, walked out upon the smooth sward, on which a faint moonlight flickered. He had shot his bolt, and saw it as it quivered in his victim's flesh. Barrington was after him in an instant, and, drawing an arm within his he said in a low voice, "You may count upon me."

Stapylton wrung his hand warmly, without speaking. After walking for a few moments, side by side, he said: "I must be frank with you, Mr. Barrington. I have little time and no taste for circumlocution; I cannot conceal from myself that I am no favorite with your sister. I was not as eager as I ought to have been to cultivate her good opinion; I was a little piqued at what I thought mere injustices on her part,—small ones, to be sure, but they wounded me, and with a temper that always revolted against a wrong, I resented them, and I fear me, in doing so, I jeopardized her esteem. If she is as generous as her brother, she will not remember these to me in my day of defeat. Women, however, have their own ideas of mercy, as they have of everything, and she may not choose to regard me as you have done."

"I suspect you are wrong about this," said Harrington, breaking in.

"Well, I wish I may be; at all events, I must put the feeling to the test at once, for I have formed my plan, and mean to begin it immediately."

"And what is it?"

"Very few words will tell it. I intend to go on half-pay, or sell out if that be refused me; set out for India by the next mail, and, with what energy remains to me, vindicate your son's claim. I have qualifications that will make me better than a better man. I am well versed in Hindostanee, and a fair Persian scholar; I have a wide acquaintance with natives of every rank, and I know how and where to look for information. It is not my disposition to feel over-sanguine, but I would stake all I possess on my success, for I see exactly the flaws in the chain, and I know where to go to repair them. You have witnessed with what ardor I adopted the suit before; but you cannot estimate the zeal with which I throw myself into it now—*now* that, like George Barring-ton himself, I am a man wronged, outraged, and insulted." For a few seconds be seemed overcome by passion and unable to continue; then he went on: "If your granddaughter will accept me, it is my intention to settle on her all I possess. Our marriage can be private, and she shall be free to accompany me or to remain here, as she likes."

"But how can all this be done so hurriedly? You talk of starting at once."

"I must, if I would save your son's cause. The India Board are sending out their emissaries to Calcutta, and I must anticipate them—if I cannot do more, by gaining them over to us on the voyage out. It is a case for energy and activity, and I want to employ both."

"The time is very short for all this," said Barrington, again.

"So it is, sir, and so are the few seconds which may rescue a man from drowning! It is in the crisis of my fate that I ask you to stand by me."

"But have you any reason to believe that my granddaughter will hear you favorably? You are almost strangers to each other?"

"If she will not give me the legal right to make her my heir, I mean to usurp the privilege. I have already been with a lawyer for that purpose. My dear sir," added he, passionately, "I want to break with the past forever! When the world sets up its howl against a man, the odds are too great! To stand and defy it he must succumb or retreat. Now, I mean to retire, but with the honors of war, mark you."

"My sister will never consent to it," muttered Barrington.

"Will you? Have I the assurance of *your* support?"

"I can scarcely venture to say 'yes,' and yet I can't bear to say 'no' to you!"

"This is less than I looked for from you," said Stapylton, mournfully.

"I know Dinah so well. I know how hopeless it would be to ask her concurrence to this plan."

"She may not take the generous view of it; but there is a worldly one worth considering," said Stapylton, bitterly.

"Then, sir, if you count on *that*, I would not give a copper half-penny for your chance of success!" cried Barrington, passionately.

"You have quite misconceived me; you have wronged me altogether," broke in Stapylton, in a tone of apology; for he saw the mistake he had made, and hastened to repair it. "My meaning was this—"

"So much the better. I'm glad I misunderstood you. But here come the ladies. Let us go and meet them."

"One word,—only one word. Will you befriend me?"

"I will do all that I can,—that is, all that I ought," said Barrington, as he led him away, and re-entered the cottage.

"I will not meet them to-night," said Stapylton, hurriedly. "I am nervous and agitated. I will say good-night now."

This was the second time within a few days that Stapylton had shown an unwillingness to confront Miss Barrington, and Peter thought over it long and anxiously. "What can he mean by it?" said he, to himself. "Why should he be so frank and outspoken with me, and so reserved with her? What can Dinah know of him? What can she suspect, that is not known to me? It is true they never did like each other,—never 'hit it off' together; but that is scarcely *his* fault. My excellent sister throws away little love on strangers, and opens every fresh acquaintance with a very fortifying prejudice against the newly presented. However it happens," muttered he, with a sigh, "*she* is not often wrong, and *I* am very seldom right;" and, with this reflection, he turned once again to resume his walk in the garden.

CHAPTER XII.

A DOCTOR AND HIS PATIENT

Stapylton did not make his appearance at breakfast; he sent down a message that he had passed a feverish night, and begged that Dr. Dill might be sent for. Though Barrington made two attempts to see his guest, the quietness of the room on each occasion implied that he was asleep, and, fearing to disturb him, he went downstairs again on tiptoe.

"This is what the persecution has done, Dinah," said he. "They have brought that stout-hearted fellow so low that he may be the victim of a fever to-morrow."

"Nonsense, Peter. Men of courage don't fall sick because the newspapers calumniate them. They have other things on their minds than such puny attacks."

"So he may, likely enough, too. He is bent heart and soul on what I told you last night, and I 'm not surprised if he never closed his eyes thinking of it."

"Neither did I!" said she, curtly, and left the room.

The doctor was not long in arriving, and, after a word or two with Barrington, hastened to the patient's room.

"Are we alone?" asked Stapylton, cutting short the bland speech with which Dill was making his approaches. "Draw that curtain a bit, and take a good look at me. Are my eyes bloodshot? Are the pupils dilated? I had a bad sunstroke once; see if there be any signs of congestion about me."

"No, I see none. A little flushed; your pulse, too, is accelerated, and the heart's action is labored—"

"Never mind the heart; if the head be well, it will take care of it. Reach me that pocket-book; I want to acquit one debt to you before I incur another. No humbug between us;" and he pressed some notes into the other's palm as he spoke. "Let us understand each other fully, and at once. I 'm not very ill; but I want *you*."

"And I am at your orders."

"Faithfully,—loyally?"

"Faithfully,—loyally!" repeated the other after him.

"You've read the papers lately,—you've seen these attacks on me?"

"Yes."

"Well, what do they say and think here—I mean in this house—about them?

How do they discuss them? Remember, I want candor and frankness; no humbug. I'll not stand humbug."

THE CONSULTATION

"The women are against you."

"Both of them?"

"Both."

"How comes that?—on what grounds?"

"The papers accused you of cruelty; they affirmed that there was no cause for the measures of severity you adopted; and they argued—"

"Don't bore me with all that balderdash. I asked you how was it that these women assumed I was in the wrong?"

"And I was about to tell you, if you had not interrupted me."

"That is, they believed what they read in the newspapers?"

"Yes."

"And, of course, swallowed that fine story about the Hindoo fellow that I first cut down, and afterwards bribed to make his escape from the hospital?"

"I suspect they half believed it."

"Or rather, believed half of it, the cutting down part! Can you tell me physiologically,—for I think it comes into that category,—why it is that women not otherwise ill-natured, in nine cases out of ten take the worst alternative as the credible one? But never mind that. They condemn me. Is n't it so?"

"Yes; and while old Barrington insists—"

"Who cares what he insists? Such advocacy as his only provokes attack, and invites persecution. I 'd rather have no such allies!"

"I believe you are right."

"I want fellows like yourself, doctor,—sly, cautious, subtle fellows,—accustomed to stealing strong medicines into the system in small doses; putting the patient, as you call it in your slang, 'under the influence' of this, that, and t'other,—eh?"

Dill smiled blandly at the compliment to his art, and Stapylton went on:—

"Not that I have time just now for this sort of chronic treatment. I need a heroic remedy, doctor. I 'm in love."

"Indeed!" said Dill, with an accent nicely balanced between interest and incredulity.

"Yes, and I want to marry!

"Miss Barrington?"

"The granddaughter. There is no need, I hope, to make the distinction, for I don't wish to be thought insane. Now you have the case. What 's your prescription?"

"Propose for her!"

"So I have, but they hesitate. The old man is not unfavorable; he is, perhaps, more: he is, in a measure, friendly; but what avails such advocacy? I want another guess sort of aid,—a clever man; or, what is better still, a clever woman, to befriend me."

He waited some seconds for a reply, but Dill did not speak; so he went on: "A clever woman, to take a woman's view of the case, balancing this against that, never ignoring an obstacle, but inquiring what there may be to compensate for it Do you know such a one, doctor?"

"Perhaps I may; but I have my doubts about securing her services."

"Even with a retainer?"

"Even with a retainer. You see, Major,"—here Dill dropped his voice to a most confidential whisper,—"my daughter Polly,—for I know we both have her in mind,—Polly is a strange sort of girl, and very hard to understand; for while, if the case were her own, she 'd no more think of romance than she would of giving ten guineas for a dress, if she was advising another whose position and prospects were higher than hers, it's the romantic part of it she'd lay all the stress on."

"From which I gather that my suit will not stand this test!" said Stapylton, with a peculiar smile. "Eh, is n't that your meaning?"

"You are certainly some years older than the lady," said Dill, blandly.

"Not old enough to be, as the world would surely say, 'her father,' but fully old enough to give license for sarcasm."

"Then, as she will be a great fortune—"

"Not a sixpence,—she'll not have sixpence, doctor. That bubble has burst at last, and can never be blown again. The whole claim has been rejected, refused, thrown out, and there's an end of it. It amuses the old man to sit on the wreck and fancy he can repair the shattered timbers and make them seaworthy; and, for the time he is likely to last, it is only kindness to leave him to his delusion; but he is ruined,—ruined beyond recall, and as I have told you, the girl will have nothing."

"Do they know this,—has Barrington heard it?"

"Yes, I broke it to him last night, but I don't think he fully realized the tidings; he has certain reserves—certain little conceits of his own—which are to supply him with a sort of hope; but let us talk of something more practical. How can we secure Miss Dill's services?"

"A few days ago, the easiest way would have been to offer to befriend her brother, but this morning brings us news that this is not needed,—he is coming home."

"How so?"

"It is a great event in its way; at least, it may be for Tom. It seems there was a collision at sea, somewhere near the Cape, between the ship 'St. Helen's,' that carried out General Hunter and his staff, and the 'Regulus,' with the Forty-ninth on board. It was at night, and a terrible sea on at the time. In the shock the 'St. Helen's' took fire; and as the two ships were inextricably locked together, the danger was common to each. While the boats were being lowered and manned,—for it was soon seen the vessel could not be saved,—a cry was raised that the fire was gaining on the fore-hold, and would soon reach the magazine. The woful news spread at once, and many jumped overboard in their terror. Just then Tom heard that there was a means of drowning the powder by opening a certain sluice, and, without waiting for more, he clambered across into the sinking vessel, made his way through smoke and fire, gained the spot, and succeeded, just as the very ladder itself had caught the flames. How he got back he cannot tell, for the vessel foundered in a few minutes, and he was so burned—face, cheek, and one shoulder—that he was unconscious of everything; and even when the account came, was still in bed, and not able to see."

"He was a wild sort of lad, was he not,—a scamp, in short?"

"No, not exactly that; idle—careless—kept bad company at times."

"These are the fellows who do this kind of thing once in their lives,—mark you, never twice. They never have more than one shot in their locker, but it will suffice in this case."

Though the worthy doctor was very far from enthusiastic about his son's gallantry, there was a degree of coolness in the Major's estimate of it that almost shocked him; and he sat staring steadily at the stern bronzed face, and the hard lineaments of the man, and wondering of what strange stuff such natures were fashioned.

"It's quite clear, then, that for Master Tom we can do nothing half so good as chance has done for him," said Stapylton, after a short interval.

"Chance and himself too," added the doctor.

Stapylton made no answer, but, covering his eyes with his hand, lay deep in thought.

"If you only had the Attorney-General, Mr. Withering, on your side," said Dill. "There is no man has the same influence over this family."

"It is not what *you* call influence I want, my good sir. It is a far more subtle and more delicate agent. I require the sort of aid, in fact, which your daughter could supply, if she would. An appointment awaits me in India, but I must occupy it at once. I have no time for a long courtship. I 'm just as hurried as that boy of yours was when he swamped the powder-magazine. It's a skirmish where I can't wait for the heavy artillery, but must do my best with the light field-guns,—do you understand me?"

Dill nodded, and Stapylton resumed: "The thing can be done just by the very road that you have pronounced impossible,—that is, by the romantic side of it,—making it a case of violent love at first sight, the passion of a man past the heyday of youth, but yet young enough to feel a most ardent affection. I am, besides," said he, laughing with a strange blending of levity and sarcasm, "a sort of Brummagem hero; have been wounded, led assaults, and that kind of thing, to a degree that puffery can take the benefit of. And, last of all, doctor, I am rich enough to satisfy greater ambitions than ought to live under such a roof as this. Do you see the part your daughter can take in this drama?"

"Perhaps I do."

"And could you induce her to accept it?"

"I'm not very certain,—I'd be slow to pledge myself to it."

"Certainly," said Stapylton, mockingly; "the passing glimpses we bachelors obtain of the working of that vaunted institution, The Family, fail to impress us with all its imputed excellence; you are, it seems to me, just as powerless within your own doors as I am regarding what goes on in a neighbor's house. I take it, however, that it can't be helped. Children, like colonies, are only governable when helpless."

"I suspect you are wrong, sir; at least, I fancy I have as much of the sort of influence you speak of as others; but still, I think, here, in this particular case, you would yourself be your best ambassador, if you were strong enough to come down with me in the boat to-day."

"Of course I am!" cried Stapylton, starting up to a sitting posture; "and what then?"

"You would be better in my house than this," said Dill, mysteriously.

"Speak out, and speak clearly, doctor; I have very little the matter with me, and am in no want of change of air. What I need is the assistance of one dexterous enough to advocate my plans with persons and in places to which I have no access. Your daughter is just such a one,—will she do it?"

"We can ask her."

"Well, how will you explain my absence to these people here? What will you say for my not appearing at breakfast, and yet being able to take an airing with you?"

"I will put it on hygienic grounds," said Dill, smiling acutely. "My profession has a number of sanctuaries the profane vulgar can never enter. I 'll just step down now and ask Barrington to lend me his boat, and I 'll throw out a dark hint that I 'd like to manage a consultation on your case without alarming you, for which purpose I 'd ask Dr. Tobin to be at my house, when we arrive there, by mere accident, so that a conference would follow as a matter of course."

"Very wily,—very subtle all this, doctor. Do you know, I 'm half frightened at the thought of trusting myself to such a master of intrigue and mystification."

"Have no fears; I reserve all my craft for my clients." And with this he left the room, but only for a few minutes; for he met Barrington on the stairs, and speedily obtained permission to take his boat to Inistioge, having first pledged himself to come back with Stapylton to dinner.

"We shall see, we shall see," muttered Stapylton to himself. "Your daughter must decide where I am to dine today."

By the way—that is, as they glided along the bright river—Dill tried to prepare Stapylton for the task before him, by sundry hints as to Polly's temper and disposition, with warnings against this, and cautions about that. "Above all," said he, "don't try to overreach her."

"Perfect frankness—candor itself—is my device. Won't that do?"

"You must first see will she believe it," said the doctor, slyly; and for the remainder of the way there was a silence between them.

CHAPTER XIII.

CROSS-PURPOSES

"Where 's Miss Polly?" said Dill, hastily, as he passed his threshold.

"She's making the confusion of roses in the kitchen, sir," said the maid, whose chemistry had been a neglected study.

"Tell her that I have come back, and that there is a gentleman along with me," said he, imperiously, as he led the way into his study. "I have brought you into this den of mine, Major, because I would just say one word more by way of caution before you see Polly. You may imagine, from the small range of her intercourse with the world, and her village life, that her acuteness will not go very far; don't be too sure of that,—don't reckon too much on her want of experience."

"I suppose I have encountered as sharp wits as hers before this time o' day," replied he, half peevishly; and then, with an air of better temper, added, "I have no secrets to hide, no mystery to cloak. If I want her alliance, she shall herself dictate the terms that shall requite it."

The doctor shook his head dubiously, but was silent.

"I half suspect, my good doctor," said Stapylton, laughing, "that your charming daughter is a little, a very little, of a domestic despot; you are all afraid of her; never very sure of what she will say or do or think on any given circumstances, and nervously alive to the risk of her displeasure."

"There is something in what you say," remarked Dill, with a sigh; "but it was always my mistake to bring up my children with too much liberty of action. From the time they were so high"—and he held his hand out about a yard above the floor—"they were their own masters."

Just as the words had fallen from him, a little chubby, shock-headed fellow, about five years old, burst into the room, which he believed unoccupied, and then, suddenly seeing his papa, set up a howl of terror that made the house ring.

"What is it, Jimmy,—what is it, my poor man?" said Polly, rushing with tucked-up sleeves to the spot; and, catching him up in her arms, she kissed him affectionately.

"Will you take him away?—will you take him out of that?" hissed out Dill between his teeth. "Don't you see Major Stapylton here?"

"Oh, Major Stapylton will excuse a toilette that was never intended for his presence."

"I will certainly say there could not be a more becoming one, nor a more charming tableau to display it in!"

"There, Jimmy," said she, laughing; "you must have some bread and jam for getting me such a nice compliment."

And she bore away the still sobbing urchin, who, burying his head in her bosom, could never summon courage to meet his father's eye.

"What a spacious garden you appear to have here!" said Stapylton, who saw all the importance of a diversion to the conversation.

"It is a very much neglected one," said Dill, pathetically. "My poor dear boy Tom used to take care of it when he was here; he had a perfect passion for flowers."

Whether that Tom was associated in the Major's mind with some other very different tastes or not, Stapylton smiled slightly, and after a moment said, "If you permit me, I 'll take a stroll through your garden, and think over what we have been talking of."

"Make yourself at home in every respect," said Dill. "I have a few professional calls to make in the village, but we 'll meet at luncheon."

"He's in the garden, Polly," said Dill, as he passed his daughter on the stairs; "he came over here this morning to have a talk with you."

"Indeed, sir!"

"Yes; he has got it into his head that you can be of service to him."

"It is not impossible, sir; I think I might."

"I'm glad to bear it, Polly; I'm delighted to see you take a good sensible view of things. I need not tell you he's a knowing one."

"No, sir. But, as I have heard you card-players say, 'he shows his hand.'"

"So he does, Polly; but I have known fellows do that just to mislead the adversary."

"Sorry adversaries that could be taken in so easily." And with a saucy toss of her head she passed on, scarcely noticing the warning gesture of her father's finger as she went.

When she had found her work-basket and supplied herself with the means of occupying her fingers for an hour or so, she repaired to the garden and took her seat under a large elm, around whose massive trunk a mossy bench ran, divided by rustic-work into a series of separate places.

"What a churlish idea it was to erect these barricades, Miss Dill!" said Stapylton as he seated himself at her side; "how unpicturesque and how prudish!"

"It was a simple notion of my brother Tom's," said she, smiling, "who thought people would not be less agreeable by being reminded that they had a place of their own, and ought not to invade that of their neighbor."

"What an unsocial thought!"

"Poor Tom! A strange reproach to make against *you*," said she, laughing out.

"By the way, has n't he turned out a hero, —saved a ship and all she carried from the flames, —and all at the hazard of his own life?"

"He has done a very gallant thing; and, what's more, I 'll venture to say there is not a man who saw it thinks so little of it as himself."

"I suppose that every brave man has more or less of that feeling."

"I'm glad to learn this fact from such good authority," said she, with a slight bend of the head.

"A prettily turned compliment, Miss Dill. Are you habitually given to flattery?"

"No? I rather think not. I believe the world is pleased to call me more candid than courteous."

"Will you let me take you at the world's estimate, —that is, will you do me the inestimable favor to bestow a little of this same candor upon *me?*"

"Willingly. What is to be the subject of it?"

"The subject is a very humble one, —myself!"

"How can I possibly adjudicate on such a theme?"

"Better than you think for, perhaps!" And for a moment he appeared awkward and ill at ease. "Miss Dill," said he, after a pause, "fortune has been using me roughly of late; and, like all men who deem themselves hardly treated, I fly at once to any quarter where I fancy I have found a more kindly disposition towards me. Am I indulging a self-delusion in believing that such sentiments are yours?"

Polly Dill, with her own keen tact, had guessed what was the real object of Stapylton's visit. She had even read in her father's manner how he himself was a shareholder in the scheme, and she had made up her mind for a great frankness on each side; but now, seeing the diplomatic mys-teriousness with which the Major opened his attack, that love of mischievous drollery which entered into her nature suggested a very different line. She determined, in fact, to seem to accept the Major's speech as the preliminary to an offer of his hand. She therefore merely turned her head slightly, and in a low voice said, "Continue!"

"I have not deceived myself, then," said he, with more warmth of manner. "I have secured one kind heart in my interest?"

"You must own," said she, with a half-coquettish look of pique, "that you scarcely deserve it."

"How, —in what way?" asked he, in astonishment.

"What a very short memory you are blessed with! Must I, then, remind you of a certain evening at Cobham? Must I recall what I thought at the time very particular, as they certainly were very pleasant, attentions on your part? Must I, also, bring to mind a certain promised visit from you, the day and hour all named by yourself, —a visit which never came off? And after all this, Major, are you not really a bold man to come down and take up your negotiation where you dropped it? Is there not in this a strong conviction of the greatness of Major Stapylton and the littleness of the doctor's daughter?"

Stapylton was struck dumb. When a general sees that what he meant as a feint has been converted into a real attack, the situation is often imminent; but what comparison in difficulty is there between that mistake and that of him who assails what he never desired to conquer? How he inwardly cursed the stupidity with which he had opened his negotiation!

"I perceive," said she, triumphing over his confusion, "that your calmer judgment does not reassure you. You feel that there is a certain levity in this conduct not quite excusable! Own it frankly, and at once!"

"I will own, if you like, that I was never in a situation of greater embarrassment!"

"Shall I tell you why?"

"You couldn't; it would be totally impossible."

"I will try, however, if you permit me. You do! Then here goes. You no more intended anything to come of your little flirtation at Cobham than you now do of a more serious blunder. You never came here this morning to make your court to *me,* You are much pained at the awkwardness of a situation so naturally wounding to me, and for the life of you, you cannot imagine what escape there is out of such a difficulty."

"You are wonderfully clever, Miss Dill," said he; and there was an honest admiration in his look that gave the words a full significance.

"No," said she, "but I am wonderfully good-natured. I forgive you what is the hardest thing in the world to forgive!"

"Oh! if you would but be my friend," cried he, warmly.

"What a want of tact there was in that speech, Major Stapylton!" said she, with a laugh; "but perhaps you wanted to reverse the line of our dear little poet, who tells of some one 'that came but for Friendship, and took away Love'!"

"How cruel you are in all this mockery of me!"

"Does not the charge of cruelty come rather ill from *you?* — *you,* who can afford to sport with the affections of poor village maidens. From the time of that 'Major bold of Halifax' the song tells of, I never heard your equal."

"Could you prevail upon yourself to be serious for a few minutes?" said he, gravely.

"I think not, — at least not just now; but why should I make the attempt?"

"Because I would wish your aid in a serious contingency, — a matter in which I am deeply interested, and which involves probably my future happiness."

"Ah, Major! is it possible that you are going to trifle with my feelings once more?"

"My dear Miss Dill, must I plead once more for a little mercy?"

"No, don't do any such thing; it would seem ungenerous to refuse, and yet I could not accord it."

"Fairly beaten," said he, with a sigh; "there is no help for it. You are the victor!"

"How did you leave our friends at 'The Home'?" said she, with an easy indifference in her tone.

"All well, perfectly well; that is to say, I believe so, for I only saw my host himself."

"What a pleasant house; how well they understand receiving their friends!"

"It is so peaceful and so quiet!" said he, with an effort to seem at ease.

"And the garden is charming!"

"And all this is perfectly intolerable," said he, rising, and speaking in a voice thick with suppressed anger. "I never came here to play a part in a vaudeville! Your father led me to believe, Miss Dill, that you might not be indisposed to lend me your favoring aid in a suit which I am interested in. He told me I should at least find you frank and outspoken; that if you felt inclined to assist me, you'd never enhance the service by a seeming doubt or hesitation—"

"And if I should not feel so inclined, what did he then give you to expect?"

"That you'd say so!"

"So I do, then, clearly and distinctly tell you, if my counsels offer a bar to your wishes, they are all enlisted against you."

"This is the acme of candor. You can only equal it by saying how I could have incurred your disfavor."

"There is nothing of disfavor in the matter. I think you charming. You are a hero,—very clever, very fascinating, very accomplished; but I believe it would be a great mistake for Fifine to marry you. Your tempers have that sort of resemblance that leave no reliefs in their mutual play. You are each of you hot and hasty, and a little imperious; and if she were not very much in love, and consequently disposed to think a great deal of you and very little of herself, these traits that I speak of would work ill. But if every one of them were otherwise, there would still be one obstacle worse than all!"

"And that is—"

"Can you not guess what I mean, Major Stapylton? You do not, surely, want confidences from me that are more than candor!"

"Do I understand you aright?" said he, growing red and pale by turns, as passion worked within him; "do I apprehend you correctly? These people here are credulous enough to be influenced by the shadowy slanders of the newspapers, and they listen to the half-muttered accusations of a hireling press?"

"They do say very awkward things in the daily press, certainly," said she, dryly; "and your friends marvel at the silence with which you treat them."

"Then I *have* divined your meaning," said he. "It is by these cowardly assailants I am supposed to be vanquished. I suspect, however, that Colonel Barrington himself was, once on a time, indulged with the same sort of flattery. They said that he had usurped a sovereignty, falsified documents, purloined jewels of immense value. I don't know what they did not charge him with. And what do they say of me? That I exhibited great severity—cruelty, if you will—towards a mob in a state of rebellion; that I reprimanded a very silly subaltern for a misplaced act of humanity. That I have been cashiered, too, they assert, in face of the 'Gazette,' which announces my appointment to an unattached majority. In a word, the enormity of the falsehood has never stayed their hand, and they write of me whatever their unthinking malevolence can suggest to them. You have, perhaps, seen some of these paragraphs?"

"Like every one else, I have read them occasionally; not very attentively, indeed. But, in truth, I'm not a reader of newspapers. Here, for instance, is this morning's as it came from Dublin, still unopened;" and she handed it as she spoke.

"Let us see if I be still honored with their notice," said he, unfolding the paper, and running his eyes hastily over it. "Debate on the Sugar Bill—Prison Reforms—China—Reinforcements for Canada—Mail Service to the Colonies—Bankruptcy Court. Oh, here we have it—here it is!" and he crushed the paper while he folded down one part of it. "Shall I read it for you? The heading is very tempting: 'Late Military Scandal.—A very curious report is now going through our West-end Clubs, and especially such as are the resort of military officers. It is to the purport that a certain Field-officer of Cavalry—whose conduct has been the subject of severe strictures from the Press—will speedily be called to answer for a much graver offence than the transgression of regimental discipline. The story which has reached us is a very strange one, and we should call it incredible, if we were not informed, on author-ity, that one of our most distinguished Indian generals has declared himself fully satisfied of its truth in every particular.' Can you fancy anything worse than that, Miss Dill? An unknown somebody is alleged to be convinced of an unknown something that attaches to me; for, of course, I am designated as the 'Field-officer of Cavalry,' and the public is graciously pleased to hold me in abhorrence till I have found out my calumniator and refuted him!"

"It seems very hard. Who do you suspect is the Indian General alluded to?"

"Tell me, first of all,—does he exist?" "And this, too, you will not reply to, nor notice?" "Not, certainly, through such a channel as it reaches me. If the slanderer will stand forth and avow himself, I may know how to deal with him. But what has led us into this digression? I am sure it is as little to your taste as to mine. I have failed in my mission, and if I were able to justify every act of my life, what would it avail me? You have pronounced against me; at least, you will not take my brief."

"What if I were retained by the other side?" said she, smiling.

"I never suspected that there was another side," said he, with an air of extreme indifference. "Who is my formidable rival?"

"I might have told you if I saw you were really anxious on the subject."

"It would be but hypocrisy in me to pretend it. If, for example, Major McCormick—"

"Oh, that is too bad!" cried Polly, interrupting. "This would mean an impertinence to Miss Barrington."

"How pleasant we must have been! Almost five o'clock, and I scarcely thought it could be three!" said he, with an affected languor.

"'Time's foot is not heard when he treads upon flowers,'" said she, smiling.

"Where shall I find your father, Miss Dill? I want to tell him what a charming creature his daughter is, and how wretched I feel at not being able to win her favor."

"Pray don't; or he might fall into my own mistake, and imagine that you wanted a lease of it for life."

"Still cruel, still inexorable!" said he, with a mockery of affliction in his tone. "Will you say all the proper things—the regrets, and such like—I feel at not meeting him again; and if he has asked me to dinner—which I really forget—will you make the fitting apology?"

"And what is it, in the present case?"

"I 'm not exactly sure whether I am engaged to dine elsewhere, or too ill to dine at all."

"Why not say it is the despair at being rejected renders you unequal to the effort? I mean, of course, by myself, Major Stapylton."

"I have no objection; say so, if you like," said he, with an insulting indifference. "Good-day, Miss Dill. This is the way to the road, I believe;" and, with a low bow, very deferential but very distant, he turned away to leave the garden. He had not, however, gone many paces, when he stopped and seemed to ponder. He looked up at the sky, singularly clear and cloudless as it was, without a breath of wind in the air; he gazed around him on every side, as if in search of an object he wanted; and then, taking out his purse, he drew forth a shilling and examined it. "Yes," muttered he, "Chance has been my only counsellor for many a year, and the only one that never takes a bribe! And yet, is it not taking to the raft before the ship has foundered? True; but shall I be sure of the raft if I wait for the shipwreck? She is intensely crafty. She has that sort of head that loves a hard knot to unravel! Here goes! Let Destiny take all the consequences!" and as he flung up the piece of money in the air, he cried, "Head!" It was some minutes ere he could discover where it had fallen, amongst the close leaves of a border of strawberries. He bent down to look, and exclaimed, "Head! she has won!" Just as he arose from his stooping attitude he perceived that Polly was engaged in the adjoining walk, making a bouquet of roses. He sprang across the space, and stood beside her.

"I thought you had been a mile off by this time, at least," said she, calmly.

"So I meant, and so I intended; but just as I parted from you, a thought struck me—one of those thoughts which come from no process of reasoning or reflection, but seem impelled by a force out of our own natures—that I would come back and tell you something that was passing in my mind. Can you guess it?"

"No; except it be that you are sorry for having trifled so unfeelingly with my hopes, and have come back to make the best reparation in your power, asking me to forgive and accept you."

"You have guessed aright; it was for that I returned."

"What a clever guess I made! Confess I am very ready-witted!"

"You are; and it is to engage those ready wits in my behalf that I am now before you."

"'At my feet,' sir, is the appropriate expression. I wonder how a gentleman so suited to be the hero of a story could forget the language of the novel."

"I want you to be serious," said he, almost sternly.

"And why should that provoke seriousness from *me* which only costs *you* levity?"

"Levity!—where is the levity?"

"Is it not this instant that you flung a shilling in the air, and cried out, as you looked on it, 'She has won'? Is it not that you asked Chance to decide for you what most men are led to by their affections, or at least their interests; and if so, is levity not the name for this?"

"True in part, but not in whole; for I felt it was *I* who had won when 'head' came uppermost."

"And yet you have lost."

"How so! You refuse me?"

"I forgive your astonishment. It is really strange, but I do refuse you."

"But why? Are you piqued with me for anything that occurred this morning? Have I offended you by anything that dropped from me in that conversation? Tell me frankly, that I may, if in my power, rectify it."

"No; I rather felt flattered at the notion of being consulted. I thought it a great tribute to my clear-headedness and my tact."

"Then tell me what it was."

"You really wish it?"

"I do."

"Insist upon it?"

"I insist upon it."

"Well, it was this. Seeing that you were intrusting your future fortune to chance, I thought that I would do the same, and so I tossed up whether, opportunity serving, I should accept you or a certain other, and the other won!"

"May I ask for the name of my fortunate rival?"

"I don't think it is very fair, perhaps not altogether delicate of you; and the more since he has not proposed, nor possibly ever may. But no matter, you shall hear his name. It was Major McCormick."

"McCormick! You mean this for an insult to me, Miss Dill?"

THE MAJOR IS ALL "ATTENTION"

"Well, it certainly is open to that objection," said she, with a very slight closure of her eyes, and a look of steady, resolute defiance.

"And in this way," continued he, "to throw ridicule over the offer I have made you?"

"Scarcely that; the proposition was in itself too ridiculous to require any such aid from me."

For a moment Stapylton lost his self-possession, and he turned on her with a look of savage malignity.

"An insult, and an intentional insult!" said he; "a bold thing to avow."

"I don't think so, Major Stapylton. We have been playing a very rough game with each other, and it is not very wonderful if each of us should have to complain of hard treatment."

"Could not so very clever a person as Miss Dill perceive that I was only jesting?" said he, with a cutting insolence in his tone.

"I assure you that I did not," said she, calmly; "had I known or even suspected it was a jest, I never should have been angry. That the distinguished Major Stapylton should mock and quiz—or whatever be the name for it—the doctor's daughter, however questionable the good taste, was, after all, only a passing slight. The thought of asking her to marry him was different,—that was an outrage!"

"You shall pay for this one day, perhaps," said he, biting his lip.

"No, Major Stapylton," said she, laughing; "this is not a debt of honor; you can afford to ignore it."

"I tell you again, you shall pay for it."

"Till then, sir!" said she, with a courtesy; and without giving him time for another word, she turned and re-entered the house.

Scarcely had Stapylton gained the road when he was joined by McCormick. "Faith, you didn't get the best of that brush, anyhow," said he, with a grin.

"What do you mean, sir?" replied Stapylton, savagely.

"I mean that I heard every word that passed between you, and I would n't have been standing in your shoes for a fifty-pound note."

"How is your rheumatism this morning?" asked Stapylton, blandly.

"Pretty much as it always is," croaked out the other.

"Be thankful to it, then; for if you were not a cripple, I 'd throw you into that river as sure as I stand here to say it."

Major McCormick did not wait for a less merciful moment, but hobbled away from the spot with all the speed he could muster.

CHAPTER XIV.

STORMS

When Stapylton stepped out of his boat and landed at "The Home," the first person he saw was certainly the last in his wishes. It was Miss Dinah who stood at the jetty, as though awaiting him. Scarcely deigning to notice, beyond a faint smile of acquiescence, the somewhat bungling explanation he gave of his absence, she asked if he had met her brother.

"No," said he. "I left the village a couple of hours ago; rather loitering, as I came along, to enjoy the river scenery."

"He took the road, and in this way missed you," said she, dryly.

"How unfortunate! — for me, I mean, of course. I own to you, Miss Barrington, wide as the difference between our ages, I never yet met any one so thoroughly companionable to me as your brother. To meet a man so consummately acquainted with the world, and yet not soured by his knowledge; to see the ripe wisdom of age blended with the generous warmth of youth; to find one whose experiences only make him more patient, more forgiving, more trustful—"

"Too trustful, Major Stapylton, far too trustful." And her bold gray eyes were turned upon him as she spoke, with a significance that could not be mistaken.

"It is a noble feeling, madam," said he, haughtily.

"It is a great misfortune to its possessor, sir."

"Can we deem that misfortune, Miss Barrington, which enlarges the charity of our natures, and teaches us to be slow to think ill?"

Not paying the slightest attention to his question, she said, —

"My brother went in search of you, sir, to place in your hands some very urgent letters from the Horse Guards, and which a special messenger brought here this morning."

"Truly kind of him. They relate, I have no doubt, to my Indian appointment. They told me I should have news by to-day or to-morrow."

"He received a letter also for himself, sir, which he desired to show you."

"About his lawsuit, of course? It is alike a pleasure and a duty to me to serve him in that affair."

"It more nearly concerns yourself, sir," said she, in the same cold, stern tone; "though it has certainly its bearing on the case you speak of."

"More nearly concerns myself!" said he, repeating her words slowly. "I am about the worst guesser of a riddle in the world, Miss Barrington. Would you kindly relieve my curiosity? Is this letter a continuation of those cowardly attacks which, in the want of a worthier theme, the Press have amused themselves by making upon me? Is it possible that some enemy has had the malice to attack me through my friends?"

"The writer of the letter in question is a sufficient guarantee for its honor, Mr. Withering."

"Mr. Withering!" repeated he, with a start, and then, as suddenly assuming an easy smile, added: "I am perfectly tranquil to find myself in such hands as Mr. Withering's. And what, pray, does *he* say of me?"

"Will you excuse me, Major Stapylton, if I do not enter upon a subject on which I am not merely very imperfectly informed, but on which so humble a judgment as mine would be valueless? My brother showed me the letter very hurriedly; I had but time to see to what it referred, and to be aware that it was his duty to let you see it at once, — if possible, indeed, before you were again under his roof."

"What a grave significance your words have, Miss Barrington!" said he, with a cold smile. "They actually set me to think over all my faults and failings, and wonder for which of them I am now arraigned."

"We do not profess to judge you, sir."

By this time they had sauntered up to the little garden in front of the cottage, within the paling of which Josephine was busily engaged in training a japonica. She arose as she heard the voices, and in her accustomed tone wished Stapylton good-evening. "*She*, at least, has heard nothing of all this," muttered he to himself, as he saluted her. He then opened the little wicket; and Miss Barrington passed in, acknowledging his attention by a short nod, as she walked hastily forward and entered the cottage. Instead of following her, Stapylton closed the wicket again, remaining on the outside, and leaning his arm on the upper rail.

"Why do you perform sentry? Are you not free to enter the fortress?" said Fifine.

"I half suspect not," said he, in a low tone, and to hear which she was obliged to draw nigher to where he stood.

"What do you mean? I don't understand you!"

"No great wonder, for I don't understand myself. Your aunt has, however, in her own most mysterious way, given me to believe that somebody has written something about me to somebody else, and until I clear up what in all probability I shall never hear, that I had better keep to what the Scotch call the 'back o' the gate.'"

"This is quite unintelligible."

"I hope it is, for it is almost unendurable. I am sorely afraid," added he, after a minute, "that I am not so patient as I ought to be under Miss Barrington's strictures. I am so much more in the habit of command than of obedience, that I may forget myself now and then. To *you*, however, I am ready to submit all my past life and conduct. By you I am willing to be judged. If these cruel calumnies which are going the round of the papers on me have lowered me in your estimation, my case is a lost one; but if, as I love to think, your woman's heart resents an injustice,—if, taking counsel of your courage and your generosity, you feel it is not the time to withdraw esteem when the dark hour of adversity looms over a man,—then, I care no more for these slanders than for the veriest trifles which cross one's every-day life. In one word,—your verdict is life or death to me."

"In that case," said she, with an effort to dispel the seriousness of his manner, "I must have time to consider my sentence."

"But that is exactly what you cannot have, Josephine," said he; and there was a certain earnestness in his voice and look, which made her hear him call her by her name without any sense of being off ended. "First relieve the suffering; there will be ample leisure to question the sufferer afterwards. The Good Samaritan wasted few words, and asked for no time. The noblest services are those of which the cost is never calculated. Your own heart can tell you: can you befriend me, and will you?"

"I do not know what it is you ask of me," said she, with a frank boldness which actually disconcerted him. "Tell me distinctly, what is it?"

"I will tell you," said he, taking her hand, but so gently, so respectfully withal, that she did not at first withdraw it,—"I will tell you. It is that you will share that fate on which fortune is now frowning; that you will add your own high-couraged heart to that of one who never knew a fear till now; that you will accept my lot in this the day of my reverse, and enable me to turn upon my pursuers and scatter them. To-morrow or next day will be too late. It is now, at this hour, that friends hold back, that one more than friend is needed. Can you be that, Josephine?"

"No!" said she, firmly. "If I read your meaning aright, I cannot."

"You cannot love me, Josephine," said he, in a voice of intense emotion; and though he waited some time for her to speak, she was silent. "It is true, then," said he, passionately, "the slanderers have done their work!"

"I know nothing of these calumnies. When my grandfather told me that they accused you falsely, and condemned you unfairly, I believed him. I am as ready as ever to say so. I do not understand your cause; but I believe you to be a true and gallant gentleman!"

"But yet, not one to love!" whispered he, faintly.

Again she was silent, and for some time he did not speak.

"A true and gallant gentleman!" said he, slowly repeating her own words; "and if so, is it an unsafe keeping to which to intrust your happiness? It is no graceful task to have oneself for a theme; but I cannot help it. I have no witnesses to call to character; a few brief lines in an army list, and some scars—old reminders of French sabres—are poor certificates, and yet I have no others."

There was something which touched her in the sadness of his tone as he said these words, and if she knew how, she would have spoken to him in kindliness. He mistook the struggle for a change of purpose, and with greater eagerness continued: "After all I am scarcely more alone in the world than you are! The dear friends who now surround you cannot be long spared, and what isolation will be your fate then! Think of this, and think, too, how, in assuring your own future, you rescue mine."

Very differently from his former speech did the present affect her; and her cheeks glowed and her eyes flashed as she said, "I have never intrusted my fate to your keeping, sir; and you may spare yourself all anxiety about it."

"You mistake me. You wrong me, Josephine—"

"You wrong yourself when you call me by my Christian name; and you arm me with distrust of one who would presume upon an interest he has not created."

"You refuse me, then?" said he, slowly and calmly.

"Once, and forever!"

"It may be that you are mistaken, Miss Barrington. It may be that this other affection, which you prefer to mine, is but the sickly sentiment of a foolish boy, whose life up to this has not given one single guarantee, nor shown one single trait of those which make 'true and gallant gentlemen.' But you have made your choice."

"I have," said she, with a low but firm voice.

"You acknowledge, then, that I was right," cried he, suddenly; "there is a prior attachment? Your heart is not your own to give?"

"And by what right do you presume to question me? Who are you, that dares to do this?"

"Who am I?" cried he, and for once his voice rose to the discordant ring of passion.

"Yes, that was my question," repeated she, firmly.

"So, then, you have had your lesson, young lady," said he; and the words came from him with a hissing sound, that indicated intense anger. "Who am I? You want my birth, my parentage, my bringing up! Had you no friend who could have asked this in your stead? Or were all those around you so bereft of courage that they deputed to a young girl what should have been the office of a man?"

Though the savage earnestness of his manner startled, it did not affright her; and it was with a cold quietness she said, "If you had known my father, Major Stapylton, I suspect you would not have accused his daughter of cowardice!"

"Was he so very terrible?" said he, with a smile that was half a sneer.

"He would have been, to a man like you."

"To a man like me,—a man like me! Do you know, young lady, that either your words are very idle words or very offensive ones?"

"And yet I have no wish to recall them, sir."

"It would be better you could find some one to sustain them. Unfortunately, however, you cannot ask that gallant gentleman we were just talking of; for it is only the other day, and after passing over to Calais to meet me, his friends pretend that there is some obstacle to our meeting. I owe my tailor or my bootmaker something; or I have not paid my subscription to a club; or I have left an unsettled bill ar Baden. I really forget the precise pretext; but it was one which to them seemed quite sufficient to balk me of a redress, and at the same time to shelter their friend."

"I will not believe one word of it, sir!"

"Well, we have at least arrived at a perfect frankness in our intercourse. May I ask you, young lady, which of your relatives has suggested your present course! Is it to your aunt or to your grandfather I must go for an explanation?"

"I suspect it is to me, Major Stapylton," said Barrington, as he came from behind Josephine. "It is to me you must address yourself. Fifine, my dear, your aunt is looking for you; go and tell her, too, that I am quite ready for tea, and you will find me here when it is ready. Major Stapylton and I will take a stroll along the river-side." Now this last was less an invitation than a sort of significant hint to Stapylton that his host had no intention to ask him to cross his threshold, at least for the present; and, indeed, as Barrington passed out and closed the wicket after him, he seemed as though closing the entrance forever.

With a manner far more assured thau his wont, Barrington said: "I have been in pursuit of you, Major Stapylton, since four o'clock. I missed you by having taken the road instead of the river; and am much grieved that the communication I have to make you should not take place anywhere rather than near my roof or within my own gates."

"I am to suppose from your words, sir, that what you are about to say can scarcely be said to a friend; and if so, cannot you hit upon a more convenient mode of making your communication?"

"I think not. I believe that I shall be dealing more fairly with you by saying what I have to say in person."

"Go on," said Stapylton, calmly, as the other paused.

"You are aware," continued Barrington, "that the chief obstacle to a settlement of the claims I have long preferred against the India Company has been a certain document which they possess, declaring that a large portion of the territory held by the Rajah of Luckerabad was not amenable to the laws that regulate succession, being what is called 'Lurkar-teea,'—conquered country,—over which, under no circumstances, could the Rajah exercise prospective rights. To this deed, for their better protection, the Company obtained the signature and seal of the Rajah himself, by means which, of course, we could never discover; but they held it, and always declared that no portion of my son's claim could extend to these lands. Now, as they denied that he could succeed to what are called the 'Turban lands,' meaning the right of sovereignty—being a British subject—on the one hand, and rejected his claim to these conquered countries on the other,—they excluded him altogether."

"My dear sir," said Stapylton, mildly, "I'm shocked to interrupt you, but I am forced to ask, what is the intimate bearing of all this upon me, or on your position towards me?"

"Have a little patience, sir, and suffer me to proceed. If it should turn out that this document—I mean that which bears the signature and seal of the Rajah—should be a forgery; if, I say, it could be shown that what the India Board have long relied on to sustain their case and corroborate their own view could be proved false, a great point would be gained towards the establishment of our claim."

"Doubtless," said Stapylton, with the half-peevish indifference of one listening against his will.

"Well, there is a good prospect of this," said Barring-ton, boldly. "Nay, more, it is a certainty."

"Mr. Barrington," said Stapylton, drawing himself haughtily up, "a few hours ago this history would have had a very great interest for me. My hopes pointed to a very close relationship with your family; the last hour has sufficed to dispel those hopes. Your granddaughter has rejected me so decidedly that I cannot presume to suppose a change in her opinion possible. Let me not then, obtain any share in your confidence to which I have no right whatever."

"What I am about to say will have more interest for you, sir," continued Barrington. "I am about to mention a name that you will recognize,—the Moonshee, Ali Gohur."

Stapylton started, and dropped the cigar he was smoking. To take out another and light it, however, sufficed to employ him, as he murmured between his teeth, "Go on."

"This man says—" continued Barrington.

"Said, perhaps, if you like," broke in Stapylton, "for he died some months ago."

"No; he is alive at this hour. He was on board the Indiaman that was run down by the transport. He was saved and carried on board the 'Regulus' by the intrepidity of young Dill. He is now recovering rapidly from the injuries he received, and at the date of the letter which I hold here, was able to be in daily communication with Colonel Hunter, who is the writer of this."

"I wish the gallant Colonel honester company. Are you aware, Mr. Barrington, that you are speaking of one of the greatest rascals of a country not famed for its integrity?"

"He lays no claim to such for the past; but he would seem desirous to make some reparation for a long course of iniquity."

"Charmed for his sake, and that of his well-wishers, if he have any. But, once again, sir, and at all the risk of appearing very impatient, what concern has all this for me?"

"A great deal, sir. The Moonshee declares that he has been for years back in close correspondence with a man we long since believed dead, and that this man was known to have communicated constantly with the law advisers of the India Board in a manner adverse to us, he being none other than the son of the notorious Sam Edwardes, whom he always addressed under cover to Captain Horace Stapylton, Prince's Hussars."

"This is—strange enough, when one thinks of the quarter it comes from—perfectly true. I came to know Edwardes when on my voyage home, invalided. He took immense trouble about me, nursed and tended me, and, in return, asked as a favor to have some letters he was expecting addressed to my care. I neither knew who he was, nor cared. He got his letters, and I suppose read them; but of their contents, I, it is needless to say, know nothing. I am speaking of a dozen years ago, or, at least, eight or ten, for since that time I have never heard of either Edwardes or his friend."

"He tells a different story. He asserts that to his letters, forwarded to the same address up to the period of last March, he regularly received replies; but at last finding that the writer was disposed to get rid of him, he obtained means to circulate a report of his death, and sailed for Europe to prefer his claims, whatever they be, in person."

"And if every word of this were true, Mr. Barrington, which I don't suspect it is, how, in the name of common sense, does it concern me? I don't suppose I ever took my own letters at a post-office twice in my life. My servant, who has lived with me fourteen years, may, for aught I know, have been bribed to abstract these letters on their arrival; they would be easily recognized by the very superscription. This is one way the thing might have been done. There may have been fifty more, for aught I know or care."

"But you don't deny that you knew Edwardes, and had a close intimacy with him?—a circumstance which you never revealed to Withering or myself."

"It is not at all improbable I may have known half a dozen of that name. It is by no means an uncommon one, not to say that I have a singularly infelicitous memory for people's names. But for the last time, sir, I must protest against this conversation going any further. You have taken upon you, I would hope without intending it, the tone of a French *Juge d'Instruction* in the interrogation of a prisoner. You have questioned and cross-questioned me, asking how I can account for this, or explain that. Now, I am ready to concede a great deal to your position as my host, and to your years, but really I must entreat of you not to push my deference for these beyond the limits of the respect I owe myself. You very properly warned me at the opening of this conversation that it ought not to have the sanction of your roof-tree. I have only to beg that if it is to go any further, that it be conducted in such a shape as is usual between gentlemen who have an explanation to ask, or a satisfaction to demand."

There was consummate craft in giving the discussion this turn. Stapylton well knew the nature of the man he was addressing, and that after the passing allusion to his character as a host, he only needed to hint at the possibility of a meeting to recall him to a degree of respect only short of deference for his opponent.

"I defer to you at once, Major Stapylton," said the old man, with a bland courtesy, as he uncovered and bowed. "There was a time when I should scarcely have required the admonition you have given me."

"I am glad to perceive that you understand me so readily," said Stapylton, who could scarcely repress the joy he felt at the success of his diversion; "and that nothing may mar our future understanding, this is my address in London, where I shall wait your orders for a week."

Though the stroke was shrewdly intended, and meant to throw upon Barrington all the onus of the provocation, the Major little suspected that it was the one solitary subject of which his opponent was a master. On the "duello" Barrington was an authority beyond appeal, and no subtlety, however well contrived, could embarrass or involve him.

"I have no satisfaction to claim at your hands, Major Stapylton," said he, calmly. "My friend, Mr. Withering, when he sent me these letters, knew you were my guest, and he said, 'Read them to Major Stapylton. Let him know what is said of him, and who says it.'"

"And, perhaps, you ought to add, sir, who gives it the sanction of his belief," broke in Stapylton, angrily. "You never took the trouble to recite these charges till they obtained your credence."

"You have said nothing to disprove them," said the old man, quickly.

"That is enough,—quite enough, sir; we understand each other perfectly. You allege certain things against me as injuries done you, and you wait for *me* to resent the imputation. I 'll not balk you, be assured of it. The address I have given you in London will enable you to communicate with me when you arrive there; for I presume this matter had better be settled in France or Holland."

"I think so," said Barrington, with the air of a man thoroughly at his ease.

"I need not say, Mr. Barrington, the regret it gives me that it was not one of my detractors himself, and not their dupe, that should occupy this place."

"The dupe, sir, is very much at your service."

"Till we meet again," said Stapylton, raising his hat as he turned away. In his haste and the confusion of the moment, he took the path that led towards the cottage; nor did he discover his mistake till he heard Barrington's voice calling out to Darby,—

"Get the boat ready to take Major Stapylton to Inistioge."

"You forget none of the precepts of hospitality," said Stapylton, wheeling hastily around, and directing his steps towards the river.

Barrington looked after him as he went, and probably in his long and varied life, crossed with many a care and many troubles, he had never felt the pain of such severe self-reproach as in that moment. To see his guest, the man who had sat at his board and eaten his salt, going out into the dreary night without one hospitable effort to detain him, without a pledge to his health, without a warm shake of his hand, or one hearty wish for his return.

"Dear, dear!" muttered he, to himself, "what is the world come to! I thought I had no more experiences to learn of suffering; but here is a new one. Who would have thought to see the day that Peter Barrington would treat his guest this fashion?"

"Are you coming in to tea, grandpapa?" cried Josephine, from the garden.

"Here I am, my dear!"

"And your guest, Peter, what has become of him?" said Dinah.

"He had some very urgent business at Kilkenny; something that could not admit of delay, I opine."

"But you have not let him go without his letters, surely. Here are all these formidable-looking despatches, on his Majesty's service, on the chimney-piece."

"How forgetful of me!" cried he, as, snatching them up, he hastened down to the river-side. The boat, however, had just gone; and although he shouted and called at the top of his voice, no answer came, and he turned back at last, vexed and disappointed.

"I shall have to start for Dublin to-morrow, Dinah," said he, as he walked thoughtfully up and down the room. "I must have Withering's advice on these letters. There are very pressing matters to be thought of here, and I can take Major Stapylton's despatches with me. I am certain to hear of him somewhere."

Miss Barrington turned her eyes full upon him, and watched him narrowly. She was a keen detector of motives, and she scanned her brother's face with no common keenness, and yet she could see nothing beyond the preoccupation she had often seen. There was no impatience, no anxiety. A shade more thoughtful, perhaps, and even that passed off, as he sat down to his tea, and asked Fifine what commissions she had for the capital.

"You will leave by the evening mail, I suppose?" said Miss Barrington.

"No, Dinah, night travelling wearies me. I will take the coach as it passes the gate to-morrow at five; this will bring me in time to catch Withering at his late dinner, and a pleasanter way to finish a day's travel no man need ask for."

Nothing could be more easily spoken than these words, and Miss Dinah felt reassured by them, and left the room to give some orders about his journey.

"Fifine, darling," said Barrington, after a pause, "do you like your life here?"

"Of course I do, grandpapa. How could I wish for one more happy?"

"But it is somewhat dull for one so young,—somewhat solitary for a fair, bright creature, who might reasonably enough care for pleasure and the world."

"To me it is a round of gayety, grandpapa; so that I almost felt inclined yesterday to wish for some quiet days with aunt and yourself,—some of those dreamy days like what we had in Germany."

"I fear me much, darling, that I contribute but little to the pleasure. My head is so full of one care or another, I am but sorry company, Fifine."

"If you only knew how dull we are without you! How heavily the day drags on even with the occupations you take no share in; how we miss your steps on the stairs and your voice in the garden, and that merry laugh that sets ourselves a-laughing just by its own ring."

"And you would miss me, then?" said he, as he pushed the hair from her temples, and stared steadfastly at her face, — "you would miss me?"

"It would only be half life without you," cried she, passionately.

"So much the worse, — so much the worse!" muttered he; and he turned away, and drew his hand across his eyes. "This life of ours, Fifine, is a huge battle-field; and though the comrades fall fast around him, the brave soldier will fight on to the last."

"You don't want a dress-coat, brother Peter, to dine with Withering, so I have just put up what will serve you for three days, or four, at furthest," said Dinah, entering. "What will be the extent of your stay?"

"Let me have a black coat, Dinah; there 's no saying what great man may not ask for my company; and it might be a week before I get back again."

"There's no necessity it should be anything of the kind, Peter; and with your habits an hotel life is scarcely an economy. Come, Fifine, get to bed, child. You'll have to be up at daybreak. Your grandpapa won't think his coffee drinkable, if it is not made by your hands."

And with this remark, beautifully balanced between a reproof and a flattery, she proceeded to blow out the candles, which was her accustomed mode of sending her company to their rooms.

CHAPTER XV.

THE OLD LEAVEN

Withering arrived at his own door just as Barrington drove up to it. "I knew my letter would bring you up to town, Barrington," said he; "and I was so sure of it that I ordered a saddle of mutton for your dinner, and refused an invitation to the Chancellor's."

"And quite right too. Iam far better company, Tom. Are we to be all alone?"

"All alone."

"That was exactly what I wanted. Now, as I need a long evening with you, the sooner they serve the soup the better; and be sure you give your orders that nobody be admitted."

If Mr. Withering's venerable butler, an official long versed in the mysteries of his office, were to have been questioned on the subject, it is not improbable he would have declared that he never assisted at a pleasanter tête-â tête than that day's dinner. They enjoyed their good dinner and their good wine like men who bring to the enjoyment a ripe experience of such pleasures, and they talked with the rare zest of good talkers and old friends.

"We are in favor with Nicholas," said Withering, as the butler withdrew, and left them alone, "or he would never have given us that bottle of port. Do you mark, Barrington, it's the green seal that John Bushe begged so hard for one night, and all unsuccessfully."

"It is rare stuff!" said Barrington, looking at it between him and the light.

"And it was that story of yours of the Kerry election that won it. The old fellow had to rush out of the room to have his laugh out."

"Do you know, Tom," said Barrington, as he sipped his wine, "I believe, in another generation, nobody will laugh at all. Since you and I were boys, the world has taken a very serious turn. Not that it is much wiser, or better, or more moral, or more cultivated, but it is graver. The old jollity would be now set down simply for vulgarity, and with many people a joke is only short of an insult."

"Shall I tell you why, Peter? We got our reputation for wit, just as we made our name for manufacture, and there sprung up a mass of impostors in consequence,—fellows who made poor jokes and rotten calicoes, that so disgusted the world that people have gone to France for their fun, and to Germany for their furniture. That is, to my taking, the reason of all this social reaction."

"Perhaps you are right, Tom. Old Joe Millers are not unlike cloth made out of devil's dust. One can't expect much wear out of either."

"We must secure another bottle from that bin before Nicholas changes his mind," said Withering, rising to ring the bell.

"No, Tom, not for me. I want all the calm and all the judgment I can muster, and don't ask me to take more wine. I have much to say to you."

"Of course you have. I knew well that packet of letters would bring you up to town; but you have had scarcely time to read them."

"Very hurriedly, I confess. They reached me yesterday afternoon; and when I had run my eyes hastily over them, I said, 'Stapylton must see this at once.' The man was my guest,—he was under my roof,—there could not be a question about how to deal with him. He was out, however, when the packet reached my hands; and while the pony was being harnessed, I took another look over that letter from Colonel Hunter. It shocked me, Tom, I confess; because there flashed upon me quite suddenly the recollection of the promptitude with which the India Board at home here were provided with an answer to each demand we made. It was not merely that when we advanced a step they met us; but we could scarcely meditate a move that they were not in activity to repel it."

"I saw that, too, and was struck by it," said Withering.

"True enough, Tom. I remember a remark of yours one day. 'These people,' said you, 'have our range so accurately, one would suspect they had stepped the ground.'" The lawyer smiled at the compliment to his acuteness, and the other went on: "As I read further, I thought Stapylton had been betrayed,—his correspondent in India had shown his letters. 'Our enemies,' said I, 'have seen our despatches, and are playing with our cards on the table.' No thought of distrust,—not a suspicion against his loyalty had ever crossed me till I met him. I came unexpectedly upon him, however, before the door, and there was a ring and resonance in his voice as I came up that startled me! Passion forgets to shut the door sometimes, and one can see in an angry mind what you never suspected in the calm one. I took him up at once, without suffering him to recover his composure, and read him a part of Hunter's letter. He was ready enough with his reply; he knew the Moonshee by reputation as a man of the worst character, but had suffered him to address certain letters under cover to him, as a convenience to the person they were meant for, and who was no other than the son of the notorious Sam Edwardes. 'Whom you have known all this while,' said I, 'without ever acknowledging to us?'

"'Whom I did know some years back,' replied he, 'but never thought of connecting with the name of Colonel Barrington's enemy.' All this was possible enough, Tom; besides, his manner was frank and open in the extreme. It was only at last, as I dwelt, what he deemed too pertinaciously, on this point, that he suddenly lost control of himself, and said, 'I will have no more of this'—or, 'This must go no further'—or some words to that effect."

"Ha! the probe had touched the sore spot, eh?" cried Withering. "Go on!"

"'And if you desire further explanations from me, you must ask for them at the price men pay for inflicting unmerited insult.'"

"Cleverly turned, cleverly done," said Withering; "but you were not to be deceived and drawn off by that feint, eh?"

"Feint or not, it succeeded, Tom. He made me feel that I had injured him; and as he would not accept of my excuses, — as, in fact, he did not give me time to make them —"

"He got you into a quarrel, is n't that the truth?" asked Withering, hotly.

"Come, come, Tom, be reasonable; he had perfect right on his side. There was what he felt as a very grave imputation upon him; that is, I had made a charge, and his explanation had not satisfied me, — or, at all events, I had not said I was satisfied, — and we each of us, I take it, were somewhat warmer than we need have been."

"And you are going to meet him, — going to fight a duel?"

"Well, if I am, it will not be the first time."

"And can you tell for what? Will you be able to make any man of common intelligence understand for what you are going out?"

"I hope so. I have the man in my eye. No, no, don't make a wry face, Tom. It's another old friend I was thinking of to help me through this affair, and I sincerely trust he will not be so hard to instruct as you imagine."

"How old are you, Barrington?"

"Dinah says eighty-one; but I suspect she cheats me. I think I am eighty-three."

"And is it at eighty-three that men fight duels?"

"' Not if they can help it, Tom, certainly. I have never been out since I shot Tom Connelly in the knee, which was a matter of forty years ago, and I had good hopes it was to be my last exploit of this kind. But what is to be done if a man tells you that your age is your protection; that if it had not been for your white hairs and your shaking ankles, that he 'd have resented your conduct or your words to him? Faith, I think it puts a fellow on his mettle to show that his heart is all right, though his hand may tremble."

"I 'll not take any share in such a folly. I tell you, Barrington, the world for whom you are doing this will be the very first to scout its absurdity. Just remember for a moment we are not living in the old days before the Union, and we have not the right, if we had the power, to throw our age back into the barbarism it has escaped from."

"Barbarism! The days of poor Yelverton, and Ponsonby, and Harry Grattan, and Parsons, and Ned Lysaght, barbarism! Ah! my dear Tom, I wish we had a few of such barbarians here now, and I 'd ask for another bottle or two of that port."

"I'll not give it a milder word; and what's more, I'll not suffer you to tarnish a time-honored name by a folly which even a boy would be blamed for. My dear old friend, just grant me a little patience."

"This is cool, certainly," said Barrington, laughing. "You have said all manner of outrageous things to me for half an hour unopposed, and now you cry have patience."

"Give me your honor now that this shall not go further."

"I cannot, Tom,—I assure you, I cannot."

"What do you mean by 'you cannot'?" cried Withering, angrily.

"I mean just what I said. If you had accepted a man's brief, Tom Withering, there is a professional etiquette which would prevent your giving it up and abandoning him; and so there are situations between men of the world which claim exactly as rigid an observance. I told Stapylton I would be at his orders, and I mean to keep my word."

"Not if you had no right to pledge it; not if I can prove to you that this quarrel was a mere got-up altercation to turn you from an inquiry which this man dare not face."

"This is too subtle for me, Withering,—far too subtle."

"No such thing, Barrington; but I will make it plainer. How if the man you are going to meet had no right to the name he bears?"

"What do I care for his name?"

"Don't you care for the falsehood by which he has assumed one that is not his own?"

"I may be sorry that he is not more clean-handed; but I tell you again, Tom, they never indulged such punctilios in our young days, and I 'm too old to go to school again!"

"I declare, Barrington, you provoke me," said the lawyer, rising, and pacing the room with hasty strides. "After years and years of weary toil, almost disheartened by defeat and failure, we at last see the outline of land; a few more days—or it may be hours—of perseverance may accomplish our task. Since I arose this morning I have learned more of our case, seen my way more clearly through matters which have long puzzled me, than the cost of years has taught me. I have passed four hours with one who would give his life to serve you, but whose name I was not at liberty to divulge, save in the last necessity, and the reasons for which reserve I heartily concur in; and now, by a rash and foolish altercation, you would jeopardy everything. Do you wonder if I lose temper?"

"You have got me into such a state of bewilderment, Tom, that I don't know what I am asked to agree to. But who is your friend,—is n't it a woman?"

"It is not a woman."

"I'd have bet five pounds it was! When as sharp a fellow as you takes the wrong line of country, it's generally a woman is leading the way over the fences."

"This time your clever theory is at fault."

"Well, who is it? Out with him, Tom. I have not so many stanch friends in the world that I can afford to ignore them."

"I will tell you his name on one condition."

"I agree. What is the condition?"

"It is this: that when you hear it you will dismiss from your mind—though it be only for a brief space—all the prejudices that years may have heaped against him, and suffer me to show you that *you*, with all your belief in your own fairness, are not just; and with a firm conviction in your own generosity, might be more generous. There's my condition!"

"Well, it must be owned I am going to pay pretty smartly for my information," said Barrington, laughing. "And if you are about to preach to me, it will not be a 'charity' sermon; but, as I said before, I agree to everything."

Withering stopped his walk and resumed it again. It was evident he had not satisfied himself how he should proceed, and he looked agitated and undecided. "Barrington," said he, at last, "you have had about as many reverses in life as most men, and must have met with fully your share of ingratitude and its treatment. Do you feel, now, in looking back, that there are certain fellows you cannot forgive?"

"One or two, perhaps, push me harder than the rest; but if I have no gout flying about me, I don't think I bear them any malice."

"Well, you have no gouty symptoms now, I take it?"

"Never felt better for the last twenty years."

"That is as it should be; for I want to talk to you of a man who, in all our friendship, you have never mentioned to me, but whose name I know will open an old wound,—Ormsby Conyers."

Barrington laid down the glass he was lifting to his lips, and covered his face with both his hands, nor for some moments did he speak a word. "Withering," said he, and his voice trembled as he spoke, "even your friendship has scarcely the right to go this far. The injury the man you speak of did me meets me every morning as I open my eyes, and my first prayer each day is that I may forgive him, for every now and then, as my lone lot in life comes strongly before me, I have need to pray for this; but I have succeeded at last,—I have forgiven him from my heart; but, dear friend, let us not talk of what tears open wounds that bleed afresh at a touch. I beseech you, let all that be a bygone."

"That is more than I can do, Barrington; for it is not to me you must acknowledge you have forgiven this man,—you must tell it to himself."

"That is not needed, Tom. Thousands of long miles separate us, and will in all likelihood separate us to the last. What does he want with my forgiveness, which is less a question between him and me than between me and my own heart?"

"And yet it is what he most desires on earth; he told me so within an hour!"

"Told you so,—and within an hour?"

"Yes, Barrington, he is here. Not in the house," added he, hastily, for the suddenness of the announcement had startled the old man, and agitated him greatly.

"Be calm, my dear friend," said Withering, laying a hand on the other's shoulder. "He who is now come to claim your forgiveness has never injured you to the extent you believe. He asks it as the last tribute to one he loved only less than you loved him. He has told me everything; never sparing himself, nor seeking by any subtlety to excuse a particle of his conduct. Let me tell you that story as I heard it. It will be some solace to you to know that your noble-hearted son inspired a friendship which, after the long lapse of years, extracts such an atonement as one act of disloyalty to it could demand. This was Ormsby Conyers's one and only treason to the love that bound them. Listen to it!"

Barrington tried to speak, but could not; so he nodded an assent, and Withering continued. His story was that which the reader has already heard from the lips of Conyers himself, and the old lawyer told it well. If he did not attempt to extenuate the offence and wrong of Conyers, he showed the power and strength of an affection which could make one of the haughtiest of men come forward to accuse himself, and at every cost of humiliation vindicate the noble nature of his friend.

"And why not have avowed all this before?—why not have spared himself years of self-accusing, and me years of aggravated misery?" cried Barrington.

"He did make the attempt. He came to England about eighteen years ago, and his first care was to write to you. He asked to be allowed to see you, and sent you at the same time an admission that he had injured you, and was come to seek your forgiveness."

"That's true, Tom; all strictly true. I remember all about it. His letter was such a one as an enemy might have used to crush him. My own temper at the time was not to be trusted too far; sorrow was making me cruel, and might make me vindictive; so I sent it back to him, and hinted it was safer in *his* hands than *mine*."

"And he has never forgotten your generosity. He said, 'It was what well became the father of George Barrington.'"

"If he is here in this city, now, let me see him. Remember, Withering, when a man comes to my age his time is short. Cannot we go to him at once?"

"Not feeling certain of your coming up to town to-day, I had arranged with Conyers to start for 'The Home' tomorrow; we were to await the post hour, and, if no letter came from you, to leave at ten o'clock. I was to take him up at Elvidge's Hotel. What say you if I drive him down to Reynolds's? You stop there, I know."

"With all my heart, Tom. I am fully as impatient as he can be to sign and seal our reconciliation. Indeed, I feel myself already less sinned against than sinning; and an act of forgiveness is only an exchange of prisoners between us. If you knew how young I feel again at all this, Withering," said he, grasping his friend's hand. "What a happiness to know that poor George's memory is so revered that one who has failed towards him in fidelity should come to expiate the wrong thus openly! My fine noble-hearted boy deserved this tribute! And he told you how they loved each other; in what a brotherhood they lived; and what a glorious fellow George was? Did he tell you of his gentleness?—womanly softness it was, Tom. A careless observer might have said there was no stuff in him to make a soldier, and yet where was there his equal? You heard what he did at Naghapoor and Meerutan, where he held a mountain-pass with three squadrons against a whole army corps, and never owned to being wounded till he fell fainting from his horse on the retreat. Oh, let me not speak of these things, or my heart will burst I must leave you, old friend; this agitation will unfit me for much that is before me; let me go, I beseech you, and when you see me to-morrow, you 'll find I am all myself again."

It was in silence they grasped each other's hand, and parted.

CHAPTER XVI.

A HAPPY MEETING

Barrington scarcely closed his eyes that night after he had parted with Withering, so full was he of thinking over all he had heard. "It was," as he repeated to himself over and over again, "'such glorious news' to hear that it was no long-laid plot, no dark treachery, had brought poor George to his grave, and that the trusted friend had not turned out a secret enemy. How prone we are," thought he, "to suffer our suspicions to grow into convictions, just by the mere force of time. Conyers was neither better nor worse than scores of young fellows entering on life, undisciplined in self-restraint, and untutored by converse with the world; and in his sorrow and repentance he is far and away above most men. It was fine of him to come thus, and become his own accuser, rather than suffer a shade of reproach to rest upon the fame of his friend. And this reparation he would have made years ago, but for my impatience. It was I that would not listen,—would not admit it.

"I believe in my heart, then, this confession has a higher value for me than would the gain of our great suit. It is such a testimony to my brave boy as but one man living could offer. It is a declaration to the world that says, 'Here am I, high in station, covered with dignities and rich in rewards; yet there was a man whose fate has never interested you, over whose fall you never sorrowed; hundreds of times my superior.' What a reward is this for all my life of toil and struggle,—what a glorious victory, when the battle looked so doubtful! People will see at last it is not an old man's phantasy; it is not the headlong affection of a father for his son has made me pursue this reparation for him here. There is a witness 'come to judgment,' who will tell them what George Barrington was; how noble as a man, how glorious as a soldier."

While the old man revelled in the happiness of these thoughts, so absorbed was he by them that he utterly forgot the immediate object which had occasioned his journey,—forgot Stapylton and the meeting, and all that had led to it. Thus passed the hours of the night; and as the day broke, he arose, impatient to actual feverishness for the coming interview. He tried by some occupation to fill up the time. He sat down to write to his sister an account of all Withering had told him, leaving the rest to be added after the meeting; but he found, as he read it over, that after the mention of George's name, nothing dropped from his pen but praises of him. It was all about his generosity, his open-heartedness, and his bravery. "This would seem downright extravagant," said he, as he crushed the paper in his hand, "till she hears it from the lips of Conyers himself." He began another letter, but somehow again he glided into the self-same channel.

"This will never do," said he; "there's nothing for it but a brisk walk." So saying he sallied out into the deserted streets, for few were about at that early hour. Barrington turned his steps towards the country, and soon gained one of those shady alleys which lead towards Finglas. It was a neighborhood he had once known well, and a favorite resort of those pleasant fellows who thought they compensated for a hard night at Daly's by sipping syllabub of a morning on a dewy meadow. He once had rented a little cottage there; a fancy of poor George's it was, that there were some trout in the stream beside it; and Barrington strolled along till he came to a little mound, from which he could see the place, sadly changed and dilapidated since he knew it. Instead of the rustic bridge that crossed the river, a single plank now spanned the stream, and in the disorder and neglect of all around, it was easy to see it had fallen to the lot of a peasant to live in it. As Barrington was about to turn away, he saw an old man—unmistakably a gentleman—ascending the hill, with a short telescope in his hand. As the path was a narrow one, he waited, therefore, for the other's arrival, before he began to descend himself. With a politeness which in his younger days Irish gentlemen derived from intercourse with France, Barring-ton touched his hat as he passed the stranger, and the other, as if encouraged by the show of courtesy, smiled as he returned the salute, and said,—

"Might I take the liberty to ask you if you are acquainted with this locality?"

"Few know it better, or, at least, knew it once," said Barrington.

"It was the classic ground of Ireland in days past," said the stranger. "I have heard that Swift lived here."

"Yes; but you cannot see his house from this. It was nearer to Santry, where you see that wood yonder. There was, however, a celebrity once inhabited that small cottage before us. It was the home of Parnell."

"Is that Parnell's cottage?" asked the stranger, with eagerness; "that ruined spot, yonder?"

"Yes. It was there he wrote some of his best poems. I knew the room well he lived in."

"How I would like to see it!" cried the other.

"You are an admirer of Parnell, then?" said Barrington, with a smile of courteous meaning.

"I will own to you, sir, it was less of Parnell I was thinking than of a dear friend who once talked to me of that cottage. He had lived there, and cherished the memory of that life when far away from it; and so well had he described every walk and path around it, each winding of the river, and every shady nook, that I had hoped to recognize it without a guide."

"Ah, it is sadly changed of late. Your friend had not probably seen it for some years?"

"Let me see. It was in a memorable year he told me he lived there,—when some great demonstration was made by the Irish volunteers, with the Bishop of

Down at their head. The Bishop dined there on that day."

"The Earl of Bristol dined that day with me, there," said Barrington, pointing to the cottage.

"May I ask with whom I have the honor to speak, sir?" said the stranger, bowing.

"Was it George Barrington told you this?" said the old man, trembling with eagerness: "was it he who lived here? I may ask, sir, for I am his father!"

"And I am Ormsby Conyers," said the other; and his face became pale, and his knees trembled as he said it.

"Give me your hand, Conyers," cried Barrington,—"the hand that my dear boy has so often pressed in friendship. I know all that you were to each other, all that you would be to his memory."

"Can you forgive me?" said Conyers.

"I have, for many a year. I forgave you when I thought you had been his enemy. I now know you had only been your own to sacrifice such love, such affection as he bore you."

"I never loved him more than I have hated myself for my conduct towards him."

"Let us talk of George,—he loved us both," said Barrington, who still held Conyers by the hand. "It is a theme none but yourself can rival me in interest for."

It was not easy for Conyers to attain that calm which could enable him to answer the other's questions; but by degrees he grew to talk freely, assisted a good deal by the likeness of the old man to his son,—a resemblance in manner even as much as look,—and thus, before they reached town again, they had become like familiar friends.

Barrington could never hear enough of George; even of the incidents he had heard of by letter, he liked to listen to the details again, and to mark how all the traits of that dear boy had been appreciated by others.

"I must keep you my prisoner," said Barrington, as they gained the door of his hotel. "The thirst I have is not easily slaked; remember that for more than thirty years I have had none to talk to me of my boy! I know all about your appointment with Withering; he was to have brought you here this morning to see me, and my old friend will rejoice when he comes and finds us here together."

"He was certain you would come up to town," said Conyers, "when you got his letters. You would see at once that there were matters which should be promptly dealt with; and he said, 'Barrington will be my guest at dinner to-morrow.'"

"Eh?—how?—what was it all about? George has driven all else out of my head, and I declare to you that I have not the very vaguest recollection of what Wither-ing's letters contained. Wait a moment; a light is breaking on me. I do remember something of it all now. To be sure! What a head I have! It was all about Stapylton. By the way, General, how you would have laughed had you heard the dressing Withering gave me last night, when I told him I was going to give Stap-ylton a meeting."

"A hostile meeting?"

"Well, if you like to give it that new-fangled name, General, which I assure you was not in vogue when I was a young man. Withering rated me soundly for the notion, reminded me of my white hairs and such other disqualifications, and asked me indignantly, 'What the world would say when they came to hear of it?' 'What would the world say if they heard I declined it, Tom?' was my answer. Would they not exclaim, 'Here is one of that fire-eating school who are always rebuking us for our laxity in matters of honor; look at him and say, are these the principles of his sect?'"

Conyers shook his head dissentingly, and smiled.

"No, no!" said Barrington, replying to the other's look, "you are just of my own mind! A man who believes you to have injured him claims reparation as a matter of right. I could not say to Stapylton, 'I will not meet you!'"

"I *did* say so, and that within a fortnight."

"You said so, and under what provocation?"

"He grossly insulted my son, who was his subaltern; he outraged him by of-fensive language, and he dared even to impugn his personal courage. It was in one of those late riots where the military were called out; and my boy, intrusted with the duty of dispersing an assemblage, stopped to remonstrate where he might have charged, and actually relieved the misery he had his orders to have trampled under the feet of his squadron. Major Stapylton could have reprimanded, he might have court-martialled him; he had no right to attempt to dishonor him. My son left the service,—I made him leave on the spot,—and we went over to France to meet this man. I sent for Proctor to be my boy's friend, and my letter found him at Sir Gilbert Stapylton's, at Hollowcliffe. To explain his hurried departure, Proctor told what called him away. 'And will you suffer your friend to meet that adventurer,' said Sir Gilbert, 'who stole my nephew's name if he did not steal more?' To be brief, he told that this fellow had lived with Colonel Howard Stapylton, British Resident at Ghurtnapore, as a sort of humble private secretary. 'In the cholera that swept the district Howard died, and although his will, deposited at Calcutta, contained several legacies, the effects to redeem them were not to be discovered. Meanwhile this young fellow assumed the name of Stapylton, gave himself out for his heir, and even threatened to litigate some landed property in England with Howard's brother. An intimation that if he dared to put his menace in action a full inquiry into his conduct should be made, stopped him, and we heard no more of him,—at least, for a great many years. When an old Madras friend of Howard's who came down to spend his Christmas, said, "Who do you think I saw in town last week, but that young scamp Howard used to call his Kitmagar, and who goes by the name of Stapylton?" we were so indignant at first that we resolved on all manner of exposures; but learning that he had the reputation of a good officer, and had actually distinguished himself at Waterloo, we relented. Since that, other things have come to our knowledge to make us repent our lenity. In fact, he is an adventurer in its very worst sense, and has traded upon a certain amount of personal courage to cover a character of downright ignominy.' Proctor, on hearing all this, recalled me to England; and declared that he had traced enough to this man's charge to show he was one whom no gentleman could meet. It would appear that some recent discoveries had been made about him at the Horse Guards also; for when Proctor asked for a certain piece of information from one of his friends in office there, he heard, for answer, 'We hope to know that, and more, in a day or two.'"

"Do you know that I 'm sorry for it,—heartily sorry?" said Barrington. "The fellow had that stamp of manliness about him that would seem the pledge of a bold, straightforward nature."

"I have a high value for courage, but it won't do everything."

"More 's the pity, for it renders all that it aids of tenfold more worth."

"And on the back of all this discovery comes Hunter's letter, which Withering has sent you, to show that this Stapylton has for years back been supplying the Indian Directors with materials to oppose your claims."

"Nothing ever puzzled us so much as the way every weak point of our case was at once seized upon, and every doubt we ourselves entertained exaggerated into an impassable barrier. Withering long suspected that some secret enemy was at work within our own lines, and repeatedly said that we were sold. The difficulty is, why this man should once have been our enemy, and now should strive so eagerly to be not alone our friend, but one of us. You have heard he proposed for my granddaughter?"

"Fred suspected his intentions in that quarter, but we were not certain of them."

"And it is time I should ask after your noble-hearted boy. How is he, and where?"

"He is here, at my hotel, impatiently waiting your permission to go down to 'The Home.' He has a question to ask there, whose answer will be his destiny."

"Has Josephine turned another head then?" said Barring-ton, laughing.

"She has won a very honest heart; as true and as honorable a nature as ever lived," said Conyers, with emotion. "Your granddaughter does not know, nor needs ever to know, the wrong I have done her father; and if you have forgiven me, you will not remember it against my boy."

"But what do you yourself say to all this? You have never seen the girl?"

"Fred has."

"You know nothing about her tastes, her temper, her bringing up."

"Fred does."

"Nor are you aware that the claim we have so long relied on is almost certain to be disallowed. I have scarcely a hope now remaining with regard to it."

"I have more than I need; and if Fred will let me have a bungalow in his garden, I'll make it all over to him tomorrow."

"It is then with your entire consent he would make this offer?"

"With my whole heart in it! I shall never feel I have repaired the injury I have done George Barrington till I have called his daughter my own."

Old Barrington arose, and walked up and down with slow and measured steps. At last he halted directly in front of General Conyers, and said, —

"If you will do me one kindness, I will agree to everything. What am I saying? I agree already; and I would not make a bargain of my consent; but you will not refuse me a favor?"

"Ask me anything, and I promise it on the faith of a gentleman."

"It is this, then; that you will stand by me in this affair of Stapylton's. I have gone too far for subtleties or niceties. It is no question of who was his father, or what was his own bringing up. I have told him I should be at his orders, and don't let me break my word."

"If you choose me for your friend, Barrington, you must not dictate how I am to act for you."

"That is quite true; you are perfectly correct there," said the other, in some confusion.

"On that condition, then, that I am free to do for you what I would agree to in my own case, I accept the charge."

"And there is to be no humbug of consideration for my age and my white hairs; none of that nonsense about a fellow with one leg in the grave. Mark you, Conyers, I will stand none of these; I have never taken a writ of ease not to serve on a jury, nor will I hear of one that exempts me from the rights of a gentleman."

"I have got your full powers to treat, and you must trust me. Where are we to find Stapylton's friend?"

"He gave me an address which I never looked at. Here it is!" and he drew a card from his pocket.

"Captain Duff Brown, late Fifth Fusiliers, Holt's Hotel, Charing Cross."

"Do you know him?" asked Barrington, as the other stood silently re-reading the address.

"Yes, thoroughly," said he, with a dry significance. "The man who selects Duff Brown to act for him in an affair of honor must be in a sore strait. It is a sorry indorsement to character. He had to leave the service from the imputation of foul play in a duel himself; and I took an active part against him."

"Will this make your position unpleasant to you, — would you rather not act for me?"

"Quite the reverse. It is more than ever necessary you should have some one who not only knows the men he is to deal with, but is known himself to them. It is a preliminary will save a world of trouble."

"When can we set out?"

"To-night by the eight-o'clock packet, we can sail for Liverpool; but let us first of all despatch Fred to 'The Home.' The poor boy will be half dead with anxiety till he knows I have your permission."

"I'll accredit him with a letter to my sister; not that he needs it, for he is one of her prime favorites. And now for another point. Withering must be made believe that we are all off together for the country this evening. He is so opposed to this affair with Stapylton, that he is in a mood to do anything to prevent it."

"Well thought of; and here comes the man himself in search of us."

"I have been half over the town after you this morning, General," said Withering, as he entered; "and your son, too, could make nothing of your absence. He is in the carriage at the door now, not knowing whether he ought to come up."

"I'll soon reassure him on that score," said Barrington, as he left the room, and hastened downstairs with the step of one that defied the march of time.

CHAPTER XVII.

MEET COMPANIONSHIP

In a very modest chamber of a house in one of the streets which lead from the Strand to the Thames, two persons sat at supper. It is no time for lengthened introductions, and I must present Captain Duff Brown very hurriedly to my reader, as he confronted his friend Stapylton at table. The Captain was a jovial-looking, full-whiskered, somewhat corpulent man, with a ready reply, a ready laugh, and a hand readier than either, whether the weapon wielded was a billiard-cue or a pistol.

The board before them was covered with oysters and oyster-shells, porter in its pewter, a square-shaped decanter of gin, and a bundle of cigars. The cloth was dirty, the knives unclean, and the candles ill-matched and of tallow; but the guests did not seem to have bestowed much attention to these demerits, but ate and drank like men who enjoyed their fare.

"The best country in Europe,—the best in the world,—I call England for a fellow who knows life," cried the Captain. "There is nothing you cannot do; nothing you cannot have in it."

"With eight thousand a year, perhaps," said Stapylton, sarcastically.

"No need of anything like it. Does any man want a better supper than we have had to-night? What better could he have? And the whole cost not over five, or at most six shillings for the pair of us."

"You may talk till you are hoarse, Duff, but I'll not stay in it When once I have settled these two or three matters I have told you of, I'll start for—I don't much care whither. I'll go to Persia, or perhaps to the Yankees."

"*I* always keep America for the finish!" said the other. "It is to the rest of the world what the copper hell is to Crockford's,—the last refuge when one walks in broken boots and in low company. But tell me, what have you done to-day; where did you go after we parted?"

"I went to the Horse Guards, and saw Blanchard,—pompous old humbug that he is. I told him that I had made up my mind to sell out; that I intended to take service in a foreign army,—he hates foreigners,—and begged he would expedite my affairs with his Royal Highness, as my arrangements could not admit of delay."

"And he told you that there was an official routine, out of which no officer need presume to expect his business could travel?"

"He told me no such thing. He flatly said, 'Your case is already before the Commander-in-Chief, Major Stapylton, and you may rely on it there will be no needless delay in dealing with it.'"

"That was a threat, I take it."

"Of course it was a threat; and I only said, 'It will be the first instance of the kind, then, in the department,' and left him."

"Where to, after that?"

"I next went to Gregory's, the magistrate of police. I wanted to see the informations the black fellow swore to; and as I knew a son of Gregory's in the Carbiniers, I thought I could manage it; but bad luck would have it that the old fellow should have in his hands some unsettled bills with my indorsements on them, — fact; Gregory and I used to do a little that way once, — and he almost got a fit when he heard my name."

"Tried back after that, eh?"

"Went on to Renshaw's and won fifty pounds at hazard, took Blake's odds on Diadem, and booked myself for a berth in the Boulogne steamer, which leaves at two this morning."

"You secured a passport for me, did n't you?"

"No. You'll have to come as my servant. The Embassy fellows were all strangers to me, and said they would not give a separate passport without seeing the bearer."

"All right. I don't dislike the second cabin, nor the ladies'-maids. What about the pistols?"

"They are yonder under the great-coat. Renshaw lent them. They are not very good, he says, and one of them hangs a little in the fire."

"They 'll be better than the old Irishman's, that's certain. You may swear that his tools were in use early in the last century."

"And himself, too; that's the worst of it all. I wish it was not a fellow that might be my grandfather."

"I don't know. I rather suspect, if I was given to compunctions, I'd have less of them for shaking down the rotten ripe fruit than the blossom."

"And he 's a fine old fellow, too," said Stapylton, half sadly.

"Why didn't you tell him to drop in this evening and have a little écarté?"

For a while Stapylton leaned his head on his hand moodily, and said nothing.

"Cheer up, man! Taste that Hollands. I never mixed better," said Brown.

"I begin to regret now, Duff, that I did n't take your advice."

"And run away with her?"

"Yes, it would have been the right course, after all!"

MEET COMPANIONS

"I knew it. I always said it. I told you over and over again what would happen if you went to work in orderly fashion. They'd at once say, 'Who are your people,—where are they,—what have they?' Now, let a man be as inventive as Daniel Defoe himself, there will always slip out some flaw or other about a name, or a date,—dates are the very devil! But when you have once carried her off, what can they do but compromise?"

"She would never have consented."

"I'd not have asked her. I'd have given her the benefit of the customs of the land she lived in, and made it a regular abduction. Paddy somebody and Terence something else are always ready to risk their necks for a pint of whiskey and a breach of the laws."

"I don't think I could have brought myself to it."

"*I* could, I promise you."

"And there 's an end of a man after such a thing."

"Yes, if he fails. If he's overtaken and thrashed, I grant you he not only loses the game, but gets the cards in his face, besides. But why fail? Nobody fails when he wants to win,—when he determines to win. When I shot De Courcy at Asterabad—"

"Don't bring up that affair, at least, as one of precedent, Duff. I neither desire to be tried for a capital felony, nor to have committed one."

"Capital fiddlesticks! As if men did not fight duels every day of the week; the difference between guilt and innocence being that one fellow's hand shook, and the other's was steady. De Courcy would have 'dropped' me, if I'd have Jet him."

"And so *you* would have carried her off, Master Duff?" said Stapylton, slowly.

"Yes; if she had the pot of money you speak of, and no Lord Chancellor for a guardian. I 'd have made the thing sure at once."

"The money she will and must have; so much is certain."

"Then I 'd have made the remainder just as certain."

"It is a vulgar crime, Duff; it would be very hard to stoop to it."

"Fifty things are harder,—no cash, no credit are harder. The Fleet is harder. But what is that noise? Don't you hear a knock at the door? Yes, there's some one without who hasn't much patience." So saying, he arose and walked to the door. As he opened it, he started back a little with surprise, for it was a police constable stood before him.

"Not you, Captain, not *you*, sir! it's another gentleman I want. I see him at the table there,—Major Stapylton." By this time the man had entered the room and stood in front of the fire. "I have a warrant against you, Major," said he, quietly. "Informations have been sworn before Mr. Colt that you intend to fight a duel, and you must appear at the office to-morrow, to enter into your bond, and to give securities to keep the peace."

"Who swore the informations?" cried Brown.

"What have we to do with that?" said Stapylton, impatiently. "Isn't the world full of meddling old women? Who wants to know the names?"

"I 'll lay the odds it was old Conyers; the greatest humbug in that land of humbugs,—Bengal. It was he that insisted on my leaving the Fifth. Come, Sergeant, out with it. This was General Conyers's doing?"

"I'm sorry to be obliged to declare you in custody, Major," said the policeman; "but if you like to come over to Mr. Colt's private residence, I 'm sure he 'd settle the matter this evening."

"He'll do no such thing, by George!" cried Brown. "The sneaking dogs who have taken this shabby course shall be exposed in open court. We 'll have the names in full, and in every newspaper in England. Don't compromise the case, Stapylton; make them eat the mess they have cooked, to the last mouthful. We 'll show the world what the fighting Irishman and his gallant friend are made of. Major Stapylton is your prisoner, Sergeant?"

The man smiled slightly at the passionate energy of the speaker, and turned to Stapylton. "There 's no objection to your going to your lodgings, Major. You 'll be at the chief office by ten to-morrow."

Stapylton nodded assent, and the other retired and closed the door.

"What do you say now?" cried Brown, triumphantly. "Did n't I tell you this? Did n't I say that when old Con-yers heard my name, he 'd say, 'Oh, there 'll be no squaring this business'?"

"It's just as likely that he said, 'I 'll not confer with that man; he had to leave the service.'"

"More fool you, then, not to have had a more respectable friend. Had you there, Stapylton,—eh?"

"I acknowledge that. All I can say in extenuation is, that I hoped old Barrington, living so long out of the world, would have selected another old mummy like himself, who had never heard of Captain Duff Brown, nor his famous trial at Calcutta."

"There's not a man in the kingdom has not heard of me. I 'm as well known as the first Duke in the land."

"Don't boast of it, Duff; even notoriety is not always a cheap luxury."

"Who knows but you may divide it with me to-morrow or next day?"

"What do you mean, sir?—what do you mean?" cried Stapylton, slapping the table with his clenched hand.

"Only what I said,—that Major Stapylton may furnish the town with a nine-days wonder, *vice* Captain Duff Brown, forgotten."

Evidently ashamed of his wrath, Stapylton tried to laugh off the occasion of it, and said, "I suppose neither of us would take the matter much to heart."

"I 'll not go to the office with you to-morrow, Stapylton," added he, after a pause; "that old Sepoy General would certainly seize the opportunity to open some old scores that I'd as soon leave undisturbed."

"All right, I think you are prudent there."

"But I 'll be of use in another way. I 'll lay in wait for that fellow who reports for the 'Chronicle,' the only paper that cares for these things, and I 'll have him deep in the discussion of some devilled kidneys when your case is called on."

"I fancy it does not matter what publicity it obtains."

"Ah, I don't know that. Old Braddell, our major, used to say, 'Reputation, after forty, is like an old wall. If you begin to break a hole in it, you never know how much will come away.'"

"I tell you again, Duff, I'm past scandalizing; but have your way, if you will 'muzzle the ox,' and let us get away from this as soon as may be. I want a little rest after this excitement."

"Well, I 'm pretty much in the same boot myself, though I don't exactly know where to go. France is dangerous. In Prussia there are two sentences recorded against me. I 'm condemned to eight years' hard labor in Wurtemberg, and pronounced dead in Austria for my share in that Venetian disturbance."

"Don't tell me of these rascalities. Bad enough when a man is driven to them, but downright infamy to be proud of."

"Have you never thought of going into the Church? I 've a notion you 'd be a stunning preacher."

"Give up this bantering, Duff, and tell me how I shall get hold of young Conyers. I 'd rather put a ball in that fellow than be a Lieutenant-General. He has ever been my rock ahead. That silly coxcomb has done more to mar my destiny than scores of real enemies. To shoot him would be to throw a shell in the very midst of them."

"I 'd rather loot him, if I had the choice; the old General has lots of money. Stapylton, scuttle the ship, if you like, but first let *me* land the cargo. Of all the vengeances a man can wreak on another the weakest is to kill him. For my part, I 'd cherish the fellow that injured me. I 'd set myself to study his tastes and learn his ambitions. I 'd watch over him and follow him, being, as it were, his dearest of all friends,—read backwards!"

"This is tiresome scoundrelism. I'll to bed," said Stapylton, taking a candle from the table.

"Well, if you must shoot this fellow, wait till he's married; wait for the honeymoon."

"There's some sense in that. I 'll go and sleep over it."

CHAPTER XVIII.

AUNT DOROTHEA.

"You must come down with me for one day, Tom, to see an old aunt of mine at Bournemouth," said Hunter to young Dill. "I never omitted going to see her the first thing whenever I landed in England, and she 'll not forgive me if I were to do so now."

"But why should I go, sir? My presence would only trouble the comfort of a family meeting."

"Quite the reverse. She 'll be delighted to see you. It will be such a triumph to her, amongst all her neighbors, to have had a visit from the hero of the day,—the fellow that all the print-shops are full of. Why, man, you are worth five hundred pounds to me. I 'm not sure I might not say double as much."

"In that case, sir, I 'm perfectly at your orders."

And down they went, and arrived late on the day after this conversation at an old-fashioned manor-house, where Miss Dorothy Hunter had passed some sixty-odd years of her life. Though to Tom she seemed to bear a great resemblance to old Miss Barrington, there was really little likeness between them, beyond an inordinate pride of birth, and an intense estimation for the claims of family. Miss Hunter's essential characteristic was a passion for celebrities; a taste somewhat difficult to cultivate in a very remote and little visited locality. The result was that she consoled herself by portraits, or private letters, or autographs of her heroes, who ranged over every imaginable career in life, and of whom, by mere dint of iteration, she had grown to believe herself the intimate friend or correspondent.

No sooner had she learned that her nephew was to be accompanied by the gallant young soldier whose name was in every newspaper than she made what she deemed the most suitable preparations for his reception. Her bedroom was hung round with portraits of naval heroes, or pictures of sea-fights. Grim old admirals, telescope in hand, or with streaming hair, shouting out orders to board the enemy, were on every side; while, in the place of honor, over the fireplace, hung a vacant frame, destined one day to contain the hero of the hour, Tom Dill himself.

Never was a poor fellow in this world less suited to adulation of this sort. He was either overwhelmed with the flattery, or oppressed by a terror of what some sensible spectator—if such there were—would think of the absurd position in which he was forced to stand. And when he found himself obliged to inscribe his name in a long column of illustrious autographs, the sight of his own scarce legible characters filled up the measure of his shame.

"He writes like the great Turenne," said Miss Dorothy; "he always wrote from above downwards, so that no other name than his own could figure on the page."

"I got many a thrashing for it at school, ma'am," said Tom, apologizing, "and so I gave up writing altogether."

"Ah, yes! the men of action soon learn to despise the pen; they prefer to make history rather than record it."

It was not easy for Hunter to steer his bashful friend through all the shoals and quicksands of such flattery; but, on the plea of his broken health and strength, he hurried him early to his bed, and returned to the fireside, where his aunt awaited him.

"He's charming, if he were only not so diffident. Why will he not be more confiding, more at his ease with me,—like Mungo Park, or Sir Sidney Smith?"

"After a while, so he will, aunt. You 'll see what a change there will be in him at our next visit All these flatteries he meets with are too much for him; but when we come down again, you 'll see him without these distracting influences. Then bear in mind his anxieties,—he has not yet seen his family; he is eager to be at home again. I carried him off here positively in spite of himself, and on the strict pledge of only for one day."

"One day! And do you mean that you are to go tomorrow?"

"No help for it, aunt. Tom is to be at Windsor on Saturday. But for that, he would already have been on his way to Ireland."

"Then there's no time to be lost. What can we do for him? He'snot rich?"

"Hasn't a shilling; but would reject the very shadow of such assistance."

"Not if a step were purchased for him; without his knowledge, I mean."

"It would be impossible that he should not know it."

"But surely there is some way of doing it A handsome sum to commemorate his achievement might be subscribed. I would begin it with a thousand pounds."

"He'd not accept it. I know him thoroughly. There's only one road to him through which he would not deem a favor a burden."

"And what of that?"

"A kindness to his sister. I wish you saw her, aunt!"

"Is she like him?"

"Like him? Yes; but very much better-looking. She's singularly handsome, and such a girl! so straightforward and so downright It is a positive luxury to meet her after all the tiresome conventionalities of the every-day young lady."

"Shall I ask her here?"

"Oh, if you would, aunt!—if you only would!"

"That you may fall in love with her, I suppose?"

"No, aunt, that is done already."

"I think, sir, I might have been apprised of this attachment!" said she, bridling.

"I didn't know it myself, aunt, till I was close to the Cape. I thought it a mere fancy as we dropped down Channel; grew more thoughtful over it in the Bay of Biscay; began to believe it as we discovered St. Helena; and came back to England resolved to tell you the whole truth, and ask you, at least, to see her and know her."

"So I will, then. I'll write and invite her here."

"You're the best and kindest aunt in Christendom!" said he, rushing over and kissing her.

"I'm not going to let you read it, sir," said she, with a smile. "If she show it to you, she may. Otherwise it is a matter between ourselves."

"Be it entirely as you wish, aunt."

"And if all this goes hopefully on," said she, after a pause, "is Aunt Dorothea to be utterly forgotten? No more visits here,—no happy summer evenings,—no more merry Christmases?"

"Nay, aunt, I mean to be your neighbor. That cottage you have often offered me, near the rocks, I'll not refuse it again,—that is, if you tempt me once more."

"It is yours, and the farm along with it. Go to bed now, and leave me to write my note, which will require some thought and reflection."

"I know you'll do it well. I know none who could equal you in such a task."

"I'll try and acquit myself with credit," said she, as she sat down to the writing-desk.

"And what is all this about,—a letter from Miss Dorothea to Polly," said Tom, as they drove along the road back to town. "Surely they never met?"

"Never; but my aunt intends that they shall. She writes to ask your sister to come on a visit here."

"But why not have told her the thing was impossible? You know us. You have seen the humble way we live,—how many a care it costs to keep up that little show of respectability that gets us sufferance in the world, and how one little attempt beyond this is quite out of our reach. Why not have told her frankly, sir, 'These people are not in our station'?"

"Just because I acknowledge no such distinction as you want to draw, my good fellow. If my aunt has asked your sister to come three hundred miles to see her, she has thought over her request with more foresight than you or I could have given it, take my word for it. When she means kindly, she plans thoughtfully. And now I will tell you what I never meant to have spoken of, that it was only last night she asked me how could she be of use to you?"

"To *me!*" said he, blushing, "and why to *me?*"

"Can you never be brought to see that you are a hero, Tom,—that all the world is talking of you just now, and people feel a pride in being even passingly mixed up with your name?"

"If they only knew how much I have to be ashamed of before I can begin to feel vain, they 'd not be so ready with their praise or their flattery."

"I 'll talk over all that with your sister Polly," said Hunter, gayly; for he saw the serious spirit that was gaining over the poor fellow.

"Do so, sir; and you'll soon see, if there's anything good or hopeful about me, where it comes from and who gave it."

CHAPTER XIX.

FROM GENERAL CONYERS TO HIS SON

Beddwys, N. Wales.

My dear Fred,—How happy I am that you are enjoying yourself; short of being with you, nothing could have given me greater pleasure than your letter. I like your portrait of the old lady, whose eccentricities are never inconsistent with some charming traits of disposition, and a nature eminently high-minded and honorable; but why not more about Josephine? She is surely oftener in your thoughts than your one brief paragraph would bespeak, and has her due share in making the cottage the delightful home you describe it to be. I entreat you to be more open and more explicit on this theme, for it may yet be many days before I can explore the matter for myself; since, instead of the brief absence I calculated on, we may, for aught I know, be detained here for some weeks.

It is clear to me, from your last, a note of mine from Liverpool to you must have miscarried. You ask me where you are to address me next, and what is the nature of the business which has called me away so suddenly? I gave you in that letter all the information that I was myself possessed of, and which, in three words, amounted to this: Old Barrington, having involved himself in a serious personal quarrel with Stapylton, felt, or believed, that he ought to give him a meeting. Seeing how useless all attempt at dissuasion proved, and greatly fearing what hands he might fall into, I agreed to be his friend on the occasion; trusting, besides, that by a little exercise of tact and temper, extreme measures might be avoided, and the affair arranged. You may well believe, without my insisting further upon it, that I felt very painfully how we should both figure before the world,—a man of eighty-three or four, accompanied to the ground by another of sixty-odd! I know well how, in the changed temper of the age, such acts are criticised, and acquiesce, besides, in the wiser spirit that now prevails. However, as I said before, if Barrington must go on, it were better he should do so under the guidance of a sincere friend than of one casually elevated to act as such, in a moment of emergency.

We left Dublin, by the mail-packet, on Wednesday; and after

a rough passage of twenty-three hours, reached Liverpool too late to catch the evening coach. Thus detained, we only arrived here on Sunday night late. At my club I found a note from Stapylton, stating that he had daily called there to learn if we had come, but the boisterous state of the weather sufficiently explained our delay, and giving an address where he might be found, as well as that of "his friend." Now, it so chanced that this friend was a very notorious person well known to me in India, where he had been tried for an unfair duel, and narrowly escaped—I should say unjustly escaped—being hanged. Though I had fully made up my mind not to be placed in any relations with such a man, I thought it would be as well that Barrington should know the character of his antagonist's friend from other sources, and so I invited an old Bengal companion of mine to dine with us the day after we arrived. Stamer was a judge of the criminal court, and tried Duff Brown, the man I speak of. As we sat over our wine together, we got upon this case, and Stamer declared that it was the only criminal cause in his whole life wherein he regretted the escape of the guilty party. "The fellow," said he, "defended himself in a three hours' speech, ably and powerfully; but enunciated at times—as it were unconsciously—sentiments so abominable and so atrocious as to destroy the sympathy a part of his discourse excited. But somehow boldness has its fascination, and he was acquitted."

Barrington's old-fashioned notions were not, however, to be shocked even by this narrative, and he whispered to me, "Unpleasant for *you*, Conyers. Wish it might have been otherwise, but it can't be helped." We next turned to discuss Duff Brown's friend, and Stamer exclaimed, "Why, that's the man they have been making all this fuss about in India. He was, or he said he was, the adopted son of Howard Stapylton; but the family never believed the adoption, nor consented to receive him, and at this moment a Moonshee, who acted as Persian secretary to old Stapylton, has turned up with some curious disclosures, which, if true, would show that this young fellow held a very humble position in Stapylton's household, and never was in his confidence. This Moonshee was at Malta a few weeks ago, and may be, for aught I know, in England now."

I asked and obtained Barrington's permission to tell how we were ourselves involved with this Major Stapylton, and he quickly declared that, while the man stood thus accused, there could be no thought of according him a satisfaction. The opinion was not the less stringent that Stamer was himself an Irishman and of a fighting family.

I am not very sure that we made Barrington a convert to our opinions, but we at least, as we separated for the night, left him doubtful and hesitating. I had not been in bed above an hour, when Mr. Withering awoke me. He had followed us from Dublin as soon as he learned our departure, and, going straight to a magistrate, swore informations against both Barrington and Stapylton. "My old friend will never forgive me, I know," said he; "but if I had not done this, I should never have forgiven myself." It was arranged between us that I was to mention the fact of such informations having been sworn, without stating by whom, to Barrington, and then persuade him to get privately away from town before a warrant could be served. I leave you to imagine that my task was not without its difficulties, but, before the day broke, I succeeded in inducing him to leave, and travelling by post without halt, we arrived at this quiet spot yesterday evening. Barrington, with all his good temper, is marvellously put out and irritable, saying, "This is not the way such things were done once;" and peevishly muttered, "I wonder what poor Harry Beamish or Guy Hutchinson would say to it all?" One thing is quite clear, we had got into a wasps' nest; Stapylton and his friend were both fellows that no honorable man would like to deal with, and we must wait with a little patience to find some safe road out of this troublesome affair.

A letter came to B. from the India House the evening before we left town, but he handed it to me before he finished reading it, merely remarking, "The old story, 'Yours of the ninth or nineteenth has duly been received,' &c." But I found that it contained a distinct admission that his claim was not ill-founded, and that some arrangement ought to be come to.

I now close my very lengthy epistle, promising, however, that as soon as I hear from town, either from Withering or Stamer, you shall have my news. We are, of course, close prisoners here for the present, for though the warrant would not extend to Ireland, Barrington's apprehensions of being "served" with such a writ at all would induce him to hide for six months to come.

I scarcely ask you to write to me here, not knowing our probable stay; but to-morrow may, perhaps, tell us something on this head. Till when, believe me,

Yours affectionately,
Ormsby Conters.

My most cordial greeting to Miss Barrington, and my love to her niece.

FROM PETER BARRINGTON TO HIS SISTER
MISS DINAH BARRINGTON.

Long's Hotel, Bond Street.

My dear Dinah,—I hardly know how to tell you what has

happened, or what is happening around me. I came over here to meet Major Stapylton, but find that there is no such person,— the man who calls himself so being a mere adventurer, who had taken the name, and, I believe, no small share of the goods, of its owner, got into the Bengal army, thence into our own service, and though not undistinguished for gallantry, seems to have led a life of ceaseless roguery and intrigue. He knew all about poor George's business, and was in correspondence with those we believe to be our friends in India, but who now turn out to be our inveterate enemies. This we have got at by the confession of one of those Oriental fellows they call Moonshees, who has revealed all their intercourse for years back, and even shown a document setting forth the number of rupees he was to receive when Stapylton had been married to Josephine. The Moonshee is very ill, and his examination can only be conducted at intervals; but he insists on a point of much importance to us, which is, that Stapylton induced him to tear out of the Rajah's Koran the page on which the adoption of George was written, and signed by the Meer himself. He received a large sum for this service, which, however, he evaded by a fraud, sending over to England not the real document itself, but a copy made by himself, and admirably counterfeited. It was the possession of this by Stapylton which enabled him to exercise a great control over our suit,—now averring that it was lost; now, under pledge of secrecy, submitting it to the inspection of some of the Indian authorities. Stapylton, in a word, saw himself in a position to establish our claim, whenever the time came that by making Josephine his wife, he could secure the fortune. This is all that we know up to this, but it is a great deal, and shows in what a maze of duplicity and treachery we have been involved for more than twenty years. The chief point, however, is that the real deed, written in the Meer's Koran, and torn out of it by the Moonshee, in his first impulse to forward it to Stapylton, is now extant, and the Koran itself is there to show the jagged margin of the torn-out leaf, and the corresponding page on the opposite side of the volume. Stapylton refuses to utter one word since the accusation against him has been made; and as the charges stand to falsifying documents, abstraction of funds, and other derelictions in India, he is now under a heavy bail to appear when called on.

The whole business has made me so nervous and excitable that I cannot close my eyes at night, and I feel feverish and restless all day. It is very shocking to think of a man one has never injured, never heard of, animated with a spirit so inimical as to pass years of life in working ill to us. He would appear to have devoted himself to the task of blackening poor George's character and defaming him. It would seem that Mr. Howard Stapylton was one of those who took an active part against George. Whether this young fellow caught the contagion of this antipathy, or helped to feed it, I cannot tell; but it is certain that all the stories of cruelty and oppression the India Board used to trump up to us came from this one source; and at the end of all he seeks to be one of a family he has striven for years to ruin and to crush! I am lost in my efforts to understand this, though Stamer and Withering assure me they can read the man like print. Indeed, they see inferences and motives in fifty things which convey nothing to me; and whenever I feel myself stopped by some impassable barrier, to *them* it is only a bridge that conducts to a fresh discovery.

The Stapyltons are all in arms now that another sportsman has winged the bird for them; and each day increases the number of accusations against this unfortunate fellow. It is true, dear Dinah, that our own prospects brighten through all this. I am constantly receiving civil messages and hopeful assurances; and even some of the directors have called to express sympathy and good wishes. But how chilled is the happiness that comes dashed with the misfortune of another! What a terrible deal it detracts from our joy to know that every throb of pleasure to ourselves has cost a pang of misery elsewhere! I wish this fellow could have gone his way, never minding us; or, if that could n't be, that he 'd have grown tired of persecuting those who had never harmed him, and given us up!

They are now assailing him on all sides. One has found that he forged a will; another that he falsified a signature; and a miserable creature—a native Indian, who happened to be in that Manchester riot the other day—has now been ferreted out to swear that Stapylton followed him through a suburb, down a lane, and into a brick-field, where he cut him down and left him for dead. There seems a great deal of venom and acrimony in all this; and though the man is unquestionably not my friend, and I see that this persecution continues, I find it very hard not to stand by him.

As for Withering, it has made the veteran ten years younger. He is up every morning at five, and I hear that he never goes to his room till long past midnight. These are the pastimes that to such men replace the sports of the field and the accidents of the chase. They have their vacillations of hope and fear, their moments of depression and of triumph in them; and they run a fellow-creature to earth with all the zest of a hard rider after a fox.

Tell my darling Fifine that I am longing to be at home again,— longing for the quiet roof, and the roses at the window, and the murmur of the river, and her own sweet voice better than them all. And what a deal of happiness is in our power if we would only consent to enjoy it, without running after some imaginary good, some fancied blessing, which is to crown our wishes! If I could but only have guessed at the life of anxiety, doubt, and vacillation the pursuit of this claim would have cost me,—the twenty years of fever,—

I give you my word, Dinah, I 'd rather have earned my daily bread with a spade, or, when too old for that, taken to fishing for a livelihood.

But why do I complain of anything at this moment? When have I been so truly happy for many a long year? Conyers never leaves me,—he talks of George from morning to night. And I now see that with all my affection for that dear boy, I only half knew his noble nature, his fine and generous character. If you only heard of the benevolent things he has done; the poor fellows he has sent home to their families at his own cost; the sums he has transmitted to wives and widows of soldiers in England; the children whose care and support he has provided for! These were the real drains on that fortune that the world thought wasted and squandered in extravagance. And do you know, Dinah, there is a vein of intense egotism in my heart that I never so much as suspected! I found it out by chance,—it was in marking how far less I was touched by the highest and best traits of my poor boy than by the signs of love to myself! and when Conyers said, "He was always talking about you; he never did anything important without the question, 'How would "Dad" like this, I wonder? would "Dad" say "God speed" in this case?' And his first glass of wine every day was to the health of that dear old father over the seas."

To you who loved him only a little less than myself, I have no shame in the confession of this weakness. I suppose Conyers, however, has hit upon it, for he harps on this theme continually, and, in sheer pride of heart, I feel ten years younger for it.

Here comes Withering to say, "Some more wonderful news;" but I have begged him to keep it till I have sealed this letter, which if it grows any longer, I 'll never have courage to send to you. A dozen kisses to Fifine I can, however, transmit without any increase to the postage. Give my love to young Conyers; tell him I am charmed with his father,—I never met any one so companionable to me, and I only long for the day when the same roof shall cover all of us.

Yours, my dearest sister, ever affectionately,
Peter Barrington.

FROM T. WITHERING, ESQ., TO MISS DINAH BARRINGTON, "THE HOME."

Long's Hotel, Bond Street.

My dear Miss Barrington,—If your brother has deputed me to

write to you, it is not that he is ill, but simply that the excitement caused by some late events here has so completely mastered him that he can neither sit quiet a moment, nor address him steadily to any task. Nor am I surprised it should be so. Old, weather-beaten sailor on the ocean of life as I am, I feel an amount of feverishness and anxiety I am half ashamed of. Truth is, my dear Miss Dinah, we lawyers get so much habituated to certain routine rogueries that we are almost shocked when we hear of a wickedness not designated by a statute. But I must not occupy your time with such speculations, the more since I have only a brief space to give to that report of proceedings to which I want your attention. And, first of all, I will entreat you to forgive me for all want of sequence or connection in what I may say, since events have grown so jumbled together in my mind, that it is perfectly impossible for me to be certain whether what I relate should come before or after some other recorded fact In a word, I mean to give you an outline of our discoveries, without showing the track of our voyage on the map, or even saying how we came by our knowledge.

You are aware, Barrington tells me, how Stapylton came by the name he bears. Aware that he was for some of his earlier years domesticated with old Howard Stapylton at Ghurtnapore, in some capacity between confidential valet and secretary,—a position that was at once one of subordination and trust,—it would now appear that a Moonshee, who had long served Colonel Barrington as Persian correspondent, came into Howard Stapylton's service in the same capacity: how introduced, or by whom, we know not. With this Moonshee, the young fellow I speak of became an intimate and close friend, and it is supposed obtained from him all that knowledge of your nephew's affairs which enabled him to see to what his claim pretended, and what were its prospects of success. It is now clear enough that he only regarded this knowledge at first as a means of obtaining favor from the Indian Government. It was, in fact, by ceding to them in detail certain documents, that he got his first commission in the Madras Fusiliers, and afterwards his promotion in the same regiment; and when, grown more ambitious, he determined to enter the King's service, the money for purchase came from the same source. Being, however, a fellow of extravagant habits, his demands grew at last to be deemed excessive and importunate; and though his debts had been paid three several times, he was again found involving himself as before, and again requiring assistance. This application was, however, resisted; and it was apparently on the strength of that refusal that he suddenly changed his tactics, turned his attention towards us, and bethought him that by forwarding your grandniece's claim,—if he could but win her affections in the mean while,—he would secure as a wife one of the richest heiresses in Europe. An examination of dates proves this, by showing that his last application to the Indian Board was only a few weeks before he exchanged into the regiment of Hussars he lately served with, and just then ordered to occupy Kilkenny. In one word, when it was no longer profitable to oppose Josephine's claim, he determined to support it and make it his own. The "Company," however, fully assured that by the papers in their possession they could prove their own cause against Colonel Barrington, resisted all his menaces,—when, what does he do? It was what only a very daring and reckless fellow would ever have thought of,—one of those insolent feats of boldness that succeed by the very shock they create. He goes to the Secret Committee at the India House and says: "Of the eighteen documents I have given you, seven are false. I will not tell you which they are, but if you do not speedily compromise this claim and make a satisfactory settlement on Colonel Barrington's daughter, I'll denounce you, at all the peril it may be to myself." At first they agree, then they hesitate, then they treat again, and so does the affair proceed, till suddenly—no one can guess why—they assume a tone of open defiance, and flatly declare they will hold no further intercourse with him, and even threaten with exposure any demand on his part.

This rejection of him came at a critical moment. It was just when the press had begun to comment on the cruelty of his conduct at Peterloo, and when a sort of cry was got up through the country to have him dismissed from the service. We all saw, but never suspected, why he was so terribly cut up at this time. It was hard to believe that he could have taken mere newspaper censure so much to heart. We never guessed the real cause, never saw that he was driven to his last expedient, and obliged to prejudice all his hope of success by precipitancy. If he could not make Josephine his wife at once, on the very moment, all was lost. He made a bold effort at this. Who knows if he might not have succeeded but for you, as Josephine was very young, my old friend himself utterly unfit to cope with anything but open hostility? I say again, I 'd not have answered for the result if you had not been in command of the fortress. At all events, he failed; and in the failure lost his temper so far as to force a quarrel upon your brother. He failed, however; and no sooner was he down, than the world was atop of him: creditors, Jews, bill-discounters, and, last of all, the Stapyltons, who, so long as he bore their family name thousands of miles off, or associated it with deeds of gallantry, said nothing; now, that they saw it held up to attack and insult, came forward to declare that he never belonged to them, and at length appealed formally to the Horse Guards, to learn under what designation he had entered the service, and at what period taken the name he went by.

Stapylton's application for leave to sell out had just been sent in; and once more the newspapers set up the cry that this man should not be permitted to carry away to Aix and Baden the proceeds of a sale which belonged to his "creditors." You know the world, and I need not tell you all the pleasant things it told this fellow, for men are pretty nigh as pitiless as crows to their wounded. I thought the complication had reached its limit, when I learned yesterday evening that Stapylton had been summoned before a police magistrate for a case of assault committed by him when in command of his regiment at Manchester. The case had evidently been got up by a political party, who, seeing the casual unpopularity of the man, determined to profit by it. The celebrated radical barrister, Hesketh, was engaged for the plaintiff.

When I arrived at the court, it was so full that it was with difficulty I got a passage to a seat behind the bench. There were crowds of fashionables present, the well-known men about town, and the idlers of the clubs, and a large sprinkling of military men, for the news of the case had got wind already.

Stapylton, dressed in black, and looking pale and worn, but still dignified and like a gentleman, had not a single friend with him. I own to you, I felt ashamed to be there, and was right glad when he did not recognize me.

Though the case opened by a declaration that this was no common assault case, wherein in a moment of passion a man had been betrayed into an excess, I knew the cant of my craft too well to lay any stress on such assertion, and received it as the ordinary exordium. As I listened, however, I was struck by hearing that the injured man was asserted to be one well known to Stapylton, with whom he had been for years in intimacy, and that the assault was in reality a deliberate attempt to kill, and not, as had been represented, a mere passing act of savage severity committed in hot blood. "My client," said he, "will be brought before you; he is a Hindoo, but so long a resident of this country that he speaks our language fluently. You shall hear his story yourselves, and yourselves decide on its truthfulness. His wounds are, however, of so serious a nature that it will be advisable his statement should be a brief one." As he said this, a dark-complexioned fellow, with a look half-frightened, half defiant, was carried forwards in a chair, and deposited, as he sat, on the table. He gave his name as Lai Adeen, his age as forty-eight, his birthplace Majamarha, near Agra. He came to this country twelve years ago, as servant to an officer who had died on the passage, and after many hardships in his endeavor to earn a livelihood, obtained employment at Manchester in the mill of Brandling and Bennett, where he was employed to sweep the corridors and the stairs; his wages were nine shillings a week. All this, and much more of the same kind, he told simply and collectedly. I tried to see Stapylton while this was going on, but a pillar of the gallery, against which he leaned, concealed him from my view.

I omit a great deal, not without its interest, but reserving it for another time, and come to his account of the night on which he was wounded. He said that as the cavalry marched on that morning into Manchester, he was struck by seeing at the head of the regiment one he had never set his eyes on for years, but whose features he knew too well to be deceived in.

"I tried to get near him, that he might recognize me," said he; "but the crowd kept me back, and I could not. I thought, indeed, at one moment he had seen me, and knew me; but as he turned his head away, I supposed I was mistaken.

"It was on the following evening, when the riot broke out in Mill Street, that I saw him next. I was standing at the door of a chemist's shop when the cavalry rode by at a walk. There was a small body of them in front, at about forty or fifty paces, and who, finding a sort of barricade across the street, returned to the main body, where they seemed to be reporting this. A cry arose that the troops had been blocked up at the rear, and at the same instant a shower of stones came from the side-streets and the house-tops. Thinking to do him a service, I made my way towards him I knew, in order to tell him by what way he could make his escape; and jostled and pushed, and half ridden down, I laid my hand on his horse's shoulder to keep myself from falling. 'Stand back, you scoundrel!' said he, striking me with the hilt of his sword in the face. 'Don't you know me, master?' cried I, in terror. He bent down in his saddle till his face was almost close to mine, and then, reining his horse back to give him room for a blow, he aimed a desperate cut at me. I saw it coming, and threw myself down; but I rose the next instant and ran. The street was already so clear by this time, I got into Cleever's Alley, down Grange Street, up the lane that leads to the brick-fields, and at last into the fields themselves. I was just thinking I was safe, when I saw a horseman behind me. He saw me, and dashed at me. I fell upon my knees to ask mercy, and he gave me this;" and he pointed to the bandages which covered his forehead, stained as they were with clotted blood. "I fell on my face, and he tried to make his horse trample on me; but the beast would not, and he only touched me with his hoof as he sprang across me. He at last dismounted to see, perhaps, if I were dead; but a shout from some of the rioters warned him to mount again; and he rode away, and I lay there till morning. It is not true that I was in prison and escaped,—that I was taken to the hospital, and ran away from it. I was sheltered in one of the clay-huts of the brickmakers for several weeks, afraid to come abroad, for I knew that the Sahib was a great man and could take my life. It was only by the persuasions of others that I left my hiding-place and have come here to tell my story."

On being questioned why this officer could possibly desire to injure him, what grudge one in such a station could bear him, he owned he could not say; they had never been enemies, and, indeed, it was in the hope of a friendly recognition and assistance that he approached him in Mill Street.

Stapylton's defence was very brief, given in an off-hand, frank manner, which disposed many in his favor. He believed the fellow meant to attack him; he certainly caught hold of his bridle. It was not his intention to give him more than a passing blow; but the utterance of a Hindoo curse—an expression of gross outrage in the East—recalled prejudices long dormant, and he gave the rascal chase, and cut him over the head,—not a severe cut, and totally unaccompanied by the other details narrated.

"As for our former acquaintance I deny it altogether. I have seen thousands of his countrymen, and may have seen him; but, I repeat, I never knew him, nor can he presume to say he knew me!"

The Hindoo smiled a faint, sickly smile, made a gesture of deep humility, and asked if he might put a few questions to the "Sahib."

"Were you in Naghapoor in the year of the floods?"

"Yes," said Stapylton, firmly, but evidently with an effort to appear calm.

"In the service of the great Sahib, Howard Stapylton?"

"In his service? Certainly not. I lived with him as his friend, and became his adopted heir."

"What office did you fill when you first came to the 'Residence'?"

"I assisted my friend in the duties of his government; I was a good Oriental scholar, and could write and speak a dialect he knew nothing of. But I submit to the court that this examination, prompted and suborned by others, has no other object than to insult me, by leading to disclosures of matters essentially private in their nature."

"Let me ask but one question," said the barrister. "What name did you bear before you took that of Stapylton?"

"I refuse to submit to this insolence," said Stapylton, rising, angrily. "If the laws of the country only can lend themselves to assist the persecutions of a rascally Press, the sooner a man of honor seeks another land the better. Adjudicate on this case, sirs; I will not stoop to bandy words with these men."

"I now, sir," said Hesketh, opening his bag and taking out a roll of papers, "am here to demand a committal for forgery against the person before you, passing under the name of Horace Stapylton, but whose real designation is Samuel Scott Edwardes, son of Samuel Edwardes, a name notorious enough once."

I cannot go on, my dear friend; the emotions that overpowered me at the time, and compelled me to leave the court, are again threatening me, and my brain reels at the recollection of a scene which, even to my fast-fading senses, was the most trying of my life.

To General Conyers I must refer you for what ensued after I left. I cannot even say who came home with me to the hotel, though I am aware I owed that kindness to some one. The face of that unhappy man is yet before me, and all the calm in which I have written up to this leaves me, as I think over one of the most terrible incidents of my life.

Your brother, shocked of course, bears up bravely, and hopes to write to you to-morrow.

One word of good cheer before I close this miserable record. The Indian directors have written to offer excellent terms—splendidly liberal terms, Conyers calls them, and I agree with him. We have had a very busy week of it here, but it will be well requited if all that I now anticipate be confirmed to us. Barrington begs you will tell your neighbors, the Dills, that Tom—I think that is the name—has just arrived at Southampton with General Hunter, and will be here to-morrow evening.

I have cut out a short passage from the newspaper to finish my narrative. I will send the full report, as published, to-morrow.

Your attached friend,
T. Withering.

"The chief police-office in Marlborough Street was yesterday the scene of a very shocking incident. The officer whose conduct at the head of his regiment in Manchester has of late called for the almost unanimous reprobation of the Press, was, while answering to a charge of aggravated assault, directly charged with forgery. Scarcely was the allegation made, than he drew a pistol from his pocket, and, placing the muzzle to his mouth, pulled the trigger. The direction of the weapon, however, was accidentally turned, and the ball, instead of proceeding upwards, passed through the lower jaw, fracturing the bone, and created a terrible wound. It is supposed that the large vessels are not injured, and that he may yet recover. All who witnessed the scene describe it as one of intense horror.

"The unhappy man was at once removed to the Middlesex Hospital. He has not uttered a word since the event; and when asked if there were any relatives or friends whom he wished might be sent for, merely shook his head negatively. It is said that when the result of the consultation held on him was announced to him as favorable, he seemed rather grieved than otherwise at the tidings."

FROM PETER BARRINGTON TO DINAH, HIS SISTER.

My dear Dinah,—How glad am I to tell you that we leave this to-morrow, and a large party of us, too, all for "The Home." Put young Conyers in my dressing-room, so that the large green bedroom can be free for the General, at least for one of the generals—for we have another here, Hunter, who will also be our guest. Then there will be Withering. As for myself, I can be stowed away anywhere. What happiness would there be to us all at such a meeting, if it were not for that poor wretch who lies in all his agony a few streets off, and who is never out of my thoughts. I went twice to the hospital to see him. The first time I lost courage, and came away. The second, I sent up my name, and asked if he would wish to see me. The only answer I got was my visiting-card torn in two! How hard it is for an injurer to forgive him he has injured! I have arranged with the Stapyltons, however, who instigated the charge of forgery, not to press it; at least, they are to take bail, and the bail will be forfeited, so I understand it; but Withering will explain all more clearly.

Our own affairs are all as bright and prosperous as our best wishes could desire. The Council have had all the evidence before them, and the Moonshee has produced his copy of the Koran, with the torn leaf fitting into the jagged margin, and George is vindicated at last in everything. His loyalty, his disinterestedness, his honesty, all established. The ceremony of his marriage has been fully recognized; and General Conyers tells me that the lowest estimate of our claim is a little short of a quarter of a million sterling. He counsels me not to be exigent in my terms; if he knew me better, perhaps, he would not have deemed the advice so necessary.

What will Fifine say to all this wealth? Will she want to go back to India, and be a princess, and ride about on an elephant; or will she reconcile herself to such humble ways as ours? I am most eager to hear how she will take the tidings. Withering says it will not spoil her; that knowing nothing of life in its moneyed relations, she runs no risk of being carried away by any vulgar notions of her own importance through riches.

Conyers has never once hinted at his son's pretensions since Fifine has become an heiress; and I fancy—it may be only fancy—is a shade or so cool towards me, so that I have not referred to them. But what can I do? I cannot offer him my granddaughter, nor—if what you tell me be true, that they are always quarrelling—would the proposal be a great kindness to either.

Here is Tom Dill, too, and what a change! He is the image of Polly; and a fine, well-grown, straight-figured fellow, that looks you manfully in the face,—not the slouching, loutish, shamefaced creature you remember him. Hunter has had him gazetted to an Ensigncy in the 10th Foot, and he will, or I much mistake him, do honest credit to the recommendation. Hunter takes him about with him wherever he goes, telling all about the shipwreck and Tom's gallantry,—enough to turn the lad's head with vanity, but that he is a fine, simple-hearted creature, who thinks very little of himself or his achievement. He seems to have no other thought than what Polly, his sister, will say and think of him.

He also will be one of our party; that is if I can persuade him to make "The Home" his headquarters while our friends are with us. What a strong muster we shall be; and how we 'll astonish that old bin of Madeira, Dinah! By the way, I have been rather boastful about it to Conyers, and let some bottles have the sun on them for a couple of hours every day.

I should like to try my chance once more of seeing that poor fellow at the hospital, but Withering will not hear of it; he got positively ill-tempered at the bare mention of such a wish. Even Conyers says, "Better not," with an air that may mean for the sick man's sake as much as my own.

A little more of this life of noise, confusion, and excitement would finish me. This city existence, with its incessant events and its never ending anxieties, is like walking in a high wind with the chimney-pots falling and crashing on every side of one,—while I am pitying the fellow whose skull is just cracked, I am forced to remember that my own is in danger. And yet there are people who like it; who tell you that out of London there is no living; that the country is a grave, aggravated by the consciousness that one is dead and buried there!

On Tuesday,—Wednesday, at farthest,—Dinah, look out for us. I do not believe there is that prize in the wheel that would tempt me again away from home! and till I reach it, believe, my dear Dinah,

Your loving brother,
Peter Barrington.

I have just seen Conyers. He met Sir Harvey Hethrington, the Home Secretary, this morning, and they got into a talk over our business, and H. said how cruelly I had been treated all this time back, and how unfairly poor George's memory was dealt with. "We want," said he, "to show your friend our respect and our sympathy, and we have thought of submitting his name to the King for a Baronetcy. How do you think Mr. Barrington himself would take our project?" "I 'll find out," said Conyers, as he told me of the conversation. "If they don't let me off, Conyers," said I, "ask them to commute it to Knighthood, for the heralds' fees will be smaller; but I'll try, meanwhile, if I can't escape either." So that now, Dinah, you may expect me on Saturday. I told you what a place this was; you are never sure what may befall you from one moment to another!

CHAPTER XX.

THE END

Fortune had apparently ceased to persecute Peter Barrington. The Minister did not press honors upon him, and he was free to wait for his companions, and in their company he returned to Ireland.

The news of his success—great as it was, magnified still more—had preceded him to his own country; and he was met, as all lucky men are met, and will be met to the end of time, by those who know the world and feelingly estimate that the truly profitable are the fortunate!

Not that he remarked how many had suddenly grown so cordial; what troops of passing acquaintances had become in a moment warm friends, well-wishing and affectionate. He never so much as suspected that "Luck" is a deity worshipped by thousands, who even in the remotest way are not to be benefited by it. He had always regarded the world as a far better thing than many moralists would allow it to be,—unsteady, wilful, capricious, if you like—but a well-intentioned, kindly minded world, that would at all times, where passion or prejudice stood aloof, infinitely rather do the generous thing than the cruel one.

Little wonder, then, if he journeyed in a sort of ovation! At every change of horses in each village they passed, there was sure to be some one who wanted to shake his hand. People hobbled out on crutches and quitted sick-beds to say how "glad they were;" mere acquaintances most of them, who felt a strange mysterious sort of self-consequence in fancying themselves for the moment the friends of Peter Barrington, the millionnaire! This is all very curious, but it is a fact,—a fact which I make no pretence to explain, however.

"And here comes the heartiest well-wisher of them all!" cried Barrington, as he saw his sister standing on the roadside, near the gate. With thoughtful delicacy, his companions lingered behind, while he went to meet and embraced her. "Was I not a true prophet, Dinah dear? Did I not often foretell this day to you?" said he, as he drew her arm, and led her along, forgetting all about his friends and companions.

"Have they paid the money, Peter?" said she, sharply.

"Of course they have not; such things are not settled like the fare of a hackney-coach. But our claim is acknowledged, and, fifty thousand times better, George Barrington's name absolved from every shadow of an imputation."

WELCOME TO BARRINGTON

"What is the amount they agree to give?"

"Upon my life, I don't know,—that is, I don't recollect, there were so many interviews and such discussions; but Withering can tell you everything. Withering knows it all. Without *him* and Conyers I don't know how I could have got on. If you had heard how he spoke of George at the Council! 'You talk of *my* services,' said he; 'they are no more fit to be compared with those of Colonel Barrington, than are *my* petty grievances with the gross wrongs that lie on *his* memory.' Withering was there; he heard the words, and described the effect of them as actually overwhelming."

"And Withering believes the whole thing to be settled?"

"To be sure, he does! Why should he oppose his belief to that of the whole world? Why, my dear Dinah, it is not one, nor two, but some hundreds of people have come to wish me joy. They had a triumphal arch at Naas, with 'Welcome to Barrington' over it. At Carlow, Fishbourne came out with the corporation to offer me congratulations."

She gave a hasty, impatient shake of the head, but repressed the sharp reply that almost trembled on her lips.

"By George!" cried he, "it does one's heart good to witness such a burst of generous sentiment. You'd have thought some great national benefit had befallen, or that some one—his country's idol—had just reaped the recompense of his great services. They came flocking out of the towns as we whirled past, cheering lustily, and shouting, 'Barrington forever!'"

"I detest a mob!" said she, pursing up her lips.

"These were no mobs, Dinah; these were groups of honest fellows, with kind hearts and generous wishes."

Another, but more decisive, toss of the head warned Peter that the discussion had gone far enough; indeed she almost said so, by asking abruptly, "What is to be done about the boy Conyers? He is madly in love with Josephine."

"Marry her, I should say!"

"As a cure for the complaint, I suppose. But what if she will not have him? What if she declares that she'd like to go back to the convent again,—that she hates the world, and is sorry she ever came out into it,—that she was happier with the sisters—"

"Has she said all this to you, sister?"

"Certainly not, Peter," said Dinah, bridling up. "These were confidences imparted to the young man himself. It was he told me of them: he came to me last night in a state bordering on distraction. He was hesitating whether he would not throw himself into the river or go into a marching regiment."

"This is only a laughing matter, then, Dinah?" said Peter, smiling.

"Nothing of the kind, brother! He did not put the alternatives so much in juxtaposition as I have; but they lay certainly in that manner on his thoughts. But when do your friends arrive? I thought they were to have come with you?"

"What a head I have, Dinah! They are all here; two carriages of them. I left them on the road when I rushed on to meet you. Oh, here they come! here they are!"

"My brother's good fortune, gentlemen, has made him seem to forget what adversity never did; but I believe you all know how welcome you are here? Your son, General Conyers, thought to meet you earlier, by taking boat down to the village, and the girls went with him. Your friend, Polly Dill, is one of them, General Hunter."

Having thus, with one sweep of the scythe, cut down a little of all around her, she led the way towards the cottage, accepting the arm of General Conyers with an antiquated grace that sorely tried Hunter's good manners not to smile at.

"I know what you are looking at, what you are thinking of, Barrington," said Withering, as he saw the other stand a moment gazing at the landscape on the opposite side of the river.

"I don't think you do, Tom," said he, smiling.

"You were thinking of buying that mountain yonder. You were saying to yourself, 'I 'll be the owner of that beech wood before I'm a month older!'"

"Upon my life, you 're right! though I have n't the remotest notion of how you guessed it. The old fellow that owns it shall name his own terms to-morrow morning. Here come the girls, and they 've got Tom Dill with them. How the fellow rows! and Fifine is laughing away at Conyers's attempt to keep the boat straight. Look at Hunter, too; he 's off to meet them. Is he 'going in' for the great heiress prize, eh, Tom?" said he, with a knowing smile.

Though Hunter assisted the ladies to land with becoming gallantry, he did not offer his arm to Josephine, but dropped behind, where Tom Dill brought up the rear with his sister.

"We have no confidences that you may not listen to," said Polly, as she saw that he hesitated as to joining them. "Tom, indeed, has been telling of yourself, and you may not care to hear your own praises."

"If they come from *you*, I 'm all ears for them."

"Isn't that pretty, Tom? Did you ever hear any one ask more candidly for—no, not flattery—what is it to be called?"

Tom, however, could not answer, for he had stopped to shake hands with Darby, whose "May I never!" had just arrested him.

"What an honest, fine-hearted fellow it is!" said Hunter, as they moved on, leaving Tom behind.

"But if *you* had n't found it out, who would have known, or who acknowledged it? *I* know—for he has told me—all you have been to him."

"Pooh, pooh! nothing; less than nothing. He owes all that he is to himself. He is one of those fellows who, once they get into the right groove in life, are sure to go ahead. Not even *you* could make a doctor of him. Nature made him a soldier."

Polly blushed slightly at the compliment to those teachings she believed a secret, and he went on,—

"What has the world been doing here since I left?"

"Pretty much what it did while you were here. It looked after its turnips and asparagus, took care of its young calves, fattened its chickens, grumbled at the dear-ness of everything, and wondered when Dr. Buck would preach a new sermon."

"No deaths,—no marriages?"

"None. There was only one candidate for both, and he has done neither,—Major M'Cormick."

"Confound that old fellow! I had forgotten him. Do you remember the last day I saw you here? We were in the garden, talking, as we believed, without witnesses. Well, *he* overheard us. He heard every word we said, and a good deal more that we did not say."

"Yes; so he informed me, a few days after."

"You don't mean to say that he had the impertinence—"

"The frankness, General,—the charming candor,—to tell me that I was a very clever girl, and not to be discouraged by one failure or two; that with time and perseverance—I think he said perseverance—some one was sure to take a fancy to me: he might not, perhaps, be handsome, possibly not very young; his temper, too, might chance to be more tart than was pleasant; in a word, he drew such a picture that I had to stop him short, and ask was he making me a proposal? He has never spoken to me since!"

"I feel as if I could break his neck," muttered Hunter, below his breath; then added, "Do you remember that I asked leave to write to you once,—only once?"

"Yes, I remember it."

"And you would not answer me. You shook your head, as though to say the permission would be of no service to me; that I might write, but, you understand, that it would only be to indulge in a delusion—"

"What an expressive shake of the head that meant all that!"

"Ah! there it is again; never serious, never grave! And now I want you to be both. Since I landed in England, I ran down for a day to Devonshire. I saw an old aunt of mine, who, besides being very rich, has retained no small share of the romance of her life. She always had a dash of hero-worship about her, and so I took down Tom with me to show her the gallant fellow whose name was in all the newspapers, and of whom all the world was talking. She was charmed with him,—with his honest, manly simplicity, his utter want of all affectation. She asked me ten times a day, 'Can I not be of service to him? Is there no step he wishes to purchase? Is there nothing we can do for him?' 'Nothing,' said I; 'he is quite equal to his own fortune.' 'He may have brothers,' said she. 'He has a sister,' said I,—'a sister who has made him all that he is, and it was to repay her love and affection that he has shown himself to be the gallant fellow we have seen him.' 'Tell her to come and see me.—that is,' said she, correcting herself, 'give her a letter I shall write, and persuade her, if you can, to oblige me by doing what I ask.' Here is the letter; don't say no till you have read it. Nay, don't shake your head so deploringly; things may be hard without being impossible. At all events, read her note carefully. It's a droll old hand, but clear as print."

"I'll read it," said she, looking at the letter; but the sorrowful tone revealed how hopelessly she regarded the task.

"Ask Tom about her; and make Tom tell you what she is like. By Jove! he has such an admiration for the old damsel, I was half afraid he meant to be my uncle."

They reached the cottage laughing pleasantly over this conceit, and Polly hurried up to her room to read the letter. To her surprise, Josephine was there already, her eyes very red with crying, and her cheeks flushed and feverish-looking.

"My dearest Fifine, what is all this for, on the happiest day of your life?" said she, drawing her arm around her.

"It's all *your* fault,—all *your* doing," said the other, averting her head, as she tried to disengage herself from the embrace.

"My fault,—my doing? What do you mean, dearest, what can I have done to deserve this?"

"You know very well what you have done. You knew all the time how it would turn out."

Polly protested firmly that she could not imagine what was attributed to her, and only after a considerable time obtained the explanation of the charge. Indeed it was not at first easy to comprehend it, given, as it was, in the midst of tears, and broken at every word by sobs. The substance was this: that Fifine, in an attempted imitation of Polly's manner,—an effort to copy the coquetting which she fancied to be so captivating,—had ventured to trifle so far with young Conyers, that, after submitting to every alternative of hope and fear for weeks long, he at last gave way, and determined to leave the house, quit the country, and never meet her more. "It was to be like you I did it," cried she, sobbing bitterly, "and see what it has led me to."

"Well, dearest, be really like me for half an hour; that is, be very patient and very quiet. Sit down here, and don't leave this till I come back to you."

Polly kissed her hot cheek as she spoke; and the other sat down where she was bade, with the half-obedient sulkiness of a naughty child.

"Tell young Mr. Conyers to come and speak to me. I shall be in the garden," said she to his servant; and before she had gone many paces he was beside her.

"Oh, Polly dearest! have you any hope for me?" cried he, in agony. "If you knew the misery I am enduring."

"Come and take a walk with me," said she, passing her arm within his. "I think you will like to hear what I have to tell you."

The revelation was not a very long one; and as they passed beneath the room where Josephine sat, Polly called out, "Come down here, Fifine, we are making a bouquet; try if you can find 'heart's-ease.'"

What a happy party met that day at dinner! All were in their best spirits, each contented with the other. "Have you read my aunt's note?" whispered Hunter to Polly, as they passed into the drawing-room.

"Yes. I showed it also to Miss Dinah. I asked her advice."

"And what did she say,—what did she advise?"

"She said she 'd think over it and tell me to-morrow."

"To-morrow! Why not now, — why not at once?" cried he, impatiently. "I 'll speak to her myself;" and he hurried to the little room where Miss Dinah was making tea.

It was not a very long interview; and Hunter returned, fond, radiant, and triumphant. "She's the cleverest old woman I ever met in my life," said he; "and the best, besides, after my Aunt Dorothy. She said that such an invitation as that was too cordial to be coldly declined; that it meant more — far more — than a politeness; that you ought to go, yes, by all means; and if there was any difficulty about the journey, or any awkwardness in travelling so far, why, there was an easy remedy for it, as well as for meeting my aunt a perfect stranger."

"And what was that?"

"To go as her niece, dearest Polly, — to be the wife of a man who loves you."

"Is it possible that you have so much to say to each other that you won't take tea?" cried Aunt Dinah; while she whispered to Withering, "I declare we shall never have a sociable moment till they're all married off, and learn to conduct themselves like reasonable creatures."

Is it not the best testimony we can give to happiness, that it is a thing to feel and not describe, — to be enjoyed, but not pictured? It is like a debt that I owe to my reader, to show him "The Home" as it was when blissful hearts were gathered under its roof; and yet, for the life of me, I cannot acquit myself of it. To say that there were old people with their memories of the past, and young ones with their hopes of the future; that there were bygones to sigh over, and vistas to gaze at, conveys but little of the kindliness by which heart opened to heart, and sorrow grew lighter by mutual endurance, and joys became brighter as they were imparted to another.

"So I find," said Barrington, as they sat at breakfast together, "that Josephine insists on going back to the convent, and Fred is resolved on an exchange into the Infantry, and is off for Canada immediately."

"Not a bit of it!" broke in Hunter, who remarked nothing of the roguish drollery of old Peter's eye, nor even suspected that the speech was made in mockery. "Master Fred is coming with me into Kilkenny this morning, for a visit to the Dean, or whatever he is, who dispenses those social handcuffs they call licenses."

"Why, they were quarrelling all the morning," repeated Harrington.

"So we were, sir, and so we mean to do for many a year," said Josephine; "and to keep us in countenance, I hear that General Hunter and Polly have determined to follow our example."

"What do I hear, Miss Dill?" said Miss Barrington, with an affected severity.

"I'm afraid, madam, it is true; there has been what my father calls 'a contagious endemic' here lately, and we have both caught it; but ours are mild cases, and we hope soon to recover."

"What's this I see here?" cried Fred, who, to conceal his shame, had taken up the newspaper. "Listen to this: 'The notorious Stapylton, *alias* Edwardes, whose case up to yesterday was reported all but hopeless, made his escape from the hospital, and has not since been heard of. It would appear that some of the officials had been bribed to assist his evasion, and a strict inquiry will be immediately set on foot into the affair.'"

"Do you think he has got over to France?" whispered Peter to Withering.

"Of course he has; the way was all open, and everything ready for him!"

"Then I am thoroughly happy!" cried Barrington, "and there's not even the shadow of a cloud over our present sunshine."

THE END.

Lector House believes that a society develops through a two-fold approach of continuous learning and adaptation, which is derived from the study of classic literary works spread across the historic timeline of literature records. Therefore, we aim at reviving, repairing and redeveloping all those inaccessible or damaged but historically as well as culturally important literature across subjects so that the future generations may have an opportunity to study and learn from past works to embark upon a journey of creating a better future.

This book is a result of an effort made by Lector House towards making a contribution to the preservation and repair of original ancient works which might hold historical significance to the approach of continuous learning across subjects.

HAPPY READING & LEARNING!

LECTOR HOUSE LLP
E-MAIL: lectorpublishing@gmail.com

9 789390 294428

Lightning Source UK Ltd.
Milton Keynes UK
UKHW011828030820
367624UK00003B/606